# *FOREST H ALL*

## The Seventh of the
## Chronicles of Martindale

**John Blaylock**

# Also by John Blaylock

## (The Martindale Chronicles)

*The Gates of Brass*

*The Women at the Gates*

*The Gates Flung Wide*

*The Gates of Wrath*

*Strangers at the Gates*

*Love At Large*

*****

*A Murder of Little Account*

*How Far Is It To Dunkirk?*

With love and
fondest regards.

John

*This Book Is Dedicated to*

*The Memory Of*

# LESLEY FRANKS
## *(1942 - 2020)*

*The Girl With The Voice Of An Angel*

*****

# List of Characters

**Gideon Sturgis** and **Jervis Esprey;** in the aftermath of the American Civil War, have left their wives without a word in order to purchase as cheaply as possible the Knightsbridge Plantation which is the home of Sturgis' first love, Deborah Talisker.

**Sir Charles Martin Bt** was the joint developer of Martindale along Hannibal Wright who was the father of his first wife. His current wife is **Marian** who was previously his housekeeper. She is also the sister of Frank and Richard Turner.

**George Murphy** was orphaned at a young age though he was soon unofficially adopted by **Annie** and **Geordie Cook.** Together they are the joint owners of a pie shop which was originally the brain child of George. However, he recently fell out with them over his infatuation with the local girl **Lucy Greenwood**.

**John Losser** once pursued George Murphy from Liverpool to Martindale after the latter had escaped from an horrific orphanage there. However, through the kindness of the Cooks Losser's character was reformed and he became one of the finest hewers in Martindale.

**Clara Miller** is also an orphan who was also taken in by the Cooks.

**Venetia Lander** is the wife of **Edwin** the Rector of Martindale. She has two daughters, **Amelia** who is married to **Fred Schilling** the brother of **Helmuth**. The other is **Arabella** the wife of local businessman **Douglas**

**Brass**.   Their third daughter; Abigail recently died prematurely whilst on a tour of Europe with **Elysia, the Marchioness of Studland.**

**Caroline Schilling** is the mistress of her childhood home Blanchwell.   Previously, due to poor investment advice, her father lost almost everything and decided to go to America where he hoped to regain his fortune.   However, he died in Nebraska, though Caroline was rescued from there by   **Helmuth Schilling** whose business acumen eventually allowed her to return to Blanchwell as his wife.

**Elysia Scott-Wilson, the Marchioness of Studland** was the first wife of **Sir Charles Martin**, until he divorced her on the grounds of her unfaithfulness.   She is extremely rich and resides at Winterbourne Abbey.   Over the intervening years she has become friendly with the ladies of Martindale and frequently visits them there.   Her father was **Sir James Hannibal Wright** the co-founder and chief mover of the development of the town of Martindale.

**Richard Turner** is the brother of both **Lady Martin** and **Frank Turner**.   He is part owner of a newspaper and recently was elected as the local Member of Parliament. His wife is **Jane** who inherited a considerable fortune from her uncle, though despite her wealth she is an enthusiastic radical, champion of the rights of women and an undoubted free spirit.

**Johnie Corsica** is the general-factotum of the Marchioness of Studland and also her lover.   He has proved to be willing to carry out any order issued by the marchioness – legal or not.

**Virgil Kent** is an ex-cavalryman who is now the butler of Martin Hall and the husband of **Cissy** who is the housekeeper there.

**Sarah Nicholson** is the widow of Jack Nicholson, a much respected collier. She is a teacher who spends her time between the school room at Martin Hall and the Martindale Education Association. **Harry (Harold) Nicholson** is the illegitimate child of Jack who was taken in by Sarah at the request of Janet Goundry his birth mother.

**Roderick Villiers** is the director of the *Martindale Civic Theatre*, his wife is **Roberta (Bobbity)** the sister of the schoolmaster **John Fisher.** **Solomon Vasey** is Villiers' friend and right-hand man.

**Elizabeth Esprey** was an actress who was brought to Merrington Hall as the wife of Colonel Henry Galvin. After his death in India during the Mutiny she married Lieutenant-Colonel Jervis Esprey. She was the prime mover behind the creation of the *Martindale Civic Theatre.*

**Matthew Priestly** is the leader of one of the two local Workers' Associations, though he is more concerned about the pay and conditions his members work under than supporting any political movement. He is living under an assumed name due to his previous involvement in a failed conspiracy against the government. Only Sarah Nicholson knows of this.

**Kevin O'Dowd** is an associate of Johnie Corsica.

**Inspector Roland Mason** is a policeman who has worked for many years trying to bring to justice both Hannibal

Wright and his daughter, though without being provided with sufficient resources to succeed in this. He is supported by **Constable George Dodds**.

# PART ONE: *Virginia and the Knightsbridge Plantation*

Lieutenant-Colonel Jervis Esprey was not feeling particularly happy as he scanned the extensive forest which lay to either side of him. This was the same terrain through which General Grant's army had fought its way towards Richmond the previous year. The casualties on both sides had amounted to nearly thirty-thousand men and many of those killed still lay unburied where they'd fallen. Even at noon it was dark under the trees and the atmosphere was steamily oppressive, where above everything there remained a sickly, sweet, unavoidable stench.

"It seems to me that the smell of death will linger here for ever," muttered his companion, Major Gideon Sturgis, late of the Confederate cavalry.

"I've not come across anything so bad since the Bibighar," reflected Esprey, more to himself than to his companion.

"The Bibighar?"

"It was a pleasure palace where the local native prince kept his lady friends in comfort, however, when I arrived there the well in the courtyard was filled to the brim with bodies and parts of bodies."

"Soldiers?"

"No, women and children, captured at Cawnpore during the Mutiny."

"India, I suppose."

Jervy nodded but added nothing further.

"War always brings with it atrocity."

"Though we stubbornly remain steadfastly loyal to our individual units," pointed out Jervy softly.

"It's what soldiers are supposed to do," Sturgis shrugged his shoulders as he spoke.

"Loyalty to the regiment always comes first."

"It's funny, isn't it, that we both speak of the units we served in as though they still existed."

"The Company's Indian troops still serve Her Majesty," observed the colonel.

"Though the East India Company itself was dissolved seven or eight years ago, so its army must have disbanded at that time."

Esprey coughed, wheezed and then eventually nodded his head in agreement, "Though many of its finest regiments now serve in the British Army."

These veteran soldiers were driving a wagon which contained their belongings and necessaries, but hidden beneath it all there lay a fortune in gold and species. Their destination was Cardinal Woods, the childhood home of Sturgis near the city of Petersburg.

"Why don't we check to see if the owner of the first suitable plantation we pass is willing to do business with us," suggested Jervy who was aching to see his wife and hoping that she would forgive him for disappearing to

America without him having left so much as a word for her.

"It's got to be Talisker's place, I *must* have Knightsbridge."

"Suppose he won't sell? What are you going to do then – kill him?"

"He murdered my beautiful Deborah, she died because of the love she held for me," the major's voice adopted a grim monotone.

"It was suicide, wasn't it," reminded the colonel.

"Maybe killing him is out of the question, but I'll be damned if I can't bring him to ruin."

Giddy shivered as a sudden breeze swept by as though sent by his lovely, Deborah, but its breath carried on it not that of her perfume but instead the stench of corruption.

They travelled on in a contemplative silence for a while and then Esprey complained, "We're travelling along one long, lonely road after another and I'm sure you've no idea where we are."

"We're still in Virginia and heading for Petersburg."

"It's a pity we couldn't have taken the shorter route through Washington," said Esprey as his hand stretched to the comforting feel of his Smith & Wesson revolver which he had concealed beneath a handkerchief on the seat beside him.

"With Judge Mattheson still determined to wreak his vengeance upon me, you know that was impossible."

Esprey nodded, "Yes, there are some areas of Northern India and Afghanistan that I'd not enter again without a very good reason."

"The last time I was hereabouts was with Fitzhugh Lee when we discovered that Hooker's flank was in the air, which allowed old Stonewall's corps to smash through the Union line, sending Howard's men tumbling back to Fredericksburg, with Hooker and the rest of the Union army following close behind them."

"It's a pity that Jackson was killed that same night, for he may have made a decisive difference at Gettysburg."

"Even though Stonewall was an alarming eccentric, he couldn't be replaced and especially not by Old Baldy Ewell," replied Giddy who went on, "Still, Chancellorsville was a famous victory."

"Remembering a victory is always sweet – once one is separated in both time and space from the futility of it all," replied Jervy.

"There's nothing quite like a battle won, though."

"Unless it's one lost, according to Wellington."

"Confusing business battle, most of the time at Chancellorsville I had no idea where we were, nor what we were supposed to be doing."

"I believe that this is *still* the case," remarked Jervy drily.

"We're amidst the Virginia wilderness, though Cold Harbor can't be far away," Giddy defended himself.

"Harbour? Harbour you say, then where's the sea?" Jervy looked around as he spoke, sniffing the air as though for the tang of salt.

Giddy laughed, "It isn't an actual harbour."

Their conversation came to a startled halt as the cries of a woman - of a woman in distress reached them.

The major picked up his revolver and then felt beneath his seat to check that his shot-gun was still in place, fully loaded and ready.

Again the girl; whoever she was, screamed though this time even more plaintively.

"Is this really our business?" Asked Jervis, "It may merely be some incident of domestic strife."

A third scream rent the air, even louder than the previous ones.

At the sound of it Sturgis urged the horses forward over a low rise and soon came into sight of a dilapidated shack, outside of which a naked boy was desperately trying to pull free of a much larger man who was attempting to beat him with what appeared to be a piece of fencing.

"Hey, you there," commanded Gideon, "stop that at once."

The man hardly glanced around, "You mind yer business and I'll take care o' my own."

The naked boy turned towards the interlopers and screamed for help again.

At that moment it became clear that the boy was; as they had initially believed, a girl, but a very young and scrawny one. Her body was cut and bruised whilst her hair had been irregularly sheered very short, except on the top where it stuck up in spikes.

Gideon wasted no further time and jumped from the wagon determined to prevent any further punishment of a woman.

The aggressor grabbed the girl by the neck and began to squeeze.

"*Oh, uggh*, stop," she begged.

"Come a mite closer an' I'll finish with her," warned the brute.

"You do so and a second later you'll be a dead man," the colonel called from the wagon in a friendly enough tone, as though it was of great indifference to him were he to shoot a complete stranger dead or not.

"Look y'here, this gal is mine. I won her fair and square at blackjack, so jest get about your business an' leave me t'enjoy my winnings."

"It is illegal to buy or own human flesh, no matter what colour it is nor how you acquired it," reminded Giddy as he took a cautious couple of steps closer to the girl.

The man worked out the odds and with a loud guffaw thrust the lassie from him, "You take her then, she's just nought but hassle anyways."

Seizing her chance, the girl picked up a nearby chunk of rock and threw it with a deadly aim at her captor's head.

"You little….," he screamed as the rock bounced off his left ear, which began to stream blood.

By this time Gideon was close enough to stand between the man and his would be victim, "Leave it, I reckon you and her are evens now."

"I got clothes in the shack, don't leave me, ya' hear," cried the girl as she ran off.

The man sat on the ground, rocking and holding his hands to his head, "She's a thief an' a trouble maker, so hold tight t'yer belongings an' remember what I've told you."

"What's her name?" Asked Esprey, who had dismounted from the wagon.

"How'd I know that? She was just a free fuck t'me."

"Kitty, I'm Kitty Hawes," shouted the girl as she left the cabin fastening the last of a long line of buttons on a grey worsted dress which had seen better days.

"Hawes by name an' *whore* by nature," put in the man with a guffaw.

"I ain't nothin' men haven't made me," Kitty picked up the fence post with which she had been beaten and was about to take her revenge.

The colonel took her in a bear-hug and ignored the kicks she was inflicting on his shins.

"What can we possibly do with her?" Asked the major.

"Neither of you are having your way with me, if that's what y'think," put in Kitty with determination.

"Not unless you pay her," opinioned the man, still nursing his head.

"I've told you, I'm no whore," shouted the girl.

The colonel took Kitty gently by the shoulders and turned her towards the wagon, "Climb aboard, my dear, we'll drop you off at the next town."

"I ain't going to no orphanage."

"We shall find shelter for you somewhere safe," promised Esprey.

"How old are you?" Asked Giddy.

"That's no business o'yours."

"She ran off from an asylum," informed the man, "that's how she ended up as my winnings. I should ha' taken ole Simms's stopped tin clock I was offered instead."

"I ain't going back there – they beat me worse than he was going to," she pointed at the shack dweller.

Not wishing to waste any further time, Sturgis lifted the girl and plonked her on to the tailboard of the wagon, her legs dangling over the edge.

"Come on, Jervy, we've no further time to waste," called Sturgis who had taken up the reins again.

A minute or two later they had left the shack behind and were hoping they'd soon find somewhere to drop off their unexpected and unlooked for guest.

"I'm hungry, you got any food?" Asked Kitty sharply.

"We're not stopping until we find a town," replied Giddy shortly.

"*Ha*, just my luck to hitch up with a pair o' foreigners who are lost."

*****

"I presume we're still in your home state, or perhaps we've reached the dark side of the moon," sighed Lieutenant-Colonel Jervis Esprey, as their wagon trundled along a seemingly unending forest trail.

"I was brought up around here, fought here and damn nearly died here too," replied Major Gideon Sturgis, lately an officer of Fitzhugh Lee's Brigade who had been wounded and taken prisoner at Gettysburg.

"Then why is it that you've no idea where we are?"

"I told him t'take the last left fork we passed," this voice was a shrill one and belonged to Kitty Hawes who was proving to be something of an irritant.

"Shut up, girl," the colonel growled, he being both tired and hungry.

"If ye'd gone where I telt ye, we'd be eating supper by now."

"Do you wish to shoot the child yourself or should I?" Asked Sturgis.

"I ain't no child."

"You're no lady either," returned Esprey.

Miss Hawes ignored them and from the back of the wagon shouted, "There's fresh water down by this here stream, why don't you stop an' get yer frying pan out?"

"What part do you intend to play in this camping frolic, your ladyship?" Asked Jervy with heavy sarcasm.

"Why, I can handle a skillet, that's if you've got one, which I doubt."

Giddy reined in the team and sighed, "That's the best offer we've had to-day."

Half an hour later they were eating bacon and beans and drinking hot coffee.

"She's a better cook than you, Jervy," pointed out Sturgis.

"I'm an officer of field rank, what should I know of menial tasks such as cooking?"

"In that case, who's gonna wash up?" Put in Kitty quickly.

"You're the hired help," returned Giddy.

"Hired? So ye're gonna pay me?"

"Young lady, we rescued you, we are taking you to safety, fed you and now you expect money," retorted Jervy.

"I ain't no slave and I'm worth it to you. I can cook, wash, see to the horses and not only that, I know where we are."

"You're certain that you know where we are?" The colonel sounded hopeful.

"Sure do," she pointed to her left, "Petersburg's over there, not ten miles away."

"She has no idea, by my reckoning it's only five miles that way," replied Sturgis, flinging out his right arm.

Esprey's head dropped in thought for a second and then he looked up and said, "My money's on the lassie."

18

\*\*\*\*\*

The next day, after eventually following Kitty's advice, Major Gideon Sturgis was driving steadily along the cottonwood shaded drive he recalled so well from his childhood. He soon came into sight of his family home and became very eager to reach it, shaking the reins and urging on his team.

"This it?" Queried a less than impressed Major Esprey.

"Yes," he replied in a faraway voice as memories of his childhood tumbled through his mind.

"It's nearly falling down," observed Kitty Hawes with some accuracy.

"It has been through a war," defended Sturgis.

"I expect the Union Army came this way," put in Jervy.

"Sure looks like it," added Kitty.

"Cardinal Woods never matched Blanchwell or Merrington, but I was happy here."

"*Cardinal*, you say. Papist, are you? I never realised," put in the colonel.

"You ain't set eyes on a cardinal *bird* afore?" Asked Kitty, with a heavy sigh.

"The house is named for the birds which roost hereabouts. They are also a symbol of the Commonwealth of Virginia," explained Giddy.

"When are we going to eat?" Asked Kitty who had got her way and was now being paid to do the cooking and washing-up. Though she was still negotiating over the level of renumeration she expected for looking after the horses, of which there were five.

Esprey ignored her and asked, "How far are we from Knightsbridge?"

"Six or so miles, but I reckoned on getting news of my folks before taking on Talisker."

"Do you think you'll find them still at Petersburg?"

Sturgis shook his head, "Only God knows that."

"Suppose Talisker gets to hear that you're back?"

"I'll just have to risk it."

"Ye'd best bring home some vittles, I can't feed you on fresh air," complained the cook.

"I'll do my best, but who knows what conditions are like in a city which has just come through a siege."

"Perhaps we should come too," said Esprey.

"No, it's best if I go alone."

The colonel eventually nodded his acceptance of this.

"Are we staying here?" Questioned Kitty as she studied the damage which had been done to the building.

"We may as well, for at least the roof appears intact," observed Sturgis.

"There's maybe some food hereabouts," said Kitty, though doubtfully.

"Not after a hungry army's passed through," Esprey shook his head.

"There'll not be a broken cracker left," predicted Giddy, he being well aware that marching armies picked clean every place they passed through.

Kitty decided to see for herself, she jumped from the wagon and ran into the house.

As the officers were unhitching the team she appeared from around the back to report, "It's an empty shell."

"Nothing there at all?" Gideon wasn't surprised, but had hoped that *something* of his early life was still in place.

"Just a broken jug and shards o' pottery."

Kitty saw how affected Major Sturgis was and tried to cheer him up, "Oh, there's what looks like it was once a rocking-chair over by the fireplace."

"That was my grandma's, she died in it when I was seven or so,"

Jervy broke the silence which followed by suggesting, "We'd better bring saddles and blankets inside, they're the best we've got for beds."

"You two do that while I find kindling to set a fire away, then we can have bacon and beans," ordered Kitty.

"Couldn't you grub about in the garden and find the makings of a salad or something," the colonel was becoming tired of beans as he had no fondness for the effect they had on his digestive system.

"I like beans," shouted Kitty as she disappeared to bring a bag of them indoors.

"Sound like we have a new CO," commented Giddy dryly.

"I've known worse ones," put in the colonel.

"What ought we to do with the gold, now that we have a base?"

Esprey gave it some thought and said, "You must have played around here as a child, can't you recall somewhere safe to hide it?"

"There used to be an ice-house in the woods, but no doubt the Yankees will have been there already looking for drink."

"Which means they may not return to look again."

"It could be full of snakes by now," mused the major.

Esprey shivered, "Don't care for snakes myself – found a cobra coiled up in my bath house once."

"There are venomous ones around here too, but they'll stay out of your way if you stay out of theirs."

"Maybe we should bury our valuables," suggested the colonel.

"That's the simplest solution, we'll do it to-night when the child's asleep."

As if on cue Kitty shouted from the veranda, "Grub's up.".

"We're coming," returned Esprey.

"Do you think she heard us?" Asked Giddy.

The colonel thought for a moment and then replied, "We just need to make sure she's not about when we begin digging."

Two hours later they all sat pleasantly full around the fire Kitty had made up in the drawing room hearth.

"This must once have been a pleasant room," suggested Esprey, "fine dimensions and plenty of light too."

"Pity there's no glass in the windows," grunted Kitty.

"You're nothing other than a hanger-on or at best a servant and so should keep quiet," admonished the Englishman, though in a friendly, joshing sort of way.

"An' you're just a foreigner who don't even speak proper American," replied the girl swiftly.

Giddy then put in quickly, "Whatever he is, it'll be dark soon and I'll be off to Petersburg, so we'd best sort our beds out whilst we can still see our way around."

"There ain't no beds," pointed out Kitty.

"I can barely remember when I last slept on a decent mattress, such as the one I share with Eliza," nodded the colonel sadly.

"Any corner'll do me, I'm more tired than I was after Chancellorsville," smiled Giddy, pleased that once he had visited his home city he would continue to sleep under his own roof, no matter what condition it was in.

*****

"Did ya find your folks?" Called Kitty Hawes the following day as she returned from the water pump after washing up the breakfast things.

"No," replied Sturgis shortly.

"You were away long enough…," she paused and pointed at the Englishman, "and after that you and him went off like thieves in the night."

23

"We thought you were asleep, as all good girls should be at midnight," admonished Esprey.

Kitty shook her head, "I ain't interested in your doings, s'long as I get my pay."

Somehow Giddy doubted this but said nothing.

"As we agreed, our next business is down to me," said Jervy putting his foot into the stirrup, "so I'd best be away."

"I should be off to Knightsbridge myself," said Gideon Sturgis.

"We've been through this umpteen times, even were Talisker not to shoot you out of hand, he'd refuse to deal with you."

"Though he may be willing to negotiate when he learns what we have to offer."

"I doubt that."

"You're forgetting that the war has changed everything here, he may be desperate to sell up and move on."

"It don't make no difference anyways," put in Kitty Hawes.

Both men took on puzzled looks.

"What makes you say that?" Asked the major.

"'Cos neither of you will be able to find your way to Knightsbridge."

Gideon laughed derisively, "I was brought up here, I know every side turning and dip in the road for miles around."

"Colonel Englishman don't though, do he?"

24

"I could draw him a map from memory."

It was Kitty's turn to laugh mockingly, "Betcha' don't know where the Yankee road blocks are."

"Union troops would have no reason to stop a British citizen, especially one of Her Majesty's officers of field rank."

"Maybe not, but sure as shootin' they'd want to know what's in the wagon."

"I'm not taking the wagon, perhaps just a few samples to make my case."

"All nice an' clean an' dandy."

"Yes, that's how it will be."

"The Yankees'll be mostly drunk, maybe all o' them will be."

"What about their officers, surely...," began the colonel.

"There'll maybe be a sergeant and half a dozen men, they'll likely search you and take anything you have of value."

"They wouldn't dare."

Kitty shrugged her shoulders, "They won the war, they run things round here and there ain't no sayin' *no* to 'em."

"The British consul in Washington would lodge a complaint as soon as he was informed that such an outrage had occurred," replied the colonel with a degree of pomposity.

"By which time the Yankee thieves would be well away spending your valuables, that's if they ain't kilt you for the fun of it."

"You know this from experience?" Interrupted Gideon.

"My bruises remind me of it all the time."

The two men contemplated in silence for a moment and then Jervy said, "This makes things more difficult."

"Though I suppose the army'll be pulled out soon enough," declared Giddy.

"Not in time to acquire the plantation for anywhere near the figure we have in mind."

Kitty shook her head, "How you both managed t'survive a battle or two, I don't reckon I know. I've told you, I can lead you around the road-blocks, sweet as a midsummer whistle."

"Saddle-up the spare draft horse for yourself, then," Giddy gave way.

Later that day, after they'd ridden through the steamy heat for half-an-hour, Kitty Hawes said, "We're being followed, the tips o' my toes are tingling."

"It'll be Giddy, he's seeing us safely on our way," replied the colonel knowingly.

"He's a real kindly old grandma', ain't he."

*****

In fact, Sturgis was shadowing them from half a mile behind and continued to do so until he came to a road he was familiar with, which he took without a second thought.

The road was open and the weather fair so he nudged his steed into a canter and began to enjoy the rush of fresher, cooler air across his face.

On rounding a bend he found himself cantering into the middle of a unit of Union soldiers who were in the process of establishing a camp.

In a flash his mind revisited times recently past and he instinctively leaned forward to grip the butt of his horse-pistol. He began to breath more quickly and could feel the heat of his blood as it began to course through his veins in a well-remembered way. His dander was up now and he kicked his mount into a gallop. His mouth opened wide as he prepared his throat to make a series of Rebel yells.

Then, as soon as his searching fingers were unable find the weapon they were seeking, he was pitched back to reality, "It's over. The war's over and done with," he gasped aloud. As these stark memories faded away he sighed with relief that he had no need to risk life and limb ever again.

Still breathing heavily he pulled hard back on the reins and fought his mount to a shuddering stop.

A sergeant came into the middle of the road, his palm raised high and with several black infantrymen ready to back him up.

*Damn girl promised she knew where all the Federal road-blocks were,* thought Sturgis as he settled his mount down.

"I'm a citizen of the Commonwealth of Virginia going about my lawful business," he stated quietly.

"And what business would that be, sir?" Enquired the white captain of the company in a friendly sort of way as he approached.

"The resumption of normal commerce of course, which is required here most urgently," as he spoke Giddy climbed from the saddle and shook hands with the Union officer.

"I see you're armed," the captain continued to smile.

"What sensible man wouldn't be in the backwoods these days?"

The captain laughed and then invited, "Join me for coffee," at the same time pointing towards a tent with an open flap where a coffee pot was already steaming.

Shortly thereafter the officers were sipping hot drinks and discussing the current situation in and around Petersburg.

"You have your men in better order that some I've seen or heard about," congratulated the major.

"You're a military man yourself, I think."

Giddy smiled and sat rigidly erect to introduce himself, "Major Gideon Sturgis, late of Fitzhugh-Lee's Brigade."

"The way you handled your mount I thought you must be cavalry. Though I'm surprised you managed to survive the war in so hard a fighting unit."

"A thigh wound at Gettysburg probably saved my life."

"I was there too, out on the right-flank with the Pennsylvania Cavalry, took a hit on the third day – stray bullet I think – but that's how I ended up in the infantry."

"Which Pennsylvania cavalry outfit were you with?"

"Seventeenth."

Giddy's memory began to stir, "You weren't with a Captain Helmuth Schilling I suppose."

At this the Union officer took off his hat and flung it to the ground as a physical indication of his amazement, "Cap'n Schilling had me promoted from sergeant."

"He's now my brother-in-law, and residing in England."

"Yes, I knew that he was living in some style, *Blankway, Blotching* – or some such place."

"*Blanchwell*. You'll remember his servant too, Andy Jackson, the fellow who escorted him home to his wife and family – he came back here to fight."

At this Crittenden shook his head sadly, "A brave man he was indeed, and never one to let his friends down. Poor fellow took the typhus and was dead in less than twenty-four hours."

At this Sturgis took from his pocket a silver flask, "Perhaps a toast to his memory?"

Crittenden smiled but shook his head, "Still on duty, but at any other time I'll be pleased to accommodate you."

"What regiment are you now?" Queried Giddy, flapping a hand towards the soldiery.

"Still with the Nineteenth Infantry, United States Colored Troops."

"What on earth are you doing out here in the backwoods?"

"Senior officers intend to keep my boys away from the towns as they don't wish to rub the noses of the Rebs....," he paused and then added quickly, "No offence intended."

"None taken."

"Anyway, the rest of our outfit was ordered off to Texas leaving 'J' Company high and dry in the middle of what was recently hostile territory."

"The ways of the high command," Giddy shook his head slowly in time with his words.

"The regiment is to be disbanded soon enough, I suppose the politicians don't like the idea of too many well trained black troops about – especially in sensitive areas."

Giddy nodded his agreement and then asked, "What's for you after that? Back home, I suppose."

Again the Union officer shook his head, "My pa' is a poor dirt farmer with no chance of getting any bottom land, besides which soldiering is in my blood now."

"Staying on then."

"The story is that the War Department is to establish two cavalry regiments of Negro troopers."

"Were you to join them it's unlikely you'd be accepted socially, outside of your own regiment that is."

"Makes no difference to me as I've never been invited to fine tea-parties anyhow."

"Peacetime army though, you'll have to drop a rank."

"Two I expect, and though the pay's not great at least I won't have to worry about crops not growing or the weather ruining them."

"There's that to it."

Gideon waved towards the troops, "Do you think the Negroes will be prepared to soldier on?"

Crittenden thought for a short while, smiled and then replied, "These boys are fine soldiers, I'd back them against anything they come up against, whether they be Mexicans, British or Sioux Indians."

*****

"It would be best if you were to remain here," suggested Colonel Esprey as he reined in his mount at the gateway to the Knightsbridge Plantation.

"I'm sticking with you – else you'll be lost after half a mile," Kitty's tone was determined.

The colonel spoke more forcefully, "You will do as you're told."

"You can't stop me following you – unless you use that pistol o'yours on me," she flung her head enough to make her short hair ruffle in the breeze.

Jervy softened his voice, "I've obviously overestimated your maturity, for it was my expectation you'd easily understand the vital part you have to play in this escapade."

"Maybe so, but I *still* want to see Knightsbridge," she stuck out her lower lip.

"Your duty is to act as my rear-guard, for by all accounts Talisker is a most unpleasant person and if he were to do me down, then you must return to warn Major Sturgis."

"Then he'll come in shootin' an' I'll be charging with him."

"Exactly, my dear," called Esprey kindly as he trotted off.

Kitty smiled as she watched him depart and as soon as he was out of sight she kicked her own mount into motion, "I'll be watching his back, but from closer in than he thinks," she muttered to herself.

A few minutes later the colonel was fast approaching Knightsbridge, he was pleased to see that the house was completely intact, untouched by the war. However; during his journey along the driveway, he had noticed that there was no activity at all to be seen in the surrounding fields.

"What'ya, want?" The voice was a very loud one and the colonel immediately saw why when its owner stepped from behind a tree, shot-gun levelled to fire.

"I'm here to meet with the owner of this plantation," replied Esprey, his tone unfazed.

The man in front of him was young and very large. In girth he reminded Jervy of a Waziri chieftain he'd had uneasy dealings with back in the 40's.

"What fer?"

"Business – not that it's any of yours, unless you are the titleholder of this property."

"Nope."

"I'm hoping to meet a Mister Tobias Talisker."

The man guffawed, "Then ye'd best visit the family plot, it's over there, in that grove of trees."

"He's dead?"

"Sure is, unless we buried him alive," the sentry chuckled gruffly.

"Then who's in charge now?"

"Madame de Friese."

"A lady? Is she receiving visitors this morning?"

The guard laughed, "*Receiving*? She's done naught else since the war ended."

"Then perhaps you'll take me to her, I'm Lieutenant-Colonel Esprey of the British Army."

"She won't want no doin's with a redcoat," the guard; whose name turned out to be Buster Bailey, shook his head vigorously.

"You couldn't possibly know that, and I'm very sure that Madame de Friese will wish to discuss my proposition."

"She don't give no carpetbaggers the light o' day."

"I'm an officer of the British Army, do I *look* like a carpetbagger?"

The large man contemplated for a second or two and then ordered, "All right, you go ahead o' me, steady like, and I'll check t'see if she's *receiving.*"

A short while later, Jervy was led into a beautifully and recently decorated drawing room which was filled with fine pieces of furniture, pictures and *objects d'art*.

"This is a splendid apartment, ma'am."

33

The lady nodded and he could see that; like the room, she was very well dressed and also sparklingly bejewelled.

*Madam is doing very well for herself, this may take many more dollars than we expected,* he thought to himself.

"Please do take a seat, colonel, and I shall have tea brought – you English like it hot and strong, or so I believe."

"Very kind of you, ma'am."

The lady of the house turned out to be the most attractive woman Jervy had come across in a long while. Her figure was full, though not too full, her complexion had never suffered from an overdose of sunlight and her eyes were dark but sparkled nonetheless. Her hair though was her crowning glory, it was piled high in a succession of intricate waves and curls.

"I don't suppose Knightsbridge compares very well with the country houses you're used to."

"I half expected this mansion to be a charred wreck," commented Jervy, "like so many of the others I've come across."

Madame de Friese laughed shortly, "Fortunately, I'm a distant relative of General Sherman as well as being able to play the part of a damsel-in-distress more than adequately."

"My wife was once an actress, so yes, I can easily picture you in that part too."

34

"Well, then, colonel, what is your business?" She asked once the tea had been served and the time for small-talk was over.

"I was expecting to meet a Mister Tobias Talisker."

"My father died early last year."

The colonel hoped that he didn't look as puzzled as he felt, for he had a feeling that this could be the woman that Giddy believed to be dead.

"You have a sister? Other family?" He asked.

"No, I'm an only child."

"Your papa obviously believed that perfection couldn't be improved upon," the colonel meant every word.

She gurgled with laughter, in the style of a little girl who has just been told that she is pretty, but then her expression  swiftly became business-like and she said, "You still haven't explained what it is you want."

"My partner and I hoped to be able to purchase Knightsbridge."

Again she laughed, "With all your fine talk you're yet another carpetbagger."

"No, ma'am, I hold the rank of colonel in the British Army and my partner and I wish to purchase and return this plantation to a state of prosperity."

"What makes you think that this is not already the case?"

Esprey thought for a while and then spoke clearly, "There are no crops growing, nor are there any field hands to be seen labouring to produce them."

"This is obviously so, as it is no longer possible to hold slaves and presently I haven't the resources to pay the number of workers  required to successfully cultivate tobacco."

"My partner and I have sufficient capital to take on your ex-slaves and pay them the going rate."

"I see," Mrs de Friese now sounded much more interested.

"We shall also ensure that decent quarters are available for them and that a school is built to educate their children."

"That won't sit very well with some of my neighbours, who still hanker for everything to be as it once was."

"These are inducements we propose are to encourage hard work and we would expect to be exporting tobacco by the end of next year."

"This is your plan?"

"A feasible one, don't you think?"

Deborah de Friese thought for a while and then asked, "Who is your partner and why hasn't he accompanied you?"

Esprey was now in a quandary. *Should he tell or refuse to tell her?* He wasn't sure which.

"Come on, colonel, don't be shy.  For all I know you may be the hired representative of some slimy Yankee with a bag full of dollars."

"My partner is Major Gideon Sturgis, recently of the Army of Northern Virginia," Jervy came to a sudden decision.

To say that Deborah de Friese was taken aback would be an understatement as a multitude of expressions crossed her face in rapid succession.

"Giddy's alive. Where is he?"

"Not ten miles from here, at Cardinal Woods."

"I was sure he'd been killed at Gettysburg."

"That's strange, because he thinks you're dead too."

*****

The following day when Sturgis set off to visit Deborah, he was hoping that he would no longer find her physically attractive. Though only an hour later he discovered that in this he was to be disappointed. From the instant he set eyes on her his heart began to pound and he could feel his limbs trembling more violently than they had at Drewrey's Bluff, where he had first come under hostile fire.

"Your father told me you were dead, that was just before his men opened up on me with their shotguns," he managed to scramble out some words at last.

"It was only birdshot, or at least that's what papa told me they were using."

"He didn't give me a moment to discuss things with him," Giddy spread his hands in a gesture of helplessness.

"At the time I was locked in the attic with the windows battened shut. I heard everything that was happening and my heart nearly broke – I refused to eat for a week."

"As long as that?" He spoke cynically.

"I was compelled to take food when a quack doctor; accompanied by a very large nurse, was called in. They force fed me through a rubber tube."

"I didn't mean to sound so callous, I'm sorry."

They sat in silence for a minute or so and then he asked, "When did you become Madame de Friese?"

"I had no choice in the matter and when the news came after Gettysburg that you were amongst the fallen, I had little else to care about."

"It is true that I may well have died, but my leg and life were saved by Grace Schilling, the lady I later married."

"You're wed to a *Yankee?*" Deborah was finding this difficult to believe.

"My wife is a fine woman, honest, caring and loyal."

"I suppose she's a pale skinned, blonde beauty too."

"She would never describe herself as such," he shook his head.

After a few long seconds Deborah spoke again, "You have children to this woman?"

"Her name is Grace."

"Has *Grace* given you children?"

"She recently suffered a miscarriage, but we continue to live in hope."

After another long pause Deborah spoke up strongly, "*I* would have presented you with several healthy male children by now."

"Though we can never know the truth of that," Giddy shrugged his shoulders.

Deborah considered for a long moment and then suggested, "From what I gathered from Colonel Esprey you live in England, and in some comfort too."

"My brother-in-law is a man of means."

"He is supporting your proposal to buy Knightsbridge?"

Giddy shook his head negatively at first as he had no desire to tell the truth, but he came out with it at last, "My wife has a reasonable fortune which she is willing to venture."

Deborah nodded sagely, "Suppose I were unwilling to sell, especially to the wife of the man who once promised me his eternal love?"

"I believed you were dead," returned Giddy plaintively.

Her face hardened, "I may wish to keep Knightsbridge for myself."

"Then Esprey and I will have to look elsewhere for a similar property."

"I could be persuaded to deal with you and your partner, but there is a tiny problem," she had softened her tone to reply.

"There always is, whether it be in love, war or commerce."

"My husband, Claude, insists that my property became his on marriage."

"That is the normal arrangement," put in Sturgis who then went on to ask, "Will he agree sell do you suppose?"

"I've no idea, I've not seen him for some months – since Sherman's troops ravaged Georgia on their way to the sea in fact."

"Could he have been caught up in the fighting?"

Deborah laughed derisively, "Claude would do his damnedest to stay well away from a battlefield, even were the fighting to be across his own property."

"Then I guess he never felt obliged to take up arms for the Cause?"

"You'd be quite correct in that assumption."

"In which case why isn't he here with you? If you were mine I couldn't bear to be parted from you," as soon as he had spoken thus Gideon wished he hadn't.

"I can see that you still yearn for me, even though you married another woman," the timbre of her voice warmed and softened even further.

Sturgis shook his head as his mind was battered by a rapid series of emotions.

"You may kiss me, if you wish, for were we not always at least friends?"

He leaned forward and pecked her cheek.

"Not like that, *like this*," she whispered hoarsely as she pressed her lips firmly on to his and her tongue began a darting exploration of his mouth.

He moved closer to her and then pulled away again.

"Faint heart never won fair lady nor desirable property either," she taunted.

He rose and at the same time pulled her to her feet and held her firmly in his arms, then he began kissing her as though he meant it, releasing the pent up passion for her which had been held in check for many years.

\*\*\*\*\*

"For goodness sake stop fiddling with your saddle straps, your nerves must really be on edge," commented an irritated Colonel Esprey.

"Not particularly."

"Expecting trouble ahead I suppose."

Giddy said nothing for a while and then admitted, "I'm fretting over Grace, I'm concerned how my feelings for Deborah could affect her."

"Don't let a pretty face overrule your common sense."

"But I loved Deborah from the moment I first met her, we go back years."

"Years of heartbreak as far as I can tell."

"I love Deborah, I always have and always will."

"I can easily see the attraction of Madame de Friese; for any red blooded man it would be the same, but it's best that you maintain your distance from her, both mentally and physically."

"I keep telling myself that, but I can hardly sleep for thinking of her."

"Madame de Friese is *not* your woman – push her from your mind."

"I'll try, but I'm not sure that I can."

"Just keep remembering that we both have fine ladies waiting for us at home."

"Yes, and we left them without a single word or even a note."

"Nonetheless, we should keep them to the forefront of our minds," said Jervy forcefully.

Riding just behind the two men, Kitty's ears were flapping as she took in everything they had said but she made no comment.

A short while later Knightsbridge came into sight, however it now bustled with activity. At least a dozen horses were hitched nearby and six or seven men were lounging around on the veranda eating, drinking and seemingly making a jolly good time of it.

As Gideon's party dismounted they were approached by Buster Bailey who was still clutching his shotgun, "The missus definitely ain't *receiving* today," he greeted them with a smirk.

"Though Monsieur de Friese has returned," presumed the colonel.

"The *monsieur* sure has," he poked a thumb towards the crowd on the veranda, all of whom had turned their attention to the visitors.

"Is Madame de Friese at home too?" Asked Giddy with something of a catch in his voice.

"No she ain't, the master has sent her off down to Georgia – he has holdings there."

"It's of no matter, we're here to see whoever owns this place," interrupted Esprey as he took a step towards the front door of the mansion.

"Now, hold on there...," cried Buster as he scrambled to catch up with the much taller British colonel.

Sturgis quickly joined his partner, *"Georgia,"* he whispered to himself sadly, torn between his desire to see Deborah and the necessity of concluding their present business successfully.

With an ungainly scramble Buster Bailey caught up with the visitors just as they had reached the front door.

"Yer can't go no further," he ordered.

Sturgis ignored him and rattled the knocker hard.

Conversation on the veranda ceased and those men who weren't drunk checked that their side-arms were resting easy in their holsters and looked on with interest.

A few long seconds went by and then the door was flung open by the largest and most impressive black woman either of them had ever seen, statuesque wasn't in it.

"The master was expecting you to call," her voice was soft and warm, a combination of honey and melting chocolate.

"Now hold on there," cried Buster, "it's my job t'see to strangers – I've bin here since..."

The black woman turned a pair of glittering green eyes upon him, "Jest shut up and go about your business." The previous softness and warmness of her voice had packed their bags and fled the scene, to be replaced by a sharpness which brooked no denial.

Buster took a step backwards whilst the audience on the veranda renewed their interest.

Bailey could see that the other men were laughing at him, "Black bitch," he shouted as he stepped forward again.

With the speed of a striking rattler a black arm with a clenched fist at the end of it struck Buster squarely between the eyes. He staggered back, his hands covering his face and he hoping that his nose wasn't broken.

"Don't you mess with me ag'in," commanded the black woman as she waved the visitors inside.

Bailey made a last desperate effort to get the better of the servant but had the door firmly shut in his face long before he was able to reach it.

"I trust that Madame de Friese is well," said Esprey, once he'd recovered from the surprise of Buster's downfall.

"As I've already telt you, she ain't here, but the master'll maybe see you if he ain't too busy. Follow me."

This impressive servant, whose name turned out to be Willow, eventually led them into the drawing room where waiting to greet them was Claude de Friese who turned out to be an very tall, thin man.

"Greetings, gentlemen," when he spoke his voice was high pitched and had no trace of a French accent.

The visitors were waved to seats and then Claude's gaze was fixed on Kitty, "She your whore?" He enquired, raising his eyebrows.

"Certainly not," returned the colonel quickly.

"No," backed up Sturgis.

"I ain't nobody's plaything," added Kitty very firmly.

"Twenty or so miles back there's a man still nursing a sore head who would confirm what the child has said," backed up the major.

De Friese nodded and then came straight to the point, "I believe you wish to purchase Knightsbridge."

"Is Deborah not to join us, for I believe the plantation belongs to her?" Enquired Sturgis.

"You need have no concerns over the position of *Madame* de Friese in this affair."

"Nonetheless, she told us that this plantation is *hers* and hers alone."

"Perhaps she dreamt that – besides which the law here is that a woman's property passes to her husband as soon as he's slipped a wedding ring on to her finger."

"Unless there has been some previous legal arrangement made," returned Giddy firmly.

"However, if your price is the right one, then perhaps a deal can be done," interrupted Jervy swiftly, wishing to get on with the business in hand.

"I will not sell," pronounced Claude resolutely, but then continued, "though a partnership could prove to be a profitable arrangement for us all."

The colonel laughed gently, "You expect us to buy into a plantation that has nothing growing nor even planted yet?"

"No field hands either," pointed out the major.

De Friese snorted loudly, "This is all by-the-by, for I must see the colour of your money before we discuss the matter any further."

"We easily have capital enough to satisfy you," replied Jervy.

"I hope your wealth is in something other than Confederate dollars," Claude smiled wryly.

"We are in a position to invest using English pounds or Yankee dollars," informed the colonel.

"Eighteen Fifty-four gold eagles too?" Replied Sturgis casually.

Noticing the avaricious expression which then crossed de Friese's face, Esprey wished that his partner had not mentioned the availability of gold.

"I should expect to see with my own eyes the colour of your money," as he spoke de Friese smiled widely, the idea of gold being available was a very attractive one to him.

Giddy nodded slowly and his words followed the same cadence, "Maybe..," he turned to his partner, "with the agreement of Colonel Esprey, of course."

"Every penny is currently deposited in a Yankee bank, quite secure," lied the colonel quickly.

De Friese watched closely the conflicting expressions crossing the faces of his visitors and knew for certain that the fortune carried by these would-be investors was secured within a short distance of Knightsbridge.

"I need to pee," trilled Kitty, who had followed the conversation carefully and who also knew where the cash of her rescuers was concealed.

"Should I take the little girl to the privy, sir?" Asked Willow.

De Friese said nothing for a second or two and then nodded his acquiescence before suggesting, "Perhaps we should discuss our business over luncheon."

Willow nodded and indicated that Kitty should follow her.

"Send in a selection of *aperitifs,* and whilst you're about it some *hors d'oeuvres* too," de Friese amended his orders.

As they were waiting for lunch, Esprey said, "You seem to have recruited a good number of armed men."

"These are difficult times, sir. Banditry is rife. There's no law and order unless you provide your own."

"There's a whole company of Union infantry just down the road," pointed out Giddy, his glass poised momentarily at his lips.

De Friese's eyes hardened, "Our Yankee overlords have had the temerity to send *black* soldiers to police this area."

"They appeared to be more than capable of securing this district when I met up with them," put in Sturgis.

"Their presence is nothing other than an attempt to humble us further, to thrust our faces into the dust," Claude's voice was pitched even higher than normal.

"They'll keep the peace for you, though."

"I will keep the peace here and the black Yankees will be dealt with soon enough."

"All of this is irrelevant to the business at hand," interrupted Esprey, who was keen to keep the negotiations for Knightsbridge at the top of the agenda.

De Friese smiled broadly, "Of course, the black soldiers are of little import."

"What sort of partnership had you in mind?" Asked Giddy, as he finished off a glass of fine madeira.

"It is one which will prove to be very lucrative within two or three years."

"Each of us owning a third of Knightsbridge?" Queried Esprey doubtfully.

"That won't do for me," warned the major.

"The partnership I envisage is a much, *much* grander concept."

"What *is* your plan, then?" Asked Jervy, becoming interested and putting aside for the moment his distrust of de Friese.

"I have tobacco at Knightsbridge and also a cotton plantation in Georgia."

"Combining the two? This sounds interesting," returned the colonel, against his better judgement.

"It's much more than that, for I also own a sugar plantation in Barbados."

Sturgis caught on quickly, "So no matter how erratically the commodity markets are swinging at least one product will maintain its price or even better it."

"By God, yes, if sugar's down then tobacco may be up – and so on," the colonel nodded positively as he spoke.

De Friese beamed and clapped his hands, "Excellent."

"Nonetheless, I must have Knightsbridge. I *must* own it," Giddy's voice was powerful and determined.

A short silence followed after which de Friese suggested, "Perhaps there is a compromise you would find acceptable."

"What do you suggest?" Queried the colonel, wishing to speed their business up.

"It may be possible, if Major Sturgis will agree to compromise."

"Very well, then, what do you propose?"

"Sturgis takes fifty-one percent of Knightsbridge but only twenty-five percent of each of the other properties," de Friese directed his words specifically to Giddy.

"That works well enough for me," agreed the Englishman who was keen for a positive outcome.

"Very well, though there is still the hurdle of your wife to be overcome," replied Sturgis after a moment or two.

"Deborah is of no account in this, but if you must have her present at the signing of the contracts then she shall attend, as long as you are willing and able to do business."

"To-morrow?" Asked Giddy quickly.

De Friese laughed, "She's down in Georgia, next week or the one after perhaps, travelling being as uncertain as it is. Before the end of the month, to be sure."

"*Two weeks.., End of the month...,*" exploded Sturgis, but then felt his arm restrained by his partner.

"Anyway," began Claude slyly once the major had settled down, "You will need to visit – New York is it not - to access your money."

"Philadelphia," corrected Esprey, developing his original lie.

"That will take you some time – what with the poor condition of the highways, road blocks and such."

"Indeed, yes," put in the colonel, "it will take us some days."

"I shall send a messenger to Cardinal Woods as soon as I have news."

Gideon shrugged his shoulders, "As you wish, I suppose."

Three hours later; after a leisurely lunch had been taken, the visitors were approaching the main entrance of the estate when they were halted by a shout from one of the rowdies standing there.

"Hey, that you Major Sturgis?"

Giddy looked around to see an old comrade hobbling towards him, he smiled and replied "Well, Fergie, I guess you didn't come out of the war in one piece either."

"Never got a scratch fighting the Yankees, major, but I fell off my horse drunk last week."

Giddy turned to the colonel, "This is Company Sergeant-Major Anthony Fergus," he introduced.

"Pleased t'meet y'all," Fergus nodded rapidly.

After a minute or two of recollections Sturgis asked, "What's the set-up here?"

The sergeant shook his head, "Money's good and haven't had to do much to earn it so far."

"What about Mr de Friese? He's a strange sort of fellow, don't you think?"

"As you well know, sir, I don't question orders, I jest follows 'em."

"To where was Madam de Friese smuggled away?" Asked Sturgis.

"Yes, our business was originally with her," added the colonel.

Fergus scratched his head, "I'd tell you if I knew, major, but I don't."

"She's still in the house," interrupted Kitty.

Giddy turned on her immediately, "How do you know that?"

"I didn't take a pee nor a sip o' water; even though my throat were parchin', I could have done with the fresh pair of boots that were lying around too…."

"For goodness sake, child, what about…" the colonel tried to interrupt.

"Where's my Deborah?  Has she been locked away?"
The major became impatient.

Kitty shrugged her shoulders, "I couldn't tell whether she were locked up or not, but I did hear her crying."

"Are you certain it was she?"

"Sure am, I can see straight through walls and doors, she was lying on the bed in a silken nightgown bubbling her big black eyes out…"

"Don't waste any more of our time, child," the Colonel's voice brooked no further prevarication.

"It was her, who else could it have been?"

"The swine's locked Deborah away so that she can't interfere."

"Which means that de Friese is afraid because she *does* have the power to upset his plans."

"Can we get her away, do you suppose?"  Suggested Giddy, his eyes betraying the recklessness he felt.

"Yes, I'll send forward the Grenadier Guards if you bring on the Blues and Royals."

Sturgis thought for a moment and then, looking directly at Fergie said, "I can't bring any British troops, but I think I know where I can recruit some American ones."

The ex-sergeant shook his head, "You know I'd follow you anywhere, major, but I'm not so sure about the others – most of 'em ain't troopers at all, more like red legs or bushwhackers."

"Are none of them reliable?"

Fergus thought for a while and then shook his head and replied meaningfully, "A few, but we're all well paid by Monsieur de Friese and mostly contented."

"What are you gossipin' wi' strangers over, Fergus, y'know the boss'll not like it?" This question was shouted by Buster Bailey who was approaching at; what was for him, high speed.

"Mind your own business and show some courtesy when in the hearing of an officer of General Fitzhugh-Lee's brigade."

"Just you never mind who *was* your boss, jest take your orders straight from Monsieur de Friese himself," returned Buster.

"Miss Willow seemed able to disregard you at will," pointed out Jervy with a smile.

"I'm the master o'her anytime, I can take her buck naked whenever I like," blustered Bailey who then turned to Sergeant Fergus, "You'd best get back where you belong."

"I'll go when I'm good and ready to and if you want to do anything about it, then go ahead and see what you get," the ex-sergeant wasn't about to take orders from an overweight lacky.

"We're just off anyway," put in Esprey, wishing to avoid trouble.

"Just see ye do," replied Buster as he turned away quickly, relieved that he had been able to see off these strangers without any further loss of face.

"What is de Friese planning?" Asked Giddy softly, wondering if a raid on Cardinal Woods was a possibility.

Fergus smiled, "The Yankees down the road have been mentioned. We could get some of our own back there."

"The war's over, sergeant," pointed out Sturgis.

Fergus thought for a while before he said softly, "Maybe it is, maybe it ain't."

*****

"You two going to do something about poor Mrs de Friese or not?" Asked Kitty once they were clear of the plantation.

Jervy shook his head doubtfully, "Odds are against us."

"Night time action, maybe. In and out just before dawn?" Suggested Sturgis with the hint of an appeal in his tone.

The colonel knew what the sensible answer to his friend's suggestion was, but he'd recognised early on in his career that a battlefield required luck just as much as it did courage, skill and common sense.

"If we have Deborah with us we also have Knightsbridge," pointed out Sturgis.

Esprey thought more a moment and then said, "No killing, mind, unless we have to."

"Have you a gun for me?" Asked Kitty enthusiastically.

Their answers came at once and together, "Certainly not. No."

Kitty knew that her companions were well armed and, as they couldn't use all their weapons at the same time, there was bound to be a gun left over for herself.

"When should we go? I think it should be as soon as possible – there's no sense pondering on it," proposed Giddy firmly, not wishing to give his friend time for a change of mind.

"Let's go now," urged Kitty, her eyes afire with excitement.

"De Friese may be expecting us to make an attempt to-night, so let's wait a couple of days," suggested the colonel calmly.

"Time is of the essence, de Friese might get it into his head to actually send Deborah to Georgia."

"Though if we wait he'll believe that we have no heart for any more fighting – we being two old soldiers whose best days are well behind them."

"He's sure right about that," muttered Kitty from the corner of her mouth.

"In addition, should his men spend two or three nights on watch waiting for nothing to happen, they would become much less vigilant."

Sturgis thought for a while and then agreed, "Oh, very well, I suppose a short delay may be for the best."

"Why don't I go to-night and cause a ruckus, keep them on their toes, make them nervous," suggested Kitty enthusiastically.

"*Hush*, child," replied Giddy.

"Be a *good* girl and I'll take you into town with me for provisions," offered Esprey.

"You two ain't much fun at all," growled Kitty.

*****

The next day a very worried Jervis Esprey was relieved to see Cardinal Woods come into sight as he drove back from the supply run to Petersburg. He urged on his team and didn't slacken their pace until he pulled up by the front porch.

"Is Kitty in there with you?" He shouted, his face twisted with anxiety and dread.

There was no answer, but then the main doors were swept open and Claude de Friese strode out on to the veranda, accompanied by a pair of his troopers.

"Young Miss Hawes definitely isn't here," he smirked as he spoke.

"Where's Major Sturgis?"

"I'm here, Jervy and I'm very sorry to find that the girl isn't with you," Giddy dropped his head as he came outside.

"I sent her off to buy whatever fruit and vegetables she could find, though she didn't return and I couldn't find her," explained Esprey.

Claude turned to Sturgis, "You'll see now that I was speaking the truth, which is that my men invited her to re-visit Knightsbridge."

"He *has* Kitty," said Giddy, his tone sombre.

"Kidnapping wee lassies now, is it? Very brave, very daring," Jervy's tone was edged with contempt.

"One way or another, I get what I want."

"He may be lying and Kitty is wandering around town still looking for me," suggested Esprey, though with little confidence.

"I do have your young friend, and to preserve her in good health you must bring every penny you have to Knightsbridge tomorrow morning."

"How can we possibly do that? Our wealth is tucked away…"

"You will do it or life for the little slut you had the temerity to bring into my home will worsen rapidly."

"It will takes us some days to get to our bank," appealed Sturgis.

"Your hoard is not in Philadelphia, nor anywhere else other than…" de Friese waved his arms around vaguely, "somewhere here."

"The child is nothing to us, so she's not much of a bargaining chip," pointed out the colonel.

"Oh dear me, that is unfortunate, for in that case I shall hand her over to Willow, she enjoys a white trash play-thing for a day or two."

Giddy shrugged his shoulders in as carefree a manner as he could manage, "In that case, let her get on with it."

"Hold on," put in Jervy, "I expect our deal will stand from the moment we hand over our cash."

"Yes, the three plantation arrangement," put in Giddy.

Claude de Friese flung his head back and snorted with laughter, "Don't be ridiculous, there is no Georgia plantation nor one on Barbados either. You'll both be as poor as church mice by this time to-morrow."

"In that case, do your worst," replied Giddy, though with not much force.

"Yes, we'll not submit to blackmail," agreed his partner, though his tone too lacked determination.

"That's such a pity for the little girl, Willow is very adept with a horsewhip. I've seen her peel a man of his skin, one strip at a time. Took her a while and her victim was still alive at the end of it."

"Harm that child and I'll kill you," the colonel's tone had changed to one as hard as steel.

A derisive laugh began to form in Claude de Friese's throat until he noticed the expression and glaring eyes of the British colonel and he could feel a steadily increasing tingle of fear run through his body. He coughed to clear his confusion and then said, "I wish the girl no harm, just do as I say and she'll go as free as a bird back to the whorehouse she originated from."

Giddy took his companion's arm, "We've no other choice."

Jervy sighed deeply, "It shall be as you say, we'll bring what we have tomorrow."

"Excellent," de Friese applauded lightly, "Bring every cent you have to Knightsbridge tomorrow morning and the girl will be returned to you – and I wish you well of her."

"Wait, there are only two of us and it will take us some time to recover our cash and coin," returned Esprey.

De Friese thought for a second and then said, "Very well, I've an accommodating nature, shall we say by to-morrow evening then?"

Both Jervy and Giddy nodded their acceptance; though each was hoping that the other had a better plan, and watched as their enemy and his followers rode off.

"I suppose we'd better start digging," suggested Esprey.

"No, I think we should visit Knightsbridge to-night, accompanied by a company of Union troops to arrest a kidnapper."

"Won't we be putting Kitty into even greater danger?"

"What makes you think de Friese will honour his side of the deal even if we do hand over the gold?"

Jervy thought for a second and then said, "Yes, he is probably planning to kill us all. We'd best check our weapons."

"You do that and I'll ride over to the Union camp and have a word with Captain Crittenden," shouted Giddy as he went to saddle up his horse.

*****

"Your husband won't really harm us, will he?" Asked Kitty.

Deborah de Friese screwed up her face into a thoughtful one, "Not ordinarily, but he will have his way and will go to any length to get it."

"That doesn't help much."

"What about Gideon and the British colonel? You've spent time with them, will they give in easily or is their fortune too precious to them?"

Kitty shook her head gently, "I met them on the road where I was in the process of being beaten with a fence pole. They could have rode on and not thought anymore about it…"

"But they didn't they stayed and rescued you."

"Yes and then they hired me as their cook, it's the first time anyone's paid me for working. I was worked to the bone at the orphanage and in return never received so much as a kind word."

"You never knew your parents, I suppose."

"Never seen them, as far as I know I just appeared out of thin air."

"What will you do when this present trouble is over – one way or another?"

"I guess I'll stick with my pardners."

"Are they aware that they have a prospective companion?"

"Nope, but they have."

*****

"It is unfortunate that Captain Crittenden was unavailable," reflected Jervis the following morning as they rode towards Knightsbridge.

"He'd gone off to the telegraph office, but I left a note warning him of the danger to his troops posed by de Friese as well as a request for assistance," replied Giddy.

"*Mmm*, I'm sure you realise that this makes the execution of our plan much more difficult."

"Indeed yes, but the company sergeant looked a reliable type, whom I'm sure will pass on my message."

"Can they arrive at Knightsbridge in time though – they being infantry?"

"It's an easy march for seasoned foot soldiers."

Just then Esprey came to a jerky halt and looked back over his shoulder, "Someone is following us."

Giddy turned his horse, looked around and replied, "I can't see anyone."

"Though I'm sure you'll have that familiar feeling running up and down your spine, the one you have no explanation for, but one you dare not ignore."

"Whoever it is will be a couple of hundred yards back, I suppose. Should we pull into the trees and wait to see who turns up?"

The colonel shook his head, rode his horse back a dozen yards and shouted; in a friendly enough tone, "Whoever is there behind us you can show yourself, we're honest travellers."

The sound of a cantering horse filled their ears and there then appeared the figure of Sergeant-Major Fergus.

"I expect de Friese has put you on to us?"

Fergie pulled his mount to a halt beside the two officers, "Yes, sir. He said I was to follow you and if you *weren't* coming in with a heavily loaded wagon, then I was to report back at once."

"It's taken you a while to obey your orders, we must be half way to Knightsbridge by now."

"I never was one to strike out at women."

"Women?"

"Sure, Madame de Friese and the little girl as was taggin' along with you."

"Then Deborah wasn't sent south at all," said Jervis.

"Nor is she in partnership with her husband," Sturgis was obviously pleased to learn this.

"Nope, she's locked away with the child – as far as I know."

Esprey looked hard at the sergeant and spent some time weighing him up, "I gather, then, that your loyalty to your employer is wavering a little."

"Maybe so, maybe not,  but some of the things Monsieur de Friese does, well, they don't sit happy on my shoulders."

"Very well, you've explained your positions to us and we're very grateful, so you may as well get on your way," said Esprey.

"Sure, we'll trust you not to make too early a report to de Friese," Giddy smiled and winked.

"Oh, there's nuthin' going to happen up at Knightsbridge until to-night, then it's one last strike at the Yankees for me an' the boys."

"De Friese plans to attack the Union infantry?" Asked Sturgis.

Fergie took off his hat and scratched his thinning hair, "I reckon on making one last charge before my time's up."

"You intend to go at 'em bald headed?" The colonel was puzzled.

"My hair's a bit scarcer than it were, but I *ain't* bald yet," the sergeant narrowed his eyes and spoke sharply.

"It's just a saying we use in England, no insult intended."

"Anyways, like always, I'm with the troop – death or glory."

"But the war is *over*," the major's tone became regimental.

"Maybe so, but the Union has no right to send black troops to lord it over us whites in our own backyard."

"General Lee signed for us all in good faith at Appomattox, what will he think when he hears that he has been dishonoured by the very troops he was so inordinately proud of?"

The sergeant laughed, "How will he know of it?"

"Were you to kill a company of Union troops he'd be bound to hear of it soon enough."

"In that case ol' Bobby'll cheer an' wave his hat, like he did on the battlefield," Fergie's tone was less than certain now.

Sturgis' expression turned very grave, "He will be distraught, sir, as he will consider himself dishonoured."

Esprey believed it was time for him to interrupt what could become a rather nasty argument. "Nevertheless, thank you, sergeant-major, for giving us fair warning of what lies ahead."

"I trust you'll take your time to inform de Friese that we're travelling light," added Sturgis, managing to keep his tone level.

"Well, as I've said, I don't hold with ill-treating womenfolk. De Friese is making it hard for his wife, she holds the deeds and won't say where they're stashed – I reckon he's planning to get what he wants any way he can – the boys reckon he'll let that hellcat Willow loose on her."

"We understand your position and thank you for it," said the colonel.

Fergus nodded and turned his horse, "It's time I took a drink or two of something stronger than water," he said before galloping off.

"Do you trust him?" Queried Esprey.

"I did once, but I figure he's gone a little bad since then."

"Then let's away, we've no time to lose," Jervy kicked his horse into movement.

*****

Captain James Crittenden returned to camp where his sergeant immediately handed over the warning note which had been delivered earlier by Major Sturgis.

"I think Monsieur de Friese's outlaws will be in for a very nasty surprise," laughed the officer grimly.

"The men need a taste of action, sir," replied the sergeant, "loafing about does them no good."

Crittenden laughed, "*Loafing?* Why, you never give them so much as a moment to take breath."

"Best to keep 'em busy, sir, all sergeants know that."

"Though I suppose they're eager to go home."

"The southerners amongst them aren't sure what sort of welcome they'll receive – I think most of 'em are planning to set up home north of Maryland."

Crittenden merely nodded, for he wasn't sure just how warm a welcome his men would receive anywhere north of the Mason-Dixon Line.

"Any of them plan to stay on?"

The sergeant nodded, "We hear a few black regiments are to be formed, I'm interested and so are some of the younger men."

"Good, they're all really fine soldiers."

They stood in silence for a while thinking of past battles and their comrades who had fallen in them.

"Let's be fully prepared for tonight, sergeant," ordered Crittenden after he'd sniffed to hold back the tears which so readily came into his eyes these days when his mind lingered on things past for longer than it should have.

"I hope we don't suffer too many casualties, especially as the war is over," said the sergeant.

"I had my fill of carnage at the siege of Petersburg."

"Especially the Crater, sir."

"It's just as well that we weren't as fully involved in that fiasco as was planned for us."

"Thank the Good Lord for our salvation."

They both stood in thoughtful silence for a while and then Crittenden ordered "Right, let's get ourselves prepared. Order the troops to build up the camp fires and fetch straw and any old or unused pieces of uniform they can find."

*****

"There's a lot going on at Knightsbridge, both back and front. Men tumbling all over the place, their mounts are restless too, and there's that pre-battle excitement and dread in the air," reported Gideon Sturgis on his return from a reconnaissance.

"All for us, you think?" Jervy had hoped that the plantation would be quiet.

"I don't think so, I believe they're going off to hit Crittenden's little force."

"Though de Friese is surely expecting us to turn up too, so why would he send most of his men off on a most unnecessary side-show?"

"He may be right in thinking that we're second on the bill, especially as he has our womenfolk held captive."

"Unless it's a blind hatred of black troops, or over confidence, maybe."

"Whatever it is the odds are still in his favour," suggested Esprey.

As they watched from the cover of a shrubbery, the front door of the house was flung open and a wide beam of light illuminated the veranda, into which strode Claude de Friese smoking an havana and looking as though he was soon to be crowned King of the World.

The tumult from his men and horses ceased as Fergus marched up and gave a poor representation of a salute, "We're all ready to go, sir," he informed.

"Then get on your way and make sure that you kill *all* the blacks, I don't want any survivors left to tell tales."

"What about the officer, sir? He's a white man."

"Kill him anyway."

"Sir," returned Fergie before he turned on heel and ordered, "Mount up."

Not very far away, Esprey whispered, "Once they've gone we could take de Friese easily."

"What about warning the Yankee infantry, though?"

"You're an ex-Reb, what do you care?"

"The war's over and, anyway, I've since realised that I spent two and a half years fighting on the wrong side."

"One of us should try to warn them you think?"

"Whoever goes will have to be damned quick to catch up with the raiding party or better still get ahead of them."

The colonel thought for a second and then said, "We can't split up, for de Friese won't have left his prisoners unguarded nor himself unprotected."

"I suppose Crittenden's men are able to look after themselves, especially as they've been warned of what's afoot," said Sturgis as he drew out his favourite revolver, the one which had never misfired or let him down in any way during the war.

"Okay, let's set the women free and then ride hell for leather to Crittenden's camp."

That decided they worked their way through the shrubbery until they had a view of the rear of the mansion, which was in complete darkness apart from a light shining in what they took to be an attic room.

"They could be up there…," began Esprey.

"*Shh,*" Giddy grabbed his partner's arm and whispered, "look, just by the door, in the shadow of the veranda."

Jervy looked closely and picked out the shape of a man.

As he spoke the guard came forward, armed with what looked like a repeating rifle, "Who's out there," he called.

"I'll put a shot over his head and keep him busy, whilst you rush around to the front and make use of my diversion," suggested Esprey.

"Wait," hushed Sturgis as he cleared the bushes and walked boldly towards the sentry with his arms in the air.

"Who the fuck are you and what are you doing back here."

"I didn't fancy charging into the unknown in the dark, so I came back. Thought there might have been some vittles left around."

"De Friese won't like that," the guard paused and then continued suspiciously, "Say, I don't believe that I recognise you."

Sturgis took off his hat, "How's that?" He asked coming still closer.

"When did you join up?" Asked the guard who was still plagued with doubt and began to raise his rifle ready to fire from the hip.

"Just yesterday, it seemed a good deal then, but now I'm not so sure."

"You frightened o' black Yankees?"

"I'm frightened of anyone with a gun, the war taught me that – who were you with?"

"Fourteenth Virginia Cavalry."

"I was with Fitzhugh Lee."

"Top of the tree, *huh*?"

By this time Giddy was very close to the guard, he took a further step forward and then stunned the man by hitting him across the head with the side of his pistol and then hit him again to render him unconscious.

"Okay," he half shouted.

As he was waiting for his partner, Sturgis tried the back door and found that it was unlocked.

"We're in, I see," muttered Jervy as he arrived and had inspected the body of the guard for any sign of consciousness.

A few minutes later they had carefully passed through various rooms and found themselves at the bottom of the rear stairs which appeared to lead to the attic room they were interested in.

They climbed a step at a time upwards and paused on each tread, their nerves jarred by every creak of the woodwork. Once they'd reached the top floor they soon came to a door which had light shining from under it.

"This must be it," whispered Sturgis.

"Yes, but where is everyone? De Friese wouldn't have left himself totally unprotected."

"There's only one way to find out," replied Giddy as he turned the door handle and found to his surprise that it was unlocked.

It only took a second or two for their eyes to become accustomed to the light and they saw, seemingly waiting for them, Claude de Friese who was waving a pistol in their direction.

"Welcome, gentlemen," he called in a conversational sort of way.

"Hand over the ladies and we'll be on our way," offered Esprey as he ventured further into the room, his revolver also at the ready.

"Come in, we'll smoke, drink and discuss the womenfolk," as he spoke de Friese pocketed his gun which was a Sharps Pepperbox.

Not expecting so hospitable a welcome, both Esprey and Sturgis accepted the offer of a bourbon whisky and a choice cigar and waited to hear what de Friese had to say.

"Down to business, I think, gentlemen."

"Fair enough," replied Jervy, before he added, "Where are the ladies?"

"They're both chained up in the cellar."

"Bring them here, let us see for ourselves that they are unharmed."

"Not until we've concluded our business – which will begin with clear instructions as to where I must dig for your treasure trove."

"We must first see that both Madame de Friese and Miss Hawes are in good health."

"You've no bargaining power, I'll do as I please."

"We easily out-gun you and we know where our cash is and you don't."

"This is true, but I hold the trump card, which is that the ladies are *my* prisoners and I know that you will not allow any harm to come to them."

"If you did harm either…," responded Giddy with some heat.

De Friese held up both hands in a placatory way, "My dear fellow, how can you think such a thing, not a hair on their heads will be touched, as long as I end up with your combined fortune – all of it."

Both officers laughed and shook their heads.

"We're both fighting men, we have weapons and know how to use them, we'd fill you full of holes before you'd even cocked that toy pistol of yours," Giddy's words were full of fire and came out in a flood.

De Fries clucked his tongue several times and shook his head gravely, "Between you and the ladies I have… a good number of guardians, besides which they have orders to kill the women if any attempt to rescue them is made."

"You're a lower dog than I ever imagined possible," retorted Esprey.

"I'll take great pleasure in battering the life out of you if…," responded Giddy, furiously.

"Oh, dear, so much wind and fire. Perhaps you should give thought to the ladies who are languishing in the cellar. This is an old house and its underpinnings are extensive and deep. There are rats down there and probably some snakes too."

Giddy's face paled, for he knew that this abductor of women was speaking the truth.

"We must have proof that you have both ladies and that they are in good condition," demanded Esprey.

"Then first, put your gun away, Major Sturgis."

"Do as he says," advised Esprey.

Reluctantly; after the passage of a few long seconds, Giddy did as had been asked.

Then de Friese called quietly towards a door at the other side of the room, "Willow, tell Buster to bring the ladies up here."

"Yes, sir," came a reply followed by the sound of heavy feet on the stairs.

"Willow will bring them up shortly, in the meantime let me top up your glasses."

As de Friese stooped to pour whiskey, Sturgis thought about striking him over the head, but then decided that for the safety of the women it was too dangerous a move.

Five or so minutes later the door was opened and both Deborah de Friese and Kitty Hawes were pushed into the room. They both looked bedraggled but otherwise none the worse for wear.

"Here they are, sir," said Willow who at the same time gave Deborah a rough push forward.

"Touch her again and I'll kill you where you stand," said the Giddy in a low, deadly tone.

"Idle threats carry no weight with me, major," returned Willow with a sneer.

Once the atmosphere in the room had settled down, de Friese suggested, "In the morning we shall all ride over to Cardinal Woods and dig up your loot."

"Don't listen to him, he hasn't got his hands on the Knightsbridge deeds yet and without them and your money he is lost."

Before anything more could be said, Buster Bailey pushed his way into the room and covered the ex-soldiers with a shotgun.

"We seem to have little other choice," sighed the colonel.

"I've told you, without my deeds he's finished," cried Deborah desperately.

"I shall have them beaten out of you. Willow would enjoy such a task and I'll look on with; I must admit, a considerable degree of pleasure."

"I'm stubborn by nature and what's mine I'll keep," Deborah was defiant, though to a perceptive listener there was an uncertain catch in her voice.

"You won't be so brave when you find yourself bound naked across a bench and so very vulnerable? I doubt you'll hold out for longer than half-a-dozen strokes," de Friese was smiling as he spoke.

Even the idea of this was more than Major Sturgis could stand, he flung himself forward powerfully into de Friese and carried him half-way across the room. Then they fell rolling and tumbling on the floor.

Bailey discharged his shot-gun, but the barrel was pushed upwards by the very agile Miss Hawes so that it was only the ceiling which was punished by the pellets, causing a shower of dust and plaster to fall.

Willow took out her knife and balanced herself, stepping from foot to foot until she was in the right position to strike in support of her master.

Wasting not a second further, Esprey took up the whisky bottle and cracked it across the head of the black woman who fell groaning in a heap at his feet.

From the attic landing there was heard the sound of several pairs of boots and a gruff male voice shouted, "You Okay Monsieur de Friese? What's going on in there?"

"I've got your boss here and I'll choke the miserable life out of him if you so much as turn the door handle and it won't take more than a couple of squeezes, 'cos I'll be enjoying it," returned Giddy.

"Do as he says… Quickly, he'll throttle me to death," Claude managed to deliver these words but only with great difficulty.

"Check to see if he has another gun on him," Sturgis instructed.

The colonel did as he was asked and then shook his head negatively.

Giddy then let loose of his prisoner and pushed him to the floor to join the still unconscious Willow.

As soon as de Friese had cleared his throat and got his breath back, he asked, "What do you plan now, this house is surrounded by my men and they outgun you many times over?"

"That maybe so, but with you leading the way, with a choker around your neck, would you wish them to open fire?"

"I've some sharp-shooters."

"In the dark into a tight cluster of folks? Who'd end up shooting who?"

At that point, Willow groaned and rolled over on to her side and raising her hands to her wounded head.

"Can I give her a good, hard kick?" Asked Kitty with some eagerness.

"Leave the woman be, child," instructed Jervy.

"I'm not a child, I'm sixteen… At least I think I am."

"Let's get going, I'm tired of him," at this Deborah aimed a kick at her husband's ribs which struck home with some force.

De Friese yelped and then offered in a pathetic whine, "I'm sure we can come to some arrangement over this – perhaps a deal can be done after all."

"The time for an agreement has long passed," Deborah had her husband where she wanted him and there was now no deal which would satisfy her, apart from one which ended with him beneath the ground.

"How do you expect to get away? My men are stationed all around, why in one quick rush they could deal with every one of you in an instant."

At this Bailey grunted and nodded his agreement.

Sturgis spoke up decisively, "You will order your men to the barn, which Kitty will bolt once they're safely inside. After which we shall mount up and be on our way."

"*Ha*, you will have to return to Cardinal Woods as everything you have is there, so I'll know exactly where you are," cried de Friese.

"Sure we will, but *you'll* be coming with us too, as a hostage," returned Giddy, pouring cold water over de Friese's triumph.

These exchanges were interrupted by Willow who sat up rubbing her head and moaning gently to herself.

"What's happened? Who hit me?" She eventually asked, though seemingly still in a daze.

"You were put to sleep with whiskey," informed Jervy truthfully.

Willow's hands went to her head and she began to rock unsteadily back and forth, "I think I'm... I don't know...," she muttered.

Kitty leaned forward and touched the black woman's shoulder, "You'll be all right...," she began sympathetically.

Without warning, Willow growled like a tiger, launched herself at Kitty and took her by the neck.

"Let the master go, let him go, 'cos I can squeeze the life out of this kitten in the shake of a fist," she threatened, rising at the same time and dragging the young girl with her.

Kitty began to kick with her heels into the shins of her captor, but further pressure on her throat subdued her quickly.

"Keep tight hold on her," ordered de Friese rising to his feet with a leer of triumph crossing his face.

Willow manoeuvred her captive towards the door where she indicated with a nod to both her boss that he should join her.

Bailey also wasted no time in retrieving his shotgun and hurrying for the stairway.

De Friese followed quickly ordering at the same time, "Bring the little whore with you."

Hearing this, Kitty jerked herself free of her captor and ran into the waiting arms of Sturgis.

As soon as she'd lost her bargaining chip, Willow wasted no time in dashing off down the stairs hot on the heels of her master.

"Quick, along the corridor, before he comes back with reinforcements," cried Deborah decisively, who then led them to her boudoir, where she rummaged through a set of drawers until she came out with a six-shot revolver and a full box of ammunition.

"Are you planning that we shoot our way out?" Asked Giddy.

"*Yeah*," cried Kitty, "gimme the little pop-gun de Friese had… *Please.*"

"I'm a hopeless pistol shot at distance," admitted Gideon.

"I've had plenty of practice, especially from the saddle…," began the colonel before he was interrupted by Deborah.

"I can hit a target ten times out of ten and tonight I'm going to revel in the use that skill."

"The trouble is, in a rough and tumble one generally pushes the barrel of one's gun into the stomach of the foe before pulling the trigger," pointed out the colonel knowingly, "not much skill is required."

They were then reduced to silence as the sound of heavy footsteps were heard from the staircase. This turned out to be Willow, whose voice reverberated around the confined space, "The master wants to know whatcha gonna do now?"

"Send for him to come half-way up and I'll discuss the situation with him," returned Deborah.

After some time Claude de Friese appeared on the landing.

"You've lost, Claude, so why don't you just push off back to Georgia – or where ever it is you came from," suggested Deborah loudly.

"I could starve you out or send my men in, either way you're done for," countered her husband.

"Were you to do that, then you would never have Knightsbridge nor would the combined wealth of Major Sturgis and Colonel Esprey end up in your pocket."

"Then my only option is to take my revenge on all of you."

"*Ha*, in that case say goodbye to everything you yearn for," sneered Deborah.

"There's no victory at all in death," shouted de Friese as he retreated down the stairs.

"I hope you two fighting men have not forgotten any of your battle skills," said Deborah seriously.

*****

"You men ready," called out Captain James Crittenden several times as he strode the length of the double line formed by his troops.

Every one of his soldiers nodded, smiled or answered him cheerfully in the affirmative.

The captain's men were veteran troops who had been blooded in several battles and skirmishes and were especially looking forward to firing upon a rabble of unreconstructed Rebs.

Crittenden took his time surveying the site he had chosen for the forthcoming action, though he never hurried nor appeared to be the least bit concerned. To his left burned the company camp fires, which had been piled high with wood and were burning fiercely. Scattered between and around the tents were the dummies his men had fabricated using straw and spare items of uniform. These wouldn't have stood up to scrutiny in daytime, but at night, with just flickering firelight illuminating them, he was sure they would work very well.

All of the troops standing-to stiffened as they heard the sounds of a number of horses approaching.

"Steady men," ordered Crittenden quietly, though he knew it was unnecessary.

The gentle thunder of hooves became louder and harder as the horsemen approached.

*Careless, they hold us in such contempt that they haven't even bothered to muffle the hooves of their horses*, thought Crittenden to himself.

"They ain't sneaking up on us, sir," pointed out a nearby soldier.

"No scouts sent out either, they will soon pay the price for that," returned Crittenden.

Then all became still and time appeared to stop ticking by. The waiting veteran troops recognised that this was that brief period before all Hell broke loose.

All at once, de Friese's men burst into sight in a column which rapidly deployed itself into a line of battle as it reached the open ground before the camp.

There then followed from the attackers a rattle of gunfire as they shot the  harmless dummies to pieces.

"*FIRE*," ordered Crittenden and immediately his line was alive with flame and sound as their first volley went off. This  had obviously taken effect, for several rider less horses galloped into and then through the camp.

Yells and cries of pain and confusion could be distinguished above the racket of the second volley, which was delivered accurately and proved to be as effective as the first had been.

The ex-Rebs were firing too, but most of them were using their pistols wildly and their shots were; for the most part, ineffective.

"Come on, come you villains," shouted Sergeant-Major Fergus, "come on, they're only black slave scum, they'll run if we hit them hard enough."

After shouting this, he spurred his horse forward and took the reins between his teeth in order to draw out his second revolver.

The Rebels were thus somewhat encouraged and began to shout and scream their feared war cries, but these had not the force nor the effect that they had had early in the Civil War.

As he glanced behind him, Fergus could see and sense that not many of his men were with him and at this decisive point they were hit by a third Yankee volley, which turned out to be just as devastating as the others had been.

"Come on, for the Old South, we're nearly amongst them," cried Fergie just before a rifled-musket ball struck him in the throat, crashed against his spine and from there was directed upwards into his brain. He fell from his horse into the dirt of his home state, his blood running away into the soil he'd spent four years hopelessly defending.

Once their leader had gone down, what little heart which remained in his men disappeared without trace and they scattered in every direction, apart from that from which the terrible, disciplined fire had come.

As the sound of galloping hooves drifted away Captain Crittenden shouted, "Well done, men, well done indeed."

Grunts of triumph were returned from along the length of the skirmish line.

"Anyone injured?" Asked the officer.

It was soon apparent that none of the troopers had received so much as a scratch.

"Very well, full kit, marching order and off we go to Knightsbridge where we shall arrest a certain Monsieur de Friese."

*****

"How many men would you say that de Friese sent off against the Union infantry," asked Esprey slowly.

"Twenty, maybe," returned Gideon after a thoughtful second or two.

The colonel turned to Deborah de Friese, "Have you any idea how many chaps he has altogether?"

She thought for a moment to calculate and then said with confidence, "No more than twenty-four – that's if you count Bailey as a man."

"Willow makes up for him," pointed out Kitty.

"That leaves only four, plus Bailey and Willow."

"De Friese too," added Giddy.

"Even so, that leaves only five if they're all counted in."

"There's one chap who'll still have a sore head who may not be in any state to bother us," Giddy reminded them of the sentry he'd knocked out on the porch.

"You have a suggestion?" Asked Deborah.

"Yes, there are three of us, all armed," began Esprey.

"*Four*," interrupted an indignant Kitty.

"In which case, if we stormed out shouting and screaming we could beat double our number."

"Then it's hey-ho and away for Cardinal Woods," said Sturgis.

"Then, if you can agree terms with me, all will be well," said Deborah.

"Can I lead?" Kitty shook with impatience and eagerness.

The colonel thought for a while and then replied, "I have a much more vital mission in mind for you."

"I'm keeping my gun."

"Of course, you may need it, though I have grave doubts about your ability to carry out the task I have in mind," he replied, shaking his head negatively at the same time.

"What doubts? I can do anything y'want doing."

"You're a girl and not used to climbing," the colonel grimaced and again shook his head vigorously.

"I can climb as long as I keep my skirts out o' the way."

"Very well, then, for there is a trellis attached to the wall, just beside the window here, and I wondered if you were up to shinning to the ground using it? It would be a long fall were you to slip."

"I can climb like no other girl in the Confederacy."

"Good, in which case, before the rest of us begin a ruckus, you are to find and secure our mounts."

"If anyone gets in my way can I shoot them?" It was plain that Kitty quite liked the idea of this.

"Of course, but the real skill in this mission is *not* to be noticed by the other side."

Kitty gave her version of a quiet Rebel yell, smiled broadly and began to shove the hem of her skirt into the top of her underdrawers, much to the embarrassment of the gentlemen who both looked away.

Ten minutes later, she had squeezed through the window and had found the lattice work which existed to give support to a virginia creeper.

Hanging from the shrub were clusters of small black berries which looked tempting to Kitty so she stretched her free hand to grab a bunch.

"Leave them alone, they're poisonous," a hoarse whisper was directed to her by Deborah who stood next to the window.

"Birds eat 'em, though, I've seen them do it," returned Kitty, though she pulled her hand away from the fruit.

This argument ended when a guard appeared from around the corner of the building and began to patrol its length.

Fortunately for Kitty, he hadn't the wit to check what lay above him.

*"Go on, move off,"* Kitty whispered to herself.

However, the sentry decided to smoke a thin cigar and sat himself down on the porch to enjoy it in comfort.

*Move before I kill you,* Kitty's eyes narrowed at the thought of this.

What seemed to the young girl to be hours later, the guard flicked away the stub of his cigar and stood up. He stamped his feet a few times before he groaned and sat down again.

"What's he doing now? Kitty whispered to herself as she continued to hang on to the trellis, though somewhat precariously.

The guard then began to remove debris from the soles of his boots using several twigs, none of which were suitable for the task. Eventually, however, he gave up, picked up his rifle, looked all around for a few seconds and then moved off, soon to disappear around a corner of the house.

Once she was sure he'd gone she climbed further down and then dropped the last few feet to earth. Then, without wasting any further time, she headed for the shrubbery to begin her search for the horses.

*****

"Back or front stairs?" Asked Giddy as he spun the well-oiled chamber of his Colt 'Navy' pattern revolver.

"Both sets of stairs at the same time, perhaps. Two go shooting and yelling down the back, the other waits a minute or so and then goes quietly down the main."

"Hitting them from *two* directions may make all the difference."

"I'll take the main staircase by myself," offered Deborah, "I know every nook and cranny of this house."

"Alone?" Queried the colonel doubtfully.

"Yes, that's if you brave soldier boys can face the wrath of the enemy until I arrive to help you out."

Giddy and Jervy looked at each other and then nodded their agreement.

"We'll go quietly until we're discovered then it's a thunderclap of noise and speed the rest of the way," suggested the colonel.

"Sounds sensible to me," returned Sturgis.

"Good luck," whispered Deborah, who then impulsively took Gideon into her arms and kissed him hard.

At first he wanted to free himself from her, but the scent and feel of her body soon overpowered his senses and he kissed her back.

"Things to do," grumbled the colonel as he found a corner where he noisily checked his own revolvers.

The warmth and intensity of Deborah's body pressing into his own made Sturgis forget everything else – the job in hand, his partner and above all his wife.

"When this is over stay here with me. Don't go back to England, please, we could be so happy – I know I can make you happy," whispered Deborah urgently.

Gideon pulled away and shook his head, "I don't know…"

She took his hand and pulled it on to her breast, "*Everything* I have is yours and only yours."

Feeling the warm softness of her and finding that her nipple was hardening, he pulled her firmly into him where his member soon began to make an impression on her.

"Don't stop," she whispered hoarsely.

"We're both married and this is hardly the ideal time," he replied, as common sense suddenly returned to him.

"There is an easy solution to that," she replied, her tone changing from the softness of a butterfly's wing to the harshness of a raging storm.

"Kill your husband, you mean."

"Just do what's right, for both of us," she whispered hoarsely, hugging him tightly at the same time and trying to squeeze her own determination into him.

"There isn't any more time for this," interrupted the colonel, who had decided to keep an eye on his friend to make sure that he didn't do anything he'd regret in the future.

Giddy pulled away from the woman who had once been his only true love, giving her a squeeze and one last kiss.

"Good luck, *kill him* for both our sakes," she whispered as he took to the stairs.

*****

It took Kitty some time to find the horses, but eventually she heard them snuffling and stamping a dozen yards away and soon came up to them.

Just as she was patting the muzzle and forehead of *Suzie*, which was Gideon's mount, she was grabbed from behind and thrown to the ground.

"Now I've got you," growled and puffed Buster Bailey, pointing his shotgun at Kitty's belly.

She kicked out hard at his ankles and struck home firmly enough for him to start hopping about on one foot.

"You'll suffer for that you little bitch, I'll teach you a lesson you won't forget in a hurry...," he paused for a breath and then continued, "but before that I'll service you."

"You're not up to seeing to the needs of a nanny-goat," returned Kitty with a derisory laugh.

Bailey settled his injured foot down and waved the nozzle of his gun straight at Kitty's face, "Strip, take everything off. Do it now or I'll blast y'to pieces."

Kitty got to her feet and began to fiddle with the numerous buttons of her dress, and feeling at the same time; as surreptitiously as she could, for the pocket which held de Friese's Pepper-pot pistol.

"Hurry up," cried Buster who began to unbuckle his belt, as well as trying to keep a tight grip on his shotgun at the same time.

"I'm going as fast as I can, a lady needs time to strip off."

"You, a lady, I've seen sows in labour that were more ladylike than you," as he spoke his engorged penis appeared

"It ain't big enough," cried Kitty scornfully.

"It's big enough for you, just you wait and see," in his eagerness Buster lurched forward his manhood leading the way.

Then, from the direction of the house loud and prolonged gunfire opened up.

Bailey gripped his shotgun tighter, "Just you stay quiet or else," he threatened before he looked towards the sound of the firing.

Taking her chance, Kitty pulled the gun clear of her pocket, cocked it and pointed it at the would-be rapist. Then she found she couldn't bring herself to squeeze the trigger. The idea of killing anyone, even someone as crude and unpleasant as Bailey was beyond her.

"Drop your gun and hold your hands up," she ordered.

With his pants still hanging around his thighs, Buster swung around as quickly as he was able, raising his scatter-gun at the same time.

Kitty looked into her adversary's eyes and saw that he intended to finish with her, so she aimed the pistol at his legs, closed her eyes and squeezed the trigger.

The report of the gun was much louder than she thought it would be and as a result she involuntarily jerked the barrel upwards.

The bullet sped into Buster's right eye and carried on through and into his brain. He was dead well before his body hit the ground.

Kitty's emotions were turbulent, she felt elated and then ashamed that she had taken something so precious as a human life, she couldn't decide whether she should laugh out loud or cry but ended up doing both several times in rapid succession.

*****

As they crept down the backstairs Giddy was suddenly alarmed by a very loud noise and he was just about to leap into action when he felt the restraining arm of his companion.

"That was a snore or I'm a deaf man."

The major chuckled gently in embarrassment, nodded his agreement and carried on to the ground floor where they found the source of the noise.

The guard they came across had propped his chair against the wall, pushed his hat over his eyes and was dreaming happily.

Giddy pushed his revolver into the ribs of the sentry, whilst at the same time the colonel covered the man's mouth.

The fellow's hat fell from his head and he awoke with fear in his eyes whilst his hand went for the rifle which leaned against the wall beside him.

"Don't," the voice, which was an authoritative one, belonged to Esprey.

Giddy stared into the eyes of the guard, "Do you want to die here and now or would you prefer to gallop off to the nearest saloon never to return?" He questioned.

The man nodded and Esprey removed his gagging hand.

"I'll be to hell and gone, just give me a chance," promised the guard, his Adam's apple pulsing up and down.

"Okay, git, but leave that rifle just where it is," ordered Giddy.

The sentry needed no further instructions, fleeing into the night as fast as he was able.

"Can we trust him, do you think? Or is age softening us?" Asked Jervy.

"We'll soon find out if we're wrong. Anyway, let's get this done, you kick the door open and I'll go in shooting."

Esprey had just raised his boot when he heard a voice from the other side of the door.

"You there, Sampson? Get yer lazy ass in here."

"What's your beef?" Returned Giddy promptly, hoping the door would disguise his voice.

"I've just heard a shot fired, come on out and get yourself over to Buster, he's by the Englishman's horses but I wouldn't trust him to wipe his own ass if his shit was on fire."

"I'll be right there," returned the major.

"Your voice is kinda strange," this reply was accompanied by the squeaking of rarely oiled hinges.

Esprey wasted no time, for just as a curious head was about to be poked into the backstairs hall he kicked shut the door.

A scream of pain was followed by a tirade of loud abuse, though this came to an abrupt end when Giddy stepped forward and shot the offender in the head.

Almost immediately, the two officers ran straight into a third guard who; when he saw them, curled up swiftly into the space between the stove and a large welsh dresser, thrusting his head between his knees.

"Do you wish to leave here in one piece or should I kill you as you squirm?" Again, it was Giddy who was asking the life or death question.

In reply the man threw forward his six-gun, "I guess I don't get paid enough to die."

"If you've a knife or any other weapon you'd be well advised to give it up now," warned Jervy, his eyes glistening with threat.

"No... *No...*, Honest, the six-shooter is it – it's all they gave me – I'm no soldier," the man garbled frantically.

"On your way, then, and don't come back," ordered the major.

"De Friese's men have turned out to be a poor quality lot," observed the colonel who seemed disappointed that they hadn't so far enjoyed a real shoot-out.

Just as he finished speaking three loud shots were heard coming from the area of the hallway.

Both men dashed together to find Deborah standing over a guard who was obviously seriously wounded.

"Get me a doctor," begged the man, "I'm gut shot... I'm done...," as he spoke he doubled up in agony and began to weep.

Deborah took a step forward, looked down on him without pity and then fired a shot into the back of his head from so close a range than her hands and costume became bespattered with blood and brain tissue.

"How many have you dealt with?" She asked sharply.

"Three, though the guards were talking of hearing a shot coming from round about where Kitty may be, we'd best get over there...."

Almost on cue Kitty arrived, holding her pistol before her.

"Are you all right, child," asked the colonel who had immediately noticed how drained of colour her face was.

"Sure....," she returned with a catch in her voice.

"We heard a shot?" Put in Deborah.

"Buster's dead – shot dead," she replied, deadpan.

"Oh, my dear child, that is so...," began the colonel.

"What fer? I just killed my first varmint," interrupted Kitty who was trying hard to regain her normal composure and not really succeeding very well.

"Let's hope he's your last," said the colonel who could see that for all her bravado she was as sick inside as he himself had been when he'd killed an Afghan horse thief back in the 1830's.

"Where's de Friese?" Asked Giddy, who was keen to get this whole business finished.

"Gone off to the barn for horses, he went off like a jack-rabbit the moment the first shots were fired," replied Deborah, her voice dripping with her contempt for her husband.

Giddy looked at his childhood sweetheart who was still full of blood lust and suddenly realised that all he *really* wanted to do was to get back home to Grace, peace and quiet as soon as he could.

Jervis ordered Kitty to bring forward the horses then added, "Take your time about it, you've seen enough blood for one night."

"It's getting light now," she replied, looking out at the sky, "so I guess I'll be all right."

The colonel nodded and then led the rest of the party to find de Friese.

The barn, when they reached it, was quiet with no sign of movement and so it appeared to them that their birds had flown.

"Come on, I expect you two warriors aren't shy for we must make sure that Claude doesn't get away to trouble us in the future," said Deborah as she entered the building.

Esprey became even more certain now that Mrs de Friese had no intention of allowing her husband to see the dawn of another day.

Wasting no further time, Sturgis followed Deborah into the gloom where he stopped and listened carefully for sounds of movement.

"We should have brought a lamp or sent Kitty for one," said Jervis.

"There are several in here, it's just a matter of finding them," replied Deborah.

Sturgis became impatient and called loudly, "Come out, de Friese, we know you're in here."

"Why should I, you'll just kill me – or my bitch of a wife will at any rate," the voice came from the rear of the building where there were stacked multiple bales of hay.

"You're done for, you know that," returned the colonel, "we've no reason to harm you."

"I may punch him a few times, though," muttered Giddy softly.

A peal of nervous laughter came from the plantation owner, "The rest of my men will be back shortly and they'll deal with you as easily as they will have with the black Yankees."

"Unfortunately for you," the voice this time belonged to Sturgis, "the Federal troops will be ready and waiting for your rabble to turn up."

"So you are now in the place you least like to be - *on your own*," Deborah laughed mockingly.

"Come on man, the game's up and the stumps have been drawn," ordered Esprey in the friendliest, most reassuring tone he could muster.

There followed complete silence for a while and then, from the rear of the barn, they heard the striking of a match as a lantern was lit. Shortly after that the shadowy figure of the planter came into sight.

"Don't shoot, I'm unarmed," he called.

"This has turned out to be a lot easier than I feared," muttered Esprey to his companions.

Deborah nudged Giddy, "Now's the time," she whispered from the side of her mouth.

"He's surrendering, it'd be murder," Sturgis returned softly.

"This is no gentleman's game," said Deborah as she began to raise her own gun, only to find herself restrained by Gideon's arm.

Colonel Esprey looked around sharply and then asked, "Where is the Willow woman?"

"Deserted me, just like the rest. She's gone," returned Claude de Friese as he came closer to the barn doors.

At this point, Giddy started forward cautiously to make de Friese their prisoner.

Then the quiet was abruptly shattered by a scream of siren proportions as; coming running from behind them, appeared Willow. Her face was contorted with hate and her hair was flung long and wide behind her. She carried a stable-fork and was pointing it straight at Deborah with a murderous glint in her eyes.

"Look out," yelled Jervis as he raised his revolver, but soon realised that he was afraid to fire it in case he hit the wrong woman.

Meanwhile, Willow's mind was fully focused on the form of her mistress, whom she was determined to kill.

In this she was interrupted  by Giddy, who flung himself in defence of the woman he had once loved, raising his gun at the same time.

Willow was not dismayed, she continued on at full pace and stopped only once she'd run her pitch-fork deep into the stomach of Major Sturgis.

Giddy screamed and doubled up in pain, though he continued to raise his revolver, but before he could fire, Willow had pulled out the fork and was preparing to use it against her mistress.

All of this happened in seconds but Giddy somehow managed to get two shots away, neither of which hit their mark, before he fell to the floor where he lay in an ever increasing pool of blood.

Willow's eyes then focused on Deborah again, who shrunk away in both fear and horror as she saw the life seeping away from Major Gideon Sturgis.

The atmosphere in the barn was rent again as Esprey fired two aimed shots at the murderous Willow, both of which went exactly where they were aimed, into the chest of the serving woman.

Even with two fatal wounds, Willow's hate drove her on towards her mistress, being determined that she too should die.

Deborah managed to shake off her fear and raised her pistol, though it was trembling in her hand.

Then a further shot rang out from the revolver of the colonel which hit Willow in the side of her head, continued through her brain and then blew off the other side of her skull.

Deborah screamed and dropped her own revolver, before she sank to the floor and began to howl and cry.

In the confusion, de Friese himself slipped away into the night, determined not to face a charge of; he presumed, treason against the United States of America.

Esprey and Deborah hardly noticed his departure and even if they had they would have let him go.

"*Jesus Christ*," profaned Esprey as the full import of what had just happened hit him, "I need a drink or two… Large ones."

# PART TWO: *Return to Martindale*

## Chapter One

### *(September, 1865)*

Inspector Mason sighed as he closed yet another file, leaned back in his chair and hoped that time was moving along a lot faster than the office clock indicated it was.

He found himself in limbo, awaiting retirement but still mired in the everlasting investigation into the shady affairs of Elysia Scott-Wilson, the Marchioness of Studland.

How sick and tired he was of this woman who had always managed to stay a hitch and a step ahead of him. Though he had no choice other than to press on as his superiors greatly feared the unsavoury stories she could reveal were the mood to take her.

As for himself, Mason had a sneaking admiration for her, even though she'd made a fool of him on more than one occasion.

"Where's the marchioness' father now do you suppose?" He asked himself aloud.

"On balance, probably where he deserves to be," put in Constable George Dodds who was working at a table few feet away.

"True, though whatever *did* happen to Sir James it was certainly done without recourse to the Law."

"There's no doubt that her ladyship leaves a trail of mysteries behind her, I for one would not fancy ending up in her black books," replied Dodds gravely.

"Everyone in the building must have had a good laugh when the news of how she made a fool of me at Winterbourne came through."

Dodds shook his head fervently, "Oh no, sir. Though I must admit that it was greeted with some amusement in certain quarters."

"She had me utterly convinced that her father's body was sealed up in the dungeon of the old keep at Winterbourne."

"Though there turned out to be nothing there."

"Just the dust of ages, but she'd put on such an artful act that I was sure I had nabbed her at last."

"At the time you must have felt very…," the constable brought himself up sharply.

"Foolish? Stupid? Perhaps even idiotic is the word you're looking for."

Cursing himself for being so gauche, Dodds suddenly remembered a newspaper article he'd read a few weeks previously and asked, "Doesn't the marchioness own some place called Forest Hall too?"

"Yes she does, what of it?"

"The *Wessex Star* recently ran a story about a priest hole which is believed to be hidden there."

The inspector became rapidly more interested for he suspected that somewhere at Forest Hall there lay the last resting place of both Sir James Hannibal Wright and the German woman who had been; amongst other things, the family nanny.

"Some local historians wished to conduct a search to find out; once and for all, whether a priest hole ever existed but were denied access and with a distinct lack of courtesy too."

"*Mmm*, I visited Forest Hall myself once and found nothing, but it is certainly worth a second look."

"Especially when we've something solid to search for – such as a priest-hole."

"Put it on our list of possibilities," ordered the inspector.

They sat in silence for a few minutes and then Roland Mason; tapping his desk top with the end of his pencil in time with his words, said, "The two heirs of the second husband – the previous marquis – were both erased from the line of succession to the title within a very short time."

"Both gone and each in suspicious circumstances too."

"The first heir was pushed under a train – a dozen people saw it happen and yet not one proved to be a useful witness."

"Then; as I recall it," began Dodds slowly, "heir number two – Roger wasn't it - struck up a casual relationship with a lady on a cross-Channel steamer and ended up at the bottom of a cliff. Could this lady connect with the marchioness?"

"Some sort of agent of hers, perhaps."

"Maybe the Scott-Wilson heir arranged an assignation with this woman and she pushed him over, though from the description we got she was a girl of no great size," mused the inspector.

The idea of a well-built young fellow allowing himself to go over a cliff after a push from a woman of average stature didn't work for Dodds either.

"She must have had an accomplice, who was very likely a man," muttered Mason.

"If we could find the woman involved there's no knowing what she could tell us."

"Finding her, though, that's the problem. There are tens of thousands of whores in London alone, probably several thousand even somewhere like Dover."

"Though the steamship passengers reckoned that the woman looked a decent enough body."

"A higher-class lady of the night?"

"Yes, that narrows the field considerably."

"Though several years have passed so she may well have become just another common drab by now."

"Even so, let's get out of this dammed office and do some proper police work, see what we can dig up."

\*\*\*\*\*

As his train rattled on towards Doncaster, George Murphy yawned widely and pretended that he was about to take a nap.

"This is exciting, isn't it Georgie?"

"I'm trying to sleep – and stop calling me *Georgie.*"

"But it is exciting, isn't it?" The determined speaker was Hugh Doggart, son of Irene who was the sister of Douglas Brass.

"No."

"Yes it is, here we are two young fellows on a train to adventure."

"We're not crossing Arabia on camels, we're just selling dresses."

"*Ah,* but there'll be ladies to sell them to."

"Much of our business is conducted with men, mostly old miserable ones too."

"Though there are bound to be girls buzzing around like bees, buying costumes, some behind the counters, others working in the dressing rooms...," he paused and then continued, "or better still the *undressing* rooms."

George cut his companion off, "We'll have no time to acquaint ourselves with any girls – into the shop and out of it as quickly as we can. Then we'll be straight off to the next town to sell further dresses."

This quietened Hugh for a short while and then he asked, "Have you never sneaked a look when a lady was trying one of your dresses on? You must have had chance after chance of that."

"No, I've never had either the time nor the inclination," Murphy felt like punching his companion just to shut him up.

"No frilly petticoats or glimpses of stocking? I do so like the high heeled boots girls wear these days."

"You mean you slobber over them."

"Highly polished boots with high-heels," whispered Hugh hoarsely, his eyes tight-shut.

"If you don't shut up about it, I'll shut you up," George's threat was not an idle one.

"It's all right for you, you've got the perfect lass in Miss Greenwood...," Hugh paused for a moment and then continued, "Or have you?"

"Whether I have or not is no business of yours."

Doggart considered for a moment and then clicked his fingers before suggesting, "It's fallen through, hasn't it – that's what's happened and now you're love-sick and can't bear to look at another lass."

"Rubbish, I'm my own man."

"You used to lodge at the Greenwood house, then you left to sleep in a shed with your horse."

"I've since moved up in the world and I've no need to lodge with anyone – nor trouble any horse with my snoring either."

Hugh considered for a moment and then remembered, "Though you *were* engaged to Lucy Greenwood, the banns were called at Holy Innocents – I was there."

"The second and third declarations were never announced, your uncle Dougie cancelled them for me."

"Why did he do that and why haven't you taken up with her again?"

"It's complicated."

"Gone off her have you? If that's the case I may as well try my luck with the gorgeous Lucy – they say she's a game one."

Murphy was truly irritated, "I'll wash your mouth out with carbolic soap if you don't drop the subject and shut up."

"*Aha*, I've hit a tender spot."

George nearly swore at his companion, thought about it and then tipped his hat over his eyes and pretended to sleep. However, his mind was racing, for even though he knew that Lucy had coldly targeted him as the best suitor she could expect to land, he still could think of nothing other than the sight of her naked breasts bathed in moonlight. On top of which; as he now had a place of his own, a woman waiting there for his return was an attractive idea.

"Whoever does marry Miss Greenwood is going to find it difficult to keep a grip on whatever fortune he has," commented George after a long, thoughtful, silence.

"She's still a smasher, though – she could be worth going broke for," Hugh nodded in agreement with himself as he spoke.

*Broke*, Murphy didn't like the sound of that and in an instant all thoughts of Lucy's naked, compliant body fled from his mind. *How can I possibly become wealthy with a demanding woman and no doubt a child or two holding me back?* This question required an urgent answer and he was sure he knew what it was.

"You know, Hugh, I'm certain you'd be perfect for Lucy Greenwood."

"You really think so?" Hugh sounded pathetically eager.

"I'm sure so."

"Is it not something of a coincidence that Caroline and yourself are to be in London at the same time," stated Jane Turner as she flipped though the morning edition of the *Chronicle*."

"I suppose it is, but I doubt we'll meet. She'll be busy and I've loads to do in the House before the next session begins," Richard kept his voice as even as he was able.

"But you're in government now, you'll have nothing to do until the House sits again."

"Pal has to deliver a Second Reform Bill and if our country Members are as contrary and awkward as they usually are, then  anything could happen and if it does I need to be prepared."

"Both parties are hopelessly encumbered by the wild, hairy men of the Shires," nodded Jane sadly.

"They'll be overcome sooner rather than later, for the leaders of *both* parties agree that Reform is inevitable."

"As well as being just."

"The secret ballot must come next too."

"That shouldn't take much longer than fifty years or so," sighed Jane.

Richard thought for a moment and then said, "I believe it will come within the next decade."

Jane considered this for a moment, nodded her agreement and then returned to a thornier subject, "Does Caroline really need to visit her publisher?  Her second book was never completed, though it looked promising enough when I read through a draft of it."

"I suppose all the worry she suffered when Helmuth went off to war and then came back minus his memory pushed her scribblings well down her list of priorities."

"Isn't it true that her publisher would like her to return to America to lecture? I'm sure Tom Harrington has mentioned that."

"I believe so, though she'll not easily leave Blanchwell again."

"Caroline could be very successful in America, she being the epitome of a beautiful English rose," Jane paused for a while and then stepped on to dangerous ground by suggesting, "Why don't you meet and take her to dinner?"

Richard sighed, took his wife by the shoulders and kissed her, after which he said "I've no time, Harrington and I have a lot of work to do."

"Harrington and work make an unlikely combination."

"That's why he finds me so useful."

"You've been busy on this for years."

"You wouldn't wish us to return to Westminster unprepared?"

"Prepared for what? Not the War Office again – why not use your talent and energy on something useful, social and political reform for instance?"

"The army *is* important as it is the first task of any government; whether it be radical or reactionary, to keep the nation safe."

"It also gives the power to oppress working people whenever it feel the need to – actual force being necessary or not."

Richard sighed deeply, "That has been the case previously, but with a Reformed Parliament the disgrace of the Peterloo Massacre will not re-occur. Anyway, that had more to do with local authorities  becoming terrified of a huge mob."

"*Mob?*  Can you call a meeting of ordinary, everyday people out seeking justice and democracy a mob?"

Richard shook his head, "Of course not, I didn't mean it like that."

"Tory swine they were then and still remain so," Jane virtually spat her words out before Richard calmed her with another kiss.

"You do realise that the army; *our* army, is recruited from ordinary men who require as much protection as anyone else. In addition, the British Army is the only one in Europe which is a *volunteer* force."

"The poor, weak and desperate are forced to join through hunger and want."

"I'm sure that's the case in part."

"An army in which draconian punishments are meted out to them for the slightest infraction of discipline."

Richard thought for a while and then remarked, "The army is changing though, and remember it is *impossible* to flog men to victory. Our fellows fight because they're *very good* soldiers to whom their regiment is home."

"They are cannon fodder, nothing more and nothing less."

"Whatever they are, the fact remains that in any continental war involving us; unless we can rely on finding suitable allies, our troops will always be heavily outnumbered."

"The larger the army the more useful it is to supress any sort of protest, peaceful or otherwise. Anyway, it is the navy which keeps us safe."

"I'm sure you're right about that, but our current crop of generals still insist on fighting in the manner of Marlborough and Wellington."

"They both won famous victories did they not," pointed out Jane.

Richard shook his head before he spoke, "Think ahead a little, sometime in the next decade, picture our troops deployed along a ridge, shoulder to shoulder and rank upon rank."

"In the old style which always drove off the foe."

"It did once, but say that three thousand yards from our men the enemy have deployed a battery of modern artillery. Guns which fire explosive shells."

"Three thousand yards, why that's over a mile."

"It's nearer two."

"Whatever it is, it's too far away to be effective. Why, if their gunnery officers are as short-sighted as myself the target area would be the merest blur to them."

Richard laughed and then solemnly declaimed, "Imagine the situation, the enemy opens fire. Their first shot falls short, their second is long, their third…"

"*Is dropped in between* and they've found the range, and will fire their shells between the two previous attempts," it didn't take Jane long to catch on.

"Once the range has been found, the whole battery opens up firing several rounds per minute and before very long the whole British line is thrown into confusion."

"So what should the army do?"

"Avoid fighting the next war by still using the tactics of Napoleon."

"Even though he is widely regarded as a military genius?"

"Yes, we must look to the war in America and learn the lessons it teaches. For one thing the cavalry must put away their sabres and become mounted infantry."

Jane was aghast, "The cavalry to become *infantry*, that would cause apoplexy throughout the War Office."

"British tactics *must* change, our troops need to deploy in far looser formations, make use of ground, entrench, bring in the Martini-Henry rifles sooner than planned and get rid of the red tunics for good."

"Rid ourselves of the *thin red line*," even some one as radical as Jane found herself aghast at the idea of this. She turned to face her husband and exclaimed, "My God, you too are a radical!"

\*\*\*\*\*

"I'm afraid the rector has a headache and cannot be disturbed," Venetia Lander was quite determined that her husband should be left in peace.

"What? *Again?* I've visited five times in the last week or so and have not laid eyes on him once."

"Unfortunately, you've always called at an inconvenient time, Mr Somers."

"Though I suppose Mr Hodge has had free access to the Rector of Holy Innocents," Somers spat out the name of the clergyman he thought of as being his rival and enemy.

"The Vicar of Kirkby has visited frequently, but only to ask about my husband's condition – something you've singularly failed to do."

"Hodge is working to steal what should be *my* living from beneath my very nose," the curate's voice became hotter and shriller as he spoke.

"The Cathedral alone will decide who is next to have the living of Martindale, my husband has nothing to do with it. In addition, I must remind you that he *still lives*."

"But the man can no longer preach, nor serve his parishioners, it is a disgrace that he…."

"Leave*, leave* at once, sir, before I have you thrown out," Venetia's words sliced through the air, seeming to rip it asunder in her annoyance.

For a moment Roland Somers was taken aback at the wrath which had been unleashed upon him, then a smile crossed his lips, an unpleasant smile which bore little relationship to mirth.

"You'd be well advised to remember that I *know* things."

"What things? My husband has always conducted his affairs here honestly and well above board."

"What about your Aunt, though, Mrs Prudence Hodge? Has not she much to hide?"

"Prudence? What on earth can she have to do with this?" Venetia was obviously truly puzzled.

Again, Somers smiled nastily, "Prudence could destroy me, but I wouldn't care about that were Hodge to be brought down at the same time."

Before Mrs Lander could respond or enquire further the curate had stormed out, clashing the door behind him.

Venetia decided that she would have to have a private talk with Prudence as soon as she was able to leave her husband's sick bed to visit Kirkby Vicarage.

*****

"Why don't you get rid of those silly old biddies at Forest Hall?" Asked Corsica of Elysia as they lay together, exhausted after a prolonged period of love making.

"They're harmless enough and out of the way."

"Maybe, but they are much too friendly with those Antiquarian idiots for my liking and remember what lies hidden in the priest-hole."

"You told me that you'd scared the old gentlemen out of their wits, besides which neither Flora nor Rowena would have the guts nor the gumption to disobey me."

"Though the old fellows haven't given up making inflammatory speeches to the members of their Society and also writing to the local newspapers."

"*Local* newspapers," Elysia snorted her disdain.

"Provincial stories are often picked up by Fleet Street, especially were the name of a well-known ma

rchioness to be mentioned in them."

"What would your solution be?" Elysia asked, suddenly becoming more interested.

"Bring the old girls back to Winterbourne, and put the shutters up at Forest Hall."

"Is there really a need for that?"

"It would be better still to burn the place down and smash what's left of it to pieces, hide forever what little remains of your pa' and Fraulein Kleist."

"I can't do that...," replied Elysia with a catch in her voice as she thought of her father surrounded by the huge rats which featured frequently in her worst nightmares.

"Why ever not, for sooner or later Lady Flora will be persuaded by sweet talk and flattery to allow a search to begin."

"Were she to do that she's even sillier than I thought."

"Should Mr Nelson or Mr Plantagenet be allowed access to the priest hole, we know which gruesome remains they will come across."

"Oh, shut up, Johnie, you know I hate to think of my poor papa in perpetual darkness....," Elysia came as close to sobbing as she ever had, though managed to fight the emotion off.

"Then there's Gertie, she's heard about the priest-hole too. Who knows, she may take it into her head to have a poke around at Forest Hall too."

"My mother-in-law has no right to even go there without an invitation, the property never belonged to my father and it certainly doesn't belong to her."

Corsica considered for a moment and then pointed out, "Should your papa's remains see the light of day again, Gertie would then legally become his widow, which would have wide ramifications for yourself."

"She could try to claim part of his fortune."

"Half at least, I should say."

"She'd have to fight me through the courts first, by which time…" she looked meaningfully at Corsica, "she could well have *passed away*."

"Sooner rather than later you'll have to face the fact that the priest hole is not as secure as we imagined," replied Corsica gravely as he scrambled from the bed and poured himself a stiff drink.

"Though it seemed to offer the ideal solution at the time," reminded Elysia.

"It was *then*, but now's now."

"Perhaps it's as you say, but I'm not abandoning what has become my papa's resting place, the only monument there is in remembrance of him."

"Dream along, my dear, but eventually you may be left with no other choice."

"I don't wish for gruesome discoveries to be made public any more than you do," Elysia nodded as she spoke,

Corsica thought for a while and then suggested, "What's needed until this knotty problem can be resolved is a man in residence to keep an eye on things for us."

"To keep the old girls firmly in hand, you mean?"

"Yes, and prevent any flights of fancy that may occur to the sisters on a whim, or at the suggestion of some member of the Wessex Antiquarian Society."

Elysia considered for a moment and then proposed, "What about that ugly Irishman of yours – you know, the one who looks like a rat."

"O'Dowd you mean."

"Has his jaw been reset properly yet?"

"No, he's as ugly as ever, but at least it is now possible to understand what he says."

"As long as he doesn't become too friendly with my sisters-in-law."

"I can't imagine anything is likely come of that, he being as ugly as they are plain."

"Are you in contact with Mr O'Dowd?"

"I used him on a little job of my own last year and I know exactly where he's to be found."

"Excellent, seek him out again, tell him what's expected and send him off as…," she paused and then continued, "Whatever should his title be?"

"Agent?"   Suggested Corsica with a shrug of his shoulders.

"The agent of the Marchioness of Studland."

Corsica laughed, "The *special* agent, the Irishman will like that."

*****

"It was good of Tom to invite us to luncheon," remarked Richard Turner.

"Though it's funny how he was called away to meet with his banker so precipitately," muttered Caroline, looking up from plastering *pate-de-foie-gras* on to a sliver of lightly toasted bread.

"*Mmm*, he's a devious dog," returned Richard as he took a spoonful of *vichyssoise*.

"Mischievous too, don't you think?  He was an awful little boy, I often boxed his ears for him."

"I can well imagine that, having spent hours of Parliamentary time in his company."

"You've become friends?"

"Certainly, though I never expected to be."

Caroline inhaled sharply, "You haven't told him, have you?"

"Told him what?"

"About *us* of course."

"You mean when we were…."

"Lovers."

"No, I've told no one and especially *not* an awful gossip like Tom Harrington. Anyway, you and I have never been *actual* lovers."

Caroline's expression hardened substantially, "You're looking so guilty that you *must* have been regaling Tom with tales of what went on between us all those years ago, perhaps after a drink or two," she accused.

"I'm not looking guilty at all – just amazed that you should accuse me of such treachery."

"You men are all the same, a woman's character can be defiled by you almost at will."

Richard shook his head vigorously which caused him to spill soup on to the cuff of his jacket, "Not I, no, I've never mentioned to another soul how much I love you."

Caroline saw the troubled expression on his face and realised that he was telling the truth, "I'm sorry I doubted you," she apologised quietly.

"Is it possible that he has guessed, though?"

"How could he? We hardly ever see each other."

"I must look like Little Boy Blue whenever I'm close to you."

"We've never been alone together for at least three years, since that time in the conservatory at Blanchwell," Caroline returned to her *pate*.

Richard picked up his spoon and began making lazy circles in his soup, until he asked, "Do you remember when we had that row in Durham Cathedral and you slapped my face and stormed off?"

Caroline looked up sharply and replied, "How could I forget it, though you deserved double or triple what I gave you."

Richard's fingers spontaneously touched his cheek, "That was the unhappiest moment of my entire life."

"Worse that losing the farm even?"

He considered for a moment and then replied, "It wasn't long before I forgot all about the farm, besides which its loss brought us together."

"Indeed, though I thought I'd seen the last of you when my papa ordered you from the house at Durham."

"If only your father had continued to write for the *Chronicle* he may not have become fatally obsessed with the idea of regaining his fortune in America."

"At that time it seemed to me that you were the only person in my life who had any interest in my welfare and happiness," whispered Caroline.

"I would have done anything for you, anything at all."

"You promised we'd run off together to save me from the wilds of the American prairie."

"I did so, I would have."

"That is until you'd made Jane pregnant," the harshness of Caroline's tone indicated that this was still a suppurating wound.

Richard could find nothing with which to reply. What could he say? How could he make it right? He continued morosely to make a succession of creamy rings on the surface of his soup.

"What would have been the outcome had we run off together?" Asked Caroline after a long silence had elapsed.

"Ignoring both Jane and your papa, you mean?"

"Jane was wealthy and my father was a responsible adult, so why should we have not?"

Richard thought for a second, smiled and replied, "Neither of us is the sort of person who would run away from their responsibilities."

"No, you're right, but suppose we had? Would we have been any happier than we are now?"

"Your pa' would have had to go to America on his own and I'd have sorted out a future for us. I was already well established at the *Chronicle* and I've no doubt that Jane would have continued her involvement in it too, whether I was her husband or not."

"I suppose so."

Richard thought for a second and then said, "Of course it would have meant saying goodbye to Blanchwell – probably for ever."

They sat in contemplation for a few moments and then Caroline asked, "Are you going to tell Jane that we've met for luncheon?"

"No," replied Richard without any hesitation, "Is it your intention to mention our meeting to Helmuth?"

"He wouldn't raise any objection if I did."

"Damned fool."

"Helmuth loves me deeply and he is *nobody's* fool," returned Caroline sharply.

Richard reached across the table and covered her hand with his own, "I still love you."

"I love you too and always will, but Jane adores you and she is my friend."

The silence that followed was only ended when the veal; which they'd both ordered, was served.

After a mouthful Caroline dropped her cutlery and sighed, "I'm no longer hungry."

"Nor am I," agreed Richard.

Her eyes became serious for a while and then they brightened and she asked, "Are your rooms near here?"

"They're within relatively easy walking distance."

"Is your bed a large and comfortable one?"

Richard knew at once where this conversation was leading and he could feel the heat from his loins radiating further through his body.

"It's comfortable, but not wide, though there is just about room enough for two."

"Dare we? Would we just be getting this thing between us over and done with or is there more to it than that?"

"God, I wish I knew."

"Could we ever have a future together?"

"I wish I knew that too."

Caroline rose from her chair asked, "What are we waiting for? Divine intervention perhaps? Give me ten minutes and I'll meet you in the foyer."

As he watched her glide gracefully away, Turner's mind was filled with a rapid, uneven succession of feelings, ranging from supreme joy to very deep dread.

*****

"Here we are Kitty, *Madame Soutier's Academy For Young Ladies*. It's just the place for you, and what a wonderful time you'll have here," Jervy made his tone as positive as he was able to in the circumstances.

"I don't like it," Kitty crossed her arms under her chest and hunched her shoulders towards her ears.

"This place is *not* an orphanage, I promise it's nothing like the establishments you were kept in before. You'll learn lots too and be taught how a young lady should conduct herself."

"Just 'cos you put me in fancy dresses and found a hairdresser for me it don't make me a lady. I'm not a lady, I'll never be a lady."

"There'll be lots of music and dancing," encouraged the colonel, trying a different tack.

"Who'll ever want to dance with me? Look at me, I'm a scrawny brat, the other girls will laugh fit to burst."

"If they're ladies, they won't, instead they'll support you."

Kitty said nothing for a while and then declared, "I want to come with you. You and the major are the only folk who ever troubled themselves with me."

"It is not possible," Esprey pointed towards the school once more, "life will be perfect for you here."

"The other girls will hate me and I'll hate 'em back, but more fiercely."

"We will correspond, I promise at least a letter a month," Esprey tried yet a different approach.

"I don't want letters I want *you*." Kitty never shed tears, she'd learnt early in her life that crying just brought another slap or a cuff, but now she couldn't hold them back.

Jervy took out his handkerchief and moved to dry her eyes, but she turned sharply away from him.

"Leave me be, I can dry my own cheeks with one of those fancy little 'kerchiefs y'gave me."

Jervis couldn't think of anything to say which would resolve the situation, so he tried to take her hand, but she shrugged it off.

"If I've got to go, I'll go alone, I've always been *alone*," she fired over her shoulder as she set off towards the academy.

Esprey had been an orphan himself and he recalled his own childhood, how he had been sent from one cheap boarding school to another and then; at the earliest opportunity, had been bundled off to India with five pounds in his pocket and told not to expect another penny piece from the distant relatives who laughingly called themselves his *family*.

"Goodbye," he called to her but she ignored him and went off along the drive.

He continued to watch her slight figure as she walked out of his life, the thought of which brought a wetness to his own eyes.

"Wait," he shouted, "all right, you win."

*****

"There's really no need to walk too close to me," suggested Clara Miller to her companion John Losser.

The collier noticed that her tone was not as sharp as that she normally used when speaking to him.

"I like walking with you, I like to hear you talk – it's canny different to mine, more interesting like."

Clara was about to reply *I too enjoy our strolls*, but managed to change her answer to a short, "Then that's fine by me."

They walked on in silence until they arrived at the base of a hill that during the Seventeenth Century had been a spoil heap. Over the years grass, stunted trees and shrubs had taken root and given the slopes of it a pleasant rural aspect, even so close to the smoke and noise of Martindale.

"Could you manage to climb up there?" Asked Losser, pointing towards the summit, which was only a few dozen yards or so away.

"I think so," though Clara sounded doubtful.

"I'll help you up and carry you down if need be."

"You will *not*, sir, no, *never*," this time Clara's response *was* a sharp one.

He nodded sheepishly and began to turn away.

"Don't go," she called, her tone much softer than that she had intended.

"You said…," he began until she interrupted him.

"Come on, I didn't say that I *didn't* want to enjoy a panoramic view of beautiful Martindale," she said as she set out on what she knew would be a hard slog for her to the crest.

Losser followed behind her in a hangdog sort of way until they eventually reached the highest point of the hill.

"This *is* a fine view, I never believed for a moment that it would be so grand as this," she cried.

"Aye, everything is in sight apart from the ironworks."

"I suppose this is a hill courting couples use for their assignations?"

Losser shook his head, "It's known locally as the *Green Hill* or more commonly, the *Greeny*."

Clara; her leg aching, sat down on the grass and spread her skirts around her, "You must bring me here again," she said, though she had no idea why she had suggested this.

The pitman's heart stirred because he detected something in her voice which gave him hope that one day she'd look upon him as being more than a useful nuisance.

"Anytime you like, Miss Miller," he managed to reply in an even tone.

"Clara – you must call me Clara. It's not as though we've just been introduced and we do share the same address."

Losser nodded eagerly, "Aye, that'd be good."

"Don't read too much into this, mind you," said Clara after a minute or two, though she couldn't work out why she had spoken to him as softly as she previously had.

"No, I won't," he replied, but, in his heart, he *had* read quite a lot into it.

*****

"I now know what we should put on next season," announced Roderick Villiers, the Director of the *Martindale Civic Theatre* to his friend and deputy Solomon Vasey.

"Perchance, something which has a significant role in it for yourself."

"That goes without saying, however, I feel that we should regale the township with more of the Bard, much more."

"Good, as you know I'm a Shakespeare man through and through, so which of his works do you intend to schedule?"

"Four or perhaps even five of them."

"*Four or Five*, you're a madman."

"We shall found in this town a Festival to celebrate the immortal works of the Swan of Avon. People will visit here in their thousands for it."

"I doubt that the Management Sub-Committee will agree to this manic idea of yours," returned Vasey smugly, he having recently become a member of the said group of governors.

"Why ever not? Who could possibly complain about an abundance of Shakespeare?"

"The cost, the scenery, extra lighting, and above all it would require the employment of a number of professional actors."

"We've already performed successfully the *Scottish Play* and *Romeo and Juliet* with the people we already have."

"Though they remain amateurs – talented ones in some respect – but they wouldn't be able to cope with a multitude of roles, the whole thing would be a disaster."

Villiers smiled broadly, "Our people will be able to manage easily with what I have in mind."

Vasey sighed deeply, "Yet another of your schemes."

"They generally work."

"I can think of a few that didn't."

"This idea could turn out to be my best yet."

"All right, then, out with it."

"We perform the same five plays a week for a full season."

"Why, that's impossible," Solly was becoming hot under the collar and beginning to believe that his friend was losing his mind.

"Calm yourself," Villiers tapped his temple, "The way it can be accomplished is stored in here."

Vasey sighed deeply, "Then spell it out clearly and slowly for we lesser mortals."

"We shan't perform *whole* plays, just segments of them linked together by the clever use of a narrator."

"So, we miss out the boring bits and only stage the scenes everyone knows and loves," Solly became mildly enthusiastic.

"Exactly," returned the Director smugly.

"Some good parts for us too – I may even get my fair share of them, just for a change."

"Precisely."

"Which plays have you in mind?"

"*Richard III, Henry V, Twelfth Night, King Lear* and the *Merry Wives*."

"Not *Lear*, Oh no, far too miserable."

"I once played a great Lear at the Old Vic."

"That still won't recommend it to colliers nor to their wives."

"It's a work of genius."

"Maybe, but not for Martindale, nor for any person who's not going out of his mind."

"All right, Lear is out to be replaced by which of the others?"

"*A Midsummer Night's Dream?*"

"What, offer a play packed with fairies and sprites to a town full of colliers and ironworkers? Don't be silly."

"*Othello*, then."

Villiers paused for a second or two and then spoke almost reverently, "I played a truly *brilliant* Othello opposite Eliza Vincent's Desdemona to packed houses."

"Eliza's dead now, and *King Lear* should go the same way."

Roddy nodded positively and then said, "Very well, for there are some good lines in *Othello*, yes it will do nicely."

"When do we open?"

"We shall have it ready and prepared for the coming Spring Season."

"That will be tight, even with a narrator."

"Can you recall *ever* being allowed sufficient time to rehearse any of the productions you've had a part in?"

Vasey laughed, "Very well then, I shall report to the Sub-Committee at the end of the week for their approval."

"There'll be no problem with that, Lizzie Esprey loves the Bard as much as we do."

"Though she's rather sullen and despondent at the moment, with the fine colonel having gone off without so much as a word to her," said Vasey.

"Indeed," replied Villiers who at the same time was wondering if he should pay the colonel's lady a visit to offer her comfort.

"Just leave her alone, she's important to us," warned Vasey, who knew precisely what his partner was thinking.

*****

"Well, ladies, this fine fellow has been appointed to oversee the running, upkeep and safety of Forest Hall,"

Corsica was introducing Kevin O'Dowd to the Scott-Wilson sisters.

"He looks like a rat," Lady Flora whispered to her sister.

"Indeed," Rowena murmured her agreement.

For his part, the Irishman stood looking around in wonderment at; what was in fact, a relatively shabby drawing room.

"What is he to do?" Enquired Flora.

"What is his purpose?" Rowena backed up her sister.

"He has been appointed the very *special* agent of the Marchioness of Studland."

"You mentioned that previously, Mr Corsica, but what is he to *do*?"

"What is his function?" Added the younger sister.

"Anything the marchioness desires."

"I suppose he could help out with the horses and the garden," put in Rowena who couldn't pull her eyes away from the face of O'Dowd which appeared to consist of two distinctly disparate halves, with the lower not quite married to the upper.

Corsica sharpened his tone, "Mr O'Dowd is *not* to be regarded as a servant, he is to be treated with all the favour and respect of an honoured guest."

"A *guest*?" Flora found the idea of this appalling.

"*Honoured?*" Rowena couldn't believe what she was hearing.

"Though I expect that he is to sleep in the attic with the other servants," put in Flora.

Corsica hardened his tone of voice still further, "He shall dine with you as any other guest would and when he's ready for beddy-byes he shall retire to the finest of the guest rooms."

The sisters were stunned for the Irishman was not the sort of person usually invited to dinner at Forest Hall — nor to any other fine house for that matter.

Lady Flora, with some hesitation, raised a forefinger, "I'm sure Mr O'Dowd is a very worthy young man, but..."

"You *will* carry out the instructions of the marchioness, as I do myself," Corsica was becoming increasingly irritated.

"For heaven's sake lasses old Kevin's no bother t'no man, nor t'no ladies neither," O'Dowd spoke up for himself.

"Good gracious, he can hardly be understood," Rowena's eyes widened.

"How could one possibly converse over dinner with him?" Wondered Flora aloud.

Corsica laughed and explained, "A much better man than he'll ever be broke his jaw for him."

"Watcha mean? There's no better man than me sel'," interrupted O'Dowd his face becoming red and even less symmetrically arranged than normal.

Johnie's eyes narrowed and his voice dropped to a hiss, "*Shut up.*"

The newly appointed special agent immediately did as had been told, worried that this cushy number which had been handed to him on a plate might be lost.

"Mr O'Dowd will take his place here *exactly* as the marchioness has directed," Corsica laid down the law firmly.

"But..." began Flora.

Johnie silenced her with a single glance, "If you two old hags don't wish to be returned to the shabby, broken down cottage you previously occupied at Winterbourne, then you had better do exactly as Lady Elysia wishes."

In perfect harmony the Scott-Wilson sisters nodded their acquiescence as they recalled the leaking roof of their previous dwelling and the icy chill which had blasted through its cracked and broken window panes.

*****

"Your landlady was less than polite when I left the other day," observed Caroline as she hooked her arm into Richard's as they strolled along the recently completed section of the Victoria Embankment opposite the Houses of Parliament.

Richard coughed and shook his head, "As it turned out she need not have feared for the reputation of her establishment."

"You were too excited, my dear, as was I."

"Too much hurry and not enough...," he struggled to continue.

"*Stiffness?*" Caroline finished off for him and then wished she hadn't.

"It was not a lack of desire...," he began to defend himself.

"I understand that for I'm sure the consequences of betraying Jane lay behind it."

"You must have felt the same about Helmuth."

"Indeed, yes, he is the man who rescued me from the wilds of Nebraska and brought me safely home to my beloved Blanchwell."

"You owe him a lot."

"As you do Jane."

"Could you ever even contemplate losing Blanchwell for a second time?" He felt that he had to ask this same question again.

"The hard headed side of my nature would find that a very difficult proposition."

Richard laughed ironically, *"Hard headed?* This is a trait you could never have inherited from your papa."

"My poor father was brought up in an entirely different world, as far as he was concerned the Eighteenth Century had never run its course."

Richard could see that he was beginning to tread on shaky ground and so came to an abrupt halt, leaned across the embankment and looked down at the oily brown waters of the Thames.

"You could no more leave Jane and your children than I could give up my childhood home."

"Is this not a time for boldness, though, for a final decision?" He asked, half terrified that her answer would be in the affirmative.

"To move on or to stay as we are?"

"Yes, though if we were bolder than we've managed to be so far, you'd lose Blanchwell with very little chance of ever returning to it."

"Not to mention our children and the other people who depend and rely upon us."

They stood in silence for a long time, watching the river gurgle by, their eyes unseeingly following the passage of various pieces of flotsam and jetsam.

"Will it ever be different between us?"

"Whatever fate has in store, you will always remain my first, my true love."

*****

"Is there no change in him?" Asked Arabella Brass as she entered the entrance hall of the rectory.

"I'm afraid there isn't," returned her sister, Amelia Schilling, "mama is sitting with him now."

"I'll go up then," Arabella said as she took a step towards the staircase.

"I wouldn't just yet, the doctor thinks it's not good for papa to have too many visitors at one time as he becomes ever more agitated. Anyway, Fred's taking his turn at the moment."

"Is it really so bad, the message I received was a very urgent one?"

"Doctor Grace thinks it will only be a matter of hours," replied Amelia as she led her sister into the drawing room.

"Is papa sensible at all?" Asked Bella once she'd settled herself into a chair.

Tears began to form in the corners of Amelia's eyes, "Not really, he's rambling and speaking mostly in Hebrew."

"It's a pity we only have Latin, though you've some Greek."

"Taught to me by my dear papa...," Amelia sighed and her tears began to flow thick and fast.

Once they'd both dried their eyes, the sisters stood in silence for a while and then Arabella said, "Whatever is to become of mama? She will have to give up the rectory."

"Can she afford a decent place of her own?"

"I doubt it," replied Amelia.

"Not even with Great Aunt Charlotte's money?"

"I shouldn't think there will be enough left of that to maintain mama for the rest of her life."

"Can Caroline not take her in, as there is lots of room at Blanchwell?"

"Not as much as you may think and, anyway, I don't know if I dare ask her."

"A hint here and there, now and again, might work."

"It may well, but my best approach will be via Fred."

Though the girls loved their mother dearly they both saw that many problems would surface once she had been widowed; especially regarding the attitudes of their husbands, were they to have Venetia living with them for a prolonged period of time.

Upstairs, Mrs Lander had heard the arrival of her youngest daughter, nodded to Fred and went downstairs intending to greet her and discuss the latest situation regarding her father.

Even though the girls had spoken softly, their conversation was still loud enough to be heard by someone coming quietly down the stairs.

## Chapter Two

*(October, 1865)*

As George Murphy stepped from the train at Martindale, Lucy Greenwood was disappointed to find that he had a companion with him.

"Who's this?" She asked pointedly.

"Meet Mr Doggart, he's the favourite nephew of Mr Brass."

"The *only* nephew," correct Hugh swiftly.

Lucy bobbed low, brushed a strand of hair from her forehead, made her eyes sparkle and replied, "I'm Miss Greenwood and I'm ever so pleased to meet you, sir."

Doggart was finding it difficult to speak for he'd never before been addressed by a girl so pretty as this one, and in such a friendly fashion too, "My pleasure, Miss," he managed to stutter at last.

Lucy immediately set to summing up the potential value of Mister Doggart, *Is he worth spending any of my limited youth on?* she wondered to herself and then; after assessing the quality of his clothes and especially of his boots, she decided that he was – or at least could possibly be.

"Delighted, sir," she smiled sweetly and bobbed her head once more.

"Hugh is very important to the future of *Brass Shilling*," informed Murphy with a slight smile playing across his lips.

"Is that *really* so?" Lucy contrived to look impressed.

"I expect to go far at *Brass Shilling* and maybe beyond there too," these words tumbled from Hugh.

"The further away he goes the better," muttered Murphy to himself.

"I've sold lots of dresses, but every single one of them would have looked far better on you than on any other woman in the land," Hugh managed to deliver this clumsy complement without stuttering – but only just.

Again Lucy nodded her appreciation before she said, "It's a pity that Mr Murphy; who is supposed to be my fiancé, does not appreciate me as much as you do, Mr Doggart."

"What do you mean by *fiancé?*" Asked George, for as far as he was concerned their betrothal had long since been extinguished.

"You've never once told me to my face that we're no longer engaged," she accused, "you've got me so as I don't know whether I'm coming or going."

"Our situation is clear to me, you're definitely *going*," replied George.

Lucy shook her head prettily "You left my ma's without a word and never mentioned that you intended to break off our relationship."

"You know fine well that I have my own place now along Park Parade, so I have no need for lodgings."

"With no room for me either," she flashed her eyes in the forlorn hope that he might change his mind.

As this was going on, Hugh couldn't help noticing that Lucy was breathing heavily which made her breasts swell sensually, a sight which weakened his knees almost to the point of collapse.

Lucy brought herself up to her full height and raised her nose steeply into the air, "Then you are determined to abandon me, even after what has passed between us."

"What passed between you?" Asked Doggart eagerly.

"Nothing," shouted George, "and, anyway, mind your own business."

Lucy gave her ex-fiancé a withering glance and said, "You'll be sorry for deserting me, Mister Murphy, for there's not a man alive who does not need and desire a pretty wife."

Murphy considered for a moment and then replied, "I am a sensible man of business and know that I cannot contemplate marriage until I am wealthy enough to afford and sustain it."

"I've got money," put in Doggart eagerly, "lots of it."

"His uncle has," corrected Murphy.

Lucy smiled sweetly, "There is something so reassuring about a man of means, Mr Doggart."

"Call me Hugh, please," he interrupted.

"Though you are perhaps too young for serious courtship, *Hugh*," she replied with a simpering sigh.

"I'm the same age as Mr Murphy and taller than him too."

"Not by much, though," replied Murphy who never liked his lack of inches to be commented upon.

"You're a midget compared to me…," began Hugh.

"Why you…," returned George putting up his fists.

"George, Hugh, please restrain yourselves. Remember, you are supposed to be gentlemen."

"I'm better looking than him," Hugh pointed his thumb at Murphy.

"*Ha*, to blind girls, maybe."

"Please, the truth is that neither of you are outrightly handsome, though you are both of at least pleasant appearance."

For some time George had wondered how sensible an option marriage to Lucy would be, though now he was sure he had the answer to this conundrum, he dropped his fists and smiled.

Hugh breathed a sigh of relief because he'd never been any good at fisticuffs.

"Well, George, Hugh. You may both call on me; together or singly, whenever you wish.

With that she strolled off making sure that her buttocks were leaving behind her a clear message as to her suitability for marriage and child bearing.

*****

"What a clever man you are," Roberta Villiers complimented her husband from across the breakfast table.

Roddy smiled and nodded in full agreement with her.

"Don't over egg the custard, sister," put in John Fisher, sullenly.

"Roddy *is* clever though, ever so clever."

Fisher scowled, for though in the past he had abhorred and feared the overbearing character of his sister, he had still enjoyed the roastings she'd often delivered to Villiers. However, all had changed now and Roberta's current infatuation with her *Roddy* infuriated him. On top of which he hadn't received any payment for their upkeep and lodgings for some weeks.

"The Shakespeare Festival idea is pure genius," smiled Bobbity.

"Oh, I don't know about that, the idea of linking the best parts of Shakespeare with the use of a narrator just came to me in bed one morning."

"Are there to be multiple and large parts in it for me?" Enquired Roberta, her eyes wide open and appealing.

Villiers coughed and his shoulders hunched, "Of course, my dear," he struggled to speak eventually.

Roberta giggled when she saw the expression on her husband's face, "Oh, there's no need to worry, Roddy, I wish for nothing other than a tiny part to play, I know I'm not a good enough actress to take on anything major."

Her husband heaved a sigh of relief and cracked the shell of a soft boiled egg."

"That's five eggs you've gobbled up this morning," accused Fisher.

"No, Roddy has had only three."

"Three – five, it's more than I've had."

"School is on holiday, so you don't need much sustenance," retorted his brother-in-law.

"As you've wolfed down *my* eggs perhaps it's time *I* was offered a decent part in your so called Festival."

As he scowled, Roddy's eyebrows nearly touched and he tried frantically to think of a part long enough to please his brother-in-law but not so important that he could ruin the whole production with it.

"Leave it to Roddy, he'll find something suitable for you, third spear carrier, perhaps," suggested Roberta.

Had Fisher enjoyed even half the breakfast his brother-in-law had consumed, he would have retched in disgust, "I'm a long serving member of the company…," he began.

"Don't pester Roddy so early in the morning, he's ever so busy."

"I'll come up with something to suit your talents before long," promised Villiers with yet a further sigh of relief.

Roberta looked upon her husband her eyes gleaming with love, "Roddy will always do his best for us."

Villiers nodded and sighed contentedly. Previously, his marriage had been little other than a nightmare from which there was no awakening, but when Roberta had broken her leg falling from the stage of the Civic Theatre her character had changed completely. She was no longer a fierce some harridan but instead had become his angel – his guardian angel even. She cared for him so completely that he was overwhelmed by the force and affection of it. Previously, in days now long gone, he had believed women had been created merely for him to have a good time with, after which he was free to fly off without leaving behind so much as a soft word. Everything had changed for him now, Roberta had become an excellent wife who looked after his every need and whom he knew would support him in all things. She would always be there to help no matter what disasters he faced, and he had to admit that his past was well littered with calamities.

"Yes I will," he replied at last and then his face was lit by his oft practiced theatrical smile and he continued, "Everything I do is for Bobbity and Garrick."

John Fisher tried but failed to erase the crooked smile of disbelief which had appeared on his lips.

Roddy sighed with satisfaction and quoted, "*If love is not true it is a happy invention.*"

"Shakespeare, as usual, *Romeo and Juliet* I shouldn't be surprised," cried the schoolmaster.

Villiers shook his head, "No, I quoted from a Sixteenth Century Italian, who, alas, remained anonymous."

*****

"You must have given up hope of landing Georgie Porgie by now," suggested Charlotte Webb with a knowing smile.

Lucy Greenwood sniffed, "Not yet I haven't."

"I've heard that he's waved *ta-ta* to you, though."

Lucy wasn't flustered, "I could reel wee Murphy back in anytime I wanted."

"Then why haven't ye?"

"Time's not right and I thought I'd make him suffer, to dance at the end of my strings like the little puppet he is."

"It don't look like he's much bothered, though, does it. When's the last time he came calling? At one time he was never away from your front door."

Lucy yawned and pulled her shoulders back so that her breasts stuck out prominently, "George desires to have me more than anything else in his mean, miserable life and one day I shall make him pay up for it."

"My, you're a cold, cruel one."

"Men deserve to be treated badly, we women *must* treat them badly, it's the only way to keep them on the hook. I could have any man slobbering with desire just by promising to allow him to touch the hem of my skirt with his lips."

Charlotte then came to a sudden realisation and snapped her fingers, "Murphy has already *had* you. That's it, you've let him have his way and now he's done wi' you."

"He'll be back and I'll be waiting for him, unless something better turns up in the meantime."

"You've already tried out the big belly plot but it didn't come off, did it?" Charlotte was certain that she was on the right track.

"I had a queasy tummy a while back which gossips made more of than there was."

"Aye, but whatever it was you've lost him through it."

"I've other fish to fry now."

"Not Losser – I canny fancy him myself, a big strong lad and one of the best hewers in a town full of hewers."

"You can have him, for I couldn't care less about him – anyway, he's already involved with the little cripple who tried to steal away my George."

Charlotte's face flushed with guilt, "I wish I'd had nothing to do with frightening Clara away from *Brass Schilling*. It wasn't right; I knew it at the time, and I still feel bad about my part in it."

"Aye, well, you'd better think on about who your friends are."

"Maybe it's always better to remember what's right and what's not."

"Anyway, I don't need your help to push Miss Webb's nose out of joint if I had a mind to," returned Lucy sharply.

"Why would you need to? You said that you could sweep any man up into your web whenever you liked."

"That's right, I can too," replied Lucy sharply as she turned and walked away.

*****

George Dodds entered the office of Inspector Mason and carefully spread open a newspaper on his desk, "Page five, column three," he instructed.

Roland Mason found the required article and began to read:-

*It has been brought to the attention of the editor of this journal that Forest Hall; an old and venerable house long owned by several generations of the Fitzwarren*

144

*family, is believed to hold within its walls a Sixteenth Century priest hole. Though this as yet remains to be proven.*

*However, the learned gentlemen of our esteemed County Antiquarian Society are determined to settle the veracity of this matter once and for all.*

*Unfortunately, their investigation has been delayed by the current owner of the property who is none other than the Marchioness of Studland. This well-known lady has given no rational reason for her refusal of so reasonable a request.*

*Even though the agreement of Lady Gertrude Wright; the widow of that giant of the world of commerce and industry, Sir James Hannibal Wright (who mysteriously disappeared two years ago), has given her permission for the search for the Sixteenth Century Papist bolt-hole to proceed. However, entry to the house has still been steadfastly refused.*

*In fact those renowned antiquarians the Reverend Horace Nelson and Mr Rufus Plantagenet have been most rudely dealt with by some unnamed, but nonetheless, ill-mannered minion of the current owner.*

*Forest Hall is currently occupied by Lady Flora Scott-Wilson and her sister Lady Rowena and we are further informed that these ladies were more than happy to allow the investigation to proceed.*

"That's interesting," said Mason after he'd skimmed the article.

"Why do you think the marchioness has refused permission? What difference could it possibly make to her?"

"You're thinking that perhaps she *does* have something to hide and it's not likely to be a bolt-hole for fugitive priests," returned the inspector.

"It is possible that the body of Sir James could be concealed at Forest Hall, and maybe that of the woman who disappeared at the same time too."

"Fraulein Kleist, you mean."

"Would a priest-hole be large enough for two bodies?" Wondered George Dodds.

"I've known bodies to be stuffed into some very limited spaces."

"Shouldn't we go down there with a search-warrant," suggested the constable eagerly.

"No, not until we're more certain there *is* something there. The marchioness has made a fool of me before and she's *not* going to do it again," replied Mason with determination.

"What then?"

"We carry on with our search for the Channel steamer lady and watch closely events at Forest Hall, for I don't believe that the antiquarian gentlemen will give up so easily."

"Which would put some pressure on the marchioness."

"Which in turn could lead to her making a fatal mistake."

\*\*\*\*\*

After an excellent communion service conducted by the Reverend Hodge, Mrs Venetia Lander found herself accosted by a clerical gentlemen whom she had not been introduced.

"I am told that you are the widow of the late and much lamented Reverend Lander. Is that not the case?"

"Indeed yes," replied Venetia, who was immediately put on her guard as she was expecting to have to vacate the rectory very shortly.

"I am the Reverend William St.Vincent Cowpens and I have been sent by the bishop to see if the Martindale living would suit me."

Venetia nearly staggered as though she had received a physical blow, but managed to stay upright and sound both calm and serene, "I see," she uttered at last.

"I've inspected both Holy Innocents and St. Peter's and tend to believe that they will do me nicely."

"I see," repeated Venetia, smiling as brightly as she could in the circumstances.

"That leaves only the rectory itself to be viewed."

"Would it not be wise to leave domestic arrangements to Mrs Cowpens?"

"I am unmarried, my wife died some years ago."

After a pause for thought, Venetia invited, "Then I suppose you'd better come and inspect the rectory now, if that is convenient."

"Excellent, for it will save the need for a return visit to Martindale."

147

Two hours later, after every room had been thoroughly examined, Venetia and Mr Cowpens returned to the drawing room where tea and hot toasted muffins were served to them.

"My, this is a very comfortable house," the new rector nodded positively in time with his words.

"My husband and I were very happy here this decade past."

"Hopefully, as shall I be."

"I fear that both Mr Somers and Mr Hodge will be disappointed as they both had aspirations of having this living for themselves."

Cowpens considered for a moment and then informed, "The cathedral believe that Mr Somers is best suited to become the priest of a village church rather than undertaking the wider and more subtle burdens of the Martindale rectory."

"What of Mr Hodge, I'm sure the cathedral hierarchy are impressed by his truly Christian virtues."

"Indeed they are, however, it is felt that my experience of much larger parishes will be more suited to the situation here," replied her visitor before biting into a muffin.

"By, these are excellent – are they homemade?"

"To my own recipe," replied Venetia with a hint of pride.

"Very good indeed."

"Will you keep the servants on?" Venetia asked anxiously.

"Shan't you be taking them with you?" Cowpens sounded surprised.

"In my reduced circumstances I will have neither the money nor the space for servants."

"Oh, I'm sorry to hear that," replied the new rector sympathetically.

"I'll probably end up a flying shuttlecock t'wixt the households of my daughters."

The visitor sipped tea thoughtfully and then offered, "Perhaps you would consider becoming my housekeeper – running the rectory exactly as you do now."

"I hardly... I don't...," Venetia's heart leapt with joy, but she managed to successfully restrain her enthusiasm.

"Your life could then carry on as it is – keep the master bedroom for yourself, do as you will about the household. This would certainly remove a huge load from my own rather narrow shoulders."

"What about gossip? People will talk," though Venetia could no longer supress her delight on receiving his offer.

"Of course they will, and if it wasn't about supposed goings on at the rectory it would be about something or someone else."

Venetia nodded her agreement, "That is a certainty."

"Then you will accept my offer?"

"Very well, then, I shall remain exactly as I am," it took no time for Venetia to reply for this was the best offer she'd had for many years.

"Good."

"What were you to re-marry at some time in the future?"

The new rector thought for a moment and then replied, "Perhaps we should cross that bridge if and when we come to it."

*****

"I've good news," cried Susannah Reno as soon as her husband had arrived home.

"She has that," put in Mrs Hardy who was once again their landlady.

"Villiers wants you to play Desdemona to his Othello," his tone contained within it a hint of envy.

"No, no, it's much better news than that," she stood before him beaming.

"You're not..," he began with a catch in his voice.

"No she isn't," Margaret Hardy returned impatiently, before she continued, "For goodness sake, woman, tell him."

"Phil's ship is to be put out of commission and he will soon have leave to come home," she cried waving a letter.

"That's excellent news, the last we heard from him he was at Malta."

"Here, you may as well read for yourself," replied Susannah as she handed over the mail she'd received from her brother.

*My Dear Susannah,*

*How do you do? How does the admirable Marcus do? Myself, I am very well and in fact have never felt better. Once I'd gotten clear of the sea-sickness; which afflicts most sailors at some time, I soon settled down to the unchanging routine of shipboard life.*

*Though the navy isn't for either the weak minded or willed, it suits me very well and I'm sure that I shall be able to carve out a good career for myself in it.*

*In addition, I've some excellent news. My ship, the* Royal Oak *has been ordered home to be refitted and re-armed. This work will take several months so I'm bound to be allowed sufficient leave to visit my family and friends in Martindale. Which I am looking forward to with great pleasure and longing.*

*How is dear mama? I'm not sure where she resides now and only hope that she is with you or very nearby. Our mama is well rid of our father, as indeed are we. You wrote to me that he is dead; killed by tribesmen in North Africa, but I should need to see his body to be convinced of this. Though I have no fear of running into him as I should like the opportunity to give him the pummelling he so palpably deserves.*

*There's no doubt in my mind that you are now living contentedly with your husband and I pray every day for your happiness and good fortune.*

*Please pass on my regards to all and I will be with you as soon as my relief from duty allows.*

*Your*

*devoted brother,*


   *Philip*


"He seems to have taken to the navy very well," observed Marcus.

"I'm sure that he has found it a vast improvement on life with papa."

"Even though it is a hard, harshly disciplined one?"

"Yes, even then, and I'm sure that he will make a good career out of it."

"Your brother is a fine young man," put in Mrs Hardy, "he's sure to end up an admiral."

*So long as he isn't drowned or suffers a fall from the main mast or some other high place on his ship*, thought Marcus to himself, though he merely returned her smile.

*****

"Do you really live here?" Asked an awed Kitty Hawes when she first sighted Merrington Hall from the window of their carriage.

"It belongs to my wife and was the ancestral home of her first husband, Colonel Henry Galvin."

"Your lady sure must like colonels," replied Kitty with a quizzical glance at her guardian.

"Elizabeth is a person of many and varied parts."

Kitty looked towards the rapidly approaching hall again, "It's so old… I ain't seen nuthin' so old in all my life."

"The earliest part of it was a square tower, put up in 1420, a time when border raids were common. However, there's no sign of the original building now as the rest of the house was erected around it."

"In those olden days, who was raiding who?"

"Mainly the Scots, but at the time there were always two or more claimants to the English crown, a bauble they fought over between themselves for sixty years or so – on and off."

"It looks quiet enough now," Kitty scanned the undergrowth hoping to catch sight of a wild clansman.

"Nothing much has happened here for at least four centuries."

"What about all the smoke and noise in the town we just passed through?"

"Martindale you mean? Ten years ago it didn't exist at all, though it's not as bad a place as it looks and the people are pretty special – once you get to know them."

The carriage rumbled on for a dozen more yards or so before Esprey spoke again, "You will remember always to use your new name."

Kitty made a face, "*Catherine,* I don't like it."

"Kitty is a derivative of Catherine, so your mama; whoever she was, probably chose it for you."

"I still don't like it."

"Well, you've got it now, but you can decide whether you wish to be Katherine with a *K* or Catherine with a *C*."

"Which do you prefer?"

"It's your choice, choose whichever you wish."

"Catherine Esprey; with a *C*, it looks nicer on paper."

The colonel cleared his throat to prevent the sort of sentimental tears forming he had so often suppressed, "Are you sure that you wish to take my name? You could remain a Hawes, you know." His voice began to crack slightly but he managed to disguise it with a cough.

"Sure, why not, I like Esprey better than Hawes."

Shortly thereafter, they pulled to stop by Merrington Hall's portico and wasted no time disembarking.

Corporal Carew appeared immediately, "Welcome back, colonel," he greeted, though he had a knowing look in his eye which signalled to his officer, *Look out, you're for it.*

"Where is the mistress?" Asked Jervy, wishing to get started on what he knew would be a difficult interview.

"She is not receiving this morning, sir," replied Carew as he waved forward the footmen who had accompanied him to see to the luggage.

"She'll see me, though," replied Esprey forcefully, he nodded towards Kitty, "This is my daughter, Miss Catherine Esprey, see that she is made comfortable in the largest of the rooms overlooking the garden, assign a suitable maid to her, after which she shall require luncheon. A large one."

"Yes, colonel," replied Carew though he wondered where his officer had picked up the little trollop.

A few minutes later Jervy stood at the entrance to his wife's *boudoir,* he rapped sharply and pushed open the door – which; to his surprise, was not locked.

Elizabeth was soon on her feet greeting him with little more than a cold smile.

He studied her closely, trying to discern from her demeanour which of her wide repertoire of parts she had decided to play for him, he then nodded sharply in greeting.

"I'm sorry…," he began.

Her expression became excessively judgemental, her eyes glinted and she held herself smartly erect, "*Sorry* does not cover it, sir, *sorry* will never soothe nor will it compensate for the dreadful worry and fear I've endured for these several months past."

Her words were delivered with the precision and tone of a fine actress and he listened carefully to see if he could define which of her favourite characters she had decided to play.

"I can only…," he began before being hushed to silence.

"You *swine*, you *rabid hound*, a *pox* on you, sir," her voice did not so much as catch for a second, even though her eyes were bright and full of fiery emotion.

It was at this point he recognised the role she had chosen, she had become Elizabeth the Virgin Queen who had just received news of the execution of Mary Stuart.

"I'm sorry, but it was something I needed to do."

"Admit it, you went off to *play* at being soldiers with the other idiot who got himself killed and no doubt you were shot at too."

Jervy shook his head, "I was never in any particular danger, and Giddy died when the skirmish we'd fought appeared to be over."

"When it occurred is immaterial, for Major Sturgis was shot dead."

Jervy managed to prevent himself from revealing the horrific fact that his companion had been pitchforked to death and had lingered on for some considerable time.

"Why did *you* feel it necessary to accompany him?" Her voice took on a magisterial tone again and her eyes were still as cold as ice.

"Giddy was going off alone, I wished to help him out…"

"The truth is that the pair of you deeply desired to go off soldiering again – the major had some excuse to do so, though *you*, sir, had *NONE*."

"Giddy needed my help to keep him safe."

"And what a *wonderful* job you made of *that,*" her lips curled in contempt.

Elizabeth's words stung deeply, causing the colonel to hang his head, "I know I failed him, I failed my friend… I was too old for the whole game and I understand that now," his hands came up to cover his face and; suddenly overcome with emotional exhaustion, he slumped into a chair beside the fireplace.

Elizabeth had never before seen her husband look so old nor so bent, though she was damned if she was going to sympathise with him.

Jervis eventually looked up, "How did Grace take it?" He asked, his voice cracked and broken.

"Oh, she was hardly fussed at all, took a pint of brandy and forgot all about it," Elizabeth laughed sarcastically.

"I must hurry over to Blanchwell as soon as I can to explain what happened."

"Grace has taken to her bed and hasn't left it yet, as far as I'm aware."

"Has Caroline spoken to her? Talked to her…"

Eliza's temper flared again, "*GRACE HAS LOST HER HUSBAND YOU IDIOT.* Do you not recognise the import of this to her? Have you no heart, sir, no vestige of empathy?"

He looked up, his face creased and miserable, "I'm an old dog who's seen too much of violent death ever to be shocked or surprised by the impartiality and swiftness of it."

As she watched she could see that it was all he could do to keep back the tears which were forming in his eyes.

Elizabeth swiftly abandoned the part of Elizabeth of England and fell to her knees beside him, caressed his cheek and began to smooth his hair, "Hush, it will be all right."

"But when?"

"When the Good Lord makes it so."

Silence reigned for a long while and then Jervis eventually found the courage to speak again, "I've two items of good news, though."

"What on earth could they possibly be?" Liza doubted that anything pleasing could have come of her husband's jaunt to America.

"We are now the part owners of a tobacco plantation in Virginia."

"I see," replied his wife who was not convinced that this investment would turn out to be a profitable one, "And the other?"

Jervy swallowed hard and his voice cracked, "I've brought home for us a daughter."

*****

The Reverend Mr Cowpens was visiting Byers Green in the hope of meeting with his curate, Mr Somers, but had so far failed to find him.

"Have you any idea where the curate is?" He asked the wife of the church warden.

The lady bobbed, nodded and then replied, "None, sir, I haven't laid eyes on him this week."

"Though he did conduct services on Sunday last?"

"Oh, yes, sir. He's a fine, spirited speaker – too spirited some say, but he certainly compels sinners to ponder over their misdeeds."

"I see, so he's popular in the village?"

The lady paused for thought, puckered her lips, and then declared, "Not exactly popular, but he's respected in most quarters."

"He was due at Holy Innocents to conduct Evensong on Sunday, but failed to turn up. Have you any idea what may have prevented him?"

"None, sir, I attended church twice and he was there conducting the services on both occasions."

Cowpens thanked the lady, mounted his horse and made his way back to the rectory at Martindale.

Two hours later; as he was preparing his sermon for the coming week-end, he was interrupted by a hammering at the front door. He heard the visitor; whoever it was, enter and was astounded to hear a tirade being directed at Mrs Lander.

"You, *bitch,* you awful bitch, you persuaded your idiot husband to black-ball me at Durham."

"Edwin was far too ill to have any interest in whom might succeed him," Venetia defended her husband.

"If that were the case then; you sly madam, this entire plot against me was of *your own* making."

Cowpens could stand no more, he opened the door into the hall and confronted his curate, "Mr Somers, sir, please restrain yourself. Your language is immoderate and most unbecoming in a man of the Cloth, made immeasurably worse by being directed at a lady."

"*She's* no lady, she has secrets she dare not repeat," in his fury a spray of fine spittle came flying from the curate's mouth.

Cowpens decided that the heat needed to be taken out of the situation immediately, he smiled at Venetia who was still looking dumbstruck and then said forcefully, "Mister Somers, we two shall discuss this matter in private."

At first it looked as though the curate would have no part of this, but eventually the rector took him gently by the arm and led him to the study doorway.

By now, some of the anger had dispersed from Somers' mind and he allowed himself to be conducted into the study where a glass of sherry was pushed into his hand.

"Well, now, Roland, what's this all about?"

"I've been treated unjustly."

"In what way?"

Somers thought for a few seconds and then replied, "The living to which you have been appointed should have been mine."

"As you well know that was a Cathedral decision. I had nothing to do with it and nor did Mrs Lander."

"Though you wasted no time in accepting the offer."

"Indeed not, I looked around the parish first, considered deeply and decided that it would suit me very well."

"How were you chosen though? I was the obvious candidate."

Cowpens held wide his hands and shook his head to express the level of puzzlement he himself felt.

"I'll tell you why you were chosen, Lander would not have put in a good word for me and his bitch of a wife will have plunged in her own knife and twisted it."

"You will direct no further intemperate language at Mrs Lander, especially as she is entirely innocent of any misconduct," the rector's normally mild voice took on a steely tone.

"I very much doubt that...," began Somers until he was interrupted.

"Mrs Lander has no influence with the Dean and Chapter and your use of immoderate language against her is both unjust and unbecoming."

"She's against me though, because I know all about her family."

"She has two very pleasant married daughters."

"What about the third one, Abigail, no doubt she's kept quiet about her."

Cowpens shrugged his shoulders.

"Got herself pregnant whilst abroad and killed herself. Then there's the aunt, Prudence Hodge."

"The wife of the Reverend Hodge?"

"Yes and she's a notorious wanton."

"Surely not, I've met the lady and she is the model of the ideal clergyman's wife."

161

"Aye, well I tell you she has another side, I've had her myself on several occasions – in Hodge's own bed too," now that he had begun his denunciation Somers found it hard to restrain himself.

William Cowpens began to worry, for what had seemed like a settled, trouble free parish was turning out to be the very opposite.

"We need to discuss this with a little less heat," he suggested before he topped up the sherry glasses.

"It'll take more than wine to stop me from telling the truth, I don't even care were I to ruin myself in the process."

Cowpens thought for a long moment and then considered, "The root cause of all this trouble and consternation is because you were not given the living of Martindale, is that not so?"

"Partly… Though it's also a matter of morals," Somers back-tracked a little.

"Indeed, yes, but in the wider scheme of things no harm has been done."

"Apart from to my prospects."

"Indeed, though you yourself have already confessed to indulging in behaviour far below that expected of a member of the clergy."

Somers' head dropped and he took a long gulp of sherry and absent mindedly picked up a left-over ginger-snap to go with it.

"Yes..," he confessed with a deep sigh.

"There is a way out of this, you know."

"I can't see what that could be without destroying the reputations of people, both alive and dead."

"Your fire and fury has been caused; to a great extent, by your lack of a suitable living. That is the root of it, is it not?"

Somers nodded slowly and wondered what was coming next.

"Suppose something *were* to be found for you, would that be enough to bring you back to normality and reduce the palpable anger and fury you so frequently display?"

Again the curate nodded and this time he also smiled, "I believe it would."

"Then I shall see what I can do for you."

"Have you sufficient influence to help me?"

"I believe so."

"But where is the living you suggest?"

"You know of Leadhope, I presume."

"Well west of Stanhope isn't it," Somers sounded doubtful.

"Yes, the church is a fairly recently built one, going back only as far as the 20's, and the congregation is now much smaller than it was."

"You intend to shunt me out of the way, deep into the wilds...," Somers' voice rose as he spoke.

"My dear, fellow, it *is* a living, and with your record it is the best you could ever hope for. There's no curate in place, but you could appoint one, for crucially, the value of the living is still based on the size the congregation was thirty years ago."

Somers began to smile, "So it provides a reasonable income."

"Indeed, yes. Nothing like Martindale nor even Kirkby, but very acceptable nonetheless."

"Could you really help me with this? Would you be willing to do so – knowing what you know...," the curate's voice trailed off.

Cowpens' tone became very business-like, "There are certain favours that I can call in at the Cathedral, but first you must prove yourself to be worthy of my patronage. You must begin by satisfactorily playing the role of my curate."

"Of course."

"To the very letter, and there are to be no lapses of duty of any description."

"I've been a curate for years, I know what's expected of me."

There followed a long silence after which Cowpens promised, "Then you'll be ensconced at Leadhope by Easter next."

The previous storminess of Somers' expression cleared, he looked as though he'd suddenly seen the light and could make out that the path ahead of him was now a secure one.

"What about a curate for Leadhope though? I'll need a curate if I'm to gather in the lead miners and farmers from far up the dale."

"Our *See* is full of eager clerics, you may take your pick," Cowpens laughed uproariously at his own poor play on words.

A few minutes later, once Somers had departed, Venetia appeared at the study door, "Has he gone? What did he say? What sort of threats did he make?"

Cowpens looked up from the sermon he had returned to composing, "You need fear Mr Somers no longer. All is calm with him now."

"What about the threats he made?"

"All forgotten, peace and quiet reigns."

"How on earth did you manage it?"

The rector thought for a second or two, looked up and smiled, "Bribery, my dear, nothing ever works quicker and more readily than good old fashioned bribery."

*****

"I wish you'd drop this unwarranted concern you have over Forest Hall, for now you're making me nervous about it too," demanded Elysia.

"That's easy for you to say, you had nothing to do with the physical side of it," he paused meaningfully and then continued, "the disposal of your papa was left to me and O'Dowd."

"It wasn't all your work, remember Fraulein Kleist readily played the temptress that night."

"Then she panicked and I ended up with *two* bodies to dispose of," pointed out Corsica grumpily.

Elysia covered her eyes with her hands as though trying to rid herself of a migraine, "I feel as much guilt over this whole affair as you do, probably more so. Anyway, apart from knocking him on the head, you did not harm him."

"I just left him to freeze and starve."

"Which is what had been agreed."

They stood quietly for a moment or two before Elysia mused, "At that time the priest hole seemed the ideal solution."

"Not so perfect now, though, is it."

She nodded in agreement and then began to pace back and forth in front of the fireplace, her face unsettled and expression troubled. Then she halted abruptly and said, "I now know what I must do."

"Set Forest Hall afire, raze what's left to the ground and forget about it."

Elysia stood stock still, deep in thought for several moments and then declared, "I have become determined that my papa shall have a proper funeral and be buried with all the ceremony due to him." As she spoke her tone had taken on a dreamy quality as though she had suddenly seen the true light and had to follow wherever it led.

"With a suitably inscribed head-stone – and in Latin, too," replied Corsica with a sardonic grin.

"I'm serious about this, Johnie," she replied solemnly.

"When your papa returned home to take the reins of power from yourself, you couldn't wait to be rid of him," Johnie laughed sardonically.

"I've suffered for it ever since."

"Once you'd had me deal with him, you didn't give a tinker's damn about his mortal remains," Corsica's tone now became scornful.

"I've changed my mind, my dear papa deserves a proper, dignified funeral and he *shall* have one," Elysia was adamant.

"How do you propose to do that without the pair of us ending up on the scaffold?"

"Why not though? My father disappeared completely so what's to stop him turning up again."

"Him being stone cold dead may have something to do with it."

"His body could reappear – bodies often turn up in unexpected places."

"Where though? In America maybe, or on the moon," scoffed Corsica, who still wasn't taking her seriously.

"No, but suppose his body reappeared; say in a field or washed ashore somewhere."

"Then there'd be an investigation which would prove beyond doubt that we were the guilty parties."

"*You* were the guilty one, I had nothing to do with it," Elysia suddenly changed her tune.

"Apart from your close association with me, that is, which would be enough to hang you."

Elysia screwed her eyes up in thought and then said, "If we could pull it off, though, I could build a suitable tomb for my dear papa, here at Winterbourne – or at least in the village churchyard."

"Why don't you have his corpse carried off to Egypt and have a pyramid built over it."

Elysia's expression now showed her resolve, "My father's remains *are* going to be interred in a suitable resting place – I'm determined on it."

Corsica shook his head in disbelief, "You can't think that this is anything other than a madcap proposition."

"We shall see soon enough."

*****

"Well, there go the happy couple," said Sir Charles Martin as he waved farewell to Frank Turner and his new wife Rosemary.

"It's taken him some considerable time to find happiness, but I'm sure my brother has succeeded to-day," said Marian who was keeping a tight hold of the hand of her niece Maud.

"Why can't I go off with daddy and Rosie?" Asked the little girl.

"They need to be alone to get to know each other," replied Sarah Nicholson.

"They've already been friends for years," returned Maud dismissively, who though she was very small for her age was nonetheless both mature and astute.

"Indeed they have, for Rosie was a near neighbour of ours at Cherry Tree Farm, when we were children," remembered Marian fondly.

"I knew her people well, but their farm was one belonging to Blanchwell at the time," put in Charles.

"Until Wright sold it off and eventually poor Rosy was left alone and penniless."

"Then my papa came along and everything for her became *rosy*," Maud laughed at her own joke.

Jane Turner; looking at the smallness of Maud, wondered if she could really be the offspring of parents who were both tall. Frank, in fact, was huge and Abigail had been well above female average height.

Maud waved energetically until the carriage disappeared around a bend in the drive and just as it looked as though she was about to shed a few tears, Sarah Nicholson took her hand.

"I'm delighted you are to stay with your Aunty Marian whilst your papa and new mama are away, you'll be able to help me set out the school room every morning."

Any tears which had been forming in the child's eyes dried up immediately, for there was no one in the world that she'd rather spend time with than her teacher, who she firmly believed should have been her papa's new bride.

The guests all made their way back inside the Turner home to have a final round of refreshments before they ordered their own carriages to be brought around.

*****

During his military career, Colonel Esprey had fought many desperate actions, but he'd never before felt so insecure as he awaited the appearance of the widowed Mrs Sturgis.

Waiting quietly, deep in thought, he was startled as the drawing room doors opened and Grace Sturgis arrived dressed from head to foot in black, unrelieved by any other colour nor even by the merest hint of decoration.

"Colonel Esprey," she greeted pleasantly enough, but her eyes betrayed the searing anger she felt for him.

Esprey stiffened to attention and nodded. He had made ready several phrases with which to begin this long feared interview, but now that the time was upon him none of them seemed to be even remotely adequate. Nothing he said to her could *ever* be adequate, he thought.

She stood silently, staring at him as if daring him to speak. Hoping that he would say something that she could immediately dismiss with contempt.

Then, with a suddenness which almost made him start, she took a chair and invited, "Please, sit, sir."

"Thank you, ma'am."

"Do you have any explanation?" Her voice was rough and hoarse.

"I'm so sorry…," he began.

"*Sorry?* I can understand sorry, but have you an *explanation*?"

"Your husband was determined to become the owner of the Knightsbridge plantation – he wished to take it from its previous owner, Mister Talisker."

"Though Talisker was no longer alive."

"That is correct."

There then followed a long, and to Jervis an endless, silence.

"Giddy may not have gone had you refused to accompany him," she suddenly accused forcefully.

"The way he talked of it, I'm sure he would have gone whether I was with him or not."

"Did my Giddy invite you to join him?"

Esprey's throat dried up, but eventually he replied, "No."

Grace's lips formed a grim, self-satisfied smile, "Then without you he may well have given up the idea as being impracticable."

"He may have, though I doubt it," he croaked at last.

"I see," she considered for a moment and then asked, "Then who is currently in charge at Knightsbridge? If it is ever to make a profit there must be someone in charge."

"Madame Deborah de Friese, who owns a share of the estate."

If Grace knew previously of her husband's first love, she gave no sign of it, "Is she to be trusted?"

Jervy did not think she was but merely stated, "Possibly."

"Was she not previously Miss Deborah Talisker, the girl my husband was once in love with?"

"I believe so, however, each thought the other was dead."

"In that case it must have been wonderful for them to discover that the opposite was true. Was there not a rebirth of their romance?"

Jervy shook his head vigorously, "Not only was there no time for it, but no inclination on either side. They were hardly ever alone together."

"It takes mere seconds for a romance to be rekindled, a smile or a meaningful glance can do it," her voice became both hoarse and sharp at the same time.

"As I've said, there was no time, Giddy's last words were of you."

She laughed in his face, "Even had he lived, my husband would never have returned to me. Virginia, that traitor state, would have provided him with everything he longed for, I should have been forgotten in a flash."

Esprey's head dropped, his chin nearly hitting his chest, "It all ended badly, but who could say now what may or may not have happened had he lived."

Grace shook her head wildly, "I had already lost him, lost his love, I knew that before he went off."

"No, that isn't true," put in the colonel desperately.

"I lost his love the moment my unborn child broke away from my body and entered this cruel world too early."

"No, that isn't the case…"

"Do you take me for a fool, sir?"

"Of course not, ma'am," Esprey searched for a change of subject and came up with, "At least you still have the comfort of living with your brothers."

"What comfort is there for me in that?"

"I just thought…," Esprey's words stuttered out.

"In the spring I shall return to Gettysburg to live an independent life."

"A familiar place can bring such comfort…" Jervy was struggling hard to find something comforting and at the same time uncontroversial to say.

"Once I've arranged the Gettysburg house to my satisfaction I shall move on to Virginia, to Knightsbridge and Cardinal Woods to take up my inheritance – and God help anyone who tries to stop me – especially Mrs de Friese."

"Of course…," began Jervis before his throat had completely dried up.

In a rustle of silk Grace got to her feet, "Thank-you, colonel, I hope you realise that this is the last time I shall ever speak to you. As far as I'm concerned you are as dead as both my husband and poor unborn child."

# Chapter Three

*(November, 1865)*

"That's her, that's Harriet Hardacre," hissed Constable Dodds from the corner of his mouth.

"As she's sitting at a table so far away from us there's no need to whisper," replied his chief, Inspector Mason, who then went on, "however, it may be best if you refrained from staring at her,"

"Sorry, sir, I'm a little over excited I think."

"We'll both be ecstatic if she proves to be the lead we've been searching for."

The person under observation was a very prim, dark haired and attractive woman of thirty or so years. She was immaculately turned out and her clothes had the design and cut which signalled wealth to all those who cared to study her closely.

"Who's the chap do you suppose?" Wondered Dodds.

"City gent, or maybe a bishop out of uniform."

"A bishop...," cried Dodds a little too loudly, for several heads were raised from their plates, though fortunately not from the couple they were watching.

"Many men from every walk of life indulge in occasional bouts of hanky-panky – so do their wives too, though often for different reasons."

Dodds contemplated for a while and then asked, "Aren't we going to have a word with them?"

"As soon as the gentleman goes we'll have a quiet chat with the lady."

It was then as though Mason's words had provided a theatrical cue, for the man in question rose from the table, kissed the hand of the lady and left the restaurant.

"This should prove interesting…," said Dodds as he began to rise to his feet.

"Not yet, boy, not yet, she may have another *friend* calling soon," muttered Mason who at the same time placed a restraining hand on his constable's forearm.

"There's no one else coming now," suggested Dodds ten minutes later.

"Hold on, let her make the first move, I don't want her cutting-up rough in here, it would upset the management and therefore be counter-productive."

As he was speaking Miss Hardacre got to her feet, checked that her hat was neatly in place, picked up her reticule and brolly and made for the entrance.

The policemen waited until the dining-room door had closed behind her and then followed in her wake.

Once outside they were baffled, for Harriet Hardacre was nowhere to be seen.

Dodds stared around in all directions, "Gone in a puff of smoke," he cried.

Mason turned back towards the hotel, beginning to believe that somehow she had remained inside.

"Looking for me, gentlemen?" A husky voice came from behind them.

Dodds started with surprise and turned to face Harriet who was smiling knowingly.

Mason pulled out his pipe, stuffed tobacco into the bowl and lit it before he deigned to face the lady.

"Well now, Miss Hardacre, we are police officers…"

"I recognised that the moment you followed me into the restaurant, there's something about you bobbies that can't be missed."

"That only applies to people in your own line of work," returned Mason knowingly.

"And what line of work would that be?"

"Lady of the night," put in Dodds at once.

Harriet took this coolly, "You wouldn't be idiots enough to arrest me, would you? The gentleman I lunched with is a very important…"

It was Mason's turn to interrupt, "No, nothing like that, we'd just be grateful if you would tell us all you know of a man you were seen with on a cross-Channel steamer."

For the first time Miss Hardacre looked a trifle unsettled and her eyes quickly scanned the crowded thoroughfare around her.

"I don't know what you're talking of."

"I'm sure you do," replied Mason as reassuringly as he was able.

"We also believe that you gave to the man who was travelling with you a full outfit of female apparel," added Dodds.

"I do not involve myself in *any* sort of perversion. None, it's straight up and down with me or I'm off."

Mason took her arm gently and spoke in an avuncular fashion, "We're not after *you*, Hetty, not at all. It's the man who used you, hired you for this steamer job."

"You're not planning to arrest me, then."

"For what? Having lunch with a posh gentleman? There's no crime to charge you with," Mason kept his voice soft and reassuring.

Harriet thought for a moment and then suggested, "Perhaps it would be better if we got off the street, I'd rather not be seen conversing with men who are so obviously policemen. It's very bad for business."

"There's a teashop just around the corner, we'll have a cuppa and you can tell us all you know."

Five minutes later Dodds was playing mother and hoping that he would be given the opportunity to ask Miss Hardacre some questions of his own – hard ones too.

"Right, Harriet, tell us in your own words what happened," Mason wished to get things underway.

"I was approached by a foreign looking gentleman who said that he wished to play a joke on a very good friend of his."

"What was his name?" Put in Dodds eagerly.

"Prince Albert of Saxe-Coburg-Gotha come back to life, who do you think," replied a dead-pan Hetty.

"Not now, constable, not now," as he spoke Mason turned to smile reassuringly at Miss Hardacre.

"He told me that his name was Giuseppe, not that that means anything. However, the plan was that I should make myself known to his *friend*; of course in a subtle way, and develop a relationship during which I'd make it known that I was a lonely lady who was prepared to offer him sexual favours."

"This plan obviously worked," remarked Mason.

"I had the chap nibbling out of my hand by the time we docked."

"You arranged to meet him ashore?"

"Yes, at first he wished to take me to the *Lord Warden* hotel where he said he had a suite."

"But you couldn't go there because your husband would find out," presumed the inspector.

Hetty smiled knowingly, "I can't see why you need me at all."

Mason grinned to himself and waved to his witness that she should carry on.

"The tale I told was that my husband was an aide to the Governor of Dover Castle and that I should find it difficult to turn out."

"Though you made a rendezvous with him after some discussion," put in Dodds who was pleased at last not to be interrupted by his superior.

"I agreed to meet him on the cliff top path."

"Though you had no intention of doing so?"

"As arranged, I had with me a change of clothes which I got into and handed the outfit I had previously worn to Mister Mysterious."

"Who, amazingly, was your own size," put in Dodds.

"Near enough to make no difference."

"You'd never met this foreign gentleman before you'd agreed to this *joke*?" Questioned Mason.

"No, apart from receiving his instructions the week before, he was a complete stranger to me."

"Have you seen him since?"

"No, and nor do I wish to, for there was something about his eyes, the way he stared at me, it made me shiver then and the remembrance of it sets me all a tremble now."

"What did he look like?"

"Of medium height, very well-muscled; takes care of himself I should say, olive complexion, a Mediterranean type would sum him up."

"You had no inkling of his real name, he made a slip of the tongue, perhaps?"

"No, he was a professional."

"Would you recognise him again?"

"*NO,* I would not. I would not dare to if I wished to live."

"You're dealing with the Law here, Miss Hardacre...," began Dodds.

"Leave it, constable, this lady has been very helpful and we do not wish to trouble her further."

"Thank-you," replied Miss Hardacre, with some gratitude.

"Though should this chappie turn up again, I'm sure you'll let us know," said Mason handing over his card at the same time.

*****

As was usual at the first meeting of a new theatrical year, the noise was appalling as each actor jockeyed for position, hoping against hope that this time they'd be given a role in which they could prove both their true worth and devotion to their art.

"Ladies, gentlemen, please," Roderick Villiers raised both arms into the air as his rich, deep, actor's tones filled the auditorium.

"It's time to begin casting," shouted Solly Vasey, backing up his manager.

"Once you two have taken the pick of the parts, will there be a crumb or two left for us lesser mortals," shouted the youngest of the amateur actors, though at the same time he kept his head well down.

"They'll hog the best roles, as usual," yelled a disgruntled shopworker who'd spent the previous production sewing and repairing costumes.

"SHUT UP," Vasey bawled as loudly as he knew how and was surprised to find that his intervention had had some effect.

"Thank goodness for that, I thought I'd entered a madhouse," whispered Susannah Reno to her husband.

"Just wait until folks aren't given the parts they feel they deserve," he replied with a smile.

"GET ON WITH IT THEN," shouted a peculiarly disguised voice from the rear of the hall.

Realising that he was never going to enjoy the reverent silence he believed such an occasion deserved, Roddy began to shout above the clamour and his deep, mature tones eventually gained the full attention of the assembled actors.

"Our latest production will prove to be very challenging. We have never tried anything so intricate before, but with hard work and good will from all I am sure that we shall enjoy yet another *TRIUMPH*."

There came a disappointingly short round of unsynchronised clapping.

"Are you ever going to tell us what's what?" demanded a draper's assistant.

"Aye, what's the play?"

"For God's sake put us out of our misery."

"Make sure it's summat good," yelled a stable lad who looked after the ponies at the Elysia Colliery and who'd never yet been given a part to play of any description.

Roddy's voice dropped to a reverential tone, he closed his eyes and looked up towards the heavens as though seeking the approval of the Almighty before he began to speak, "We shall present a Festival of Shakespeare which will run for the whole of next season, during which we shall perform weekly five different plays."

The auditorium was hushed to a gobsmacked silence which was ended shortly afterwards by a hub-bub of thunderous proportions.

"Why, man, that's impossible."

"Which plays?"

"Are ye meaning the same play ower an' ower again."

Roddy shook his head and then went on to explain how he planned to use a narrator to link the sections of the play together, which quietened the actors somewhat, but did not silence them.

"Why not just put the *Scottish Play* on again – it worked a treat last time," called a cellar man who'd played the Night Porter; though dreadfully, in the production he'd referred to.

Again the audience became unsettled until Solly Vasey stepped to centre-stage, raised both arms and called, "Please, ladies, gentlemen, allow our director to speak."

The cellar man got to his feet again and asked, "What does Mrs Esprey and the committee think o' yer mad plan to put five different plays on in a *single week?*"

"Indeed yes, and for a whole season too," backed up a normally quiet bank clerk.

"She is in full accord," returned Roddy quickly and untruthfully.

"How do we know that? There's been no sign of hide nor hair of her while her husband's been away," put in a grocery store assistant.

"Aye," added a colliery time-keeper, "Some say she's become a recluse."

"The colonel's back now, though," pointed out one of the older bit-part players who continued to knit as she spoke.

Vasey laughed long and loud, "Mrs Esprey is an actress to her fingertips, she'll be treading the boards like the good trouper she is as soon as she's asked to."

"Lizzie'd take her dying breath on stage were she to be granted the option," added Villiers, *sotto-voce*.

"Get on with it before we have a riot," Vasey nudged his boss.

The actor-director stepped forward, hung his head for a few long seconds and then allowed his voice once more to fill the auditorium, "We shall open with *Othello*, I shall be the narrator, Mr Vasey will play the lead and Miss Millie Hopper will be memorable; I'm sure, in the role of Desdemona."

Susannah was about to jump to her feet to complain, but was held back by her husband, "Leave it," he whispered.

"He *promised* that part to me," she spoke fiercely.

Marcus laughed, "Villiers once swore faithfully that I would play the Danish Prince and that never happened."

Susannah nodded and then added sadly, "You'd learnt all the lines too."

"And there's an awful lot of them."

The meeting rambled on for a further hour before all the parts had been given out though none of the actors were totally satisfied with what they had received, nor happy with their director's concept.

"Ladies, gentlemen, there you have it, the plan for the Spring Season."

Both actors had hoped that this announcement would be followed by monstrous applause and cries of support, but in this they were to be disappointed.

After a long silence a woman cried out from the back of the hall, "What about the pantomime? There's no pantomime been mentioned."

"That is because we shall not be staging a pantomime this year," informed Vasey.

This caused uproar and the whole building seemed to be reverberating in the noise of the disappointment and dissatisfaction which every member of the theatre group felt.

"*No* pantomime?" Yelled a young man who's greatest claim to fame lay in the fact that he was able to knock out any boxing opponent with just a single punch.

"My bairns won't be happy, they looks forward to it all year."

"This won't do… It won't do at all."

"Christmas'll not be the same."

Villiers put on a smiling, confident face and waved his arms around for silence, "Mister Vasey has already booked a Christmas Variety Show."

Solly's face soured, "I've organised no such damned thing," he whispered hoarsely.

"Tell them you have or they'll riot," returned Villiers desperately from the corner of his mouth.

"Why don't we do *The Babes In The Wood* again?" Shouted a bank clerk who had a strong Scottish accent.

"Aye, that went down a treat last year," agreed one of the colliers.

"That were *two* years back," argued one of his friends.

"I'll be seeing Dougie Brass about this," warned another of the amateur actors who worked at *Brass Shilling*.

"Aye, Dougie'll not put up wi' there being no panto."

"He's on the theatre committee and he'll make his opinion heard," backed up someone else.

Villiers cleared his throat and forced his voice to reach its most powerful volume, "There will be no pantomime this year, *Babes In The Wood* or not. Our efforts must concentrate on the planned Festival of Shakespeare."

At first a stunned silence reigned, until from the rear of the hall a very large iron-worker got up, strode down the aisle and clambered on to the stage to come face to face with the theatre manager.

"Can we not do both, Mr Villiers?" He asked in a friendly enough sort of way.

Villiers' throat dried up, for though the man was speaking moderately there was something in the glint of his eyes which transmitted a warning.

"It would be very difficult and time consuming," Villiers laughed nervously.

A huge hand reached out and grasped the shoulder of the actor, "Aye, maybe it will, but can you not see how disappointed all the little un's of the town are going to be come Boxing Day?"

"This gentleman has a point, Roddy," suggested Vasey who had very quickly assessed the situation and didn't much like the look of it.

The words of the ironworker were greeted by a huge cheer from the whole hall, who then ruffled Roddy's hair, though not roughly, "See how popular puttin' on a panto'll make ye."

The gleam in the ironworker's eyes was rekindled and made the actor decide that safety was the better part of valour.

"I'm sure we *could* do both – if everyone's willing to work twice as hard."

The theatre erupted with loud cheers and became filled with almost palpable clouds of good feeling.

Villiers nodded in time with the pats on the back he was receiving from the ironworker.

"I'd best drag out the panto scripts and dust them down, they'll be needed next week," muttered Vasey who was secretly amused and doubted that the idea of the Shakespeare Festival would ever see the light of day again.

\*\*\*\*\*

Kevin O'Dowd was whistling a cheerful Irish jig as he entered the breakfast room at Forest Hall, "Tap o' the mornin', t'ye ladies," he greeted.

"Good morning, *Kevin*," simpered Lady Rowena, smiling, for the easy ways of the Irishman had soon charmed both sisters.

Flora gave her sibling a sharp elbow nudge, "Mr O'Dowd hasn't yet given us permission to address him so informally."

"Oh, that's fine by mysel', I've never been one for formalizin'," returned Kevin with a gap toothed smile.

Flora nodded fractionally and rang the bell for breakfast to be served.

"What do you intend to do to-day?" Enquired Rowena of Kevin.

"Mr O'Dowd will be very busy, far too busy to bother with us," put in her sister quickly.

"Not at all, lasses, I'm goin' t'play the billiards," he shook his head sadly, "I've lost m'sel' a terrible amount o' money due to a lack of practice."

"Oh, now there's a game I've always wished to play but my papa would never allow it," put in Rowena quickly.

"Indeed not, as you'd have been sure to rip the baize," accused Flora.

"Oh, there's no need for that, Kevin's the boy t'teach ye both."

Rowena clapped her hands, "Will you really, Kevin?"

"Not without me there too," put in Flora.

Just then the breakfast warming trays arrived and it wasn't long before O'Dowd had piled high his plate with everything there was on offer.

"By, this is good grub – Kevin's niver had better," O'Dowd splattered the virgin white of the tablecloth with half chewed food as he spoke.

Both ladies noticed this, but merely continued to smile and nod as their agent ploughed his way through several breakfasts.

"Will you teach us to play to-day, Kevin?" Asked Rowena, once she was certain that no food remained in his mouth.

"It's a game for two or four, *not* three," pointed out Flora, "and as the elder, it is myself who shall be first to receive instruction."

"But...," began Rowena.

"No, buts, sister, no buts at all. A decision has been reached."

Rowena had suffered more than half a lifetime of subservience to Flora, and before that she had always been required to bow and scrape to her papa and brothers, so she nodded her head signalling once more her reluctant acceptance.

*****

"I'm to be Viola in *Twelfth Night*," cried Violet Grainger as soon as she had skipped joyfully back to the auditorium from Villiers' office.

"That's if it's ever put on, which I doubt," returned her friend, Millie Hopper.

"Roddy is determined that it shall proceed."

"You may remember that he has offered me a part too."

"Which one? Viola is a leading part. Have you a leading part?"

"I'm to be Desdemona in *Othello*."

188

"Oh, is that a leading part?"

"Of course it is, you're being deliberately obtuse."

"Sorry, I believed Desdemona to be one of the witches in the *Scottish Play*."

"You know fine well that it's one of Shakespeare's greatest female roles."

"Though, isn't Desdemona strangled at the very beginning of Act One, Scene One?"

Just then, as he passed them, Solly Vasey greeted, "Good morning, ladies."

They both smiled and bobbed as he disappeared towards the manager's office and then Violet suggested, "He's sweet on you, you know."

Millie went red in the face and shook her head, "He's old enough to be my papa."

Violet shook her head, "No he isn't," she paused then continued, "though a *much* older brother, perhaps."

"It's such a pity that Marcus Reno married Susannah, for at one time I was quite set on having him for myself," said Millie.

"Martindale's a dreadful town for we spinsters, there being so few marriageable men."

"A few you say? My goodness, there are *none* to speak of."

"My mama has strictly instructed me *never* to bring home a collier nor an ironworker."

"Mister Fisher, the schoolmaster, would scoop you up in a shot were you to smile at him," suggested Millie mischievously.

"*Uggh*, you can save him for yourself, I'd much rather remain a spinster."

"Besides which you'd find yourself living under the same roof as Bobbity."

They stood silently for a moment or two and then Violet considered slowly, "Our discussion is making Mr Vasey look increasingly attractive."

Millie looked thoughtfully towards the office, "I suppose you're right about that."

*****

"I don't know why you haven't introduced us to Catherine yet?" Asked Marian of her friend, Elizabeth Esprey.

"Indeed, yes," added a curious Jane Turner.

"I couldn't possibly at the moment as she's such a feral creature, not fit for civilised company," returned Lizzie after she'd taken a sip of chablis.

"We must accept that it will take some time before she becomes used to our standards and customs," said Caroline.

"But sooner rather than later, I should have thought. We must help her as much as we possibly can," added Sarah Nicholson.

"Catherine shan't be visiting anywhere civilised until she has a decent wardrobe. Jervy bought clothes for her willy-nilly in America, few of which are suitable."

"Try *Brass Shilling* their dresses are awfully good," put in Caroline.

"What? Clothes that are *ready made?* That's completely out of the question," returned Lizzie Esprey, shaking her head vigorously.

Marian plucked at the fabric of her own dress, "This is one of several I've bought from them, it fits like a glove and is comfortable all day too."

Elizabeth was taken aback and began to wonder if the age of the personal attention of a dressmaker was coming to an end, but eventually said, "Your dress is very sweet, but it's high time that I revisited the capital and I shall take Kitty with me."

"The pantomime season will have opened, I'm sure Catherine would enjoy a visit to a theatre," returned Sarah.

"The child is nothing other than a burden, for apart from making a fuss of her, Jervy's left Catherine's upbringing totally to myself."

"On top of which she must nearly have reached coming out age," Caroline said pointedly.

"I'd not thought of that, thank you kindly," returned Elizabeth with some irony.

"Though, is it not pleasant to have a child around the place? It must be a century since anyone younger than thirty resided at Merrington Hall," pointed out Marian.

"I've never had much to do with children myself and never wished for any of my own. I really can't see the point of all that grief, pain and unpleasantness," Lizzie shook her head vigorously as she spoke.

191

"I'm surprised that Harry Galvin didn't desire progeny," put in Marian.

"Oh, he tried hard enough, but I'm afraid he'd left it rather too late in life."

"I don't suppose Jervy has off springs either…," began Caroline before she stopped herself.

Lizzie threw back her head and laughed, "Oh, I'm sure he *has*, though I've no doubt that they're all neatly tucked away in Bengali mud huts."

"Or even in the palaces of maharajas," suggested Jane with a laugh.

They all enjoyed the idea of this until Elizabeth shook her head negatively, "Jervy expects me to turn Catherine into a *lady*, for goodness sake.  Not that I'm even properly speaking to him yet."

"I managed to adapt myself to the ways of society, it is achievable," pointed out Marian.

"I did the same, but being an actress it didn't take much doing, though I don't know why I bothered.  Men are always only after one thing; and it's not a cut-glass accent, at least not to begin with."

"I changed my ways for the sake of Charles, I was terrified of embarrassing him and causing people who knew no better to laugh at him for his foolishness in marrying a drab such as myself."

"With your figure, complexion and wonderful hair, no one in their right mind would describe you so," put in Jane, wishing that she herself possessed just one of the assets she had just mentioned.

"Maybe not, but it drove me on to improve my speech and manners."

"Still, our girl is an American who has no concept of what is to be expected of her as the daughter of a British colonel," said Lizzie.

Marian's tone became persuasive, "Bring her to tea here, just the two of us and we'll tell her the stories of our early lives…"

"I wouldn't dare speak of the days when I was treading the boards," as she spoke Elizabeth's neck pinkened; though only slightly, with embarrassment.

"Whatever you did it was successful. Take Jane, she is the niece of an earl and she's never snubbed either of us, not once," Marian nodded as she spoke.

"Yes, but at the same time Jane is also a radical who'd have the heads sliced off all aristocrats if she had the power," suggested Sarah with a grin.

"Even her own?" laughed Marian.

"Without a doubt, Jane would fight fiercely to be first on to the tumbril," put in Sarah.

Jane joined in with their laughter and couldn't help agreeing that what they had said was absolutely true.

They sipped tea and then Marian spoke again, "I know, why not have Catherine help Sarah out in the school room, it would make her feel needed and useful and will familiarise her with some of our quaint ways at the same time."

"I'd be delighted to have her join me," offered Sarah quickly as she needed all the help she could get as she ran both the Martin Hall schoolroom as well as the Martindale Education Association.

Lizzie nodded, "That may help, Kitty is a good reader and she is very accurate with figures."

"Well then, let's give her a try."

"It may not be easy to persuade her, she'll think it's just an excuse of mine to be rid of her for several hours a week."

"You're an actress, aren't you? Put on a performance, look upon it as an important role to be played before a packed house," encouraged Marian.

Elizabeth's eyes brightened, "You could be right there, if I can't act my way into the mind and feelings of a sixteen year old, then I really am ready to end my career on a rainy night at the *Glasgow Empire*."

They all laughed and then Marian suddenly had another bright suggestion, "I think it would be a good idea if Mr Kent were to teach Kitty to ride."

"She's already a better horsewoman than myself."

Marian nodded, "Though I'll wager that she's not using a lady's saddle."

"*Mmm*, you're right there. Perhaps if Kent taught her to ride properly she could join the hunt in December and perhaps break her neck in January."

Marian's eyes widened, for she wasn't sure whether her friend was joking or not.

*****

"When are we going to seek out this mysterious olive skinned fellow who puts the fear of God into prostitutes?" Enquired Constable Dodds.

"We've no need to, for wherever the marchioness is he will be too. I also suspect that she *enjoys* an intimate relationship with him."

"Surely, not so close a one as you're suggesting."

"You've never met her, she's a strange woman, one day an angel but the next the devil incarnate. She's utterly and completely unfathomable."

"Is it possible, though, that she'd allow a fellow who has been involved in an unknown number of crimes on her behalf to live so close to her? Surely, her common sense will demand that he stay well away from both Winterbourne and Forest Hall."

"Not to mention Isis House, though there's no easy understanding of her – or even trying to guess what she'll do next."

Dodds thought for a moment or two and then suggested, "Then let's away to Forest Hall to find the priest-hole and the bodies we believe are hidden there."

"Pour the tea, son," sighed Mason, who though he appreciated his constable's keenness, felt that he often went at things like a bull at a particularly awkward gate.

"We can't just sit around here doing nothing," said Dodds as he piled sugar into both cups.

"It's called police work, my boy, and is often boringly routine," pointed out the inspector.

"I still think we should pay a visit to Forest Hall," the constable was desperate to at least make a start on something.

"What do you suppose the Marchioness will do once she finds that we're sniffing along her trail again?"

Dodds thought for a while, "Flee the country?"

"She'll not do that for she believes herself to be untouchable."

The constable thought for a long time, rejecting one possibility after another until he came to it, "She may be feeling the need to move the bodies elsewhere, or at least of disposing of them completely."

"Yes, for, remember, we're talking about the remains of her father, she'll refuse to abandon him and this could prove to be her undoing."

"Though the old biddies would have to be got out of the way before anything could be done to clear the priest hole," pointed out Dodds, who then added, "if it exists."

"If we're not barking up the wrong tree the whole household would need to be sent elsewhere so that Mister Mediterranean can bring in his friends to do the heavy work and dispose of the corpses."

"Where do you think they would rid themselves of the bodies?"

Mason considered for a moment and then informed, "Forest Hall is surrounded by thick woodland, there's also a large lake and wide areas of marshland too. A thousand bodies could be hidden there, never to be seen again."

"Why didn't she do that in the first place?" Puzzled the constable.

"It's the final resting place…," Mason thought for a while and then snapped his fingers, "My God, they were put into the priest hole *alive*."

"Jesus, that's horrible, I've never got on with my own dad – but doing something like that to him…," Dodds dried up at the thought.

"Sir James and possibly Miss Kleist starved to death in pitch blackness," considered Mason.

"In a sound-proof box, no one would be able to hear their cries for help."

"They disappeared in the winter time so it would have been freezing cold too."

Both men shuddered and were silent for some while until the constable suggested, "We could set up a twenty-four hour, seven days a week surveillance of Forest Hall."

Mason shook his head, "How many men would be required to cover the house, back, side and front for several weeks?"

Dodds tried to add it up and then came to an inescapable conclusion, "A lot more than we have or could feasibly recruit."

"On top of which, how would our chaps be able to remain undiscovered so close to the hall for an unknown but lengthy period of time?"

The constable's face dropped, he shook his head, "It can't be done."

Mason laughed, "Cheer up, boy, for all we need is someone in the village to lets us know when the Scott-Wilson sisters and the servants are to leave home."

"How will they know?"

Mason laughed heartily, "You've never lived in a village, have you?"

"Never."

"I thought not," Mason nodded knowingly and then instructed, "Take the train tomorrow to Verdley Magna, which is the nearest town…"

"Then move on to Forest Hall," interrupted Dodds eagerly.

"No, stay well away from there, get yourself a comfortable billet somewhere nearby and make friends with the local innkeepers, shop owners and above all the station master."

"You think that the railway people will be first to know if there's any movement planned?" Dodds sounded doubtful.

"Believe me, once the evacuation starts the *whole* village will have the full details before the marchioness herself does."

"The lady will want her sisters and servants well out of the way for several days, after which she'll need to bring them back again."

"Exactly so," put in the inspector.

"Plus all their luggage," considered the constable, biting his lower lip.

"Precisely so."

"Not straightforward travel arrangements, then," the constable could see what his superior was getting at.

"Yes, and once we know when there's movement afoot we cover the place and catch the villains in full and unexplained charge of a number of dead bodies."

"There could be promotions in this for us," suggested Dodds hopefully.

"Settle yourself, boy, what you don't seem to realise is that we're at the very back of the queue, there's you, me and at a pinch we could count on another couple of constables. Settle yourself to the idea that we're both employed in a dead-end situation."

"Think of it, though, at last to have nabbed the Marchioness of Studland."

"I'll believe that's happened once she's standing in the dock at the Old Bailey."

"You don't think it's likely, then," Dodds enthusiasm was rapidly fading.

"No, the higher-ups and the lady will come to some compromise."

"What about Mr Mediterranean?"

Mason laughed shortly, "He's for the eight-o-clock walk."

*****

As much as Catherine Esprey appreciated the colonel and was astonished by the lifestyle which had so suddenly come her way, she couldn't work up the same enthusiasm for the mistress of Merrington Hall, who had treated her politely enough, but coolly on every occasion they had spent time together.

To make matters worse, her foster father was currently in something of a depression himself, this being as a result of his interview with the widow of Major Sturgis.

So that she was able to keep clear of any domestic difficulty which might arise, Kitty had begun to take long morning walks. She set off in a different direction every day and tried to avoid returning until it was time for lunch. However, on one particular morning she had decided to visit Martindale which was less than three miles away from her home.

Kitty liked this new town, which whilst it was smoky, smelly and very roughly hewn, she liked the people who seemed to know who she was and often nodded their heads in greeting or gave her a cheery wave, she being something of a curiosity to them. It also had to be said that there was always something going on there, the streets were never quiet and always busy with the hubbub of traffic and the clash of railway wagons and locomotives. Not to mention the sirens and hooters used by the surrounding works.

As she sauntered along, looking into the shop windows and inspecting the produce displayed on the market stalls, she managed to push her own problems to the back of her mind.

Eventually she came to an opening which led into a narrow alleyway and on a whim decided to find out where it went.

Very shortly thereafter she found herself confronted by a tall, raven haired boy with dark eyes and only the snub of a nose.

"I'm Billy Fowler, I suppose ye've heard of me," this was forcefully expressed.

Kitty nodded knowingly, having suffered from this sort of confrontation on more occasions than she cared to remember.

"Can't say I've had the pleasure," she replied, unfazed.

"Well, I'm top lad around here and you'd best remember that," as he spoke Billy turned to his three companions, "That's right, isn't it."

The other lads nodded in dutiful unison.

"Nice to meet you all," returned Kitty making as though to move on.

"You got any treats or owt nice t'eat on you?" Enquired one of the gang roughly.

"If ye've got any brass, ye'd best hand it over, as a gift to keep us sweet," ordered Billy.

"I've no money and even if I had I wouldn't give it to you."

"You must have coin on ye, 'cos you're the Yankee lass from Merrington Hall," cried the leader of the gang.

Kitty's eyes narrowed, "I'm no damned Yankee, I'm from Virginia, a Southerner and proud of it."

"*Naw*, ye're just a *Yankee* ragamuffin, tryin' to be posh."

"I ain't trying no such thing, and never claimed to be."

"Well don't think you can come here and lord it over us," Fowler turned to his friends, "We'll not stand for it, will we lads?"

Billy's friends nodded their agreement, though with no great enthusiasm.

"Maybe she's thinking we're goin' t'become her slaves," suggested one of them after a while.

"Aye," put in another, "she'll want us runnin' around after her, bobbin' an' scraping."

"We should throw her into the ironworks pond – see if she can swim," suggested Billy taking a step closer to her chosen victim.

A thin smile appeared on Kitty's lips, "That's not such a good idea," she warned in a low voice.

Billy turned to face his friends, "We think it is, though, don't we lads?"

"An' it's us that counts," backed up one of the accompanying gang.

At this point the quietest of the other boys noticed the expression which had appeared on the face of their chosen victim and he didn't like the look of it.

"You best leave me alone," advised Kitty, as her eyes narrowed to virtual slits.

Billy looked around and counted heads, "Why should we? There's four of us against just you."

"The odds you have in your favour are nowhere near great enough, 'cos I've got this," returned Kitty as she drew from her reticule the revolver she'd killed Buster Bailey with.

"That isn't a real one," cried Billy whose face; nonetheless, was paling rapidly.

Behind the leader of the gang, two of his friends had already decided to make a speedy departure.

"Not so long ago I killed a man," Kitty's tone was icy.

"It's not loaded, you wouldn't dare," suggested Billy, stretching out a grubby hand tentatively towards the gun which was pointed squarely at his midriff.

With a speed that made her antagonist jump backwards, Kitty raised the gun into the air and fired it. By firearm standards the report was not very loud, but it was shrill enough to clear the street of bullies.

"You're mad," screamed Billy as he fled.

"Maybe so, but I'm also effective, you'd best remember that should we meet again."

Miss Esprey replaced the pepper-pot pistol into her bag and continued her walk, though she hadn't gone very far before she was confronted by Corporal Seeton Carew.

"That was smartly done, Miss Catherine," he greeted.

"What are you doing here?"

"Keeping an eye on you and it's just as well that colonel ordered me to do so. Now hand over the gun."

Kitty shook her head fiercely, "No, I may need it again if the natives are going to be unfriendly."

Carew laughed as he took the reticule from her unresisting fingers and recovered the weapon, "Gunfire isn't often heard on the streets of Martindale."

"Suppose those rats come for me again – I'm not going to give up my walks into town."

"I suspect that they'll stay well clear of your in future, but the police may show an interest."

"Police? Why should they care?"

"The discharge of a gun in a public place is frowned upon here, you could be up before the beak."

"What beak?" Kitty feared that this must be some sort of mediaeval instrument of torture.

"A magistrate or even a judge, you could end up in court."

"Oh, nobody'd much notice a single gunshot back home."

Carew could see that his charge was becoming concerned, "Don't worry, though, for if there were to be bother the colonel would see it off. Anyway, if it comes to it, just say it was a toy."

"It made an awful noise which sounded real to me."

"Aye, maybe, but the toy makers have just brought out cap pistols, say it was one of them you brought with you from America."

"They'll want to see it."

"In fright you threw it into the undergrowth somewhere along the drive at Merrington Hall."

Kitty smiled and nodded, "Yes, I did, didn't I."

"But you can't remember where exactly," suggested Carew.

"No, not at all – it could be anywhere."

"Come to think of it," continued the corporal as he took the arm of his charge, "Why are you out on foot when there's a stable full of fine horses back at the Hall."

"They ain't mine."

"You are the colonel's daughter, so they're yours to use as you wish."

"I *can* ride, you know."

"So the mistress and Mr Kent have told me."

"Is it true that I can have a horse anytime I wish?"

"All you need to do is tell the head groom that you require a mount for the following morning."

"As easy as that?" Kitty couldn't believe her luck.

"Yes, then the next day you'll find the animal you've chosen fed, watered, groomed and saddled waiting for you."

Kitty's eyes lit up, for a mount of her own would widen her horizons enormously, she could travel for miles around.

"Besides which, the likes of Fowler are unlikely to interfere with a well mounted young lady," pointed out the corporal.

"Even if I don't have a gun."

"Even then," Carew considered for a while and then stated sombrely, "Though, the colonel will require a full report of this gunshot incident."

"Will he be mad at me?"

Carew thought seriously for a second or two and then replied, "He'll probably just say that you'd put up a damned good show."

*****

As soon as Johnie Corsica entered the freshly decorated *grande salon* at Winterbourne he could sense that Elysia was in a very resolute mood.

She ignored him at first and instead ordered the waiting maid to serve afternoon tea. Once this had been done, she continued to examine the thick file of documents which lay before her, carelessly casting each one aside after she'd spent mere seconds on it.

"You can't get your pa' out of your mind," he predicted loudly.

At first she continued to ignore him, then after reading through; this time minutely, a further document she replied, "I know that you understand quite clearly what I wish done."

"Sir James and Fraulein von Kleist are both at rest, why not leave them to eternity and should someone comes across their remains; at some time in the Twenty-first Century maybe, think of the fun they'll have trying to work out who it is they've found."

"I'm not amused and am certainly not joking," her expression was stiff and as hard as a block of ice.

Johnie groaned, "You know that removing your pa' from the priest hole, and have him turn up again out of the blue, is next to impossible."

"You may remember that it was you who set me on this track in the first place – wishing the ugly sisters to be dealt with in one way or another."

"If that's the case I wish I'd kept my trap shut."

"But you didn't, did you."

"Moving the bodies is both impracticable and risky."

"Nothing is impossible if the wit and resources are there to accomplish it."

Corsica picked up a *religieuse* and swallowed it in a single gulp, "Your father cannot just suddenly reappear after being presumed dead for the best part of three years."

"I *insist* that my papa is to be accorded a proper funeral and a monument erected to his memory which is sufficiently grand to record on it his achievements."

"It cannot be done safely."

"Why ever not?"

"Firstly because he disappeared without trace and secondly because he was murdered by us."

"*You* killed him – I was nowhere near at the time."

He shook his head in disbelief, "Look at it this way, were we to appear together in the dock we'd both end up dangling at the end of ropes."

She considered for a moment and then said, "Suppose his body was fortuitously discovered in a forest somewhere or maybe on a beach or by a river?"

"Then the authorities would investigate how it came to be there."

Elysia shook her head in irritation, "I could make up a dozen ways and means in a flash."

"Go on then," he challenged.

"He fell overboard from an unknown ship far out to sea."

"That's one," Corsica began counting.

"Very well, he blundered  into a particularly deep and disused quarry – there are lots of them littered around the countryside," she paused for thought and then added, "his body was quickly hidden by thick and thorny undergrowth."

"In which case, how did it reveal itself to a passer-by?"

"The finder's dog sniffed it out."

"Tell me, at which point in this misadventure did your papa strip himself naked?"  Asked Corsica pointedly.

She thought for a while and then replied, "This is not a problem, for papa's wardrobe is still fully stocked and readily available."

Corsica couldn't help laughing aloud, "Can you imagine what it would be like trying to get clothes on to what's left of his body once the rats had finished with it?"

Elysia hid her face in her hands as a dozen of the frequent nightmares she had suffered kaleidoscope through her mind one after another at a rapid pace.

Corsica took a further *patisserie* and swallowed it whole, afterwards licking his lips, "Not only that, but the clothes from his wardrobe wouldn't show the signs of deterioration investigators would expect to see. The police would; may I suggest, smell a rat."

At Corsica's mention of the rodent Elysia shivered slightly and pulled her jacket tighter around her, though she quickly recovered herself, "In that case, gather sufficient moth eaten clothing from; say, a rag-man to re-clothe my poor papa."

"That would help, but still may not fool a bright young coroner."

The marchioness gulped some tea and pulled her thoughts together, "Other than the nakedness, my whole scheme works perfectly well. The body of my dear papa is found and after a perfunctory examination is returned to Winterbourne and buried there with all due ceremony."

"What about Miss Kleist?"

"She's of no matter, bury her remains deep in the woods at Forest Hall, it won't trouble anyone were they never to be discovered, besides which the police will think it was she who murdered my father."

"I've always known you as a hard hearted, calculating bitch, but this takes the cake."

"It'll work – for who'll give a tuppeny damn about a German nanny."

"You were more than fond of her at one time," replied Johnie, knowingly.

"Just as I'm very fond of you – at the moment," Elysia's expression hardened and her eyes flashed.

Johnie coughed and looked away before saying, "The police have a duty to investigate and their findings will be sent on to higher authority. You know to where that will lead."

"It's years since my pa' disappeared, everyone will have forgotten all about him."

"The high-ups won't as nearly all of them were in his debt in some way, or had grudges against him. Just as you are the number one threat to them now."

"Indeed, I have a long list of very important functionaries who owe my family favours, some of them dating back many years."

"Maybe so, but there's still the problem of how to move your papa from Forest Hall."

"I pay you handsomely; and not just in coin, to solve my problems, so you'd best get on with it."

*****

Arabella Brass was pleased to be hosting afternoon tea for her mama and sister Amelia Schilling, especially as they had not met regularly since the funeral of their father.

After twenty minutes of polite, though engaging, conversation, Arabella believed that the time had come to mention the scarecrow in the room.

"How does the Reverend Mr Cowpens do? He seems to have settled into Holy Innocents and taken up papa's mantle very successfully?"

"Though he can never replace you father he is everything a clergyman should be. He's even managed to settle Mr Somers down."

"Is that really so? Then he must be very capable indeed," commented Amelia.

"Does his accommodation suit his tastes and expectations?" Asked Arabella.

Venetia sipped tea and then informed, "He has made himself very comfortable, it's as though he's lived at the rectory for years."

"Very *comfortable*, you say," Amelia's tone had an edge to it.

"William is well contented with the way his domestic life has been arranged for him. In any case he is so very easy to please."

"You *already* use his Christian name freely?" Queried Bella.

"I'm surprised that he allowed it so soon after becoming acquainted with you," suggested Amelia.

"Especially as you are so recently widowed," put in Arabella.

From the tone of their voices it became obvious that the sisters were alarmed at so early a relaxation of a long established social convention.

"Why ever should I not? We are of equal status and have settled in together virtually seamlessly."

Amelia hardened her tone even more so, "Though what will people think? What will they say about such laxness?"

"Especially concerning a lady to whom they have always looked up," added Bella.

Venetia's eyebrows shot up high in amazement, "*Laxness*, you say? The pair of you dare to suggest that I am or ever have been *permissive* – I cannot believe such a thing of you."

At this point Arabella should have known enough not to press the matter any further, however, she failed to hold her tongue, "Mama, I know *exactly* what the gossips are saying, carrying the word from one household to another, it reflects on us too, you know."

Venetia stiffened, "What on earth are you suggesting?"

"Only what virtually everyone else in Martindale will be thinking," blurted Amelia who then immediately wished she had kept quiet.

"You believe that there is some *physical* relationship between myself and the Reverend Mr Cowpens?" Venetia couldn't believe that she had had to ask this question of her own daughters.

Amelia nodded sheepishly, "It's certain to have been suggested by some folk."

"Not that we'd ever believe such a thing ourselves for a second," Bella desperately tried to backtrack.

Venetia patted crumbs from the corners of her mouth and then directed a severe glance at each of her girls in turn, "I would never have expected this of my own children – please send for my pony-trap, it is high time I returned to my foul nest of sin and debauchery."

"But we're only telling you what we've heard. We never suggested that there could ever be any truth in it," put in Amelia quickly, hoping to be able to mend a fence which had been so thoughtlessly torn down.

For a moment the hot air seemed to be on the point of dispersal, but then Arabella broke the spell, "Please mama, it would be for the best were you to leave the rectory."

"You no longer trust your own mother?" Venetia's voice sharpened again.

"Of course we do," Amelia turned to her sister, "Don't we Bella."

"Yes, though it's just not right that you are living in the household of a single gentleman."

"Where am I to go then? Perhaps to Blanchwell with you, Amelia. It is the ideal place for me, I could easily live out the rest of my life in comfort and irrefutable innocence there."

"Yes…, Of course you could, though I'd have to ask Caroline about it," Amelia replied in grudging agreement.

"Mr Brass would be no doubt happy to have me permanently settled with you at Kirkby."

"I'm sure he would be, mama," replied Arabella, dropping her head and so giving the lie to her words.

"Both of our husbands are very fond of you, mama, though Fred is not the owner of Blanchwell and so could not offer an invitation to stay without the say-so of Caroline."

Arabella began to feel the closing of a noose around her own household, "I'll ask Douglas about it when he returns home tonight."

"Neither of you need bother, I'm quite happy with my life as it presently is, and if gossips wish to spread untruths or downright lies about the relationship between the Reverend Cowpens and myself, well, they'd best get on with it."

As soon as she had finished speaking, Venetia got to her feet and left with an aggressive twirl of silk.

*****

As Elizabeth Esprey watched Catherine demolish her third slice of toast and marmalade she was appalled by the roughness of her manner.

"You ought to try a bit harder to eat more elegantly," she instructed.

Catherine looked up briefly, "I'm hungry."

"You're always hungry, but there is a civilised way to eat and then there's the other way."

Kitty clattered down her knife which was still heavily larded with butter, "I can *never* please you, so I don't see why I should even try to."

Elizabeth softened her tone, "You should do your very best for the sake of the colonel."

At the mention of her benefactor, Catherine's tone softened too, "I'm sorry, but as a child I was dragged from one horrible dumping place to another, asylums where there was never enough food for everyone."

"So you had to grab or starve," Elizabeth nodded her understanding.

Kitty smiled, "This is why I'm still so scrawny."

"I gather that you never knew your mother," Lizzie's tone was now much softer.

Kitty nodded, "Nor my pa' either," her normally bright eyes clouded over and she continued, "One of the teachers; Sister Billings, always spoke of me as *that little bastard.* She hated me and dealt me some rough treatment, If I looked closely enough I dare say I could still find signs of a bruise or two she inflicted."

"I suppose she was trying to make you cry."

"She never did though."

"Which must have infuriated her even more."

"Yes, but I wouldn't give her the satisfaction."

They continued to eat breakfast for a while longer and then Lizzie spoke softly, "My upbringing too was far from easy, I never knew my real mother either."

"I know how that feels. Were you with your pa' though?"

Lizzie laughed loudly, "Oh, yes, I knew him well enough, *intimately* even."

Kitty was well advanced for her years and completely understood the relationship Elizabeth had had with her father. She began to develop some sisterly feelings towards the colonel's lady.

"Did your father re-marry?" She asked.

"No, though he had a succession of ugly mistresses, each of them more grotesque than her predecessor."

"Didn't any of them try to mother you?"

"They all hated me, besides which ours was a transitory sort of life anyway, so they came and went. Each new town provided him with a new lady friend."

"Did your pa' have a decent job?"

"Heavens no, he was the unfunniest and least agile clown ever known in the entire history of the circus," she paused and then continued, "though I grew up to love the theatre."

"So you really were an actress."

"No," smiled Lizzie, who then paused before continuing, "I was a *great* actress."

Nodding to herself, Kitty's concentration returned to her breakfast and she continued to thickly spread butter on to a further piece of toast and was taking a huge spoonful of honey to layer it with.

Lizzie sighed loudly, "You really must try harder to achieve the standard of decorum which is expected of a well brought up young woman."

"Who'll care? Who will *really* give a damn?"

"The colonel will for one – he wishes for nothing other than you become a young lady he can be proud of."

"The colonel likes me just as I am."

"He won't when you grow up to become a smug, vulgar, ill-mannered bitch."

*****

As he was riding the country lanes between Blanchwell and Byers Green, Richard Turner felt strangely uncomfortable when he suddenly came across Helmuth and Caroline Schilling.

"How nice it is to encounter our Member of Parliament," greeted Helmuth in a most friendly way as he pulled his mount up next to Richard's.

"Serendipity indeed," added Caroline.

"Yes, isn't it," replied Richard who could feel his face turning pink, and try as he might he could not prevent it from doing so.

"We meet so infrequently these days," added Caroline.

"I know, and it's such a pity, but I seem to be spending more time on trains than I do anywhere else," Richard excused himself.

They sat in a contemplative silence for a while and then Caroline suggested, "Why not come and take coffee with us?" However, her tone and facial expression indicated that he should decline her invitation.

"I am especially pressed for time myself at the moment... The Reform Bill.., A new Army Act...," Richard tried to excuse himself.

Helmuth stretched across and grasped Richard's shoulder in a companiable way, "Come on, man, you must have an hour or two to spare for old friends."

"Indeed, yes," agreed Caroline, though her tone still indicated that she intended the complete opposite of what she'd said.

Richard felt unable to refuse, especially as Helmuth was so insistent and twenty minutes later he found himself drinking coffee and sipping brandy in front of a blazing log fire.

Soon after that Helmuth was called away to attend to the concerns of one of his tenants, and Caroline took the opportunity to accuse, "You shouldn't have come,"

"What else could I do without seeming impolite?"

"I'm sure he knows about us," returned Caroline, shaking her head.

"What is there to know? We hardly meet and when we did manage to spend time in bed together nothing much happened."

"Myself merely visiting your rooms would cause scandal enough in most quarters."

"Once you'd left my landlady told be in no uncertain terms that she would not tolerate single ladies visiting gentlemen under her roof unchaperoned."

"She looked at me pretty grimly as I left, though how did you reply?"

"I stood on my dignity and told her that your visit was at the behest of your husband who is one of my electors and therefore covered by Parliamentary Privilege and thus strictly confidential."

Caroline laughed, "I can imagine the vinegar expression which crossed the old dear's face."

Richard joined in her merriment for a moment and then remembered that she was concerned that Helmuth knew about them, "Are you sure you haven't mentioned our relationship to anyone – the damned *Coven* perhaps."

Caroline's face became red with pique, "I shan't even validate that question with an answer, besides which our group isn't currently meeting."

"What, no Christmas festivities at all?" Richard considered this to be highly unlikely.

"The violent death of poor Major Sturgis has brought our socialising to a temporary halt."

The Member of Parliament nodded, "I suppose Mrs Sturgis is still distraught."

"Hardly ever leaves her rooms, I've tried to get Helmuth to help bring his sister out of it, but he's useless too."

"Grace will have to accept eventually that her husband's gone for good."

Caroline bridled, "*Men*," she hissed, "if the world isn't completely centred on their personal needs and requirements then it is of no interest to them."

"I was as sorry as the next man when I heard of the major's death," Richard looked both irritated and cross.

"I suppose now may be a good time for us to part for good," Caroline clattered down her coffee cup in an noisy show of frustration and displeasure.

Richard covered his face with his palms, "Our whole affair is impossible, it has always been impossible."

"Then this *is* the time to finish with it for ever."

"Can we so easily give each other up?"

"Between us we should have answered that question years and years ago."

It took Richard a long time to make a reply but he managed it eventually, "It comes down to whether either of us could face divorce proceedings?"

She shook her head crossly, "There are children to consider and our spouses, both of whom love us to distraction."

They sat in silence for some long seconds, each looking into the eyes of the other, but they could find nothing reflecting there but true love, which they jointly realised would linger within them for as long as they lived.

Caroline got to her feet, nearly upsetting the coffee pot and strode to a nearby window where she stood staring out into the garden.

Richard quickly joined her, "We must...," he began before his voice broke for a second, "...end it."

Caroline shook her head, "I'm a mature woman, a wife and a mother, but I can't just...," she sighed and then continued, "leave my girlhood dreams of a real, true, heart thudding romance behind me."

"I understand how you feel," his tone highlighted the misery he too was feeling at even the thought of giving her up.

"We're no longer as young as we were when we first met on the day of Charles' wedding to Elysia."

"It was in the churchyard at Kirkby, you were miserable and I needed copy for the paper."

"But we sparked, didn't we, even then we saw something special in each other."

"Charles had let you down badly and even in the beautiful grey dress you were wearing you cut a tragic figure. You won my heart at once."

"Charles and I were supposed to be a matched-pair, our union had been planned for years. I'd marry Charles, manage Martin Hall, a son of ours would eventually inherit Blanchwell too and life would continue pacifically on its settled and well-ordered way."

"Then Martindale reared its ugly head and all was lost."

"Yes, even Blanchwell was snatched from me."

"Though just for a time."

"Thanks to Helmuth and the good fortune I had to meet him in the most unlikely of places."

"Which is perhaps another reason why we should put our love to one side, store it away in a secret part of our minds to be fondly remembered whenever we feel the need," as he spoke Richard shook his head sadly.

Caroline could feel emotion welling up inside her though she managed to coldly subdue it, "That would be for the best."

They stood together for a while and then; without further thought, he took her hand into his own and squeezed it.

From that second it was no time before they were clasped in each other's arms. Her cheek was grazing his neck whilst his fingers could feel the trembling of her body.

As a door banged somewhere in the depths of the house, they pulled apart and tried to dampen down their emotions as quickly as they could.

"We can't just *stop* loving each other," stated Caroline in what was a blatantly obvious observation.

Richard nodded his agreement and then said, "It's just not possible."

"I know we're being imprudent, reckless even, but I must agree."

"Then our only option is to get this whole business over and done with. Let's have no further prevarication, no more excuses…"

"You mean let's make love and be damned to the consequences?"

"Yes, that is exactly what I mean."

"As long as we remain discreet, then perhaps no one will be harmed," even as she spoke Caroline doubted that this would prove to be the case.

"We're much older now and could surely behave discreetly."

"Indeed, though should we take this step it will be irreversible – are we ready to risk the possibly destructive consequences of it?"

"I am, if you are willing too," nodded Richard.

"Then all we need to agree is the when and how of it."

*****

"What if I was hurt down the mine?" Asked John Losser.

"Hurt in what way?" Clara Miller responded with a question of her own.

"I dunno, maybe hurt my leg and it wasn't properly fixed."

"Like my own, you mean."

"Aye, exactly like that."

"What of it?"

"We'd be the same then."

Clara covered her eyes with the palms of her hands and sighed deeply in an exasperated sort of way.

"No we wouldn't, you'd be in a much worse position than myself."

"How's that?"

"You wouldn't be able to work and would have to rely on the kindness of Annie and Geordie for your upkeep."

"But I'd be the same as you, we'd be equals."

"Equals in misfortune but in no other way."

Losser said nothing for a long time, and then said, "I like you a lot and…"

"*Stop,*" she half shouted, "Stop at once."

Losser was preparing to make a reply, but then stood for a while with a hangdog look on his face before he was driven from the room by the acute embarrassment he felt, slamming the door on his way out.

"What's on here?" Enquired Annie who had arrived accompanied by Geordie as soon as they'd seem Losser dash off into the street.

"Just John being very silly again."

"He loves you, y'knaw," pointed out Geordie.

Clara's face flushed, "Then he is even sillier than I thought he was."

"You like him, yourself, I've watched you grow together," said Annie.

"Like brother and sister, perhaps."

"No, he's always mooned over you."

"What possible attraction can I have for him?" Clara asked more in temper than in puzzlement.

"You're a good, honest person."

"Clever, too," put in Geordie.

Much as Clara was grateful to the Cooks for their generous and continuing support, she wasn't able to soften her tone, "He's wasting his time on me, there are so many irreconcilable differences between us."

"True love overcomes all," stated Annie.

"Even should the love you speak of be hurtling to destruction towards a very black and hard dead-end?"

Annie took her lodger by the shoulders and hugged her.

At first Clara struggled to be free, but soon she settled comfortably into the arms of her friend and snuggled closer. It was a long time since she had felt so warm and safe and she began to luxuriate in it.

"Give the lad a chance, a kind word now and again will do no harm," whispered Annie.

Clara loosened Annie's grip, but did not pull free of it, "It would encourage the silly ideas his mind has conceived regarding a relationship between myself and he."

"What's wrong with that? It's obvious he'd do owt for you," put in Geordie, strongly.

"But he could have any young woman he wished for. He's a tall, handsome youth who's one of the best hewers in Martindale, girls must be throwing themselves at him every day."

"Aye, maybe, but he only has eyes for you."

"Then more fool him."

"Is it not time you came down from your seat of pain and grabbed what life has offered you. Nobody could deny that you've been dealt a poor hand, but suddenly; out of nowhere, you've been granted an ace to play," Annie spoke with conviction.

"She's right ye knaw," added Geordie.

Annie patted Clara's shoulder and then swept off in order to give her time and space for careful contemplation.

"Take heed," advised Geordie, "Annie's the wisest lass I knaw that's why I always do what she sez."

*Perhaps this is often the case, though not on this occasion I fear*, thought Clara.

*****

*"An Inquiry into the Nature and Causes of the Wealth of Nations*, on to Adam Smith now are you?" Asked Fred as he noticed the title of the book his colleague was reading.

"Yes, and very interesting it is too. Everything he wrote in his day still applies to us now, and I fully expect his words to be relevant a hundred years into the future," replied George Murphy, slightly annoyed as his concentration had been broken.

"Does he mention anything about the manufacture and distribution of dresses?"

"Not in particular, but he writes that the more goods a business produces the more it will potentially sell and thus become wealthier in the process."

They were sitting together in the office of *Brass Schilling* as from the floor below them came the constant clatter of sewing machines being operated at high speed.

"Well, our girls are certainly turning out more than we ever dreamt possible when we first set up shop," put in Fred Schilling.

"We need to move on, though, expand into larger premises, install more machines and train more machinists."

"We're doing nicely as we are, aren't we?"

"Though there are fortunes to be made for any business which is determined to look to the future."

"Money isn't everything," replied Fred.

"It *is* if you have none," George knew this from bitter experience.

Fred thought for a second or two and then asked, "Are you tiring of dresses as you did of pies?"

"I outgrew pies, the real money is in industry."

"Commerce, banking and investment too," added Fred.

Murphy nodded his agreement, "It's earning enough money to be able to bank and invest, that's my problem."

Fred shook his head, "Though in any commercial enterprise there are always ups and downs."

"Isn't that the nature of everything."

"Can you keep a secret?" Asked Fred after a thoughtful pause.

"Of course, especially if it's anything to do with the acquisition of brass."

"Four or five years from now we'll be lucky to be able to keep the iron and steel works going, which in turn will affect the *Balaclava* factory."

Murphy laughed, "Why, man, the whole town knows that, it has for months."

"It's supposed to be a secret."

"It maybe was for about forty-eight hours."

"Though there's nothing we can do except gradually reduce our iron and steel production," said Fred sadly.

"I suppose the problem is the cost of transporting both what comes into Martindale and that which eventually goes out," nodded Murphy.

"Indeed, our ironworks and factories being at least sixteen miles from the coast and thus the shipping required."

"To both import and export."

"Yes, more or less, for as things stand our iron and steel will inevitably end up being priced out of the market."

"Which means that less coal will be needed to produce it, leading to unemployment and possibly the demise of the town as we know it today."

"Exactly so, but it cannot be avoided, at least not as far as I can see."

George tapped the book he was reading, "Adam Smith would urge you to *increase* production rather than reduce it."

"He was writing a century ago."

"That doesn't figure, for the more you produce the lower your costs become and the cheaper you can sell your goods, thus negating the cost of shipping. It would also force your competitors to reduce *their* production eventually leading to an extended market for yourself."

"Mr Smith has a point there, I suppose," muttered Fred, becoming interested.

"Indeed he has."

"It's a good one, too."

"We must also remember that world trade continues to expand," added Murphy eagerly, believing that he had made a break-through.

Fred held up a hand palm outwards, "There are still frequent periods of recession, though."

"Maybe, but whether that's the case or not trading *never* stops. Overseas markets are developing and at a rapid pace too. On top of which most countries; even some of those in Europe, do not yet have a viable iron industry."

"I can see where your argument is leading, though I'm not so sure that Sir Charles and Frank would agree with you."

"As I've said, it is not my theory, but it could work for Martindale."

"It all depends on what Sir Charles decides, he and his children are the majority shareholders."

"Think how relieved the whole of Martindale would be if the current plan was to be ditched? Production would soar without management needing to do a thing," encouraged George as he wondered if he himself could find a way to become involved, despite his own resources being very limited.

Fred thought for a while longer and then decided, "I'll put it to the others."

"Make a start to-day."

Fred shook his head, "Frank is on an extended honeymoon."

"What about Sir Charles?"

"He won't move without talking it over with his agent first."

"We've no time to waste, though."

"I'll talk to Sir Charles next time I get the chance."

Murphy rubbed his hands enthusiastically, "Good, and if you can find a part for me to play in this development, then I'll be ready for the call."

*****

"How are Miss Esprey's riding lessons progressing?" Queried Marian Martin of Virgil Kent.

"Very well, your ladyship, she's a born natural on a horse."

"Even on a side-saddle?" Marian was surprised as she had taken a very long time to manage the same thing.

"I've never seen better, even in the cavalry amongst officers who'd grown up with horses and at times had maybe even *slept* with them."

Marian laughed gently, "As good as that – Fourth Hussars weren't you."

"Eleventh, ma'am, the *Cherry-pickers*."

"If only Cissy could have seen you strutting around in your red overalls, that would have made her eyes goggle."

Kent winked, "What makes you think I haven't privately displayed my *Cherry-bums* to her?"

"In that case why wasn't I invited to so colourful a viewing?" Marian pretended vexation.

"Next time, my lady, when Cissy and I celebrate our tenth wedding anniversary, it'll be an occasion for full dress uniform."

Marian laughed, "I'll make a note of that," she then paused and continued, "Still, we were discussing Miss Esprey, will she be capable of riding to hounds do you think?"

"Come New Year," Kent considered for a moment and then smiled broadly, "By then she'll have the stiffest,

230

straightest back of all the hunting ladies, and even of some of the gentlemen too."

"Remember, though, there'll be hedges, gates and fences to take," Marian sounded concerned.

"Miss Esprey has jumped more than a few of those already, it's as though she's glued to the saddle."

"So she won't fall off her horse very easily, you think."

"No, ma'am, she won't do that. She sees exactly what her animal is going to do before it knows it itself, and the creature understands exactly what it is she wants it to do too."

"I'm not a good rider myself and find that horses don't always behave as their riders wish."

"A quiet word from Miss Catherine, the gentle touch of her knee and the animal will *know* what's to come next. To sum up, my lady, she's outstanding."

"This is news that Colonel Esprey will be very happy to receive."

"She's a lass who'll one day make us all proud, there's no doubt of that in my mind."

*****

"No, m'lady, m'darlin', ye'll need t'bend yer back more," instructed Kevin O'Dowd as he took a keen interest in Lady Flora's comfortable rump as she attempted to make a shot.

"I can't bend so far over, Kevin… At least not without some assistance."

Ever ready to oblige, Kevin's left arm came around her shoulders whilst his right hand began to mould the humps of her buttocks.

Flora had never enjoyed so exciting a relationship with a man before, at least not since Tommy Woodward had shown an interest in her nearly thirty years previously. Regrettably, her father and later her brother had soon shown this impoverished lawyer the door.

"Just a tiny bit more, Flora," encouraged O'Dowd whose finger was stealing down towards the opening between her buttocks.

"*Ohh*," moaned Miss Scott-Wilson, still dreaming of events past which might have been.

Kevin had never had much success with the ladies; unless he'd been willing to pay for their services that is, but he reckoned that both of the Scott-Wilson sisters were fair game for him.

"Don't stop, Kevin. *Please*, don't stop," Flora sighed heavily at the same time dropping her cue.

The Irishman's fingers next came into contact with the rigidity of Flora's corsetry which brought him to a temporary halt, he being undecided over what was best to do next. He had secured himself a fortunate position at Forest Hall, the best he'd ever enjoyed and with no work attached to speak of. On top of which he'd also become quite fond of the sisters.

"Look, it ain't no good saying yes and meaning no, or t'other way round," cried Kevin in frustration at being denied by her voluminous clothing.

Flora stood panting for a few seconds, her breasts heaving as though they were a matched pair of wildly overheating steam engines.

"Do it, *DO ME*," she was virtually howling now.

Without further delay Kevin reached for the hem of her skirt and began to pull it up along with multiple layers of petticoats.

With a struggle, Flora heaved herself up on to the billiards table and rolled over on to her back. She stretched her arms high above her head and lay there with her thighs outspread and only what was left of her underdrawers protecting her virginity.

Kevin didn't have long to savour the sight of this as he was interrupted by a hammering at the door.

"What on earth is going on in there? Let me in, I want to know what foolishness you're up to," cried Rowena through an inch of solid oak.

"Don't open the door for her yet," Flora ordered Kevin as she tried desperately to pull her clothes back into some sort of order.

"Come on, hurry up, or I shall have to call for the spare key to be brought," threatened the younger sister.

"Just hold yer horses," returned Kevin, wondering how long he'd have to wait before enjoying the tight embrace of Flora's thighs.

"Come on, there's no time to lose, there's a telegram arrived from Mister Corsica, he coming down on the afternoon train," yelled Rowena at the top of her voice.

This news dramatically and immediately reduced the size of Kevin's erection.

"Keep her out until I'm presentable," Flora begged Kevin, whilst at the same time managing to both find her feet and begin stuffing her underwear beneath the cushions of a nearby *chaise longue.*

"If Johnie's coming the day, we'd best be ready for him," the Irishman didn't like the sound of this.

# Chapter Four

## *(December, 1865)*

With Christmas approaching, on a whim and feeling hungrily nostalgic, George Murphy changed the direction of his walk and entered the Cooks' pie-shop, sitting down at what had once been his favourite table.

It wasn't very long before he was noticed by Geordie who wasted no time in taking the seat across from him.

"Why, George lad, I canna' say how pleased I am to see you – what'll it be – your usual no doubt."

"Pie and plenty of mushy peas, I've thought of nothing else for weeks," Murphy was suddenly filled with the warm, familiar feeling which he hadn't enjoyed for so long – too long in fact, he decided.

"Ye'll be wantin' a good splash of vinegar an'all," I suppose. It's lucky I filled all the bottles this morning."

Murphy smiled but at the same time noticed how much sparer Geordie was now, on top of which he had aged significantly.

"Will Annie speak to me? It's a long time since I've seen her," George's expression illustrated how concerned he was.

"Annie will always be pleased t'see you, no matter how long you've stayed away."

Almost on cue, Annie came bustling from the kitchen, wiping sweat from her brow at the same time. She wasted no time on pleasantries, instead she pulled her foster son from his seat and into her arms, dragging him close to her bosom.

"I canna' say how much I've missed you," she cried, her eyes filling with tears of delight.

"I'm sorry, I know it seems as though I deserted you," he replied, wishing that he could think of something more appropriate to say.

"We'll not have apologies, we'll have nothing other than joy that we're together again," put in Geordie who had managed to slacken the grip of his wife and was pumping the hand of the son he was sure he'd lost.

Then it seemed that the very busy, shop came to a standstill. Some customers sat with forkfuls of pie hovering around their lips. Others ceased their gossip, their mouths agape. Every one of them knew the story of the pie-shop boy and were delighted by the joyful reunion they were witnessing.

There then followed a good hour of catch-up talk much of which was carried out in the back parlour over numerous pots of tea.

George apologised a number of times for his thoughtless and rude behaviour to the people who had taken him in and had counted him as their own son – the child they themselves had never been granted in over thirty years of marriage.

"I've brought you heartache and sorrow – I'm so sorry, I wish I had the words to describe how much I regret storming away from you."

"We shouldn't have interfered between you and Lucy Greenwood – it was wrong, your heart was set on her."

"I'm not surprised y'were taken wi' her, she's a looker a'right," put in Geordie.

Murphy shook his head, "She is, but I eventually saw that she wasn't the one for me, nor I for her."

At that moment the parlour door opened as Clara Miller returned from her teaching stint at the Education Association.

"George, how nice to see that you've come to your senses at last," she cried as she removed her gloves, hat and coat.

"I've never been so delighted for as long as I can remember," put in Annie who immediately set to pouring further mugs of tea.

"Aye, we both are," added Geordie who then nodded towards Clara and continued, "She's pleased as well – I knaw she is."

Clara's features softened and she bent forward to gently kiss Murphy's cheek.

He beamed, for he had doubted that Clara would ever give him so much as the time of day, never mind a peck on the cheek.

"It's good to be back," he said slowly and was sure that he hadn't smiled as broadly since the day he'd sold his first full tray of pies in a matter of minutes.

"We'd best get back to the shop," put in Annie.

"Aye, we should at that," added Geordie, his eyes seeming to be misting over.

"Come on, then, what are you waiting for?" Annie was giving her husband the *look* and he knew exactly what he was expected to do.

Once they'd been left alone George said, "It's so good to see you again."

"It's taken you long enough."

"I've had a lot to do."

"As have we all."

"I'm never off the railways these days, you'd be amazed how many dresses I've sold."

"Do you get commission on each one?"

"Yes, I'm doing very well and soon expect to do even better."

"That'll please Miss Greenwood."

George's face clouded for a moment and he was about to make a hot reply, but the moment passed and he smiled broadly and replied, "That's all over now, but I expect you knew that."

"I tend to keep well away from her – I've been known to cross the street just to avoid her."

"I understand clearly what she's about now."

"Though the pair of you were engaged to be married."

Murphy sighed deeply, "Everyone remembers that but no one seems to recall that the bans were never completed – didn't get any further than the first reading in fact."

"So it's all over between you and Lucy?"

"Yes and now that I really know what she's like I often breathe a deep sigh of relief."

"So, the other well-to-do rising stars of Martindale had better look out."

George laughed, "She's already taken a fancy to Hugh Doggart – Dougie Brass's nephew."

"Perhaps he will see sense before it's too late."

"He will if his uncle has anything to do with it, though Hugh's almost of an age to make his own decisions."

*****

"What did Mister Corsica have to say?" Asked Flora of Kevin O'Dowd.

"Indeed, you were away together for some days," added Lady Rowena.

"I missed you, especially as we were so abruptly interrupted in the billiards room," sighed Flora.

"You've still no idea how to play that game," accused Rowena, giving her sister a sharp look.

Kevin smiled as he wrapped his arms around both the sisters and hugged them close.

"Why, lassies, there's nought t'trouble either o'ye."

"The marchioness isn't displeased with us?" Queried Flora anxiously.

"Nay, nay, nay, she sends her regards and I've got some news."

Flora didn't much like the idea of good news coming from Elysia, for though she had rescued them from their broken down cottage at Winterbourne, she could just as easily send them to somewhere worse – an Arabian slave market for instance.

Rowena saw the concerned expression on the face of her sister and began to worry too – *what can she know that I don't?* She asked herself.

O'Dowd loosened his grip on the sisters and declared with a wide, crooked smile across his misshapen face, "Ye're to go on holiday next month."

Flora's face dropped as she was sure that her worst fears were coming true and could almost feel the cold iron of the shackles as her body was prepared to be sold in the middle of Damascus or somewhere even more outlandish.

Her sister didn't like the sound of this either, for any movement at all could find them far away from Forest Hall which was the most comfortable home she'd had since the death of her brother – who; even though he had been a swine of the first order, had tended to leave her alone.

"Come on lasses, cheer up, you're going t'Bournemouth for a week or so," Kevin was puzzled that his charges didn't seemed overjoyed at the idea of a holiday at the seaside.

"In the middle of winter," cried Flora incredulously.

"We'll freeze to death," added Rowena.

"Mr Corsica has rented a fine, cosy house for you," returned Kevin.

"Are there cliffs at Bournemouth?" Queried Rowena, remembering the fate of her brother and wondering if a fatal fall had been planned for them too.

"I believe there are, and of course a never ending succession of *huge* waves as well," Flora had always had a morbid fear of drowning.

O'Dowd laughed heartily and said as clearly as he could, "Ye're to take a holiday whilst I see t'some work that needs doin' here."

Both sisters nodded several times and smiled weakly, they hoping that this was truly all there was to it.

*****

"Not at work the day?" Asked Charlotte Webb of John Losser as he was passing by the gates of *Brass Shilling*.

"I was on early."

"How come you're so clean then? Ye should be up to your neck in grime and filth – that's if you were really working."

Losser bridled slightly, "No one can ever say that I'm not a worker," he began and then his tone changed when he realised that she was joshing him.

"Not got the little cripple hanging on to your coat-tails today?"

"Don't call Miss Miller that, she's a nice lass who will not allow her infirmities get the better of her," there was real anger in his tone.

"Sorry I spoke out of turn, I meant nothing by it. Miss Miller's no enemy of mine," Charlotte smiled and quickly changed her tune.

"That's all right, then," Losser looked Charlotte up and down as though it was the first time he'd truly noticed her.

"Like what you see?" She asked.

"Aye, I do, canny good," he returned without hardly a second of thought.

"Are you planning to go to the pantomime at the *Civic*?" She asked him.

"When does it open?"

"Boxing Day, or so I hear."

"Which one are they putting on?" He asked, though with no great interest.

"*Humpty Dumpty,* but I'd have preferred *Cinderella.*"

"They're all the same to me," he replied with a distinct lack of enthusiasm.

"Do you not like the theatre?"

"Aye, I like it canny well."

"I love the theatre." Charlotte declared, at the same time shivering in feigned anticipation. " I love being in the dark, it brings me out in goose bumps. Then I start to think exciting thoughts and imagine that all sorts of thrilling things are just about to happen."

"Like what?" She'd lost Losser off completely.

Her voice became husky, "As I sit as quiet and still as I can, my ears are filled with rolling, gentle whispers that are no more solid then a summer breeze. Then I'm sure that I can sense; more than feel, the brush of an arm against my own. I become sure that fingers are stretching out, desperate to touch mine."

Losser's mouth began to dry up once he realised what she was on about and what favours she might be willing to bestow within the dimly lit and warm embrace of the theatre.

"Does this happen every time you go to a play?" He questioned curiously.

"No, silly boy, I have to have the right feller sitting next to me."

"If ye like, I'll take you to the pantomime," this offer left his tongue before his brain had had time to weigh up the consequences of it.

"Oh, yes please, I'd enjoy that and I *know* that you will too."

*****

"I thought you'd be at home with your parents," said Inspector Mason as Constable George Dodds entered the office with a great deal of haste and very little ceremony.

"Things are on the move at Forest Hall," he panted, being out of breath from having run up several flights of stairs.

"Sit down, get your wind back and report clearly what's happened."

"Her ladyship has ordered a special train to take her relatives and *all* the servants from Forest Hall to Bournemouth."

"Over Christmas?"

"No, on January 17th, and they're to be away for a week or maybe longer," it was obvious that Dodds was very pleased with his first solo detective work.

"Why Bournemouth?"

"It'll have been a whim of the lady, I expect, they're probably lucky she hasn't sent them off to the wilds of Tibet or Timbuctoo."

"I don't suppose it was the marchioness herself who booked the train, though more likely it was her Mediterranean accomplice," mused Mason.

"Neither of them, the business was completed by a certain Mister Watkins."

The inspector shook his head, "Who's he?"

"Apparently, he's the dogsbody of a London solicitor, a certain Mister Hill."

"*Aha*, the lady's legal adviser."

"She's bound to have one – or even several."

Mason thought for a moment and then considered, "This could be the break we've been waiting for."

"I certainly hope so, it could be the beginning of the end for the ever so high and mighty Marchioness of Studland."

Mason sat with a dreamy look in his eyes as he imagined the marchioness standing in the dock at the Old Bailey, this time caught out dead to rights.

"Maybe," he said eventually, knowing from experience that they were dealing with a particularly slippery customer.

"Once the house is empty, will we be given enough men to cover it adequately?"

"I'll visit a contact I have at the Home Office next week."

"Wouldn't today be better?"

"You don't know how Whitehall works, for they would judge so early an approach to them as one made in unseemly haste."

*****

"Mister Hill has arrived, your ladyship, and desires an audience with you," informed Grenville, Winterbourne's butler.

"Whatever can he want at this time of year?" Elysia had always thought her lawyer tiresome and she had no desire at all to meet with him so close to Christmas.

"He made no mention regarding the purpose of his visit, ma'am."

"Tell him to go away and return after the holiday, *Oh*, and pass on to him my greetings for the Season."

Elysia was sure that whatever was troubling her legal representative it could wait, especially as she and Warren were to visit both Martin Hall and Blanchwell over the holiday period.

"He is very insistent, ma'am and I must say that he appears to be somewhat agitated."

"He's always worried about something or another."

"Mr Hill claims his business is *very* important," Grenville tried yet again, as he himself was filled with curiosity.

Elysia sighed, "Oh, very well, send him in but be ready to show him the door the instant I ring for you."

The butler left silently and returned shortly thereafter with the solicitor.

"Well, Hill, what on earth can your business be so close to Christmas?"

From her tone the lawyer recognised that his most important client had no wish to be troubled.

"Begging your pardon, my lady, but I have come regarding the transportation my junior clerk; Mister Watkins, has arranged from Verdley Magna to Bournemouth."

"The railway companies have run out of locomotives have they? Or perhaps there is a critical shortage of carriages. Wait, *I know*, the points have all been frozen solid."

"No ma'am, everything has been prepared for the seventeenth of next month, though Watkins returned with disquieting news."

Elysia's dark eyes flashed, "Then you'd best waste no further time and tell me what he had to say."

"As you know, ma'am, my clerk is in frequent communication with the station master at Verdley who has provided some information which may be of importance."

*"THEN TELL ME WHAT IT IS?"*

Hill quailed for the marchioness in a temper always made him nervous if not quite in fear for his life.

"Several enquiries regarding the travel arrangements from Forest Hall to Bournemouth and back again have been made by a stranger to the village."

Elysia's temper faded and her expression showed her curiosity, "Enquiries about what, precisely?"

"Those regarding the removal of the household to Bournemouth."

"Why on earth should a complete stranger have any interest in the holiday arrangements I've made for my relatives?"

"Exactly, my lady."

"Who is this inquisitive person?"

"He gave his name to several of the villagers as Mr Dodds, and told them that he was the representative of a grain merchant."

"A grain merchant, you say?"

"A local farmer suggested to my Mr Watkins that he doubted that Dodds could tell the difference between a grain of barley and a pellet of rabbit shit – begging you pardon, ma'am."

"Does this Dodds ask detailed questions about the provisions made, dates, times and such?"

"Quite indirectly, but he always returns to the same theme – Departure, length of stay and the return date."

"Strange," muttered Elysia to herself.

"Perhaps Mr Corsica and his people should investigate," suggested Hill, in the hope that the responsibility for dealing with this would be taken from his own shoulders.

Elysia was just about to agree to his suggestion when she was struck by a series of sudden thoughts, ideas of impending disaster flashed through her mind and she began to tremble. *What if this were to be the harbinger of something dreadful? What if it signalled the first stroke of the axe which would bring down her whole world?*

"I'm sure that Corsica is the man for this, my lady," proposed the lawyer for the second time.

Elysia pulled herself together, smiled sweetly and replied, "I think not, Hill, at least not at the moment."

"The nosey Mister Dodds is to be ignored or even forgotten about, perhaps?"

"Indeed not, instruct the Verdley Magna people to find out more about him. It shouldn't be difficult, you know what gossips they are down there."

"Yes, ma'am."

"Keep me fully up to date; by telegram if necessary, for there may well be more to it than we realise at the moment."

"Certainly, my lady."

"Oh, make sure that you do *not* mention any of this to Mr Corsica – he's to be kept in ignorance of this particular turn of events."

The solicitor nodded his understanding and left the room, wondering if Johnie's fall from grace was imminent.

As soon as Hill had gone, Elysia pulled out two sheets of her monogrammed writing paper and began penning notes to both Marian and Caroline asking each of them if it were possible to extend her planned visits for a week or even ten days longer.

"This should keep me well out of harm's way," she smiled to herself.

*****

"This is Mr Vasey, papa," Millie Hopper introduced the actor to her father.

Miles Hopper stepped forward and thrust out his right hand which Solly took and shook, noticing how smooth and dry it was.

"I've seen you act on stage a few times," said Hopper shortly.

Solly noticed that Millie's father had made no comment, neither positive nor negative regarding the performances he'd attended.

Then he was approached by an attractive older lady, "I'm Mildred's mother, but you may call me *Mama*," offered Alice Hopper brightly, her eyes shining with both hope and expectation.

Vasey coughed, for he hadn't had any need to use the maternal term she'd proposed for some years and it was also obvious that Millie's mama wasn't much more than five or six years older than himself.

"Don't be silly, Alice," interrupted Miles Hopper, "Mr Vasey is the same age as your brother."

Vasey had hoped as soon as he had accepted Millie's invitation to Christmas lunch that her parents would look upon him as being far too old for their daughter, which

249

he reckoned would keep him safe from any looming romantic entanglement.

The idea of making some excuse and returning to his quarters at the *Civic* crossed his mind, but then dining on a boiled ham sandwich which was turning up at the corners on Christmas Day wasn't very appealing either.

Mrs Hopper was determined that at least the possibility of a suitor for her daughter should not escape. Several young men had put in an appearance over the years but none had met the standards set by her husband.

*This one won't neither,* she thought to herself sadly.

"Let's have the dinner on the table, my love, whilst I pour a couple of drinks and have a chat with Mr Vasey.

"Just call me Solly," offered the actor.

Miles paused in his efforts to pull the sticky cork from a bottle of sherry and asked sharply, "Is that short for Solomon?"

"Yes, though Solly suits me better."

"*Solomon,* why that's a Hebrew name – you're not Jewish, are you?" It was obvious that Hopper didn't like the idea of this.

The actor wasn't feeling very humorous but laughed heartily; a skill he'd learnt when he first took to the stage, "No, my father was a stonemason who was in awe of the temple Solomon had built at Jerusalem."

"Not much of it left now, or so I believe," replied Miles, doubting the veracity of what his visitor was telling him.

"Just the Wailing Wall, I understand, anyway whatever's left my pa' was obsessed by it."

Miles nodded rapidly, "We're good Christians in this household – it's very necessary that we're seen to be so, for the sake of my business."

Vasey had no idea what Millie's pa' did for a living as he'd never been interested enough to ask. "What *is* your line of business," he enquired when Hopper failed to volunteer any further information.

"I'm the owner of the largest funeral parlour in the town. Got two hearses, each pulled by a pair of the glossiest, fittest black horses ye've ever seen," he replied as he handed Solly a thimbleful of sherry.

The actor was about to swallow this in a single gulp and then hold out his glass for more, but stopped himself just in time and took the tiniest sip he could manage.

"I remember now, of course, you buried both the late Mr Lander and his daughter Abigail."

"Not to mention Jack Nicholson, now that was one to remember. There were crowds there and his widow was looking so pale I thought I was going to have to pop her in the box beside her husband," reminisced Miles with a faraway look in his eyes.

Solly wasn't sure whether he was supposed to laugh at this, but stopped himself from doing so just in time.

"The whole town was in tears that day," continued the undertaker.

"I never knew Mr Nicholson myself – heard of him, of course."

Hopper topped up the glasses and then inspected his visitor closely, looking at his tall, broad stature and fine, noble features, "Have you ever thought of directing funerals yourself?"

"No, I'm a simple actor," returned Solly very swiftly.

"Why, man, a funeral is nothing other than a show, a play if you like and each one's different."

"Really?" Solly had never thought of it like that.

"Every time I conduct a funeral, it's a show from start to finish."

"Yes, I can see that, I suppose."

"You have the perfect voice for a funeral," suggested Hopper.

"It'll always be the stage for me."

"As I've said, that's what a funeral is, pure acting with everyone playing a part – I myself am like your Mr Villiers, orchestrating the whole production. I manage it so smoothly that nobody notices the effort and nervous tension that has gone into it," Hopper spoke with enthusiasm.

"Is the money good?" Solly began to show an interest.

Miles nearly doubled up with laughter, and then pointed around the room, "Is this the accommodation of a poor man? Is my house not large and in very good order too?"

Vasey had to agree that the Hopper home was one which could only be afforded by a man of some considerable means.

"It's a fine house, you must be proud of it."

"Oh, I am, the only thing is I have no son and heir to carry on the business. There's just our Mildred and it would be unbecoming for a woman to conduct a funeral – it's against the will of the God."

"That's most unfortunate."

"Indeed it is, so I've no one to carry on in my footsteps once I've been laid to rest myself," he laughed again and then continued, "If you happened to be present on that occasion you'd see me spinning in my grave."

Solly looked puzzled, "Why would you be doing that?"

"I'd have to be buried by one of my *competitors*," Hopper doubled up with laughter.

"Yes, that would be unfortunate," smiled the actor.

They stood in contemplative silence for a minute and then Hopper continued, "Millie's into her twenties now, too. She's in want of a husband and I need a grandson."

"Yes, well, she's a very nice person – I've always got along well with her."

Miles' eyes narrowed, "Ye're not married are you? No wife tucked away in London or somewhere? I know you theatricals criss-cross the country for work."

Solly managed to prevent himself from shuddering at the thought of matrimony, "Me married? I've had no time for it, acting is a poor foundation for a settled lifestyle."

"You're not against the institution though, if say the right girl with good looks and a decent," he winked knowingly, "income of her own came along."

Vasey had seen where this conversation was leading for some time and he had been working through a number of replies which would allow him to escape. However, he began to re-think his whole position. The idea of being free of the uncertainties of the theatre, combined with working under so unreliable a man as Villiers; who still owed him money, was making such a change look increasingly attractive.

"I don't know, treading the boards has been my life since I was twelve," he shook his head negatively.

"Why, there's no need to completely give up acting, the *Civic* won't disappear overnight were you to leave for greener pastures. Instead, my Mildred and yourself could have a fine old time, performing together in Martindale."

"Romeo and Juliet, Abelard and Heloise," muttered Vasey who was now becoming even more interested.

"Exactly so, you'd hardly notice the difference, except that you'd be much more comfortably off."

The spirit of the actor inside Solly began to fear for its future, but the sensible side of his brain was putting forward a convincing argument which after a tussle won the day, "Your offer may suit me very well, especially at the moment."

"Be warned though, I won't allow you to marry my daughter one day and then drop her the next to go off on tour," there was some steel in this from Miles Hopper.

Solly held up both hands in a gesture of appeasement, "No, sir, I meant giving up the *theatre*, not abandoning Millie – whom I have come to adore."

"Adore as her husband, perhaps?"

Vasey's throat felt restricted enough to prevent speech, but in the end he managed to stutter, "Yes... Yes, I believe that I'm ready for a change."

"Ye'll have change all right, and for the better, you mark my words," replied the undertaker knowingly.

Just then the ladies returned from the dining room, "The soup is just about to be served," announced Alice Hopper,

"We've both white *and* red wine in for the occasion," added Maisie proudly.

Alice's eyes took in the situation immediately and it appeared to her that Miles' plan had come to fruition.

Mr Hopper took his wife's arm, "We'll go into the dining room to drink a Christmas toast, my dear, and leave the young folks alone, for I believe Mr Vasey has something to ask our daughter."

Millie didn't look the least surprised as her parents left the room, she turned her eyes on to Vasey and brought forth a smile of dazzling proportions.

Vasey cleared his throat nervously and then said, "I've been discussing things with your papa and it seems he's happy for us to become engaged."

"*Married*," she replied sharply, "and soon, too."

*****

"It was most kind of you to spend your Christmas Day at the rectory," William Cowpens was extremely grateful to his housekeeper, Mrs Lander.

255

Venetia nodded to the housemaid that the soup should be served before she smiled at her host and employer, "Normally, I should have spent Christmas with Amelia at Blanchwell, but with the death of poor Major Sturgis and his wife remaining bereft, any chance of a happy Yuletide flew off in a flash."

"Then I shall count myself as the only contented person to be found in Martindale this Christmas."

Venetia took a delicate spoonful of soup and sipped it, "This could do with a touch more seasoning, I feel."

"You're probably right," agreed the rector reaching for the pepper pot.

"Oh, by the way, once Christmas Day has been fully celebrated and we've all attended Evensong, I have told the servants that they're to visit their families and to return here on the twenty-seventh."

Cowpens hardly looked up, "Good idea, very charitable of you."

"You're their employer, I just wondered if I'd done the right thing."

He looked up sharply from his soup and she noticed for the first time how deep and brown his eyes were.

"Whatever household decisions you may arrive at, I shall be perfectly happy with. In fact, I've not been so contented in my domestic arrangements for years."

"Since your wife passed on, perhaps."

"She was ill for such a long time, after she'd suffered her...," his voice caught for a second and then he carried on strongly, "third miscarriage."

"I'm so sorry to hear that, I'm sure you would have made admirable parents."

"It wasn't to be," the rector took a full spoon of soup, drank it and tried to make it appear that he was no longer emotionally concerned with the events of a decade previously.

"The idea of life without children is unbearable, it's nearly as bad as having had to put up with three daughters."

"Have Amelia and Arabella come to terms with your position here yet?"

Venetia shook her head, "Our relationships are at least cordial, but lacking their original closeness and spontaneity."

"I presume they realise that your situation here is purely a domestic one."

Venetia laughed, "It's not my daughters I'm concerned about, it's the town."

"Our parishioners have caused you no concern, I trust," Cowpens' eyes flashed and his face became stern.

"No, my connection with them is exactly the same as it ever was."

"Should that change, then let me know and I shall deliver a sermon so full of hellfire that transgressors will feel the full heat of the furnace."

Venetia laughed, but then replied, "It's best to let sleeping dogs lie, is it not?"

They sat in a friendly silence for a while, then once the fish had been served, Cowpens asked, "You eldest daughter was the first wife of Mister Turner, was she not?"

"Yes, though I believe that Abigail took him on more as a challenge than as a husband."

"Really?" William raised his eyebrows.

"Turner was then; still is in fact, a very important man in the town and a close friend of Sir Charles himself, as well as being both sensible and amiable."

"He runs everything in Martindale, does he not?"

"With the assistance of Amelia's husband Fred Schilling."

"Then, I expect, Abigail saw great promise in him."

"Not exactly, she took it into her mind that she could make a gentleman out of him and then set about her task with great determination and endeavour."

"Oh, dear, even knowing and respecting Mister Turner, I fear she must have failed."

"After a year or two her whole scheme drove them apart."

"Though you yourself still respect Turner?"

"Indeed yes, he is a very competent and admirable man – any sensible mother would be delighted to welcome him into her family."

Venetia cleared the final morsel of fish from her plate and rang the bell for the pork to be served.

Once Mr Cowpens had carved the joint he asked, "Though what happened once it became obvious that Turner was not nor ever could become a gentleman?"

"It got worse, for at the time Frank's sister was the housekeeper at Martin Hall and Sir Charles had fallen deeply in love with her."

"I've heard this story, it has the flavour of Cinderella about it."

"They were married as soon as it was possible for them to do so."

"Lady Marian is lovely in every possible way too."

"Abigail couldn't abide Molly; as Marian was known then, mainly because of her jealousy. From her point of view it appeared that her sister-in-law; seemingly without effort, had achieved everything that she wished for herself. A life of refinement with the town looking up to her – you know the sort of thing."

"I see, so Lady Marian and Abigail diametrically exchanged positions in the social scheme of things, this must have been an unbearable blow for your daughter."

"Precisely. Her relationship with Francis went from bad to worse and even though she bore him my granddaughter, Maud, she cared nothing for the child nor for the husband."

"Then went off adventuring with the first wife of Sir Charles, who is now the rather colourful Marchioness of Studland."

"She did indeed but never returned alive."

*****

"Did you enjoy the pantomime?" Asked Elizabeth Esprey of Kitty as they were leaving the *Lyceum* Theatre on Boxing Day.

Kitty nodded but said nothing.

*Ungrateful little wretch,* thought Lizzie who was particularly annoyed that she'd had to waste three precious days visiting dressmakers, milliners and shoemakers for a girl who hadn't appreciated the efforts of any of them.

They strolled in silence for a more few steps and then Elizabeth tried again, "I suppose you thought it too silly or didn't understand the plot – you being unused to the English pantomime tradition."

Kitty nodded again but still failed to speak.

Mrs Esprey sighed deeply, for she had no idea of how to deal with this child who was not far from the threshold of womanhood – which she knew from personal experience was a most dangerous time.

At the behest of Jervis, she'd spent hours seeing to it that Catherine had been properly outfitted for every possible occasion. A multitude of shoes and boots had been tried on and a dozen pairs purchased. The girl was now fully outfitted for every conceivable social event, from morning and day outfits, to formal evening wear not to mention millinery, hosiery, underwear, corsetry and nightwear.

However; no matter how much encouragement she had given, none of these purchases appeared to please Miss Kitty, for there had been no gasps of pleasure nor whoops of delight, it was as though she'd been dragging a broken mechanical doll around the finest shops and dressmakers in London.

"I wish I could think of something which would please you," announced Eliza with more than a hint of agitation.

Kitty's only response was in the form of a dumb look.

"Is nothing we've done here; in the world's greatest city, been of any interest to you?"

Suddenly, Elizabeth was pulled to a halt by her charge, who she found was looking at her with huge eyes which were visibly misting over.

"What on earth is wrong with you?" Queried the actress, hoping that Kitty wasn't going to start a scene on a very busy street.

"Nothing, there's *nothing's* wrong," Catherine's words were choked off.

"Then why can't you express some pleasure? Joy or delight even?"

Kitty's chin hit her chest and when she spoke it was in a hoarse whisper, "It's so wonderful that I have the sure dread that it will all come to an end. I'm certain that I'm only living in a dream which will become a nightmare, one in which everything is taken from me, disappearing in a whiff of smoke – like the demon in the pantomime we've just seen."

"You mean to say that you've enjoyed your visit here?" Lizzie was astonished.

"Oh, yes, it's as though I've woken up in fairyland. I can't believe that I have been so lucky. The last good fortune I had was when I stole a ham bone from the larder of the orphanage and wasn't found out."

To say that Elizabeth was surprised was a huge understatement, *"Really?* I thought you hadn't at all enjoyed anything we've done."

"I've been living in the sweetest of dreams, though this was the best," Kitty turned towards the façade of the theatre and pointed, "In there they perform magic. I really believed that the little girl was dying, I thought that the villain was going to kill the heroine. And then it turned out all right in the end."

"Though you didn't applaud at all, not once."

"I wanted to, but I couldn't…"

"Everyone else was cheering, how could bear not to join in?"

Kitty shook her head, "I wanted to desperately, but was afraid that if I joined in the spell would be broken."

Elizabeth couldn't believe what she was hearing, she having been so sure that the child cared nothing for her new life nor for the people who inhabited it.

There followed a short silence and then Kitty spoke again, "I'm trying to get things right, but there's so much to learn I don't know that I can do it."

"Of course you can, it is the colonel's wish that you become a young lady, and he is not a man to be denied."

Kitty considered what had been said for a while and then she asked plaintively, "Will you help me to become the young woman the colonel wishes for?"

Twenty minutes previously, Elizabeth would have fervently denied that she wanted anything at all to do with the child, however, that feeling disappeared immediately, "Of course, I shall do everything I can to help you make it happen."

Kitty shook her head, "I came from nowhere, I know next to nothing, I doubt...," her voice trailed off.

Lizzie took her charge's face gently in both hands and smiled, "Lady Marian Martin succeeded with this same task and I did too, so I'm sure you will be able to make the transition."

"I'll try very hard, I truly will, but there's so much to learn..."

"Regard the whole thing as a play and learn the script line by line, and before you know it you'll be able to quote perfectly the full text."

"If only I could pull it off, it would be wonderful and it would help me to repay the colonel."

Lizzie gripped her charge's shoulders and looked directly into her eyes, "In that case you'd best start by calling him *papa*."

Kitty looked puzzled, "I sure don't mind that, but..."

"It will soon be legal, for when we return home we shall be visiting our lawyer. Your name will be changed by deed-poll to Catherine Esprey."

"You mean I'll be allowed to sign my name that way, I don't need to use Hawes again?"

"It will be completely legal with the colonel as your papa."

Tears began to form in Kitty's eyes, though she fought them back successfully, "Then I will really and truly *belong* somewhere?"

"Of course, Merrington Hall will be your home for the rest of your life."

"Will it be all right to call the colonel *papa* as soon as we get home, before we've even seen the legal people?"

"There's nothing he would like better and whilst you're on about it, I shall try my hardest to become your mama." Elizabeth spoke sincerely but desperately hoped that this was a role she would be able to carry off without the cracks showing.

This time tears did flow down Kitty's cheeks as she threw herself into the waiting arms of her often wished for and now newly discovered parent.

For the first time in her life, Elizabeth returned a hug which could only be described as *matronly*.

They stood on the pavement for some time oblivious of the crowds who passed by them.

Eventually, Lizzie loosened her grip and explained, "The colonel is also to make you his heir – so, not only will you become a lady you will be an heiress too – why, I'm certain that you'll marry and end up a countess."

"I shouldn't like to leave Merrington Hall."

"That's all in the future, but for now we shall go off and celebrate with champagne and oysters."

*****

"Nothing much has changed here, there's the usual chaos," whispered Philip Butterfield to his sister as they watched the dress rehearsal of *Humpty Dumpty* at the *Martindale Civic Theatre*.

"I'm very surprised that Mr Villiers is not taking a leading role this season," she replied.

"He was too small for the Humpty outfit," informed Marcus Reno.

Philip looked closely at the pantomime figure on the stage, "Why, isn't that John Fisher in there, he's surely not big enough either."

"*Ha*," returned his sister, "He is once he's been fully padded out."

"Fisher'll steam in there, it'll be hotter than the boiler room of the *Royal Oak*."

"He's been begging for a *big* part for years and he certainly got one this time," laughed Marcus.

"This rehearsal doesn't appear to be running at all smoothly," said Phil, shaking his head in surprise for he knew that, despite his many faults, Villiers was a consummate professional.

"Roddy didn't want to put on a pantomime in the first place, so he's in something of a huff," informed his brother-in-law.

"His head's full of Shakespeare, I'm sure he believes that anything else is beneath his dignity now," added his sister.

There came a crash from the stage as John Fisher fell off Humpty's wall and was finding it difficult to rise to his feet again.

After enjoying this diversion, Philip pointed out, "Millie Hopper seems to be getting on famously with Mr Vasey."

"They're engaged to be married early next year."

"Millie with Solly? He's old enough to be her father."

"He is close to it perhaps, but not quite there by a furlong or so," returned Marcus.

"Villiers is very annoyed because Solly is to become a part-time actor like the rest of us," added Susannah.

"How is he to earn a living, then?"

Marcus doubled up with laughter so much that he couldn't return an answer.

His sister helped him out, "He is to become…," she paused dramatically, "an *Undertaker*."

Both Reno and his wife waited for the burst of hilarity they were sure would burst from Philip, but he remained silent and thoughtful for a while before responding, "Come to think of it, what a good idea that is as he's perfect for the role."

"Anyway, Millie's friend and competitor, Violet isn't taking it too well as she's still sitting on the shelf without a suitable partner in sight."

Philip remembered Miss Grainger when she had played Juliet to his brother-in-law's Romeo. In his eyes she had stolen the death scene, dressed in startling white with the limelight making her face glow almost angelically.

"I think I shall introduce myself to her as Romeo's friend and brother-in-law."

The Renos watched as Phil strode purposefully towards the girl he'd set his mind on.

"He could do a lot worse," suggested Marcus.

266

"*Hmm*, he could indeed," agreed his wife.

It wasn't long before Violet noticed that a young man was beating a path straight towards her with a *I will not be denied* look in his eyes. In those same seconds she liked what she saw, for though life in the Royal Navy was hard it had been good for Phil as he had put on some pounds, broadened out and now walked with the traditional rolling gait of the sailor. He was, without a doubt, a confident young man and handsome with it.

"Miss Grainger, you will probably not remember me, but I admired you from afar when I saw you play a memorable Juliet."

"I know you, you're Susannah Reno's brother, your papa was the awful..," she clapped a hand to her mouth and hoped she hadn't blundered too far from politeness.

"I agree completely with you, my father was nothing other than a tyrant and bully and were I to come across him now I should revel in giving him a good thrashing."

Looking at the well-muscled man before her, Violet began to feel a little weak at the knees, "I'm sure that you both could and would."

Phil laughed, "I'm sorry to appear forward, but I'm in the Navy and hope to enjoy a fine career in it."

"Oh, I'm sure that you will."

"The fact is though, I've not much time to waste on introductions and can only hope that you will forgive my forwardness in approaching you so casually."

She dipped her head slightly, "Of course, anything for Her Majesty's Navy."

"In that case, I would deem it an honour were you prepared to step out with me."

Violet smiled, for this young man was very close to being her ideal partner, "I should be delighted to."

Phil smiled broadly, his teeth very white against the tanned bronze of his complexion, "Perhaps we could arrange a rendezvous now?"

"I'm sure that my mama will be pleased to welcome you to tea. Perhaps to-morrow, if that is convenient."

Philip's laughter startled some of those actors bickering nearby to silence, "Aye, aye, ma'am, what could suite a Jolly Jack Tar more than taking tea with Juliet herself."

Violet nodded her agreement and smiled a secret smile, for with her friend settling for the much older; and obviously shop-soiled, Mr Vasey, her own capture of Philip Butterfield would place Millie's king in an inescapable checkmate.

*****

"Not far now," cried Hugh Doggart as he turned the pony trap on to the narrow lane which led to his uncle's house.

Lucy Greenwood shivered and wished that she had dressed more suitably for a winter journey. It had begun to freeze as they'd set off from Martindale and it had taken a long time to climb the hill to Kirkby, especially as the rain had frozen on the road and the pony frequently found it difficult to secure a grip. Shortly after that the wind had suddenly dropped and an iron grey sky threatened that worse was to come. Then it began to snow in large, heavy flakes which rapidly blanketed the fields and hedgerows and cut down visibility to only a few yards.

"Here we are," shouted Hugh as he eventually pulled up at his uncle's property.

"Thank goodness for that, my feet are just about frozen off," complained his passenger.

"It was a struggle, but it will be well worth it," he returned cheerfully, smiling to himself, for it looked as though they'd be blocked in for the night, the thought of which filled his imagination with dreams of the favours Lucy might grant him.

Almost as soon as they'd pulled to a stop the front door was flung open and a red faced Douglas Brass greeted them, "The way the weather's turned out I doubted you'd make it up the hill," he cried.

Arabella came out on to the drive too, she looked up at the leaden sky and suggested, "Perhaps Hugh should return Miss Greenwood home immediately, whilst the possibility of a safe journey still exists."

"There's no need for that, I wouldn't risk sending my worst enemy outside this evening. Besides which we've lots of rooms," returned Douglas.

Arabella nodded and returned a smile which was as cold as the weather.

"My mama may worry about me," put in Lucy, though there wasn't even the slightest hint of concern in her tone.

"Aye, well, that's what ma's are for," said Dougie as he shepherded the ladies inside.

As soon as she'd entered the house, Lucy was pleased to feel how warm and well-lit it was, so different to the parsimonious household run by her own mother.

"Hot rum punch, that's what the troops need," cried Douglas who at the same time nodded his order to a maid who stood nearby.

"It was very kind of you to invite me," smiled Lucy as she settled into the chair she'd been offered, which had been positioned as close to the fire as could be managed without the risk of causing flesh to burn.

"*Us*, you mean," pointed out Hugh.

The rum punch arrived soon afterwards and a series of toasts were proposed and drank to.

Arabella took this opportunity to look her female visitor over, seizing her up in one glance and considering how quickly she could be rid of her.

"Did you not introduce yourself to my sister and I recently?" she enquired.

"Yes, I did, it was on the sad occasion of your sister's funeral," returned Lucy, who was luxuriating in the both the heat of the fire and the warmness the punch was delivering to her throat and belly.

Bella nodded, "Of course," she paused pregnantly and then continued, "Though, were you not engaged to Mister Murphy at that time?"

"Yes, that is true, but it did not work out well as George was never able; or perhaps willing, to make up his mind."

"True love doesn't always run smoothly," Arabella's eyes never ceased in their cool assessment of Miss Greenwood.

Lucy had not failed to notice this careful appraisal of herself and smiled thinly, for she believed that it would take more than a vicar's daughter who had sunk low enough to marry a butcher to put her off her stride.

Douglas topped up the punch, "Christmas greetings," he toasted before raising his glass and taking a long swallow of the fiery liquid.

"I thought you'd all be at Blanchwell or Martin Hall for Christmas," suggested Lucy.

"Aye, that would ha' been the case, however, with poor Major Sturgis dead before his time and his wife in deep mourning for him, it was agreed that we'd all stop at home this year," explained Dougie.

Lucy was a somewhat disappointed, for the way Hugh had described it this party was supposed to be a rip-roarer, with food, drink, dancing, music and a pile of presents waiting for her under the tree.

Arabella continued to observe her female guest closely and was easily able to see that Lucy's aim was to secure the most advantageous partner she could. After which she'd have him off to the altar by whatever means were necessary. However, at the same time she could understand how it was that she was able to attract as many of the less discerning sort of males as she pleased. Though what concerned her most was the flinty, mercenary glint in her eyes without it being twinned by any hint of compassion.

"He's a such a nice boy, is Hugh. Mister Brass must be very proud of him," Lucy reopened the conversation.

"He is, but no more engaging than young Mr Murphy," returned Douglas, lightly punching the shoulder of Doggart, "is hat not right, Hugh?"

The nephew huffed and puffed a little, smiled weakly but made no reply.

By now the punch was having an effect on Dougie and he became a little impish, "I'm sorry that I have to admit it, but it was me who got the banns stopped. Murphy was in something of a quandary over his engagement."

If she was discomforted Lucy showed no sign of it, "It didn't work out for either of us – I've no idea why not."

"Georgie Porgie was never good enough for her," the strong punch was beginning to affect Hugh too.

"Aye, these things come and go," Dougie pointed out towards his garden, "just like the winter snow."

"Was not George led to believe that you were...," began Arabella, her eyes never leaving those of her target.

"That's all water under the bridge now, Bella, best leave it," Dougie interrupted his wife.

"George can believe or say anything he likes, he's nothing to me now," replied Lucy, presenting Hugh with a wide smile which promised much more than she ever intended to deliver.

Dinner was then served and course followed course with conversation flowing, though with little said to cause controversy or upset.

Three hours later, Lucy yawned politely, "I really ought to be taken home."

Dougie looked outside and could see that the snow still lay very deep and thick, "There's no chance of that, my dear, you're stuck with us for the night."

"Hopefully, the road will be open to-morrow," added Arabella, "though I'll have warming pans sent up to pare bedrooms at once."

"That's very kind of you, Mrs Brass," replied Lucy, she recognising that this would provide an opportunity for her to strengthen her ties to Hugh.

Dougie leaned back expansively and said, "Hugh and I will pass the port and talk men's talk."

Bella sighed, "That's the signal for us to withdraw, my dear, we shall depart and complete our toilettes."

Even though Lucy had no desire to indulge in small-talk with Mrs Brass, she understood what the convention was and with as much good will as she could muster followed her hostess into the drawing room.

"We may as well finish the evening in style," said Arabella as she sent for champagne to be served.

Lucy nodded and smiled as though she was used to drinking expensive wine every evening.

Once the champagne had been served and a few sips taken Arabella opened the conversation, "Now then, Miss Greenwood, as it's just we ladies together, what really happened between you and young Murphy?"

"As I've already said, we didn't suit each other and he could never decide whether he wanted me or not."

"Though he had agreed to a betrothal at some point, I distinctly remember my surprise when my dear papa read out the banns."

"I know that you and Mr Brass count George as one of your friends, but I'm sorry to have to say that Murphy let me down rather badly – especially as I was in a delicate situation at the time."

"Delicate situation? Whatever can you mean by that?"

Lucy dropped her head in pretended shame and embarrassment, "He took me by surprise, in my own bed, while he was lodging with my mama."

"I can't imagine George Murphy ever behaving in so oafish a manner."

"Believe me or not, he came to my room, and before I knew it he had taken my maidenhood," Lucy even managed to squeeze out a tear or two.

Arabella forced herself to nod sympathetically, but believed she knew exactly who had seduced whom.

In the dining room next door, Dougie was just lighting up a cigar and watching as his nephew poured port.

"This is a good vintage, I use the same wine merchant as Sir Charles himself now."

Hugh just nodded his agreement, he wasn't an expert and to him one port tasted much the same as any other.

"Aye, I'm going places and if you play your cards right, you can come with me," promised Dougie after he'd poured himself a further drink.

"Well, I am your *only* nephew," replied Hugh before he took a sip or two of port himself.

"Are you seriously courting this Greenwood girl?" Asked Dougie.

"She's a smasher, I couldn't do better."

Dougie nodded sagely, "You've got to remember that taking a wife is for the long haul, a bit of hanky-panky is fine on the way, but a wife has to have special qualities that young men don't think about once they've been smitten by a pretty face and a trim figure."

"Aunt Arabella is very comely too, so don't tell me you didn't notice that when you were courting her."

Brass puffed out a stream of cigar smoke, "I was lucky there. When my first wife died; sudden like, I thought I'd never find a replacement for her. Though, out of the blue, Mrs Lander suggested to me that I'd be welcome to take lunch at the rectory. I've never looked back from that time, though what Arabella ever saw in me, I'll never know."

"You're a successful businessman  and getting wealthier by the year, that must have had a bearing."

"Why aye, man, of course it had. You can't expect a lass; no matter how beautiful, not take her future standard of living into account when choosing a beau. It just made good sense to her and Bella has plenty of that and some to spare."

"I still think that Lucy'll do for me."

Dougie sighed, "Maybe, but you're not of age yet."

"I will be shortly."

"What'll your ma' say, she'll have been hoping for something more substantial than a pretty face."

"A pretty face and a luscious body to go with it will do me."

"Maybe, but remember, good looks fade with age, though character doesn't."

# Chapter Five

*(January, 1866)*

"Who on earth is that scrawny girl riding a beast which is far too powerful for her?" Percival Duncombe asked his sister.

Viviane sniffed before answering, "Her name's Catherine and she's Colonel Esprey's Yankee foundling."

"Really? What on earth possessed him to send her hunting – it's not as though she'll ever fit in."

"Fitting in or not, she's mounted on a fine hunter which she is keeping well under control. Besides which her habit is expertly cut and I'm truly envious of the quality of her riding boots."

"A rich American is she? Lots of dollars, perhaps."

"She lives at Merrington Hall which was built and extended by the Galvin family and enhanced even further by Esprey, who came back from India smelling of roses and rolling in loot – or so the story goes."

"So she's not at all related to the good colonel by blood."

"Much the same as we're only vaguely related to the Shaftos – it's a wonder they put up with us as often as they do."

"It's my eternal charm and ever willingness to fit in with whatever it is they wish."

Viviane giggled, "Apart from agreeing to marry that second cousin of theirs whom they tried to palm off on to you."

Percy joined in with her laughter, "Indeed, I had to stay away from Whitworth Hall for eighteen months to be certain of avoiding her."

"Weren't you urgently required to re-join your regiment? In Ireland, wasn't it?"

"Indeed, yes, lots of those vicious Fenian chaps over there."

"Though you've never actually visited the Emerald Isle."

"Oh, how I still mourn for sight of the Mountains of Mourne."

"In fact, you currently belong to no regiment."

Duncombe shook his head sadly, "Alas, this is true, I sold my commission as soon as the merest hint of the abolition of purchase reached me."

"Though you'll be spent up again by now, I suppose."

"It's the curse of being the youngest son of a youngest son."

"You do know of Merrington Hall, I expect?

"Should I?"

"It's within a very few miles of Whitworth and even closer to Martin Hall."

Percival nodded knowingly, "*Aha*, they're the ones we don't engage with – haven't since Sir Charles got himself a divorce. Shock! Horror!"

"Martindale must breed unorthodoxy, Caroline Bellerby of Blanchwell married an American in order to get her inheritance back and Jane Turner; who also happens to be the niece of an earl, is both a radical and married to a local nobody."

"There must be lunacy in the atmosphere here," Percy sniffed theatrically as he spoke.

"It is also said that Mr Turner once turned his hand to poaching."

"Though isn't he a Member of Parliament hereabouts?"

"Indeed and close to joining the government too, if the rumours I've heard are true."

"Then to sum up, these families may be out of favour but short of lucre they're not."

Her brother's smile and flashing eyes indicated his sudden awakening of interest in the scrawny American girl. He nodded towards her and said, "An unrelated foundling, you say."

Viviane smiled knowingly, "One of my solicitor's clerks is friendly with his opposite number in the office of Esprey's lawyer – Digby."

"Go on, don't let me languish in suspense."

"The colonel intends to make Miss Catherine his heir and he has already changed her name to his by deed poll."

"She'll eventually get Merrington and all that goes with it – though what about the current Mrs Esprey?"

"An actress with no background and no children of her own."

Percy Duncombe straightened his hat and said, "I think I'd better go and make myself known to Miss Esprey."

"Wait a moment, to begin with she's just sixteen and the story is she's very spirited if not hot-headed."

Duncombe fiddled thoughtfully with his moustache, "I see, though I'm sure I could work that to my advantage."

"I don't think you see at all, for she'll be no push over. The story is that she drove off seven or eight of the rough town toughs by firing the pistol at them which she habitually carries."

"Really?"

"The bullet she fired parted the hair of the leader of the pack, or so the tale is told."

"*Really*," he repeated, though this time with much greater gravity of expression.

"You'd best stay away from her, for she also claims to have recently killed three or four men, back in America."

Duncombe nodded, "In that case I'd best put on my iron underdrawers before I introduce myself."

Then they were interrupted by the howling of the pack and the calls of the whippers-in as the Master decided it was time to get the first hunt of 1866 underway – especially as the weather appeared to be worsening, with the rain containing elements of sleet within it.

Thirty or so yards away, Kitty was ignoring the weather and hadn't noticed the interest she was generating as her mind was firmly set on keeping up with the hounds and the leaders of the hunt.

Her concentration was broken as Duncombe rode up as close to her as he could and warned, "You'd be best advised to follow me, otherwise that damned wild creature you're on will throw you into a ditch and you'll end up covered in weed and slimy water."

"Would you care to take a wager on that?" Returned Miss Esprey who was sure that her mount would keep her well in the running to be in at the kill.

"*Tally-ho*," this cry came from some distance away and indicated that the fox had been spotted and the hounds were giving full chase.

Percival was about to explain this to Kitty when he noticed that she had left him far behind and was closing in on the master's group of elite riders.

"Nerve of the little bitch," he muttered to himself as he put spur to the flanks of his own horse.

However, try as he might his borrowed hack was not up to the mettle of his quarry's mount and he could make no headway towards her.

A hundred and fifty yards ahead of him the wind was streaming into Kitty's face and she felt that she was actually flying as free as a bird and more alive than she'd ever felt before.

Two hundred yards behind, Percy cursed and began using his riding-whip injudiciously.

"You'll never catch her until you're better mounted."

Percy turned to see that his sister was riding alongside him with something between a grin and a sneer on her lips.

"We'll see about that," he returned as he began to use his whip again.

Viviane laughed, flung back her head, used her knees to nudge her animal into movement and had no difficulty in keeping up with her brother.

Seeing this, Percival's face became red with a combination of frustration and temper.

"Told you so," she yelled and urged her own animal forward until she'd overtaken him.

Duncombe began to lash his horse furiously, the poor animal was nearly exhausted and began to buck and jump as it tried to rid itself of so inconsiderate a rider.

"Come on, you brute," he cried.

Just then Virgil Kent rode up; who had been sent by Lady Martin to keep a discreet eye on his pupil, "You'd best leave the poor animal be, it's had more than enough ill treatment."

"What business of that is yours?" Replied Duncombe harshly.

"I taught Miss Esprey to ride and I can say with certainty that even were you better mounted you'd still not catch up with her."

Sweat continued to pour down Duncombe's face and he raised his whip in temper intending to strike out at this common interloper, but as soon as he'd noticed

Kent's unwavering stare he thought better of it and pulled back on the reins.

"You have no right to interfere in the business of a gentleman," he sneered, "you're not a hunting man yourself – are you?"

"I charged with the Eleventh Hussars at Balaclava – doesn't that count?"

"A *Cherrybum*, eh?" By now, Percy had calmed himself down considerably.

"You've never been a cavalryman yourself, though, you haven't the seat for it."

"No, he hasn't," interrupted Viviane who had returned when she had seen her brother about to make a fool of himself again, "He was an infantryman. A common footslogger."

"There's nothing wrong with our infantry, ma'am," replied Kent.

"I'm sorry, I meant no slur," then Viviane giggled and continued, "Though my brother's ex-regiment is acutely short of battle honours – rival regiments have suggested that its colours should be an unadorned white."

Percy forced a smile on to his lips, "None of that matters now as I put my papers in some while ago."

"They say that his ex-regiments motto should be *Thou shalt not kill,*" Viviane giggled.

"That's a bit steep, sis," replied Percy.

Kent nodded and prepared to ride off in search of his pupil.

"Sorry, it's the hunt, I sometimes get carried away with the fury of it," Percival thought it best not to make an enemy of this man.

"Yes, sir, that's the way of it."

"I suppose you're a groom at Merrington Hall."

"I'm the butler at Martin Hall, sir, delighted to be performing favours for both my mistress and Colonel Esprey."

"Butler, you say," put in Viviane as she eyed closely the erect figure of Virgil Kent.

"And very fortunate to be holding such a position," the butler added.

"Are Sir Charles and Lady Martin receiving visitors presently?" Queried Viviane.

"The Martins are a very hospitable family, ma'am, and I've never heard of them turning away a caller."

Percy could see the way his sister's mind was working, "I've never had the opportunity to visit the Martins, perhaps the time has come to rectify that omission."

Kent tipped his hat, "I'm sure you'll both be made welcome," he replied before he urged his mount into a trot.

Two miles away, Kitty was watching as the pack finished tearing apart the vixen they'd caught and as the thrill of the chase wore off she wondered if this was really something she should be feeling quite so triumphant about.

The master was then presented with the brush; of what had once been a vibrant animal, and used it to daub blood on to the cheeks, forehead and chin of Catherine Esprey.

"There you are, m'girl, you're now a huntress and a damned good one at that, though make sure that you never become a thruster nor a hill topper, for they're both damned nuisances in their own ways."

His words were well received with loud applause and enthusiastic roars of approval for Miss Esprey, even though she was an American.

Kitty had felt quite distressed at the conclusion of the hunt but forced herself to believe that the death of the vixen had been a quick one, besides which she herself had been no stranger to cruelty in her short life.

*****

"It's very good of you to host luncheon for us and at such short notice too," Jane Turner greeted her host, Helmuth Schilling.

"Indeed yes," backed up Richard.

"We've had so difficult a year that my wife thought it was about time we cheered ourselves up."

"Absolutely," agreed Lizzie Esprey who was accompanied by Catherine.

Caroline turned to Richard, "I see you've managed to restrain yourself from dashing back to the capital."

"He was just about to leave for the station but changed his mind when I threatened him with a poker," laughed Jane.

"I was very surprised myself to discover that my brother wasn't attending to more important affairs," put in Marian.

Though her friend had laid no particular emphasis on the word *affairs,* Caroline looked up sharply and her complexion flushed, "Whatever can you mean by that..?" she began to ask, before realising that she had jumped the gun.

Marian looked startled, "Only that I know he's frequently away and is always busy."

Caroline mentally kicked herself and plastered as pleasant a smile as she could manage on to her lips, "Of course, I'm so sorry, my mind is troubled by so much at the moment."

Helmuth looked concerned, for he knew the strain his wife was currently under due to his sister showing no sign of returning to something approximating a normal life.

Noticing that this; for some reason, was an awkward moment, Elizabeth Esprey spoke up, "Anyway, we're all more than ready to indulge ourselves in a pleasant a social occasion."

"It's lovely here," put in Catherine, who had been especially impressed by the paintings on show at Blanchwell.

Caroline smiled at her most recent acquaintance, "I was born here and my fondness for it knows no bounds."

"You must have enjoyed a wonderful childhood," replied Kitty, her mind far away and long ago thinking of her own cold, cruel, miserable upbringing.

"We all need cheering up, there's no doubt about that," commented Amelia.

"Without a doubt," agreed Fred, who was standing alongside her.

"On top of poor Major Sturgis, the Reverend Lander was taken from us as well," added Marian.

"Not to mention Abigail, and in distressing circumstances too," backed up Amelia.

"Indeed, I still can't believe that Abigail died so suddenly," though Lady Martin had never enjoyed an affable relationship with her deceased sister-in-law she had the gift of seeing good in everyone, as well as always being able to forgive or ignore their faults and previous misdemeanours.

"At least the war in America is over and the slaves are free at last," put in Jane Turner with obvious satisfaction.

Richard grimaced, "Though it's a great pity that we aren't able to celebrate the Union victory with mounds of Zach Taylor's wonderful *patisseries*."

Jane's head dropped momentarily but she raised it quickly and returned, "Zachary died for the cause he believed in."

"He died of the typhus, hardly a glorious end," commented Richard flatly, who still hadn't fully forgiven his wife for providing the funds with which Zach had travelled off to his death.

"Nonetheless, he was defending what was *right* and would have regretted it had he not gone to serve," returned Jane sharply.

Helmuth Schilling could see that this topic of conversation needed to be changed, "Let's just hope that all the death and destruction makes some difference in the future."

"Cheers to that," put in Richard swiftly, keen to back up his host.

As they were speaking, Elysia Scott-Wilson, the Marchioness of Studland, made an appearance, coming elegantly down the staircase to join her hosts, "Sorry I'm late, but I went riding this morning and rode much further than I ought to have. On top of which I foolishly brought my least capable maid with me, it's taken an age to change."

"As long as you've managed to join us in the end," greeted Helmuth.

"When do you intend to visit us at Martin Hall, the children can't wait to see you," Lady Marian stepped forward as she spoke.

Elysia hugged her ex-husband's wife and asked, "Were they pleased with their Christmas presents?"

"Show me children who wouldn't have been delighted with the plethora of wonderful gifts you sent and in return I'll show you a parcel of ruined brats."

"I trust you've still a bed available once I say my farewells to Blanchwell?"

"Of course," put in Charles in as welcoming a manner as he could manage, him still finding it difficult to re-engage with his ex-wife.

"I wonder if I could burden you with my presence at Martin Hall for a while longer than I initially requested?" Elysia directed her request to Charles.

"Stay as long as you wish," put in Marian before her husband could raise any objections or excuses.

"Of course," nodded Charles as cheerfully as he could.

Elysia clapped her hands gently, "Oh, good, this is so helpful. I was expected back at Winterbourne on the thirty-first and hoped to go straight to Forest Hall, however, I've been informed that emergency repairs are needed there before the place is fit to visit again."

"I thought your sisters-in-law lived there," said Charles.

"They do, but apparently, my man-of-business, Mister Corsica, has sent them off out of the way to Bournemouth."

"A seaside holiday in January?"

"I'm sure they'll enjoy some bracing salt-air there," returned Marian who gave her husband a warning glance as she spoke.

Charles took the warning, nodded and smiled, "Of course."

"You may stay with us for as long as you wish, Elysia, the children are always delighted to have Warren with them," Marian was relieved that her husband had been so accommodating for she knew how little trust he placed in his ex-wife, always suspecting that she had some nefarious plot or another in hand.

Elysia beamed and then stepped close enough to Marian to whisper, "Before I come to you, I need to finalise some business in London – it will only take a couple of days."

"Of course, business is business, come and go whenever you wish," smiled Marian.

"It's a dreadful nuisance, especially at this time of year, but it must be completed and I'd prefer not to have Warren with me."

"Think nothing more of it," Marian smiled her agreement.

"Is everyone here yet?" Muttered Caroline stretching her neck and looking around to count heads.

"I can't see either Sarah or Grace," replied Marian who had taken careful note of the comings and goings.

"Of course, poor Grace losing her husband so horribly and both you and Amelia must still be distraught over the death of your papa," said Jane.

Just then, Caroline noticed that Mrs Sarah Nicholson had just arrived and was accepting a glass of sherry, "Sarah's looking forlorn," she observed.

"As a matter of fact, she's looking extremely glum and that's unusual for her," commented Elysia.

"Have any of you been to the pantomime yet?" Queried Caroline, hoping to shift the subject away from death and misery.

"It wasn't so good as the one we saw in London, was it Elizabeth?" Catherine found the courage to speak up again.

By this time, Lizzy Esprey had hoped that her charge would have begun to refer to her as *mama*, even if it were just for the look and sound of the thing.

"Kitty's correct, for nothing much went right with the performance we attended, it's not like Villiers to produce a dud."

"When I took the children, Mr Villiers' mind didn't appear to be very much focused on it," said Marian.

"He's currently obsessed with this idea he's had of the *Martindale Festival of Shakespeare*," returned Elizabeth, "Of course, the Theatre Sub-Committee will back him, but it will be something of a risk – and an expensive one too."

"A season of the Bard, five plays a week for... How many weeks is it?" Questioned Richard, who wasn't overly fond of the works of Shakespeare.

"Six or seven, he hasn't made up his mind yet."

The room suddenly stilled as each guest in turn became aware of the arrival of Mrs Gideon Sturgis, who none of them had seen since she'd received the news of her husband's death. She was dressed from head to foot in black, though, even seen through the veil she was wearing, her face shone pale and white as though it were being illuminated by the brightest of new moons.

Caroline stepped forward, her hands outstretched in welcome, "Oh, my dear, we're all so pleased you've joined us..."

She stopped speaking abruptly as Grace ignored her and came to a halt directly facing Catherine Esprey.

"I am told that you were present when my husband was murdered," her eyes bored into those of Kitty.

"Yes, ma'am, I was," she lied without so much as a blink.

"Are you telling me the truth child? I shall *know* if you are lying," Grace's expression was granite hard and unwavering.

Catherine slipped on the well-practiced expression of sincere innocence which she had used successfully on countless orphanage guardians, "I'd *never* lie to the widow of a man I continue to hold in such high regard."

For what seemed like many minutes, Grace continued to focus exclusively on Kitty's face, holding her eyes in an unblinking stare.

If the girl was unsettled, nervous or feeling guilty she showed no physical sign of it.

"He was shot dead cleanly?" Asked Mrs Sturgis at last, her tone softened and her expression more relaxed.

"He *was* and his final words were of you."

Another long, tense silence followed until it was broken by Grace who questioned, "You are sure of that?"

"On my mother's grave," Kitty's reply was swift and sincere.

Grace nodded sharply and then retraced her steps, saying nothing and glancing neither to her left nor to her right.

The room breathed a collective sigh of relief which was followed by a buzz of conversation.

"Well done, Catherine, dear," smiled Marian.

"Indeed so," put in Elysia, who then thought, *I couldn't have done better myself.*

"You've managed to do what I've been attempting for moths," congratulated Caroline, who was hoping that her sister-in-law might now be ready to come to terms with her loss.

Catherine nodded and smiled and then looked around to catch sight of her new mama.

As one actress to another, using only her eyes and a tight little smile, Lizzie Esprey saluted her recently acquired daughter.

*****

The Martindale Education Association was; as usual, exceedingly busy, though fortunately its full complement of helpers were present – led by Sarah Nicholson who was the only qualified teacher.

The newest recruit to the organisation was Catherine Esprey, who had quickly come to grips with the local accent and was especially adept at helping the dour women who had come to learn to read despite the obstructive opposition of their husbands.

Mrs Butterfield; who now looked years younger than she had previously, rarely missed a session and felt happier than she ever had before – especially as she was often supported by her daughter Susannah and had enjoyed several long meetings with her son during his shore leave.

"It's delightful to see the way this place succeeds, especially as so many in the town were sure it would fail," said Marian Martin.

"Including the schoolmaster, who should be doing everything in his power to help, for every person to receive a basic education is so *very* important for all our futures," nodded Sarah.

"I couldn't agree more."

Sarah was pleased to see that Marian was looking much healthier than she had during the previous winter, "I suppose your husband is going to whisk you away to the South of France again this year," she suggested.

Marian laughed gently, "There was talk of it, but I persuaded him that it was not necessary."

Sarah nodded, "That's some good news at least."

Not for the first time that morning Marian noticed how morose her friend looked, she not appearing to be the cheerful, jaunty companion she was familiar with.

"You seem to be deeply worried over something."

"The worst possible thing has come to pass," returned Sarah with a catch in her voice.

"You've received bad news?"

Sarah shook her head and dug into the pocket of her overall to bring forth a letter which she handed to her friend.

Marian looked at it quickly and said, "There's no postal address, apart from *Yarm, North Yorkshire*."

"No, I believe it is deliberately vague so that I shall be unable to reply."

Lady Martin nodded and then began to read:-

*Dear Mrs Nicholson,*

*I'm sorry to have to report to you that once again I have been let down by a <u>man</u>. As you know Jack did the same thing to me, making me with child and then running off. My current fellow, who never bothered to marry me even though he <u>promised</u> he would, has had me working my fingers to the bone to keep his house and be a nursemaid to his children as well as playing my part in other wifely duties. I was extremely grateful to you when you agreed to take in Harry and look after him when the swine I went off with wouldn't agree to take my own child into his house. However, as yet again I've been abandoned, I must make my own way somehow. I've <u>nothing</u> to live on at the moment apart from a pittance from the Poor Board. This means that I shall have to have my Harry returned to me so that he can make a living for us both in the mines, just as Jack would have had he known he had a son. I can keep going as I am for a few weeks yet, but it is my intention to visit Martindale on February 15th to collect <u>my</u> boy. I've already the promise of a position for him from another gentleman friend of mine. I would be exceedingly grateful if you would prepare him for my visit and have packed and ready such belongings as he may have.*

*Sincerely,*

"My God, this is awful," Marian's face drained of colour as she spoke.

"I'm distraught – just as the future is looking so promising for Harry," Sarah's voice caught and then she continued fiercely, "Harry's *mine*, he's *my* child and it's not far short of a crime to take him from me."

"He's such an engaging, talented fellow, my Bertie just about worships him and Drina insists that she's to marry him."

"He's exactly like his father, sometimes, when I hear him banging about the house I could swear that it *was* Jack returned to me."

"What ever can you do?"

"I can't think of a thing, Miss Goundry is his legal parent who; no doubt, registered his birth. As this is the case I have no right to keep him, no right at all." Sarah wasn't one for howling out loud, but at this moment she came very close to it.

"Will Miss Goundry take money, do you think – an allowance, say?"

"Though I've some savings they amount to no more than a few hundred pounds, I couldn't match the fortnightly amount Harry's mother will be expecting to receive from her son working as a collier."

"His pay to begin with won't amount to much and it will be some time before he can become a skilled hewer, like my poor Gareth or your Jack," replied Marian.

Sarah nodded her agreement and then said, "I'm pleased I used the money from the public subscription; organised by your brother, to purchase the house on Alexandrina Street – that at least takes some of the weight from my shoulders."

"I'm sure you won't find this a very helpful suggestion, but have you room to take in Miss Goundry? It may be a squeeze with two women and two children, but at least you'd keep Harry."

Sarah nodded thoughtfully, "Since Jack's mother died last spring, I suppose the house is big enough to accommodate four."

"Then that may be the way forward."

"It's possible, but would Miss Goundry swallow it?" Muttered Sarah thoughtfully after a few long seconds.

*****

Johnie Corsica flapped a hand in ironic farewell to the Scott-Wilson sisters as their train puffed away from Verdley Magna bound for Bournemouth.

"I should ha'been going to the seaside with them," complained Kevin O'Dowd, "them ladies won't make the right connection and they'll soon be missing me."

"I wish you'd had your neck broken rather than your jaw," returned Corsica sourly, for he was annoyed to have been saddled with so complicated and risky an undertaking as the removal of the corpses from Forest Hall, one of which had to disappear for good and all, whilst the other was to miraculously reappear from the grave. For this task he had recruited three men he'd used before and knew were capable of keeping their mouths shut.

"Flora an' Rowena'll miss me," O'Dowd continued to whine.

Johnie looked sharply at his companion who he knew from experience had very little sentiment in his make-up, "You've not been putting your cock where it shouldn't have been, have you?"

O'Dowd's face changed from its normal grubby parchment colour to a greyish pink, "We're all good friends, m'self an' them lasses."

A porter leaning on his barrow nearby coughed meaningfully for there were female passengers with flapping ears nearby waiting for the Dorchester train, which was due imminently.

"What are you staring and coughing at?" Questioned Johnie, quietly but belligerently.

The railway worker, nodded towards the waiting ladies and then picked up a nearby broom and began to sweep along the platform to put as much distance as possible between himself and Johnie.

"Time to get some work done, we've only ten days at best," said Corsica as he grasped hold of the Irishman's sleeve and led him towards the booking hall.

On a nearby bench, studiously concentrating on a newspaper, Constable George Dodds caught the attention of the porter, asking, "That him?"

"Aye, but he's the devil and I'd advise ye not to cross him – not unless you've got plenty o' mates with you."

"I'll keep that in mind, if and when."

"Just so long as you know, 'cos that boy will be no picnic."

Dodds nodded, "I'll see you all right once I'm done here," he promised.

The porter brought his fingers to the peak of his cap, "Thanks – but please *don't* mention my name to the fellow we're talking of."

"I won't, but make sure you don't go tittle-tattling to him either."

\*\*\*\*\*

After being reunited with the Cooks, George found that it was becoming an increasingly attractive option to dine at the pie shop. So much so that he rarely ate anywhere else – except when he was away on his travels of course. Though part of this was because of the his developing friendship with Clara Miller, whose conversation was both wide-ranging and interesting.

"Don't you think you ought to vary your diet a little?"

He looked up to see Clara standing beside his table and he wasted no time in pulling out the chair next to him for her, "Will you join me?" He invited.

"Why not, but surely you are becoming tired of my company by now."

This suggestion he denied quickly and they were soon served their usual tea-time fare.

A short while later the shop door opened and Charlotte Webb entered accompanied by John Losser.

Clara looked up and smiled at Losser and gave Charlotte a quick nod of recognition, whilst George ignored them both.

For a moment it looked as though Losser wished to return the way he'd come, taking hold of his companion's arm and attempting to turn her around.

However, Charlotte shook free of him and strode boldly to the table occupied by George and Clara.

"Hello Miss Miller, and how are you, George?" She greeted with a slight degree of hesitation.

Losser reluctantly joined them and stood shifting his weight from foot to foot, not knowing how wise it would be to open a conversation.

Clara smiled at Losser, "It's nice to see you John," she said, completely ignoring his companion.

Charlotte pulled up the chair opposite Clara and sat down, "It's no good putting it off, so I'll come straight out wi' it. I'm sorry. Sorry for what went on at *Brass Schilling.*"

"What happened there?" Murphy's ears pricked up as soon as his place of business was mentioned.

"This has nothing to do with you, George," intervened Clara whose eyes never left those of Miss Webb.

Charlotte sniffed and then continued, "I'm truly sorry about what I did back then and wish to make things right between us. That's if you'll allow me to."

They were then interrupted by the café's nosiest waitress, "I expect ye'll be wantin' your usuals," she said, her ears alert for any tit-bit of gossip.

"We're not together – never have been," replied Murphy.

"Hold on, George, gi' me a chance to explain," appealed Charlotte, pulling at Losser's sleeve at the same time until he reluctantly sat down next to her.

"Let's hear what Miss Webb has to say," put in Clara who had always found it more profitable to avoid confrontation if it were possible to do so.

The waitress; whose curiosity was well aroused, was happy to remain on station.

"You still here?" Questioned George with a glare at the serving girl.

"I'll fetch ye're usuals," she huffed before retreating towards the kitchen hatch, whilst at the same time nodding and widening her eyes at each customer she passed.

"I'm sorry, Clara, it was wrong of me, I knew at the time it was, but…," Charlotte began her apology.

"For what? Sorry for what?" Interrupted George, looking from face to face around the table for a clue.

"Nothing of any importance occurred," replied Clara.

"The fact is, I owed Lucy Greenwood a favour or two and she wanted Clara out of *Brass Schilling*," explained Charlotte.

"Whatever reason could she have for wanting that?" Murphy shook his head in surprise.

"Men are so dense," replied Charlotte, who then explained "it was because Lucy thought Clara was after *you*, and she was determined to have you for herself."

"In that case thank goodness Hugh Doggart came along," breathed Murphy more to himself than to the company.

"Anyway, Lucy wanted Clara away from the lasses' dormitory and got me...," at this point Charlotte's narrative dried up.

Murphy turned to his companion, "So that's why you left the workshop, that's how we lost one of our best machinists."

"I was going to leave in any case, I needed a change," put in Clara wishing the subject to be dropped.

"No she wasn't, it was down to me, I bullied her away and I'm not proud of it."

George scrambled to his feet and took Clara's arm, "Come on, let's away."

Miss Miller shrugged free of him, "What was done is in the past and I came to no harm through it – in fact life improved immeasurably for me. I've found a home here and I've made myself useful at the Education Association."

Charlotte shook her head, "Even so I'm ashamed of what I did – I've regretted it ever since."

"Please forget it, for you unwittingly did me a great favour."

"How can you bear to be so kind and forgiving?" George couldn't believe what he was hearing.

"Do we not all profess to be Christians," declared Clara, pointedly.

Losser hadn't said much but now he spoke up and once he'd begun he couldn't stop, "I did George great harm myself when he was held against his will at the asylum back at Liverpool, I was very cruel to him at that time and I wouldn't blame him if he never forgave me."

"It...," began Murphy.

John held up his hands palms forward, "But like Charlotte with Clara, George did the greatest favour that was ever granted to me. Then I was a bully and a coward too, I always picked on the weak and humbled myself to the strong – or those I thought were strong. Then I ended up here and was taken in by Annie and Geordie and as far as I'm concerned this is as near to Heaven than anywhere else I've been or can imagine going."

None of those present had ever heard Losser make so long a speech and so were too surprised to reply to him immediately.

Murphy had never truly trusted John Losser whilst they had lived in close proximity above the pie shop, feeling that he had no reason to. But now, he recognised what life had been for him and how it had made him the unpleasant youth he once had been.

"John *is* truly sorry, he told me all about it and that's why he came with me to-day – though not without some resistance," added Charlotte.

George wasn't a person to bear a grudge, "I believe I understand now," he said and stretched his hand across the table, which was grasped by Losser and firmly shook.

The entire clientele of the café froze into silence with just the occasional tinkle of cutlery to be heard. One or two female customers sniffed and dabbed their eyes with their handkerchiefs.

"All's well that ends well, then," put in Clara with a rarely seen smile crossing her face.

Shortly thereafter their meals were served and the party began to eat, slowly at first but with ever increasing gusto and conversation.

*****

As Inspector Roland Mason looked up from his desk he saw before him a very cheerful looking George Dodds.

"You've news for me, I suppose."

"Events are on the move at Forest Hall, I've no doubt about it."

Mason eased back in his chair, hoping that this would not be yet another false dawn in his pursuit of the marchioness.

"Forest Hall has been cleared of servants - butler, footmen, maids, gardeners, grooms – every damn one of them, set off early this morning for Bournemouth."

"And not expected back till later in the month," put in Mason.

"Yes, and that'll allow them plenty of time to complete whatever dirty work they have planned."

"Well done, at last it seems that we're making some progress."

"It gets even better, for I've actually *seen* Mr Mediterranean – he was at the station."

"You got his name too, I expect."

"Corsica – Johnie Corsica."

"You can't get much more Mediterranean than that," mused the inspector, then he closed his eyes in thought and muttered the name to himself several times, before he clicked his fingers and declared, "The first time I visited Forest Hall his name was mentioned by the servants."

"He's not a big fellow, but fit for anything, if you know what I mean. My informant warned me not to cross him and I suspect that his was good advice."

Mason rubbed his hands together, "I'll go upstairs and let the superintendent know that the game is afoot."

"There's a bit more. When I was taking my usual pint last night, after I'd had a busy day buying and selling corn."

Mason laughed and shook his head at the unlikelihood of this.

"I got talking to the local stonemason and he has been hired to bring his full gang to Forest Hall for a job that's expected to take a week or more."

Mason's eyes lit up, "When?"

"Not too definite, but the beginning of next month for sure."

"If the lady herself was there when Corsica begins his dirty work, that would make everything perfect."

"It's a pleasing thought."

Then Mason shook his head negatively, "She far too fly for that."

\*\*\*\*\*

Jim Watkins was crossing Waterloo Bridge to reach his lodgings by the river at Shoreditch when a hansom cab pulled up alongside him.

"*Hoy*, you, lady wants to gab with ye," hailed the driver.

"I don't know any *ladies* around here, but should I want one I'd choose my own, so fuck off and pester someone else."

"Have it your own way," returned the cabby who was then about whip up his horse.

"Please get into the cab, I have little time to spare, for I may have been followed," the voice which floated from the hansom was very feminine but, nonetheless, one which was used to being obeyed.

Watkins froze on the spot, for he recognised the voice as being that of the Marchioness of Studland, who was the most important client of his master, Mister Hill. He therefore wasted no further time in following her directive.

"Where to now, ma'am?" The driver's shouted for instructions.

"Keep driving around until I tell you to stop," returned an irritated marchioness, whose tone of voice then immediately returned to its previous softness.

A shiver of apprehension sped down the clerk's spine, for the idea of so clandestine a meeting with the marchioness unsettled him. He felt sure that the outcome of this could end in only two possible ways – good or; much more likely, *very* bad.

He looked up and was immediately hypnotised by the startling dark eyes of the marchioness, "My lady," he greeted trying hard to keep a tremor from his voice.

Then she replied soothingly, "Hill has told me that he holds you in high regard, Watkins, and I am sure that you would never disappoint nor let me down."

"Of course not, my lady," Watkins nodded vigorously to emphasise more fully his absolute sincerity.

Elysia smiled to herself, *men are so easy to manipulate*, she thought and then said, "You are very familiar with the ways of our Mister Corsica, I'm sure."

Again the clerk nodded, though at the mention of the agent's name a further tidal wave of fear sped through his body.

"He is a very dangerous man – you know that too, I expect."

"Yes, he's not someone I've come across often, ma'am, but I'm still very aware of that."

Jim Watkins was now certain that the result of this meeting could only be a negative one if not downright disastrous for him.

Elysia shook her head sadly, "I fear that poor Johnie is losing his mind."

Watkins doubted this, but thought it best to say nothing.

"I began to worry about him a while ago when he became concerned that the Scott-Wilson sisters were involved in some ludicrous plot against me."

"They're the ladies at Forest Hall who turned away the historian fellows?"

"Yes, Corsica's has it in his mind that there's some secret hidden away at Forest Hall and is worried that it will brought to light by the antiquarians, were they to get their way."

"The ladies you mention would never dare to defy you, ma'am, no one would," Jim snorted gently at the very idea of it.

"Then you agree that the notion of bodies hidden in a priest hole which may or may not exist is preposterous."

Watkins nodded positively, as he thought it the wisest response to make in the circumstances, "Even if a Papist hidey-hole was discovered, after all these years it'd be empty."

"Of course it would, but Corsica insists on believing the opposite, he truly thinks that everyone around him is plotting to betray him."

Again the clerk grunted, "I see, and he could cause trouble – even for someone so important as yourself."

"Precisely, so you realise now what my concerns are."

"You think he may do something drastic?"

"Lady Flora and Lady Rowena could end up with their throats cut as they slept – if he took it into his mind that committing a double murder was necessary to keep himself safe."

"That would be both awkward and embarrassing – two close members of your family killed," Watkins nodded as he spoke.

"I myself am in danger too," pointed out Elysia.

"I can't image that he'd ever harm you, ma'am."

"Not even to save himself from the gallows?"

This meeting was turning out to be worse than his wildest imaginings, thought Watkins, who eventually asked, "How do you intend to keep yourself safe, my lady?"

"I'll have to deal with Johnie before he has the chance to settle with me."

Jimmy could see the reasoning behind this but wasn't sure what she expected he himself could possibly do.

"Are you totally reliable, can I trust you?" Asked the marchioness with a slight tremor in her voice.

"Of course ma'am," the clerk felt that he could say no other.

"Then tomorrow you shall leave the employment of Mr Hill."

Watkins shook his head vigorously, "I can't ma'am, I'd be thrown out of my lodgings and likely starve…"

Elysia held up her hands in a calming manner, "Instead you shall work exclusively for myself, however, Hill must not become aware of this."

"I don't know about that, my lady…"

The marchioness' voice became much more business-like, "I suppose the reward of a few swift steps up the ladder of your career would appeal to you."

The clerk said nothing, though his brain was in a whirl.

"You wish to become a lawyer, do you not?"

"Aye, ma'am I'd like that above all things."

"Then you shall become one, there are members of the Law Society who owe me favours which I shall call in on your behalf."

"But I'm not even an articled clerk yet."

"That is a minor problem which can be overcome easily."

"What do you wish me to do?" James Watkins could not ignore the carrot which had been dangled before him out of the blue.

Elysia's voice took on a conspiratorial edge, "It is my belief that perhaps Corsica *does* have something he wishes to be kept hidden at Forest Hall."

The clerk's eyes widened.

"There is the possibility that he had something to do with the disappearance of my papa and Fraulein von Kleist."

"Why would he have had anything to do with that?"

"God alone knows, but are the actions of a mad man reasonable?"

"Then what do you wish of me?"

"I'm not entirely sure yet, but I think it's time the police at Verdley Magna were given a gentle nudge in the right direction."

"Should I go there tomorrow?"

Elysia's voice shifted away from softness, "Yes, but remember to keep any mention of my name out of it."

"Should I report back to Mister Hill."

"*Don't be silly,* you're never to visit Hill's office again. *Remember*, you now work only for me."

"To whom should I report?"

"I have extended my Christmas stay at Martindale for much longer than was previously arranged, wait until I have returned and meet me at Forest Hall, by which time I shall expect the whole affair to be over." replied Elysia who then passed to the clerk a soft leather money-bag.

Jim's eyes opened wide and he couldn't help smiling broadly as soon as he'd felt the weight of it.

"For any expenses you may need to meet," she said.

"Yes, ma'am," returned a delighted Jim Watkins who had never before been given money for so little effort. Or so it seemed to him.

Elysia then allowed her newly recruited agent to get down from the hansom, though at some distance from his lodgings.

*****

As Roland Mason struggled through the woods; which ran alongside the meadow which in turn sloped down to the rear face of Forest Hall, he roundly cursed both the undergrowth and the weather – which had been appalling for three full days.

His boots squelched depressingly through an endless morass and he was sure that they were beginning to let in water.

"Wet feet, and at my age too, that's all I need," he muttered angrily to himself.

Removing a long tendril of vicious bramble out of his way he came to where George Dodds was stationed to watch the kitchen yard.

"Anything happening?"

Dodds didn't turn around, keeping his eyes fully focused on the house, "Wagons coming and going, same as the last few days."

"None leaving loaded suspiciously, I suppose."

"Not a sausage, sir. Which reminds me that I forgot to bring a sandwich."

Mason pulled an oilskin wrapped package from his pocket, "Have mine, they're cheese and onion and only a day or two old."

Dodds wasn't keen on stale bread, but he was hungry, "*Ta'*, you sure you don't want them yourself?"

The inspector shook his head, "No, I just want this to be over with and our suspects in the bag."

Above them the twigs and dead leaves of a branch suddenly became so completely saturated that they sagged in unison and released a heavy shower of water which further drenched the policemen who were already very wet.

"Does it ever stop raining here?" Queried a browned-off Mason.

"Christ, I hate the countryside. What use is it, anyway," muttered the constable with feeling.

"It's nice on a sunny day."

"That's what parks are for. Give me a London park every time, a city boy born and bred, that's me."

Just then their combined attention was drawn to the arrival of a wagon, but this one differed from the others, for instead of being open to the elements it was fitted with a covered top. It then pulled up in the yard and the slim figure of Johnie Corsica jumped down and hurried to the kitchen door.

"That's him, that's Mister Mediterranean," said Dodds.

Mason's concentration on their prime suspect never wavered for a second, "I'm not so sure that I've not seen him before, possibly accompanying the marchioness, though he mustn't have registered with me."

"He's not very significant, that is until you look closely at him."

"I should say he would merge easily into a crowd."

The eyes of the policemen remained on their quarry until he entered the house.

"If only we had a few others with us," complained Dodds, after a while.

"I was lucky they allowed me to bring you along."

"Did you check all the way around the property?"

"I didn't bother to look at the front for I doubt they'll use it. If they did they'd leave one hell of a mess behind."

"Even so, just two of us for a job like this is ridiculous fringing on the ludicrous."

Mason laughed shortly, "Originally they wanted to send just the local sergeant along."

"Whose side are the top brass on?"

"God only knows, but I should think it's the one which plasters the most butter on to their tea-time crumpets."

Dodds sighed deeply, "I believed we were on to something here, but just the two of us can't pull anything useful off."

"The locals at the inn are suspicious too," pointed out Mason glumly.

"They laugh behind their hands whenever we appear."

"Corsica is bound to have received news of our arrival," sighed the inspector.

Dodds unwrapped the sandwich he'd been given and looked unhappily at it, "I bet he knows exactly what we're having for lunch too."

*****

Virgil Kent entered the library at Martin Hall and coughed politely, "There's a Mister and Miss Duncombe wishing to call upon you, sir."

Charles looked up from *Our Mutual Friend* slightly irritated at being unnecessarily disturbed, "Duncombe, you say?  Surely, they're not members of the Shafto family?"

"I was given the impression that they are, sir."

"You've met them before?" Charles' eyebrows arched.

"They rode with Miss Esprey's first hunt."

Charles sighed, "Then I suppose I'd better see them. Show them into the drawing room and tell them that I'll join them directly."

"It's too late for lunch, sir, and rather too early for tea," hinted the butler.

"Ask Mrs Cruddace if she put together a sandwich or two and dainties of any description for them."

"Of course, sir," nodded Kent as he left the room.

After completing the chapter in which an attempt is made on the life of John Harmon, Charles went to welcome his guests, after which he took a seat opposite them.

"I'm sorry my wife is not here to greet you, she teaches reading and such like at the Education Association in the town and I doubt she'll be back much before dinner."

"It is very good of you to welcome us at all, out of the blue, so to speak," said Percival.

"Complete strangers too, so we truly appreciate your kindness," Viviane put on her most winning smile.

"Indeed," added Percy, as at that moment refreshments arrived and were served.

After a few minutes of general social chit-chat Charles brought up the elephant in the room, "You're members of the Shafto family, are you not?"

"Yes," nodded Percy, "we've visited Whitworth Hall many times."

"Not to mention the Salvins at Croxdale Hall," added his sister.

"Then you are well connected to our local families, I see," replied Charles.

"Though we're only vaguely related to the Shaftos, and through the female line at that," added Viviane.

Charles nodded his understanding and continued, "You *do* realise that my neighbours currently refuse to accept invitations to visit Martin Hall, nor are they willing to receive Lady Marian and myself into their own homes?"

"We've only recently become aware of that," replied Percy.

"And were most surprised," added his sister.

"You see, I divorced my first wife – therefore, I am a *divorcee*," Charles made it as plain and clear as he could.

This made no difference whatsoever to Percy, but he shook his head, deepened his voice and replied solemnly, "A most unfortunate occurrence."

Charles' expression hardened, "You must realise that my previous wife did not oppose the divorce, the guilt; if you wish to call it that, was deemed to be hers."

Viviane realised that they had drifted into shoal water, "Of course, Lady Marian is noted hereabouts for her beauty, kindness and good sense."

"At the time of my divorce, Marian had been my housekeeper for some time."

"*I see*," put in Percy who did not see at all.

His sister shot him a look which expressed the irritation and annoyance she was feeling.

"Marian was my housekeeper, but she was *never* my concubine. Perhaps you'll mention this fact when you next see the Shaftos, Salvins or Edens."

"It was never our intention to suggest anything improper had taken place, we are virtual strangers here and have obviously misunderstood the situation," Viviane spoke softly and compassionately.

"That's right, we're all for neighbourly good will and friendship," supported her brother.

Charles now understood that his visitors had unwittingly poked a stick into a nest of wasps, "Of course, I see, for how could you possibly be aware."

"You are rarely mentioned at Whitworth Hall and we had not ridden with the local hunt before, so we hardly knew of your existence."

"We're from Berkshire, you see," again, Viviane supported her brother.

"Though we are very keen to introduce ourselves to all the families of the district."

"We are seriously thinking of moving here," added Viviane with a bright smile.

"Yes," added Percy quickly, "We hope soon to visit the Schillings of Blanchwell too."

"That's if they are willing to receive us," added Viviane.

"Not to forget Merrington Hall," supported Percy.

Charles smiled and nodded, for the idea of improving neighbourhood relationships appealed to him. However, he doubted that his visitors had enough in their shot-locker to influence people like the Shaftos who were equally as rich and important in the district as he was himself.

Suspecting that his host hadn't completely taken in their story, Viviane decided to change the subject slightly, "Didn't Mister Schilling serve in the recent war in America and return home wounded?"

"He did, but he's now fully fit once more."

Viviane turned to her brother, "As an ex-officer yourself, you'd be very interested in finding out about the war in America with someone who actually fought in it."

"Indeed," Percy immediately caught on to his sister's drift.

"Helmuth was a Captain in the 17th Pennsylvania Cavalry, though he rarely mentions his experiences these days."

"Then there's Merrington Hall – the Espreys live there I believe," put in Viviane.

Charles was by nature a sympathetic and friendly man and if he could help people out he would always do so, "I'll send a footman around with a note announcing your presence in the district."

"Very thoughtful of you, sir," beamed Percy.

"Indeed, we would be ever so grateful, Sir Charles," Viviane put on her most seductive voice which she herself believed to be irresistible to any male – and in this belief she wasn't far wrong.

"You must meet our local Member of Parliament too, who is also my brother-in-law."

"That would be Mister Richard Turner, the owner of the *Northern Chronicle*," put in Viviane.

"Yes, though it is actually owned by his wife, Jane."

Percy laughed loudly and rather coarsely, "Isn't she the filly who burned her corsets in public?"

Viviane gave her brother a sharp glance and stated with some force, "She was making an important protest against the enslavement of women."

"Of course many people found it very amusing, but she was making a serious point," supported Charles before he went on to inform, "They live at the Old Hall, Byers Green, only a few miles away from here."

"Then, with luck, we shall be invited to visit them too," smiled Viviane.

Two hours or so later the brother and sister pair were making their way back to Whitworth Hall where they were expected for dinner before they travelled south after breakfast the following morning.

"That went very well, I thought," said Percy smugly.

"You think so?"

"Yes… Certainly, I believe Sir Charles took to us immediately."

"Just because he is so obviously a very nice man, don't take him for an easily hoodwinked fool."

"Of course not, I know better than that."

"You'll need to if we are to continue to live comfortably on nothing much other than our wits."

"Our financial problem would soon disappear if you would make a determined effort to find yourself a wealthy suitor."

Viviane laughed aloud, "Where in Martindale; of all places, would I find one of those do you suppose?"

"You're not trying hard enough, God knows you've got the looks to turn any man's head."

"That would just suit you, wouldn't it? I do all the work and end up with a rich though tedious thick-head and you sit about waiting for the guineas to drop into your ever gaping maw."

Percival sighed heavily, "If only we enjoyed the full range of *proper* relatives, what a difference that would make."

"Have we enough money for the train tickets home?" This thought struck her suddenly.

"There's enough for one, so you can travel with the ticket and I'll disappear into the lavatory as and when needs must."

"God, I'm so, so tired of this sort of subterfuge," cried Viviane and then her face hardened, "If and when Sir Charles comes through with introductions, our first call had better be to Merrington Hall."

"What you'd saddle me with the scrawny, ignorant Yankee girl just so you can live in comfort?"

"Indeed I would, though I imagine that opportunity is unlikely to arise."

*****

"By 'tis dirty and dusty down the hole, the lads is complaining," reported Kevin O'Dowd.

"I pay them to get filthy and to keep quiet about it," returned Johnie Corsica who was a bit short of temper as the job in hand was proving even more difficult than he had imagined.

"There's enough bits and pieces of the dead t'turn a Christian man's stomach, all covered in rat droppings 'tis too."

"Shut up and tell the rogues they'd better get on with it or I'll shut tight the hatches over them and leave them to starve."

"I'm not complaining m'self," Kevin immediately set out to cover his own back, "I'm just tellin' you what they told me t'say."

"If you know what's good for you, just make certain that they do what's expected of them."

"Aye, well, I'm doing my best," the Irishman defended himself, feeling badly done to by his ungrateful employer.

"You have got the remnants gathered together, though?"

"Aye, them that's passed over are ready an' wating t'be shifted back into the light."

321

"Keep the lads hard at it, the stonemason and his gang are due in a couple of days' time and we must have the priest hole cleared before then."

"There's the plasterers next, not to mention carpenters, decorators and…," O'Dowd began to recite a long and depressing list.

"Shut up," growled Corsica, "and get about your business before I enjoy kicking you down the cellar stairs."

O'Dowd required no further encouragement and soon disappeared into the depths of the hidey-hole again.

Corsica breathed a sigh of relief as the only problem now was to find some place where the long lost remains of Sir James Hannibal Wright could be come across by a random passer-by, and in pretty short order too. He hoped that once Sir James' body was discovered it would be assumed that Marta Kleist had murdered him, perhaps in a lovers' tiff, or because he had refused to hand over whatever portion of his wealth he had promised her. To ensure this he would have to be certain that nothing at all remained of her corpse.

"A good bonfire and her ashes flung into a marsh would maybe do the trick," he muttered to himself.

*What to do with Wright though?* Corsica wondered about this again and wasn't at all satisfied with the list of possible options he'd come up with.

"Why should a corpse suddenly turn up out of the blue?" He asked himself, for this was a question investigators were sure to ask themselves – and as yet he had no feasible answer to this knotty conundrum.

Then he began to think about Elysia, whom he hadn't heard from since before Christmas when she'd gone off to Durham to stay with the Schillings and later the Martins too. Though he knew that she did like to have all of her children together on at least two occasions a year, her absence this time was longer than normal. Not only that but was much lengthier than had been originally planned.

"Not so much as a word from her, either," he screwed up his face in puzzlement at this, for she hadn't been in communication with him at all. No telegrams marked *URGENT*, no notes demanding this that or the other to be done yesterday. This was highly unusual and he began to wonder what her reason for this might be, for he knew that she had a motive for everything she did. Serendipity had never been her style.

"Is she ditching me? Am I losing her?" He asked himself aloud and at that moment his heart felt that it had just been snatched at by the wintry fingers of Jack Frost himself.

*****

Elizabeth Esprey was surprised to come across her recently acquired daughter in the library sewing together what looked like two pieces of rag.

"What on earth are you up to?" She asked.

"After my gallop this morning I found a tear in my second best riding skirt so I'm putting it right."

"My dear, that should be done by your maid."

"Oh, Sally was far too busy washing my stockings and smalls to bother her."

"Ladies don't repair their own clothes, it's just not done," explained Eliza.

"I'm very adept with a needle myself, having been slapped and punched often enough to ensure that I was."

"That's neither here nor there now, for remember you are a young *lady*."

Kitty thought for a while and then asked, "The Bayeux Tapestry was sewn together by the ladies of William the Conqueror's court, wasn't it?"

"I believe so," smiled Elizabeth who had no idea of the veracity of this.

"In which case they were *sewing*. On that occasion even the Queen of England herself wielded a needle too."

"Yes, but you're mixing the terms up, mending a skirt is *sewing* whilst the tapestry you speak of was worked as *needlepoint*, which is a different thing entirely. You see, embroidery is an activity ladies are *supposed* to excel at."

"I've not seen you so much as touch a needle," returned Kitty pointedly.

Elizabeth smiled, "I've never had the need to, my dear,"

Catherine shrugged her shoulders nonchalantly and dropped her sewing to the floor, "Whatever you say, *mama* , I jest follows your script."

Elizabeth winced dramatically at Kitty's deliberate Americanisation of *just*, but couldn't help smiling at the cool way it had been delivered.

*****

"I don't know if I can wait around for you much longer," declared Lucy Greenwood in a tone which she intended should illustrate her complete indifference to Mr Doggart.

"I'm doing my best with Uncle Dougie," Hugh appealed to her.

"I fear I'll be an old maid before you're able to make any progress with someone as awkward as he can be."

"You will wait for me, though, won't you," his face dropped as he spoke.

"I'm of marriageable age now and I fear being stuck on the shelf, facing a bleak future as an old maid."

He laughed; though nervously, "That can't possibly happen to you – why you're so beautiful if makes my heart glad every time I catch a glimpse of you."

"That's all very nice and sweet, but I thought our relationship would have been formalised by now," she sniffed.

"You know I'm desperate to marry you, I can't say there's anything I desire  more than taking you as my wife."

"You got *very* close to me on Boxing night, when we were snowed in at Kirkby."

Hugh laughed in pleasant remembrance of it, "The landing floorboards creaked so loudly I thought I was going to wake the whole household up."

"You woke me up with a start, I thought you were a burglar and that I was about to be...," she simpered, shaking her head shyly.

"If I had been a thief in the night I wouldn't have been able to restrain myself."

"I would have shooed *you* off soon enough, though."

"Why didn't you then? We got pretty close as I remember it," Hugh's eyes took on a far-away look as he recalled cupping Lucy's breasts and licking her nipples to hardness.

"You make me tremble with... Oh, I don't know what, whenever you touch me."

"Then wait for me, give me more time," he appealed.

"I can't wait for the promises of an immature boy to materialise, I haven't time to spare."

"I'm *not* a boy," he bridled, clenching his fists in frustration.

"I know you're not," she changed tack, "but your situation is so vexing."

"I love you, Lucy, I do, but my future prospects depend completely on retaining the goodwill of my uncle."

"Douglas Brass likes me, though, I know he does, I've seen him directing sly glances my way."

"Of course he does, any man would."

"Our real problem is that stuck-up, snob of a wife of his."

Hugh nodded his agreement, "He dotes on Bella though, especially now that she's with child..." he clapped a hand across his mouth.

"*Really?* Pregnant, you say."

"Yes, but I shouldn't have said."

"Well, well, *well,* so there's life in the old dog yet."

"Keep this to yourself, it's a secret for the time being."

"It'll be no secret once her belly swells."

"Look, if my uncle finds out that I've told you about it, that'll be me finished, he'll reckon I'm not to be trusted," he took her by the shoulders as he spoke to reinforce his words.

"Oh, don't make such a fuss," she replied airily, "I can keep a secret."

"Make sure you do."

"I will, how many times have I to say it, anyone would think we were enemies rather than lovers."

Hugh thought for a while and then promised, "Anyway, I'll do my best to straighten things out with Dougie, maybe he will agree to an autumn wedding for us."

She nodded, "All right, but be warned, I'll not be able to wait for much longer than that."

"I'll be twenty-one come October, so I'll be able to do what I want then."

Lucy smiled, "Aye, but don't upset your uncle – you'll still need him and remember, you are his heir – we don't want him to go changing his will."

"Never fear, I'll keep on the right side of him."

Lucy smiled but then realised that were Arabella to provide Dougie with an heir, then Hugh would topple from the top of greasy pole to the bottom of it.

"Tricky, risky business childbirth," Lucy smiled at the thought of it.

*****

Though it had been a bit of a trudge as the footpath was slippery and the wind had a bite to it, Marian was revelling in the freshness of the air.

"You call this air clean?" Complained Elysia, "There's more than just a whiff of sulphur in it."

"You'll soon get used to that," returned Marian, "anyway it unclogs one's sinuses."

"Is it much further?" Asked Elysia who had only agreed to walk after some persuasion over the breakfast table.

"We're nearly at the top and shall be able to look over towards Martin Hall."

"Impossible, we've trudged for miles, it must be well out of sight by now."

"Our walk so far has amounted to less than two miles," informed Marian precisely.

"The boots you kindly loaned me made it feel much further than that," Elysia raised her skirts and looked at the ugly footwear which she was sure was destroying for ever the daintiness of her feet.

"I'll wager they've kept you dry, though," Marian turned her head to shout back towards her companion as she halted at the summit of the hill.

"At least the ironworks are out of sight," commented Elysia as she arrived to join her companion, "though there is still the dreadful stench of them on the air."

"Look towards the bottom of the hill," pointed Marian, "the farmhouse where I was born used to stand there."

Elysia could see no sign of a building, just a tangle of railway lines and heaps of coal scattered untidily about.

"Not much to see now, is there?"

"Ours was a very happy home," returned Marian in soft remembrance.

"That was until Charles took it into his mind to sink a colliery."

"Though his intentions were good, as they always are," Marian defended her husband.

"Good intentions you say," grunted her companion, "however, I'm sure you're aware of which road is paved with good intentions."

"That is the one which leads to the Gates of Brass," muttered Marian, "according to the Bible, anyway."

"I think we may safely lay most of the blame at my papa's door for what came afterwards – and he showed very little interest in Martindale once he had created his monster."

As Elysia spoke, memories of her parents and her younger self filled her mind and she yearned to be transformed back into the innocent, naïve eighteen year old she'd been then. If only she could start all over again and make a succession of changes for the better on her way.

"Martindale's here now and has provided employment where previously there was none," said Marian as she looked fondly toward the roof of Martin Hall which could just be made out behind a fringe of leafless trees.

Elysia's mind was still very much focused on what had gone before, "I'm sorry I treated you so badly when I was the mistress of Martin Hall."

"I hardly noticed, anyway, it's all in the past now and my mother always advised me never to bear grudges."

"But I was so awful to you, partly because you were running the household far more efficiently than I ever could."

"You were only eighteen then."

"So were you," pointed out Elysia, who then took in the view of the town once more and continued with some feeling, "At that time I hated this place."

"So did I."

Elysia nodded and then explained, "I made my pregnancy an excuse to get away from it, then I refused to return and when I eventually did I saw immediately that my husband was deeply in love with you."

Marian took both of her companion's hands into her own, "I understand fully, for I played the part of the cuckoo in the nest."

"I was so jealous, which was silly of me as I'd never loved Charles myself, at least not in the full-blooded way you love him."

"I hope that you do realise that I was *only* the housekeeper – Charles and I never slept together until the divorce was finalised."

"I find that hard to believe, but it doesn't matter anyway."

"It matters to *me* and I hope that you will believe what I say."

Elysia smiled and nodded her agreement, "Yes, that would be typical of Charles, as he finds it so hard to stray from the straight and narrow."

"Though it is true that there were kisses, breathless moments together, but we never slept in the same bed until he had the *decree absolute*."

Looking into the clear, innocent blue eyes of her companion, Elysia understood the truth of what she had been told, "Of course, I would never doubt you," she nodded her head affirmatively as she spoke.

Marian then felt the need to hug her companion very tightly, for somehow she knew that Elysia was currently a very troubled woman. Though over what she had no idea.

"I've no friends, you know, apart from you ladies here in Martindale – it's ironic when I think about it."

"But you flit about the London social scene continuously, balls, first nights, fine dining, Ascot, Cheltenham, Henley Regatta, why your life must be conducted in a whirl of activity."

"Though it has all been *bought* and means nothing to me now."

"That can't be the case," Marian shook her head in disbelief.

"It is though, I have had to *buy* my popularity, it's all to do with money. Every London friend I possess has been *bought,* and if it was left to them none would allow me to pass through their front doors – nor the back ones either."

"Then you must visit us as often as you like and all our friends love their summer visits to Winterbourne."

"Do they? *Do they really?*" Elysia was both surprised and pleased.

"Yes, of course."

Elysia's face broke into a smile and her feet seemed to be aching much less now, "I cannot express how delighted I am to hear that."

## Chapter Six

*(February, 1866)*

Jimmy Watkins stood stamping his feet in the slush at the entrance of the Verdley Magna railway station hoping to find the London policemen who he'd been told were to be found locally.

"Next train's not due for forty-two minutes, I'd find somewhere warmer to stand if I were you," advised a passing porter.

"The waiting room is locked – even though there's a fire blazing away inside there," grumbled Jim.

"Aye, station master's took the key home with him – it's dinner time you know."

Watkins thrust his hands deeper into his overcoat pockets in the hope that it would prevent them from becoming frost bitten.

"I saw that you've got a good fire going in the ticket-office, can I not sit in there for a minute or two?" He asked plaintively.

"That's against company regulations."

"*Aw*, for goodness sake, show a morsel of pity."

"Aye, well, if you promise to pay me my wages when I get the sack, I'll think about it," returned the railwayman as he walked off whistling to himself.

A disappointed Watkins followed the porter on to the platform and huddled himself up as tightly as he could manage on a bench, wishing that he had remembered to bring a pair of gloves with him.

The marchioness had sent him to Verdley to make contact with the police whom she had been informed were watching the place. At the time her orders had sounded straight forward, but so far he'd had no luck. It had also been made plain to him that he should keep well clear of Mister Corsica who was also in the neighbourhood.

"That's all I need," he muttered, "Corsica after my blood."

Then he smiled to himself as he began to day-dream about the affluent future he'd been promised by the marchioness. She'd guaranteed that he'd soon become an articled clerk and only a year or so later be presented to the Law Society for induction as a solicitor. He continued to mull over these pleasant thoughts until he was brought crashing back to reality by the last voice on earth he wished to hear.

"What the fuck are you doing here?" His worse fears were realised when he found the slim though athletic figure of Johnie Corsica looming over him.

"Mister Hill sent me – to find you," Jimmy replied almost instantly and without too much of a tremor in his voice.

"Why didn't you come straight up to Forest Hall?"

"I don't know the way as I've never been there before."

"Didn't you think of asking someone?"

"There's been nobody about, it being such a pig of a day; except the porter that is, but he was not at all helpful. Wouldn't even let me warm up by his fire."

"Never mind that, let's return to my original question – why did Hill send you here in the first place?

Watkins shook his head, "Just to see how the work is going so that he can report to the marchioness."

"She's back at Winterbourne is she?" Corsica was puzzled by this.

"No she's not and has no plans to return 'till much later in the month – or that's how Hill heard it."

Johnie's forehead wrinkled in surprise at this, for it was unusual for Elysia to deviate from a plan of hers once it was in motion. On top of which, Hill had been given no part to play, in fact he wasn't even supposed to know about it.

"She spent the whole of Christmas with her first husband, Lord somebody or another, somewhere in the North," continued Watkins, spouting rubbish in the hope that he'd be left alone.

Corsica had come across James Watkins a few time in the past when he had visited Hill and it seemed unlikely to him the clerk been told of the gruesome goings on at Forest Hall.

"What do you know of the work being carried out up at the Hall?"

Again, Watkins shook his head negatively, "Not a thing, general repairs and decoration I supposed."

Corsica smiled, "Yes that's right, so go back to London and tell old Hill that everything is in hand and we should be finished here in a day or two."

"I'm not sure what I ought to do, Mr Hill said I was to visit the hall," replied Watkins, unwilling to leave Verdley until he'd made contact with the police.

"Fucking lawyers," these words were spat from Johnie's mouth, "just take the next train back to London and tell Hill from me to mind his own fucking business or I'll come and fucking mind it for him."

The clerk didn't doubt that the fearsome Corsica would do exactly as he had threatened and decided that he would keep out of his way at the nearest public house and hope to make contact with the police later.

"Have I made myself clear?" Demanded Johnie impatiently.

"Yes sir, I'll be off on the next train," promised the clerk, hoping that he wasn't betraying himself by displaying a guilty expression.

"Make sure you do," Corsica flung these words over his shoulder as he walked away.

Jim's heart was thumping, but he became hugely relieved at the sight of Corsica's retreating back.

As he left the station, Johnie was suddenly assailed by a deep feeling of unease. Disquiet was not something that he'd felt very often, but it was definitely there now filling ever more of his mind and he was unable to shift it.

"Why has Hill become involved?" Corsica asked himself as he approached the cottage of the stone-mason he wished to chivvy into activity.

He stopped in the road and began to mentally count to himself, firstly there was both Hill and the marchioness seeking information, secondly there were clerks arriving for no apparent reason and thirdly there were stories of policemen in the woods surrounding the village.

*What could they possibly want here, apart from answers to awkward questions about the priest hole?* He thought to himself.

"With luck the idiot clerk will ignore me and come up the hill," said Corsica to himself, "and once I have him there he'll soon be squealing out the truth."

*****

"This won't do at all," muttered Inspector Mason who had never before felt so cold nor so completely fed up.

"It's a disaster, we've nothing yet with which to make even the beginnings of a case," added Dodds.

"The wagon with the canvas top is still parked in the yard, though, so they must have some plan for it."

"Even if it's just to take away the empties."

"There are lots of those every morning," muttered the inspector, "they must have the stock of a brewery in there."

Dodds sighed long and hard, "I'm becoming ever more certain that we're going to end up with nothing."

"Be patient, we need to hang on for a day or so yet," replied Mason, who was keen for his final case to end with at least one conviction.

"Is this a bad plan or are we just plain unlucky?"

"The marchioness was never going to provide evidence against herself very easily."

"Why don't we just charge in and give the hall a good going-over? Why, I'll bet they have the priest hole open and ready for us by now."

"Suppose they haven't? What then?"

At least it would get us out of the cold," returned Dodds, hoping against hope that his superior would take a bold chance.

"We've no warrant, so even if we found half-a-dozen corpses which had obviously been murdered it would make no difference."

"Though at least we'd be doing *something*."

This idea of instant action appealed to the inspector for a short moment, but eventually he shook his head, "I'm an old fashioned, plodding policeman who knows that straying from the rules often leads to failure and sometimes to disaster."

*****

"It's happened at last," Arabella Brass spoke as soon as she'd joined her sister for lunch.

"What has? Wait, I know, Jane Turner has joined the Tory Party."

"Oh, it's far more unlikely than that," returned Bella as she took a chair and began to pull off her gloves.

Amelia raised both her arms and waggled her fingers in total puzzlement, "In that case, I've no idea."

"It's something earth shattering."

"Martindale has been voted the best town in the North of England for the viewing of *haut couture*."

Arabella shook her head, plastered a huge smile across her lips and stated simply, "I'm with child."

Amelia got to her feet in a flash and soon had her arms entwined around her sister, "That's so, *so*, wonderful."

"Douglas and I have been trying from the day we were married, however, we both soon settled ourselves to the idea that it was not going to happen."

"Wait, say no more until I have sent for champagne to be served. Helmuth and Grace should be with us to join in the celebration too."

Bella shushed her sister to silence, "No, Douglas wishes to keep it quiet at the moment. When we were married he felt sure that he was too old to squire children, so he's very nervous that it will go wrong and so wishes to keep it confidential."

"I see, then this is just to be between we two and perhaps mama?"

Arabella looked a little guilty and then said, "Our plan was to tell no one until my condition made it obvious."

Amelia couldn't help glancing at her sister's midriff which presented currently no sign of being overstuffed.

"Unfortunately, however, Douglas had a drink too many one night and it slipped out to Hugh."

"Ah, well then, that's all right for he'll know enough to keep quiet."

Bella shook her head, "I'm afraid he is often in the company of the Greenwood girl and I fear she will easily be able to wheedle the news from him."

"Greenwood?" Amelia looked puzzled, "Do we know her?"

"You may remember that she introduced herself to us after Abigail's funeral, at that time she was supposed to be the fiancée of George Murphy."

"Goodness, yes, I remember papa reading out the bans."

"Though they were never completed."

"She's a tall, blond girl, quite good to look at if it wasn't for a certain sharpness of features which warns any vigilant buyer to be wary."

"*Caveat emptor*, that's her in a nutshell."

"It seems likely that Miss Greenwood will not be able to keep your secret to herself."

Arabella thought for a moment and then said, "She has so far, though, and she does wish to remain in Dougie's good books for the sake of Hugh."

"That will certainly help to keep her quiet," nodded her sister.

"I hope so, for if it all came to nothing both Douglas and I would be bereft and wouldn't be able to bear messages of sympathy from all and sundry."

*****

Kevin O'Dowd reached the top of the cellar stairs and dumped a large sack on the hall floor.

"There she is, what's left o' the poor old nanny," he informed, "she always was a hefty lass."

"Then the priest hole is clear at last," suggested Corsica with a sigh.

"It is so, clean as a whistle – apart from the dust and rat droppings."

"You've paid off the other three and sent them on their way?"

"Just as you said, they were on the first train this morning."

Corsica breathed a sigh of relief, for it looked as though at least the first part of his scheme was working.

"You'll be wanting Sir James shifting straight away?"

"No, I shall see to him myself, but let's be rid of the lady first as she's the easiest to deal with. Use the covered wagon in the yard."

O'Dowd nodded, "Whatever ye say. I can manage her m'sel', even though she was never very light."

"Remember to weigh the silly bitch's body down, it must never see daylight again."

O'Dowd nodded his understanding, "Aye, I see, but where's she to go?"

"The wetlands, just up from where the stream enters the largest of the lakes."

"Crinkle Corner the sisters call it."

"Whatever they've named it doesn't matter, just sink the sack deep in the morass and make sure that it will *never* resurface."

Kevin puffed out his cheeks and exhaled, "Ye can't expect me to plodge up t'me knees in the middle of winter, I'll catch my death...," he stopped talking as soon as he saw the venomous look which Johnie was directing unblinkingly towards him.

"There are a set of waders in the garden shed, take them with you and dump the body as I have directed."

"It's getting dark, can we not leave her 'till the morn'?" O'Dowd whined and hung his head.

Corsica was about to deliver a slapping to his underling when he thought better of it, for it was vital that the nanny's body was dumped properly.

"Very well then, it's a job best done in the light, but make sure you're up and away with the larks in the morning."

\*\*\*\*\*

As he sat thoughtfully with a glass of cider in front of him, Jim Watkins was wondering what he was to do next. Of the policemen there had been no sign and the idea of bumping into Johnie Corsica again was becoming increasingly less attractive to him.

*Thought you were ambitious to be a lawyer? Fat chance of that if you give in now,* he considered to himself, also realising that were he to fail Lady Studland his chance of advancement would be snuffed out – probably for ever. Not to mention the fact that Hill would be bound to dismiss him as he had not shown his face at the office for several days. If the marchioness discharged him from her service destitution would soon be stalking in his shadow.

"I'd not have a reference to my name," he muttered.

Jimmy then took a long gulp of cider and decided he'd have to carry on with his mission, even against the advice and feelings of both a brain and body which were ridden with funk.

One of his problems was solved when he saw two men enter the inn, both of whom had *officialdom* written across them in bold, capital letters. Then he noticed that they were coming directly towards him and; though he panicked at first, he realised that they were the only people who could get him safely out of the trouble he was in.

"Mister Watkins isn't it?" Asked Mason politely.

Jimmy nodded after checking around that Corsica hadn't made an unexpected appearance too.

"How do you know my name?"

"Nothing can be kept secret in a village as small as this," returned the inspector who then sent Dodds off to fetch drinks whilst he took a seat and made himself comfortable.

"What do you want, though?"

"We found out that it was you who arranged the transport for the folks up at the hall to visit Bournemouth, you made a good job of that."

"I was sent down by Mister Hill – he's a lawyer, you know."

"He looks after the affairs of the Marchioness of Studland doesn't he?"

"She's a client of his – though he has others."

"Very few others I expect, and none of them near so important to him as the lady is," countered the inspector.

Just then Dodds returned and placed a tray of ciders on the table. He nodded and winked, "Mister Corsica not with you to-day?"

Watkins shook his head furiously, "I've nothing to do with him – why, I've only ever met him a couple of times back at the office."

"He's got you well frightened, I see," put in the inspector.

"With good reason," added Dodds, "he's vicious enough to terrify anybody."

Jimmy's shoulders sunk, "He is that."

"I thought you said you hardly knew him?"

"I don't, he does some work for the marchioness and; as I've said, he sometimes visits Mr Hill."

"What's he doing at Forest Hall, he seem to be very busy up there?" Questioned Dodds.

"Yes," added Mason, "there's stone-masons, builders, carpenters, painters and decorators, all ready to go in, queueing up one after the other."

"Maybe the marchioness is expecting a visit from the Tsar of all the Russias," added the constable.

"I shouldn't be surprised if it were Queen Victoria herself," Mason nodded his agreement.

"I know nothing about it, I just follow orders," Watkins shook his head vigorously.

"What are your orders? Not secret, are they?"

Watkins swallowed hard and explained, "The marchioness wants to know how the work is progressing, she had planned to visit Forest Hall at the end of this month but has been delayed at some place in County Durham,"

The clerk spoke of Durham as though it was sited trembling somewhere at the edge of the Arctic ice pack.

Mason took a long sip of cider and then came to the point, "We're not interested in you, Jim, we know you've done nothing wrong. It's Corsica we want and whoever it is who pulls his strings for him."

"Then that must be Hill," suggested Watkins, hoping to lay a false trail.

"Don't take me for a fool, at the bottom of this Hill is just another counter on the board – a pawn like yourself."

"I'll have nothing to do with anything illegal," cried the clerk plaintively, "I intend to become a solicitor."

"You're as clean as a whistle," soothed Dodds, "just another paper shuffler, but out of your depth with the company you're keeping."

"That's right, you're right about that," agreed Jimmy quickly.

"I'll tell you what," offered the inspector, "I'll make it as plain as I can. Perhaps your remember Sir James Hannibal Wright?"

"The father of the marchioness, you mean."

"Yes, he disappeared, out of the blue, went off with the family nanny and neither of them were ever seen again," Dodds explained.

"However, we feel certain that they were murdered," added Mason.

"By Corsica you think? He's your suspect, isn't he?"

Mason nodded, "He is and we believe that the bodies we need to find to prove it were shut away by him at Forest Hall."

"Then why is he making all this fuss and effort now?"

"It's probably to do with  a couple of  local historians who believe that there is a priest hole hidden somewhere within the building."

Jim blinked rapidly and shook his head in disbelief, "I can't see what that has to do with it."

"It has a lot to do with it if this hidey-hole does exist and were the bodies of Sir James and Miss Kleist to be discovered there," explained Dodds.

"The evidence would have to be removed before any inspection of the priest hole began, you mean," Watkins caught on.

"Exactly, which also explains the reason for the exodus of the household to Bournemouth," added Dodds.

"If we can catch Mister Corsica in possession of the corpses the case will be proved," stated the inspector.

"Then Mr bloody Johnie Corsica will never trouble anyone again," Dodds backed up his superior with some relish.

"Corsica will hang, you think," it was obvious that the clerk was pleased with the idea of this.

"Not to mention any others who may have been part of the murder plot," added Dodds.

"I see," muttered Watkins.

There was a long, pregnant pause and then Mason suggested, "Perhaps you would care to call at Forest Hall tomorrow and let us know what the state of play is up there."

It then looked to both policemen that Jimmy's face had turned green and he seemed about to vomit into his cider.

"We've got to go in with a warrant before the craftsmen arrive, but not too late in case the bodies have gone," explained Mason.

"Oh, no, I couldn't. I wouldn't dare go there."

"Don't worry, we'll be nearby keeping an eye on things," promised Dodds.

"Yes, should anything goes amiss we'll come charging in like the fire brigade on Guy Fawkes night," promised the inspector.

Watkins was sure that his stomach had developed within it a substantial lump of granite which was rumbling upwards into the centre of his heart, where it then lay heavy and immovable.

"I've not the nerve for it."

"Come on, you can do it, it's your public duty," encouraged the constable.

Just as he was about to refuse again he remembered that he was following the orders of the marchioness herself. The policemen were offering exactly what she wanted and he couldn't let her down, not if he wished to become one of the richest lawyers in the land.

"Corsica's a swine, I've heard that he has a lot to account for, some folk say he's insane."

"Who told you that? Asked Dodds.

"The marchioness I expect," commented Mason.

"Oh, no, I doubt she's noticed, she doesn't have much to do with him these day – or so Mr Hill says," Watkins gabbled.

"I see, so you *do* believe that our Johnie is up to no good at Forest Hall."

Watkins dropped his head, "He could be, I suppose."

"In which case you're just the chap to keep us up to date with what's happening there," suggested Mason.

"Yes, it is always sensible to help the police with their enquiries," supported the constable.

"In fact it's your public duty," pointed out Mason.

Meeting with Corsica again was the last thing Jimmy Watkins wished to do, but thoughts of his future advancement spurred him on and even though he could feel bile rising in his throat, he nodded his agreement.

*****

Sarah Nicholson was pleased that she had arranged for Elinor to visit one of her playmate's in order to keep her out of the way before the arrival of a most unwelcome visitor.

"Why is my mother coming to visit?" Enquired Harry, in a suspicious tone of voice, "She's never bothered before, why, I've never even received a birthday card from her."

"We'll know soon enough," returned Sarah with the widest smile she could manage in the circumstances.

"I've noticed you've been very downcast lately."

"Far too much to do and too little time to do it in," she replied airily.

Just then she heard the knock at the front door that she had so dreaded, "Here's your mama now," she guessed and then went off and soon brought her visitor into the front room.

"Come, kiss your mama," ordered Janet Goundry as soon as she saw her son.

Harry didn't move nor did his expression show any pleasure at seeing his mother for the first time in some years.

"Please do as your parent had requested," asked Sarah, her voice soft and encouraging.

With reluctance, Harry did as he was told, though when his mother moved to hug him he pulled away and took a seat as close to Sarah as he could get. His mind now certain that this was soon to become the blackest day of his life.

"I've come to take you away with me," Janet wasted no time in getting to the point of her visit.

"I shan't go."

"Oh, *shan't* is it? Very larty-da indeed, but it won't do you much good once you're labouring down the pit."

If Harry was shocked by this he showed no sign of it, instead he looked towards Sarah, "Is it true that I must go? Leave here, leave yourself and Elinor?"

Sara nodded, "As you are aware, this lady is your *true* mama – she *is* what I can never be."

"She deserted me though and only wants me back now because I'm old enough and tough enough to earn money for her."

"Whatever it is I want, you are still *my* son, legally you belong to me," replied Janet sharply.

"I'll not go, you'll have to drag me away and I doubt you'll have the strength to carry me off."

"The police will bring you out of here and put you on the train with me," Janet's eyes narrowed, her lips became thinner and her eyes reduced to slits.

Sarah held up both hands in a gesture of pacification, "Harry, you must do as your mother wishes – we have talked about you taking up a career in law, and it is impossible to proceed with that by ignoring what is legal to suit yourself."

"Mrs Nicholson's right," added Janet, crossing her arms across her chest.

"Though I think I have a solution," put in Sarah softly.

"You'll pay me?" Janet sounded quite keen on the idea of this.

Sarah shook her head negatively, "No, I couldn't afford to do that."

Miss Goundry tossed her head in derision, "Then I must bring him away."

"Listen to what she has to say," begged Harry who had been following events closely.

"It would be something of a squeeze," began Sarah slowly, "but why don't you stay here, we could all live together."

"I thought you had no money?" Replied Janet with a sardonic smile.

"I've enough to feed you until Harold is able to support himself."

"Yes, I promise to work like billy-oh to do it," cried Harry.

"Though I'll have no money of my own – the Poor Board Guardians will stop the pittance it pays me now," pointed out Janet.

"However, you'll have a comfortable place to live with your son and be well fed," encouraged Sarah.

"What about clothes and my other necessaries?"

"I can manage a little more for those."

"You could get a job too, maybe at *Brass Shilling,*" suggested Harry, who as he looked at his mother's expression realised that Sarah's proposal was falling upon stony ground.

"Yes, I'm sure I could persuade Mrs Schilling to help find you a situation there," added Sarah.

"No it won't do, I have already taken up a position in a gentleman's house and he has promised that he can get a job for Harry too, at one of the collieries down by the Tyne."

Young Nicholson was on the verge of running away, hiding in the woods and waiting there until his mother had gone. Though he soon realised that it was no good, for Sarah wouldn't break the law or do anything which was wrong no matter how much it might affect her personally. He would have to obey his mother and hope that one day he could return to Martindale, to the only home he'd had in which he had been both cared for and loved.

"Then I'd best get my things together," he said in a dead-pan voice as he headed for the staircase and the room he realised would soon be no longer his.

*****

Johnie Corsica watched as O'Dowd carried off what was left of Marta Kleist, he hoping that he would never set eyes on her again.

"Just the main course to swallow," he muttered to himself as his gaze shifted to the sack which contained the remains of Sir James Wright. His plan was to ride off with the corpse to the wild coast of North Devon and once there deposit it on the seashore. Where he hoped to make it appear that it had been recently washed ashore. After that, whether it was discovered or not, he didn't care, he just wished for this whole damnable affair to be over.

He'd just settled down in the kitchen to make himself a sandwich and brew a pot of coffee when he heard footsteps in the hallway above his head. He checked that his knife was to hand and also that his revolver was in his jacket pocket, before he went to discover who his visitor was.

"You there, Mister Corsica," the voice was that of Jimmy Watkins.

"Yes, stay where you are, I'm coming up."

"I can see that the works are complete so I'll just get on my way and have a report on Mister Hill's desk on Monday morning."

"I thought I told you to bugger off back to Hill yesterday," said Corsica in a low and threatening voice."

"I'm caught between two fires here, Mr Corsica – I'd happily do as you ask but what about Mr Hill, he's my boss and he might…"

"Are you sure it was Hill who ordered you here?" Johnie cut him off prematurely with a question of his own.

"Of course, who else would have?" Replied Jimmy, trying hard not to stutter.

"Could it have been the Marchioness of Studland herself by any chance?" Corsica raised his eyebrows and put on a knowing look.

Watkins shook his head vigorously and emitted a nervous little laugh, "I've only seen her twice in my life – both times at Hill's it was - I don't think she would recognise me if she tripped over me in the street."

"She's a devious bitch though, and you're just the sort of fool she'd pick for a job like this."

"Job like what?" Jim tried to put on a bewildered expression.

"Putting the police on to me."

"Come on, Mr Corsica, she'd never ask me for help with anything like that."

Johnie could easily see that the clerk was lying, he walked towards him until his own nose was nearly touching that of his visitor.

Watkins uttered a further short, anxious giggle, immediately after which Corsica punched him hard in the solar-plexus.

"Don't lie to me, unless you want more of the same."

Jimmy rolled on to the floor nursing his bruised and aching stomach.

Johnie took a step forward and gave the ribs of the fallen man a vicious kick, which he then repeated twice more.

Watkins howled, though managed to creep on to his knees, his arms and hands trying to soothe the pains in his belly and ribcage.

Corsica then rolled his victim over and forced him down again before stamping hard on his ankle.

The clerk began to shed tears, his face twisted with both pain and fear.

"I'll become an awful lot rougher once I've got you trussed up in the cellar, I could keep at you for hours on end. Once I'd finished your body would never be found, it would be as though you'd never existed," threatened Corsica icily.

Despite the pain he was in, Watkins struggled to his knees and clasped his hands in front of him as though in supplication, "I don't know anything...," he began surprised at his own bravery.

Corsica took out his knife and waved it threateningly, "In that case I shall make a beginning here and now by slitting open your nose and then carving off the fleshy parts."

The eyes which bored into those of James Watkins showed no sign of compassion nor of mercy, they appeared to him like those of a dead man, a sleepwalker who no longer connected to any of the finer human emotions.

"She did send me... The marchioness... She sent me," he cried.

"For what reason?"

"I was to hint to the police that the death of her father was of your doing and his body lay in the priest hole."

"Have you spoken to the police?"

Watkins shook his head negatively and replied quickly, "No, I wouldn't..."

"I suspect you have and I shouldn't be surprised if the peelers didn't arrive imminently."

"All right, yes, they're right behind me, so you'd best leave me be," by this time Jim was snatching at straws.

Johnie grabbed Watkins by the scruff of his neck and dragged him along the floor, "In which case we shall fix up a deadly, though interesting, surprise for them."

*****

"He's been inside for longer than I thought he would be," said Dodds as he anxiously scanned the kitchen yard of Forest Hall for sight of Jimmy Watkins.

"I didn't believe he'd go in at all," returned Mason, "I expected him to be still standing trembling at the gateway."

"Just goes to show that there's more to him than we thought."

The inspector took out his pocket watch, "He's been in there for nearly half-an-hour."

"All he had to do was assess what was happening and come out again."

"That shouldn't have taken him any longer than ten minutes," calculated the inspector.

"Maybe Corsica has already gone."

"In which case our Jim would have reappeared ages ago," said Mason as he took another look at his pocket-watch.

"You're thinking we should go in now?"

"Yes, come on," cried the inspector as he clambered over the fence into the adjoining meadow and began to run down the slope towards the rear of the hall.

Dodds wasted no time in following his boss but wished that they had been allowed to bring firearms with them.

*****

Corsica smiled grimly to himself as he inspected the helpless body of Jimmy Watkins, "I wouldn't like to be you," he remarked casually.

"Come on Mister Corsica, I've done you no harm – it's all to do with the marchioness, you know that."

Johnie was now well aware that he had been betrayed, indeed, he had suspected for some time that Elysia was tiring of him. He'd begun to recognise that his time with her was coming to an end when she'd insisted that he couple with that awful old mare Abigail Turner. It was also obvious now that it was her intention that he; and he alone, should take the blame for the murder of her father.

"Silly, bitch, she ought to know by now that I'll never give her up," he shook his head as he spoke to himself, "I just can't."

Watkins watched and listened and became sure that Corsica was on the verge of insanity, which made him even more frightened than he'd been previously – were that possible. He began to tremble which made his position even more precarious.

"Keep still, or else you'll be sorrier than you've ever been before in your life."

"Please, *please* don't do anything more to me," cried Jimmy who was becoming certain that this was to be his last day on earth.

Corsica heard rapid, multiple footsteps coming from the kitchen area, "Don't worry, help is at hand," he smiled.

Before long a young policeman pelted into the hallway, but then came to an immediate stop.

"Jesus, look at the state of him," cried Constable Dodds as his boss arrived to stand next to him.

Still breathing heavily after his run, Mason was immediately struck by the import of the scene in front of him.

A few yards away Jim Watkins was standing on a chair with a noose around his neck, the rope of which stretched upwards until it was lost from sight somewhere on the floor above.

Beside the chair, with his foot poised to kick it stood a smiling Johnie Corsica.

"Took your time, gentlemen, poor old Jimmy's been waiting here for some while."

Dodds was about to burst forward to help but was restrained by his superior, "Let's hear what Mr Corsica has to say."

"I've only a couple of questions for you," began Johnie, "firstly are you mounted or on foot?"

"Our funds won't stretch to horses, just to railway tickets."

"Third class ones too, I suspect," laughed Corsica.

"And your other question?" Queried Mason.

"Do you want this fool to live or die?" Johnie gave the chair upon which Watkins stood a gentle shove.

"*Aghh*, whatever he wants let him have it," begged the solicitor's clerk as the noose began to bite into his neck, which had already been rubbed raw.

"Never mind the dramatics, I've got your message clearly enough," called Mason.

"You'll have a set of manacles on you, I expect."

Mason nodded, "What do you want me to do with them?"

"Shackle your underling to the bannister rail over there and throw the key way down the cellar steps."

Mason had no other choice and so did exactly as he had been instructed, "What now?" He asked.

"Just this," laughed Corsica who gave the chair a vicious kick which sent it crashing along the floor and left Watkins swinging through the air like a pendulum.

Mason dashed forward and grappled with the hanging man's legs, using them to heave his body upwards to save him from strangulation.

"Cheerio, and best of luck," called Corsica as he walked leisurely away towards the front doors where his horse was saddled and waiting for him..

"For God's sake don't drop me," cried Watkins in panic.

Inspector Mason was already out of breath after his run across the meadow and he didn't know for how long he could bear the full weight of Corsica's victim.

As this was happening, a few yards away Dodds was trying to pull the banister rail free of its supports to affect an escape.

"Good Jesus, get me out of this," screamed Jimmy who was becoming redder in the face with every few seconds that passed.

"Calm down, you're safe for the moment, there's no need for panic, it'll do you no good."

"You're not the one hanging with a noose around your neck."

"Just listen, I need to retrieve the chair, but to do it I'll have to let go of you for a short while."

"*Agh*, no don't, I'll choke…,"

"I'll let you down gently – now settle yourself."

"Close your eyes and think of England," called Dodds.

"That's easy for you….," Jimmy's words came to a strangulated end as the rope began to bite into his neck again.

"Believe me, I know for a fact that it takes longer than a few seconds to strangle someone, so just don't panic and keep very still."

"Do as the inspector has instructed and it'll work out fine," shouted Dodds.

Mason's plan took only the few seconds to work, and before long Watkins was safely standing on the seat of the chair once more.

"What about me?" Asked George Dodds.

Mason searched in his pockets and brought out a set of keys, "I'll give you some good advice, never set off with handcuffs without bringing a spare key, it saves all sorts of embarrassment."

Within a few of minutes of this, the constable had been freed and a very shaky Jim Watkins was pleased to be standing on *terra firma* once more.

"Corsica, will be well away by now," suggested Dodds.

Mason glanced around until his eyes focused on a sack which lay near him. He quickly tore open its bindings and informed, "There appears to be what's left of a body in here."

"Is it recognisable?" Queried the constable.

"Hardly, but my bet is it's that of Sir James himself."

"No sign of the Nanny?"

"It's possible that what little was left of her has already been removed, the covered wagon had gone by the time we arrived this morning."

Dodds shook his head in anger and frustration, "How in God's name could just the two of us be expected to pull off a job the size of this one?"

"It was always impossible, Corsica could have moved a hundred bodies and we'd have been none the wiser."

As the policemen were talking, Kevin O'Dowd blundered into the kitchen and began clambering the stairs, "Hello, *Hello*, anyone about? I've found a set of keys down here."

On hearing this the two policemen moved silently out of sight.

The first thing O'Dowd saw on reaching the hall was Watkins, whom he'd never seen before. Then his eyes focused on the opened body-bag and he immediately stepped backwards as quietly as he could, hoping to achieve a swift, unobtrusive departure.

"Going somewhere?" These words were expressed in a friendly tone of voice as Inspector Mason appeared from behind a marble column.

"No, I live here, I'm a guest of Lady Flora and her sister."

"What's your name?"

O'Dowd was startled as PC Dodds appeared from behind him.

"Why, I'm just plain Kevin – Kevin O'Dowd."

"Who's Corsica?" Asked Mason still in a companionable manner.

"Corsica?" O'Dowd shook his head, "Who do you mean?"

"If you really do live here you'll know fine well who I mean."

"*Ah,* Oh, yes, ye're meaning Johnie – I generally know him as Johnie."

"Well, then, who is Johnie?"

"He's the agent of the Marchioness of Studland, she what owns this place."

"You've been working with him here, shifting corpses," accused Dodds who couldn't wait to take part in the questioning of a man who was so patently part of this criminal conspiracy.

Kevin smiled as if at the ridiculousness of this assertion, "I've just come back from Bournemouth where I've been checking that the ladies are faring well on their holiday."

Mason smiled and sighed wearily, he pointed towards the body-sack, "Look, we know you didn't do this killing for we're pretty sure that Corsica did. Now, save yourself a lot of bother and tell us what you know of this fellow everyone seems to be so frightened of."

Kevin looked closely at the hand he'd been dealt and decided that the time had come for as honest a confession as he dared to give, keeping in mind that as far as he knew Corsica still both alive and free.

"He runs things for the marchioness, goes all over with her – he got me my position here."

"Carries out her dirty work, does he?" Again Dodds put in a question his boss wished he hadn't.

"I wouldn't know about that – I'm just a guest, a *special* guest that is."

After a further few minutes of questioning; which Kevin answered as truthfully as he dared, Mason asked, "Where do you think our Johnie's gone off to?"

"Could be anywhere, France, Ireland, America even. He's never been short of a bob or two."

"Your best guess, then."

"London to begin with to collect what he needs, then somewhere abroad where he'll never be found."

"Shouldn't we get after him too," said Dodds to his boss eagerly.

"We should indeed, it's a three mile walk to Verdley railway station."

"What about him," Dodds pointed towards the Irishman, "aren't we going to take him to Verdley police station, get his statement down and then lock him up?"

"Mister O'Dowd isn't going anywhere, he has a nice comfortable billet here, and as far as we know he's committed no crime."

"What about the body in the sack…" began Dodds.

"You've no connection with this, have you?" Asked Mason still in an easy, friendly sort of way.

Kevin shook his head, "No, I've not seen it before."

"He's as guilty as Corsica is," spluttered Dodds, "and we know he has at least two other confederates."

"We have no time for the minnows if we wish to catch Corsica before more people die."

"But..," Dodds began to disagree, though when he looked around his superior was already halfway along the entrance hall.

"What about me?" Cried Jim Watkins, he not wishing to be left alone with someone as startlingly ugly as O'Dowd.

"As the boss says, it's only three miles to Verdley," returned Dodds over his shoulder as he was running off.

*****

Johnie Corsica did not run off to his home at Gravesend, nor did he visit London to collect his valuables, for these were not his priorities. He knew; of course, that he would have to flee abroad in order to escape the hangman's noose, but that mattered much less

364

to him than the business he needed to complete with the Marchioness of Studland.

He loved Elysia and for that reason more than any other he had carried out her orders for several hectic years. Whatever she'd wished to be done; no matter how bizarre, he had done it. When it had come down to the choice of serving her or her father, he had willingly betrayed the latter. In return she'd denied him nothing, making him rich in the process and allowing him frequent access to her body.

They had made love on numerous occasions and she was the only woman he had ever really wanted for reasons other than sex or money, for she was the only woman he had ever loved, though he knew that his love had never been; nor would ever be, reciprocated.

He was also not surprised that the only woman he had ever cared for had betrayed him. Though he did find it a little harder to bear that she also intended to make him a scapegoat, to have him accept the consequences of crimes of which she herself had been the primary source. Elysia had done the same to others; some of them very close to her – and; thanks to him, one after the other they'd fallen victim to her schemes.

"I was more than happy to be her willing tool, in fact I enjoyed it," he shook his head and smiled wryly.

These thoughts filled his mind as he took a train to Birmingham, from where he intended to travel to Carlisle. Once there it was eastward to Newcastle and then south to Durham, from whence it was an easy journey to Martindale and Elysia Scott-Wilson.

Though this was a circuitous route which he intended would take him three or four days, he hoped that it would throw the pursuing police off his trail and allow him to accomplish what he needed to do.

*****

Elysia had just taken to her bed at Martin Hall when there came an urgent hammering at her door.

"Elysia, please wake up," the voice was that of Sir Charles, who was soon joined by his wife.

The marchioness flung on a dressing gown hoping that the fuss did not indicate that all had gone wrong at Forest Hall and the police had arrived to arrest her.

"What is it?" She asked before she would risk fully opening the door.

"News from Forest Hall, Elysia, and it's serious," returned Marian.

"Oh, my God, it must be Flora or Rowena... Whatever has happened to them?" She cried out dramatically, though her brain remained as cool as ever.

"Open the door, for you could soon be in danger," Charles spoke with as much authority as he could muster.

This time Elysia did as she had been bidden and stood before them pretending to wipe sleep and tears from her eyes.

"Who on earth would wish to harm me?" She asked innocently.

*Lots of people,* thought Charles to himself, though he said nothing.

"We've just received a telegram from Inspector Mason, it's urgent," informed Marian, getting to the point.

Inside, and against her will, Elysia could feel herself trembling, "What could he possibly want with me?"

"It's Corsica, your man of affairs, apparently he's gone off his head and the inspector is sure that he is on his way here to do you harm."

"Why should he wish to hurt me?" she opened her eyes innocently wide.

Marian took both of Elysia's hands into her own and explained, "They've found the remains of what they believe to be your father, Corsica was in possession of them."

Elysia put on a quite remarkable show of sorrow and regret which was reinforced by a few sobs and tears and then she asked, "Then what purpose would it serve Johnie to kill me too?"

"He must be a madman, Elysia, who can say how his mind is working."

Elysia made her eyes flash enough for her expression to appear wild and frightened.

"We'll protect you, you're safe here," soothed Marian.

The marchioness, taking advantage of Marian's calming tones, took several deep breaths, sniffed, smiled and said, "I feel better now and safe amongst friends."

"I'll order Kent to rouse the household and station look-outs around the hall as soon as possible," decided Charles.

"You must do what you think best," backed up Marian.

"They'd better be sent out in pairs, for Corsica is a very dangerous enemy," advised Elysia.

"Don't employ any of the younger boys, remember what happened to poor Billy Russell," put in Marian, recalling the boy who had been stabbed by an unknown assailant in the grounds of the hall.

"I'll send the two youngest up on to the roof as observers," declared Charles, "and provide them with whistles to sound the alarm should they catch sight of an intruder."

"Perhaps we should gather together in the drawing room," suggested Elysia in as close to a trembling voice she could manage without over-acting.

"Yes, there's safety in numbers," agreed Marian.

Charles looked at his pocket-watch, "As we've time and to spare we'd best return to our beds. Whatever else this Corsica fellow can do, he isn't capable of flight, so he can't possibly be here until late to-morrow morning, that's if the trains are running on time for him."

*****

A hundred miles away, just before he was due to arrive at Carlisle station, Corsica stole the suitcase of a gentleman who was of about the same size as himself. Once he'd left the train he strode into the nearby *Station Hotel* and booked a room for three nights, intending to stay for only two after which he would leave without paying his bill.

*May as well have a good dinner and a decent bottle of wine on the house too*, he thought to himself as he followed the porter to his room, where he quickly changed into the outfit he had stolen.

It was his belief that his non-arrival at Durham would remove the immediacy of any precautions being taken at Martin Hall. He was sure that they'd be expecting him to come post-haste and when he failed to turn up the guards there would soon become bored, lax and lazy.

In the meantime he would both eat and sleep well and plan what he intended to do with the Marchioness of Studland once he had her in his full possession.

*****

"Where do you think Corsica lives?" Asked Dodds as they arrived in the capital.

Mason shook his head, "I doubt that he lives in London."

"Then where are we to start looking for him?"

"King's Cross Station."

Constable Dodds looked puzzled, "Though, surely; as he's heading for the continent, he must first collect whatever valuables he has."

"I don't believe he is off to foreign parts, at least not yet."

"Then where do you think he *is* heading?"

"County Durham, near the town of Martindale to be precise."

George Dodds was not one easily puzzled and was well used to the vagaries and baffling ways of senior officers, but this time Mason had him stumped.

"He has no reason to go there."

"Oh, yes he has, the marchioness is there."

"He wants his revenge perhaps."

"Possibly, but it's more likely to involve an affair of the heart."

"You believe he loves the lady even when he knows she's betrayed him?" Returned Dodds incredulously.

"Indeed he does, she's probably the only person he's truly loved in his entire life."

Dodds thought for a while and then said, "How big a place is Martindale? It can't be very large, so I suppose we've more chance of finding him there than we do here."

"We can ignore the town and go straight to either Martin Hall or Blanchwell, for the marchioness is currently a guest at one or the other of these places."

"Which, though?"

Mason laughed, "We'll just need to ask about that at Martindale Station, for the whole town will know that the marchioness is back amongst them."

"What's her first husband like?"

"A proper gentlemen – in the true sense of the word. Very well respected and I doubt that he's got a vicious bone in his body."

"That bodes ill if he's faced by our Mr Corsica."

"This is another reason why we must get to Durham as quickly as we can."

*****

"It's bleedin' boring trampin' 'round an' 'round here and my boots are pinching something shocking," complained Bobby Tyres; who was an under-footmen, as he patrolled the grounds of Martin Hall.

"Aye, and it's cold, my feet feel like they've been turned into blocks of ice," agreed Colin Smart, who was the youngest of Martin Hall's three gamekeepers.

"Nowt's happened so far and I don't think anything is going to happen."

Bobby nodded, "Young Myers fell in the beck though."

"It would ha' brightened the day up if he'd drowned," returned his companion only half in jest.

"How long have we been on wi' this now?"

"This is the third night we've wandered about the grounds to no purpose. I doubt he's coming here at all," returned Bobby.

The keeper nodded his agreement, "I reckon this Corsica fellow'll be in Belgium by now."

Bobby halted and gave serious thought to Smart's suggestion, "What's makes you think Belgium?"

"It's foreign ain't it?"

"Aye, I suppose it is. It'll be as good as anywhere for a man on the run."

A dozen yards away hidden in a shrubbery, Johnie Corsica stood listening to their prattle, which had given him ample warning of their presence when they were still a hundred yards from him.

371

He kept very still as they passed on by, still chattering like spuggies in a bush. Once they'd moved off he carried on towards the house which was now well within striking distance. Even though there was no sign of human life there were still several well-lit windows casting pools of illumination into the area of the stables, which was where he was heading.

He had visited Martin Hall on three occasions previously, the first time he had been driven off by the gamekeeper before he'd even sighted the hall itself. His second plan to kill Sir Charles Martin had also ended in failure, but only after he'd done for a young lad, wounded the gamekeeper and managed to escape from Jack Nicholson, the collier who'd broken O'Dowd's jaw for him. His most recent visit had seen him here as a legitimate member of Elysia's retinue.

He paused as he gave thought to Martin Hall's butler, Virgil Kent, knowing that he was a dangerous opponent who it would be better to avoid. With good fortune he hoped to settle with Elysia and be off with her before anyone realised that he had been anywhere near Martindale.

After a further look around, Corsica moved on towards the stable yard entrance of the building, he well remembered Kent's wife; Cissy, innocently leading him inside from there during his second attempt to finish off Sir Charles. At that time he had persuaded her that he was a harmless salesman of ladies underwear, though she had soon discovered the truth when he had overpowered and bound her to a chair.

"I should have killed the silly bitch then," he muttered to himself, shaking his head at what he believed had been his own stupidity. For after that everything had gone awry, the baronet had been dining later than normal and his housekeeper had come looking for Cissy; who was then a kitchen maid, and soon discovered that all was not well below stairs. Then he had had to flee rapidly with his mission ending in complete failure. This had taken some squaring with old Wright and his bitch of a daughter.

*The housekeeper at that time is now Lady Martin, and the kitchen maid has become the housekeeper who is also married to Kent – it's funny the way things turn out,* he thought to himself.

As the memory of these scenes passed through his mind he realised that he'd never had much luck at Martindale on any of the visits he'd made. Though just the previous year he had managed to persuade Cissy that it was in the best interests of them both not to mention that it was he who had once treated her so brutally.

He sighed and brought himself swiftly back from his reverie to find that everything remained still and a further couple of lights had been snuffed out on the first floor of the building. He crept forward very slowly, stopping after each step to look, watch and listen, before he moved on again.

Eventually, he was able to view the rear stable yard and stood for some while observing the door which he knew the servants used at all times of day and night.

He was sure that Elysia would be found in a guest bedroom, probably one situated at the front of the house.

"Damn fool," he cursed himself for not having taken the time to thoroughly investigate the layout of the hall during his previous visit.

*Cissy will know where the marchioness has been accommodated, though, and as she's the housekeeper all the keys will be in her charge,* this sudden thought came to him and he smiled to himself.

*****

After a polite but insistent knock at the door, Gil Kent, accompanied by Inspector Mason and Constable Dodds entered the library at Martin Hall.

"These police gentlemen are determined to speak with you again, sir."

Charles looked up from the atlas he was studying and then rose immediately to greet his visitors.

Mason smiled and asked, "I wonder if we may have a few words with you, sir."

"I'm hoping that you've brought me news of Corsica's arrest."

Mason shook his head, "I'm afraid not."

"This is the third night we've waited for him to appear, I doubt he's coming at all now and instead has gone off to Brazil or some such other far distant country."

"We dare not take any risks, sir, for he's a very dangerous fellow."

"He seemed a reasonable enough chap to me when he came up with the marchioness last year."

Constable Dodds smiled to himself and thought, *this man is too nice and trusting to live for long.*

374

"Nonetheless, he remains at large and is known to be deadly," replied Mason.

Charles remained determined, "Even so, I shall have to stand my people down after this evening, I can't ask any more of them. Will the local police not help?"

Mason frowned, for so far the Durham Constabulary had not offered him much in the way if support, "Perhaps if you were to have a word with the chief constable."

"I'll see what I can do tomorrow," promised the baronet.

"It's important that you realise just how lethal Corsica is, and I'm sure that he intends to carry out some sort of retaliation against Lady Studland. On top of which I'm still certain that he's here or hereabouts."

"Retaliation for what?"

"Corsica has one or two scores to settle, but chiefly he believes that she has acted as a police informer against him."

Charles laughed, for he couldn't imagine Elysia becoming engaged in any public duty which did not fit into her own agenda.

"To what effect?" He questioned at last.

"He suspects that she persuaded a third party to inform us of the presence of a corpse hidden in the priest hole at Forest Hall."

"That of her father, I presume."

"Indeed, but the fact remains that Corsica believes that he has been betrayed and will be determined to retaliate."

Charles shook his head emphatically, "He'll be well away from these shores by now, I'm sure of it."

"Under normal circumstances I'd agree with you, sir, however, our Johnie is in love with the marchioness."

Charles shook his head in disbelief, "I very much doubt that, knowing her as I do."

"We shall see," smiled Mason who then warned, "He is still on the loose and determined to seek out the lady."

"To do what exactly?"

Mason shrugged his shoulders, "I've no idea. It could be anything, though he may be planning to carry her off or to inflict serious harm of some sort."

Charles shook his head sadly, "Just when I believed Martindale was at last returning to a boring but pleasant level of peace and tranquillity."

"We'd also like a word with the marchioness, if it were convenient, sir," Dodds spoke up for the first time.

"She's retired to her room, the shock of what happened to her father has been difficult for her to bear."

"Yes, we realise that she is in mourning, but we really do need to speak to her if this whole affair is to be concluded satisfactorily," returned Mason with some authority.

"She could be harmed if Corsica *is* about," backed up the constable.

"Do you really need to speak with her at so difficult a time for her?"

"The sooner she is made fully aware of the danger she faces the better.  On top of which she may be able to answer one or two pressing questions I have regarding the disappearance and death of her father."

Charles looked at the library clock, "Why, it's late, she may be asleep."

"Then she must be woken up, for when she realises the danger she is in, I'm sure she'll be happy to help me with my enquiries."

The landowner reluctantly nodded his agreement and instructed Kent to ask the marchioness to come downstairs at her earliest convenience.

Fifteen minutes later Elysia sat alone with the two policemen, Sir Charles having tactfully withdrawn after explaining the situation to her.

It certainly didn't look as though Elysia had been awakened suddenly from her bed, her hair was precisely curled, her dress immaculate and her eyes shone black and piercing.

"I hear that my man of business, Corsica, is after my blood."

"That would appear to be the case ma'am."

"Whatever for?  I've provided a good living for him for some years now."

"We understand that you have been informed that we found the remains of your father at Forest Hall the day before yesterday," interrupted Dodds with less tact than was needed.

"For which we hope you will accept our deepest sympathy and regret," Mason quickly made amends for his underling.

Elysia feigned grief and sorrow almost professionally, so well in fact, that had her friend Liz Esprey been present she would have clapped politely.

"How on earth did he get there?" She sobbed, quite realistically.

"Whoever murdered him must have arranged it."

"How do you know he was deliberately killed?"

Mason smiled, "It's hard to say how he died, as there's – begging your pardon, ma'am – not too much of him left."

"Though he would hardly have imprisoned himself in the priest hole," put in Dodds.

"In point of fact, that would have been impossible," added Mason.

Elysia tried to attach some tears to her sorrowful demeanour, but not very successfully, so she gave up, dabbed her cheeks and said, "You can't believe that *I* had anything to do with the murder of my own, dear papa."

"It is my duty to consider every possibility, my lady."

"No matter how unlikely," she bridled slightly, "it's also not long ago that you believed my father to be concealed in the old dungeon at Winterbourne."

"It seemed likely at the time," Mason's face pinkened, "everything pointed to it."

"It's our duty to follow up any leads we may have, unlikely or not," Dodds backed up his boss.

Elysia shook her head and then spoke strongly, "You can't believe still that I had anything to do with the disappearance of my papa? What possible motive could I have?"

"You inherited a great deal from him," pointed out Mason.

"Why, in that case his second wife; Gertrude, has as much of  a motive as myself – even a greater one perhaps."

"A colleague of mine has already tried to interview Lady Wright," replied Mason, though rather haltingly.

"What did she have to say?"

"Nothing, she'd gone home to New York as she could stand no more of a damp English winter."

"*Ha*, then how suspicious is that?" Returned Elysia at once and with some relish.

"We will interview her as soon as she returns."

"That may never be, and as a bonus I'll have Isis House as my own again."

"I'm sure this can be sorted out quite quickly if you'll bear with me," said Mason, hoping to get his interview back on track.

Dodds was aching to ask another question or two himself, but he was a little overawed at being in the company of a lady of such exalted rank.

"May I ask how often you reside at Forest Hall?" Queried the inspector.

Elysia laughed dismissively, "Hardly ever. At first I thought it would be a convenient place to get away from things, far fewer servants needed and above all no visitors demanding this, that or the other."

"How often, though, your ladyship?" Dodds backed up his superior.

"As I remember it, I've only slept there once. The fabric of the house groaned and creaked and the mice were scuttling along behind the skirting boards all night – the house is riddled with spiders and mice. I hardly slept at all," she paused, cleared her throat and then continued, "There are rats too – very large ones."

"In that case, why haven't you sold the property on?" The inspector was curious.

"I decided to keep it for the use of my poor sisters-in-law, who; by an oversight, had been housed in what is virtually a derelict cottage. I thought Forest Hall might be a good place for them to end their days in peace and comfort."

"Did you know that there is said to be a priest hole there?"

Again, Elysia laughed, "I hadn't a clue, in fact I've rarely given the place a thought since I bought it."

"Though you refused permission for the local Antiquarian Society to investigate," pointed out the constable.

"Yes, at the time I saw no reason to have my in-laws disturbed. However, it turns out that they are in favour of allowing Mr Nelson and Mr Plantagenet to begin a search, as a result I have changed my mind."

"So that was the reason for the building work that is currently going on there?"

Elysia managed to look surprised, "Building work? At Forest Hall? I know nothing of it."

"Was it not undertaken in preparation for the projected search for the priest hole?" Asked Dodds.

"I've no idea what you're talking about."

Roland Mason managed to lock-eyes with his suspect, "Your father was staying at Winterbourne on the night he was last seen, was he not?"

"Yes, that is the case," if Elysia was feeling any discomfort under his gaze she didn't show it for a moment.

"This being the same and *only* evening you've ever resided at Forest Hall?"

"It was, I left early next morning happy to clear the dust and vermin droppings of the place from my feet."

"Is it not strange then that the remains of your 'pa have been discovered there – could there be some connection?"

Elysia got to her feet and stood very erect, her eyes blazing, "As I've already said, I know nothing of my father's final hours. If you are suggesting that I had anything to do with his death, then this interview is terminated and you'd best next speak to Mr Hill, my lawyer."

Mason shook his head, "No, ma'am, I'm not wilfully accusing you of anything, but you must agree that this is so strange a coincidence."

"Coincidences occur all the time, it doesn't mean that there is *always* a positive connection between them."

"Of course, ma'am," Mason settled her down with a smile.

"What about the nursemaid? The one your pa' was said to have run away with," Dodds put in his own query.

"I find your question, young man, both distasteful and disrespectful, especially as both of those you mention are no longer with us."

Mason smiled ruefully and hoped that his underling would now keep his mouth shut, "That was badly put by my colleague, my lady, however, we really do need an answer to his question – if you'd be so kind as to oblige us."

"Marta Kleist you mean? As far as I am aware she was a servant, that's all, a mere servant."

"Her body hasn't been found yet."

At this point the inspector was expecting his suspect to immediately try to connect Corsica to the still missing Kleist woman.

"No," replied Elysia slowly and after some thought, "Marta would never have stooped to murder."

"Perhaps Sir James made promises to her – cash, a nice house somewhere with a comfortable living attached," Dodds tried his hand at a question again.

"In that case she would have had no need to kill my papa, for he *always* delivered on his promises."

Sir Charles had once given Mason the opportunity to peruse documents dealing with the treasonable affairs of Sir James Hannibal Wright. These had shocked and appalled him, so he knew that the dead man would have stopped at nothing either to have his own way or to increase his wealth.

"The number of suspects in this murder case are very few," pointed out the inspector.

"I've had a lingering hope that my papa was living in peace and happiness in some secluded corner of the globe, though that hopeless dream has been finally shattered to-night." Elysia managed to sob convincingly for a second or two and then stated, "There can only be one conclusion now, which is that Johnie Corsica *did* murder my father for reasons known only to himself."

"That is possible…, I suppose," returned Mason.

"In that case, I shall bid you good evening, gentlemen, and should you wish to question me further I shall be happy to oblige you in the morning."

*****

A few dozen yards away, Corsica was determined to deal with Elysia in one way or another before he fled the country, and whatever happened to him after that he did not much care.

As he stood watching, the hall lights continued to be extinguished until only one remained lit. With the yard now dark enough he stepped from his hiding place and crept forward until he reached the cover of the deeper blackness cast by the stable buildings.

He stiffened involuntarily as; with something of a clatter, the door to the yard opened and a narrow stream of light beamed forth, which to his mind seemed to be searching him out.

Then a footman appeared who leaned against the doorpost, knocking his pipe against it at the same time. He fiddled for a while and then stuffed tobacco into the bowl, pressed it hard down and proceeded to light up.

Whilst the servant was thus engaged, Corsica took out his knife, stole silently from the shadows and very accurately drove his blade between the footman's ribs and deep into his heart.

His victim crumpled with hardly a sound, apart from that made by his pipe as it hit the flags of the yard, breaking into two as it did so.

Johnie wasted no time in dragging the corpse from the doorway and into the shadows, after which he made his way into the house and up the rear stairs to the first floor.

Fortunately for him, the house remained quiet with no one to be seen or heard. As he progressed along the corridor, he put his ear to each of the doors he came to and listened intently for a few seconds, but no sound came from any of them.

As he neared the end of the passage he was alerted to danger by the sound of multiple footsteps coming closer, he stepped quietly into what appeared to be a broom cupboard, but left the door of slightly ajar.

A few seconds later he wasn't too surprised to see the policemen who had turned up at Forest Hall pass by him and who appeared to be in something of a hurry.

"I doubt he's coming now, so maybe she was right to be unconcerned about her life being in danger," said the younger of the coppers.

"She should be though, for the slippery bugger's here somewhere, I can feel his presence," replied the senior officer.

"What if he comes in at the front door, no one's expecting that?"

"He's got the brass to stride in as though he owned the place," returned Mason thoughtfully as he came to a sudden halt.

*He's right about that,* smiled Corsica to himself as waited for them to move on.

"Shouldn't we go back and give the lady a knock, her room's just around the corner?"

The senior policeman thought for a second and then said, "Maybe you're right, but we shall leave the marchioness in peace – at least until tomorrow."

A few second later the detectives had moved on and Corsica was delighted with the information they had unknowingly provided him with.

He then realised that it wouldn't be long before they; or someone else, came across the body of the footman he had killed and then the alarm would be raised with a vengeance. This galvanised him into speedy action and it wasn't long before he came to the room mentioned by the policemen.

"*Tut-tut,*" he smiled to himself as he discovered that the door was unlocked, he entered the room and found Elysia at her dressing table brushing her hair.

"Not got a tweeny with you to help out?" He asked conversationally.

She did not so much as blink nor turn around, but continued to brush her lustrous black hair in long continuous strokes.

"I thought you'd turn up, sooner or later."

"You can't keep a good man down."

She sighed, in a bored, unconcerned sort of way, "I suppose you've come to murder me."

"You betrayed me to the police – is that not a good enough reason to punish you?"

"Oh, God, you're just *so* predictable," she gave a little toss of her head, "I've become terminally bored with your antics."

Corsica smiled cynically, "You want me out of the way so you can have your pa's body back without shouldering your own share of the blame for his killing."

"I have accomplished my purpose, then, haven't I," after she spoke she put down the brush, raised both arms into the air and yawned.

"Yours isn't going to be a quick nor an easy death," he attempted to frighten her into the normal human reaction he was seeking.

"Isn't it? Why ever not, for we both know that you love me."

Johnie's throat lumped, for what she had said was true, though he was also aware that she was unattainable, always had been and would always remain so.

Again she stifled a yawn, "You'd best get on with it then – though I'd be grateful if you'd leave my face unmarked."

"If I can't have you, then no one shall," he threatened.

"I suppose you'll kill yourself once you've done with me," her tone was business-like and devoid of any sign of fear.

"Why should I not?"

She sighed, "I can see it now when our bodies are discovered, Romeo and Juliet lying at peace their arms entwined around each other in a graphic depiction of their eternal love. Some fifth rate artist will probably paint a picture of it."

She began to laugh and her laughter stung him and he took a threatening step towards her.

Elysia turned to face him tore open her *peignoir* and ripped the neck of her nightgown, she then put on a sardonic smile and suggested, "Come on then, do it."

"I will," he threatened, though without too much assurance.

"Oh, sorry, I forgot, you wish to make me suffer first."

"Yes and I shall too."

"I'm already suffering for I cannot stand for a moment longer the tedious level of *BOREDOM* you're inflicting upon me."

He stood perplexed for a second and then; in a rapid series of actions, he put away his knife, forced one of her arms high up behind her back and wrapped his other arm around her throat.

Elysia made no sound, she relaxed her body and did nothing to stop him from pushing her towards the doorway.

Corsica found himself confused for this was not working out at all as he had planned or imagined it. Besides which the closeness of her body and the scent of her perfume set his mind reeling back to times past.

"I'll go wherever you wish, there's no need to use force," she said in the husky whisper he had heard so many times before.

He grunted in reply and loosened his grip slightly before leading her from the bedroom and along the corridor to the rear stairway.

"You should have done what you wanted to in the bedroom, you'll not get far dragging me with you," she pointed out.

"Shut up, I shall take you somewhere quiet where I can deal with you as I think fit."

Elysia smiled, for it was obvious to her that; even though he was aware that she had informed on him, he had no real desire to kill or even hurt her.

"*Ha*, I'm as cosy as a kitten in its basket with you," she managed a cutting sort of laugh, even as his fingers hovered around her throat.

"We'll see about that...," he began, but then heard some considerable disturbance coming from the passage behind them.

"Oh my goodness, it looks as though they're on to you already," she laughed mockingly.

With the sounds of shouting men coming closer, Johnie pushed his captive with some force down the stairs towards the stable yard door.

As he was doing so, at the top of the landing there appeared the figures of Inspector Mason and Constable Dodds.

"Leave the lady be and come quietly," called the inspector.

Corsica couldn't help laughing aloud, "*Come quietly? Surely, no policeman actually ever says that.*"

Then both detectives began to descend the stairway, Dodds drawing forth his truncheon at the same time.

Johnie continued to hold on to Elysia with one hand whilst with the other he pulled out his revolver, "Don't come any further," he warned.

Dodds ignored him and continued steadfastly.

"Hold on, son," ordered Mason, who didn't like the look which had appeared in their quarry's eyes.

However, the constable; determined to make a name for himself, ignored his superior and took a further couple of steps.

Johnie fired three shots in quick succession, the first narrowly missed taking off Mason left ear, the second whined above Dodds' head but the third struck him in the right shoulder breaking the scapula and sending him rolling to the bottom of the stairs.

The loud noise of the gunshots in so narrow a space was then replaced by a deathly silence which was only broken by Dodds' dropped truncheon as it made a slow series of bounces down the stairs until it came to rest at Johnie's feet.

Mason dashed forward in the hope of taking Corsica down with the weight of his momentum, but stopped when he saw that the marchioness now had the pistol barrel pointed close to her ear.

"Come on, take him you idiot, he won't harm me," she encouraged.

The inspector looked at Corsica's expression and wasn't so sure that the lady was correct in her assumption.

"What on earth's happening here," called Sir Charles; accompanied by his wife, as they appeared at the top of the stairway.

At virtually the same time as this a blast of cold air flooded into the vestibule as the outside door was flung open and Virgil Kent appeared, he having been alerted by the sound of gunfire. He swiftly summed up the situation, snatched up the wounded policeman's truncheon and knocked the pistol well away from Corsica's grasp in a single, lightning fast movement.

Johnie then pushed Elysia roughly away, causing her to blunder into Mason and thus blocking his advance down the staircase. He then withdrew his knife again and began to skip from side to side with it waving in front of the butler.

"I've eaten little shits like you for breakfast," Kent smiled as he spoke.

"I'm bigger than I look, my ma' said so."

"Give up now, there's no reason for any more killing," this appeal was made by Mason who by now had pushed Elysia to safety behind him.

In the meanwhile, Marian advanced to help the wounded Dodds, who had been trying to get to his feet.

Corsica grinned as he attempted to infuriate Kent into hasty action, "I've a working knowledge of your wife, you know, when I had her trussed-up in the kitchen, keen for it that night she was too. Tiny tits though."

Kent just laughed, "I've always thought that was the truth of it as she's exactly the sort of opponent you prefer, five foot two and skinny with it – it's a wonder she didn't black your eyes for you."

As this exchange was taking place, confronted by adversaries coming against him from opposite directions, Corsica knew that he had to act both quickly and decisively. Having once partnered Kent in the rescue Warren Scott-Wilson, he knew just how dangerous an opponent he was, a much more threatening one than an ageing, overweight policeman. So, wasting no further time he leapt forward, blade in hand, hoping to slash the butler's throat.

Kent neatly side-stepped, but; due to Johnie's speed and agility, not quite far enough and he heard the cloth of his sleeve rip and felt the hot flow of blood from the gash which had been made in the fleshy part of his upper arm.

Mason pushed Elysia further behind him; from where Charles was able to drag her to safety, he then rushed forward to make a dive for the revolver which lay at the foot of the stairs.

Seeing that he had injured Kent, Corsica became intent on finishing him off, he changed grip on the handle of his knife and lunged forward, this time aiming for the belly of his opponent.

"No, Johnie, *stop*," called Elysia, in a tone which wasn't begging for obedience, but instead was demanding it.

At this, Corsica paused only for a fraction of a second, but it gave Kent time to take him in a bear hug and begin to grapple for control of the dagger.

Mason pointed the pistol into the air and fired a single round, "In the name of the law, stop," he shouted, though to no effect, which left him feeling useless and rather silly. *I really must stop using clichés,* he thought to himself.

It wasn't long before Corsica sensed that Virgil's superior size was gaining the upper hand and knew that he had to do something in what was rapidly becoming an impossible situation for him. Gathering all the strength he had left he threw himself into his opponent knocking him down and then rolling over with him to the floor.

Kent tried to twist away to one side, but wasn't quick enough and found himself heavily obstructed by the weight of his adversary.

Again, Mason took aim with the revolver, but dared not fire in case he hit the wrong man, which seemed to him to be the most likely outcome. Instead he pointed it toward the ceiling for the second time and squeezed the trigger, firing another warning shot or causing what he hoped would be a distraction which would aid the butler.

The sound of the shot resounded around the confined space of the rear vestibule, echoing from wall to wall, though it was ignored by both Kent and Corsica. However, in the fraction of a second after the revolver was fired, Kent managed to gain some control of the knife and felt sure that he would soon have his rival where he wanted him.

Johnie, realising that his strength was failing, hung on desperately to his own section of the handle and heaved it upwards, hoping to force his opponent's hand on to the very sharp edge of its blade.

Kent could feel what his opponent was trying to do, but had become well aware that Johnie's strength was diminishing with each second that passed, so he used every muscle he had to gain complete control of the knife and could feel that its handle would soon be fully in his grasp.

By now Corsica understood that the game was up for him, so using his last reserves of strength he diverted the direction of his effort to match that of his opponent. Their joint momentum was guided by him upwards until the blade tore into the soft flesh of his own stomach, just below the ribcage.

The butler soon realised what was happening but could do little about it apart from letting go of the knife, which he did.

As the blade pushed deeper into his insides, Johnie sighed and seemed to the onlookers to be smiling.

"Oh, my God," cried Marian, though Elysia stood as immobile as a statue and as unshockable.

Kent let go of his opponent, pushed himself on to his knees and then rose shakily to his feet, clamping a hand over the bloody wound in his arm at the same time.

Each of the onlookers watched as Johnie's eyes opened very wide and a long, soft sigh came from deep within him.

"Quickly," called Marian very decisively, "Send for a doctor and let's get the wounded to bed. Take them to the servants' rooms at the top of the stairs."

Charles and Mason did as they were told and soon had Corsica lying on the narrow bed which had once been occupied by Lady Martin during her time as housekeeper.

At the same time, Marian and Elysia helped the wounded policeman to the adjoining room where they made him as comfortable as they could before they crossed to where Corsica lay.

Once there, Marian immediately set to work bandaging Kent's wounded arm with one of Charles' handkerchiefs.

"I don't think Johnie's got long," Kent whispered as she attended to him.

Hearing this, Mason knelt forward and grasped Corsica by the shoulders, "You're done for, son, now's the time to tell me the truth about what happened to Sir James Wright."

Blood bubbled from between Johnie's lips and he laughed weakly, "Wouldn't you like to know it."

Elysia hunkered down at her lover's shoulder and she squeezed it gently, "I'm sorry it's ended this way," she whispered and for once her words were sincerely meant.

"Mine was always going to be a bad end," sighed Corsica with a rueful smile on his lips.

"Come on man, before you meet your Maker, tell the truth," Mason was desperate to achieve the result for which he'd laboured for some considerable time.

Corsica laughed weakly and what little colour remained of his Mediterranean complexion paled away, he spat out some blood, looked into the eyes of Elysia for a few seconds; though to those standing by it seemed like an eternity, and said, "I killed your father. I murdered the old swine, it was me alone."

"Come on, out with the truth, man," cried Mason.

Johnie managed to smile again, and used what little energy he had left to shake his head and say, "I told old man Wright that I was going to marry his daughter… He wouldn't have it, cut up rough and threatening, so I put him out of the way."

"*Rubbish*, this is no time to lie, man, not on your deathbed," cried Mason who attempted to take the shoulders of Johnie and shake the truth from him.

"It was my plan, I did it all," he gasped before his head fell to one side and his last breath left him.

Charles stooped and pulled the policeman away, "He's dead, he can say no more."

Elysia stood erect, brushed down her nightgown, pushed her hair into place and proclaimed without a tremor of emotion, "What we've all just witnessed was a death-bed confession, and there's no court in the land which will deny it as being such."

At this, Mason had a strong urge to strike this woman who had confounded him yet again, but he managed to restrain himself and decided that he'd best prepare more fully for his retirement.

Charles nodded his head gently, he knew full well what both Elysia and her father were capable of, but it appeared that once again she'd been given an escape route by someone who foolishly had loved her.

Kent smiled to himself, for he had once been employed at Winterbourne as a footman and he had more than an inkling of what the marchioness was capable of, *It'd be best if all this was left to rest,* he thought to himself.

Whilst the Marchioness of Studland was speaking Marian had been studying her intently and could see that her black eyes were completely devoid of emotion, it was as though they had been fashioned from solid marble and were thus immutable.

*Corsica obviously loved her, he sacrificed himself for her. Can she feel nothing?  Or is the display of normal human emotions way beyond her comprehension?* Marian asked herself.

At first she was sure that this was the case, but as she gazed intently, seemingly becoming able to look into the very core of Elysia's psyche, cracks began to appear in her indifference, these were hair-line ones at first but then they rapidly expanded until they became wide and deep enough to expose the secrets of her soul. It was at this point that she realised the truth of it, *Elysia had loved Johnie Corsica.*

"Though in her own, strange, destructive way," she whispered to herself.

# Chapter Seven

## *(Spring, 1866)*

It wasn't often that Bertie and Drina visited their father and step mother as a pair, so Charles was somewhat surprised.

"Are you two actually on speaking terms?"

The twins nodded in the affirmative.

"There's a turn up for the book."

"We come on important business, papa," said Alexandrina seriously.

"Very important, especially for me," added Bertie.

"You're too young to be commissioned into the army. How many times must you be told," replied Charles sharply.

"That's not what we've come to see you about, father, though I still wish to join the army as soon as I'm able."

Charles sighed, "In that case what is it you want?"

"I think I know what it is, they're both badly missing Harry Nicholson," guessed Marian.

"Yes, we want him back with us," affirmed Drina.

"He intends to join the army with me," said Bertie.

"No he doesn't, you idiot, he plans to become a lawyer and then a Member of Parliament, like Uncle Richard," Drina's words came out in a rush.

"He's to become my troop sergeant..," began Bertie only to be interrupted sharply by his father.

"Be quiet, both of you, Harry has been taken away by his mama and she has every right to do as she has."

"Your father is absolutely correct in what he says," Marian supported her husband.

"Though we have a plan," returned Drina.

"Yes, it's a good one too, I thought of it," claimed Bertie.

"No you didn't, you're far too stupid to conceive so good a plan as this."

By this time Charles was becoming very impatient, he hardened his tone a notch further and ordered, "Cease, stop, halt, shut-up."

"Listen to your papa, children, please," Marian's soft tone produced the calming effect needed and both children stood with their heads bowed waiting to hear what their father had to say.

"I am prepared to hear what your plan is, though you must decide which of you is to deliver it."

Bertie frowned and then said grudgingly, "It'd better be Drina, she's more of a talker than myself, I'm more of a man of action."

Drina managed to supress the urge to laugh at her brother and instead explained, "It's quite simple, Bertie and I will sell a portion of our shares in the *Martindale Iron & Coal Company* and use the money to buy back Harry."

"It's a good plan, sir, don't you think?" Asked Bertie.

"Traders in human flesh now, is it?"

"Hardly that, Charles," Marian thought that Drina's plan had some merit and should not be dismissed out of hand.

Charles always took his wife's opinion seriously, "It could be a way of returning young Nicholson to us, I grant you that, but the sale of shares at the moment is ticklish."

"Aren't they worth anything now?" Queried Drina.

"They are falling at the moment, though not by much. However, were important shareholders; such as yourselves, to begin selling that could knock the bottom out of the market for them completely."

Bertie shook his head, "Does that matter, papa? The shares are only pieces of paper aren't they. Not real money."

"It's what value the paper represents," returned Drina and then whispered under her breath, "*you idiot.*"

"Currently, I cannot sell any shares without unsettling the market for them."

"But they're ours," cried Bertie.

"This is true, but they would have to be traded via my stockbroker."

"I think I have a solution," put in Marian, "Why don't you buy the shares from the children yourself which would increase your personal holding and sell them once the market settles down to recoup your outlay."

"Good-oh, Harry will be back next week," yelled Bertie.

"Well thought through, mama," cried Drina.

"A lot depends on whether or not Harry's mother wishes to give him up and if so how much she will demand."

"At the same time making sure that his transfer to Sarah's care is carried out with all the necessary legal safeguards in place," added Marian.

"Indeed, yes, that is important," agreed Charles.

"Then you'll try my plan?" Yelled a very pleased Drina.

"I will, but you must not expect Harry back to-morrow or even next month. This will take time and some careful negotiation

*****

George Murphy had never before seen the interior of Martin Hall and on his first visit his first thought had been *One day I shall own a house like this*. This day-dream was interrupted when he was greeted by Lady Marian who led him to the library where her husband was expecting him.

"Here's Mr Murphy," she introduced, "whom, I'm delighted to say, has been reunited with the Cooks."

Charles got up and shook his visitor's hand vigorously, "This is splendid news, I've long hoped for such an outcome, though you should *never* have abandoned the Cooks in the first place."

Murphy felt a tinge of shame that he had so wilfully neglected the very folk who had done so much for him and his brow wrinkled and his demeanour became downcast.

Marian could see what had happened and she took George's arm in a companionable way, "Everyone is delighted that you have worked so hard and done so well, you returning to the Cooks is but the icing on the cake."

"Absolutely, I couldn't agree more, we're all so proud of you, Mr Murphy, your rise has been nothing short of meteoric," Charles followed where his wife had led. He smiled at Marian, his eyes signalling his thanks for covering up his thoughtlessness. Smiling came second nature to him these days, for whenever he caught sight of the woman he loved he felt the need to do so.

"Everyone in Martindale is as pleased as we are," continued Marian.

George nodded in appreciation of their kind words which had swiftly ironed away the pique he had felt.

They were then interrupted by the arrival of the other guests; Fred Schilling and Matthew Priestly, who were warmly welcomed and offered seats around the fireplace.

"Was Mr Dobson not invited to this meeting?" Asked Charles.

"I did so," replied Matthew, "though his association has very few members left now and I found him deep in his cups."

"Is he to attend then?"

"I left an invitation, but have heard nothing from him since."

Charles nodded and then asked, "Refreshments?"

"All in hand, I've had a word with Kent," replied Marian as she left the room.

"It's a great pity Frank can't be here," stated Fred with a great deal of force, "He's been away ages."

"Indeed," nodded Priestly, "for I'm not so sure we can begin without having access to his intimate knowledge of the Martindale works," he then turned to Fred, "Not that I intended to belittle your own expertise."

"No, you're absolutely correct, as I too am not confident that we'll get very far without being able to dip into the well of Mr Turner's knowledge."

They sat in silence for a short while and then Charles asked, "How did this idea of a change away from our previously agreed strategy come about?"

"It's all at my instigation, Sir Charles," put in George managing to keep the nervousness he felt from of his voice.

"He's been reading Adam Smith," informed Fred.

"Has he indeed and no doubt found *The Wealth of Nations* to be both readable and interesting," replied the landowner who then added, "by the way George, you may drop the *sir*, plain Charles will do nicely."

"Charles has never been one to stand on ceremony," smiled Fred.

"The suggestion is that the present strategy should be reversed," put in Matthew hoping to make a start with the real and important business at hand.

Charles considered for a while and then said, "This would mean halting our efforts to reduce the workforce and instead make plans to increase production – especially of iron and steel."

George had believed it unlikely that the landowner had ever heard of Adam Smith, so he was somewhat taken aback, especially as Charles had already recognised what was likely to be proposed.

"That's it exactly, Charles, especially were we to export much more of our steel and steel manufactures abroad," said Fred.

"Which would increase the cost of transportation to an even higher level than it is now, and is exactly why the current policy was adopted," the baronet raised his eyebrows.

"Yes sir, it will, but increased production will make for a cheaper product – perhaps even considerably cheaper," returned George.

Charles sighed, "I do wish Frank were here, he knows so much more about costs, profits, in goings, outgoings and so on."

"There's not a trained engineer amongst us either," agreed Fred rather gloomily.

Charles laughed, "Frank has made an excellent job of guiding you to competence, just as old Sam Watson did for him."

"None of us are exactly clueless," pointed out Matthew.

"Mr Turner hasn't gone off forever, either," pointed out George, who was desperate to join this tight little group.

"I must point out that were the workers of Martindale to hear that expansion was in the offing, that alone would increase production – I'm certain of it." put in Matthew who had to carefully juggle the needs and desires of the members of his association with the hard and often disagreeable facts of commercial life.

"Yes, I can see that, for the morale factor is very important, vital even," agreed Charles, pulling hard at his chin.

"Whilst we're waiting for Frank to return, perhaps we should try to sketch out a plan outlining what we wish to achieve and how it can be done," suggested Fred.

"Would it be possible to have such a report commissioned, ready for Frank's perusal?" Asked the landowner.

"Who'd compile it?" Questioned Fred.

"You know more about Martindale than anyone else barring Frank Turner, so it should be yourself," returned the baronet.

"Perhaps a joint effort would be best, our combined skills and breadth of knowledge would produce a more balanced and comprehensive report."

"Though it is said that a camel is nothing more than a horse designed by a committee," muttered the baronet.

"Nonetheless, a camel is a very useful animal in its own environment," returned Priestly quickly.

George began to feel that this meeting was slipping away from him and there was not much he could do about it. He was sure that this could be his great opportunity; perhaps the only one which would come his way, so he spoke up.

"I know that I have no financial stake in this enterprise, but I'm willing to put in as many hours as necessary to make the outcome a successful one."

"I don't suppose you've any shares in the company," surmised Charles.

"None, though I'm willing to use what capital I have to purchase a stake of my own."

"*Ha*, don't do that, for you may end up losing every penny," advised Charles in a kindly fashion.

"In which case I'd have to start all over again, I've done it before and what I've done before I can do again."

Fred clapped lightly, "George would too, I know him and there's nothing that will stand between him and success."

"What will happen to *Brass Schilling* if you spend most of your time toiling on behalf of the *Martindale Iron & Coal Company*?" Charles asked of Murphy.

"Unpaid too," Fred pointed out.

"I'll do both, for I've Hugh Doggart to help now."

"I thought you said he was useless," replied Fred, raising his eyebrows high.

Murphy considered for a second, "He's coming on now and as he seems to be in Lucy Greenwood's sights she'll give him the hearty pushes he so often needs."

"Very well, then," considered Charles slowly, "Fred will begin work on a draft report with Matthew, George and any other person of expertise who it is felt can make a contribution," he paused briefly for thought and then continued, "I suggest we meet here again in; shall we say, a fortnight, by which time Frank is certain to be back."

"A week," jumped in Matthew, "this is urgent."

"That would be possible," encouraged Fred.

*I'd have made it forty-eight hours,"* thought Murphy to himself, but said nothing.

*****

"This gathering of the *Coven* is rather a thin one," pointed out Marian Martin as she sipped a pre-luncheon drink at Merrington Hall.

Elizabeth Esprey sighed, "Originally, everyone intended to come, but one or two have had to send in their apologies due to pressing business elsewhere."

"Yes, Grace wished to be here, but now she's busy packing and making arrangements for her return to America," put in Caroline Schilling.

"I suppose she'll have lots of business to attend to once she gets there," said Marian.

"Helmuth is travelling with her and he's sworn not to return until all is in order at both Cardinal Woods and Knightsbridge."

"That's sure some chore, Cardinal Woods is a wreck," put in Catherine Esprey who was then about to comment on the mortal danger possibly involved but thought better of it.

"Good grief, that'll take him months," declared Eliza.

"He reckons weeks."

Kitty snorted her disbelief in as ladylike way as she could manage, and then pointed out, "Major Sturgis couldn't find his own way there and he was a native of the district."

"Perhaps you should return with Mr Schilling in order to keep his party on track," suggested Elizabeth Esprey with a knowing smile.

"No, I'm staying just where I am," replied Kitty without a pause.

Marian then turned to Caroline and suggested, "At least you'll be able to enjoy a quiet time, you'll could do whatever you wish."

*Does she suspect an affair exists between Richard and myself?* Caroline's eyes narrowed as this thought crossed her mind, but then she noticed that Marian's expression was as open and innocent as always, "Oh, I'll find lots to do," she replied lightly.

"Come and stay with us for a week or two, it'll be very pleasant to have some company and perhaps you'd be willing to instruct Catherine in the art of water colouring," put in Elizabeth.

"Oh, I would enjoy that, please say you'll come," cried Kitty who had admired Caroline's artwork whenever she'd visited Blanchwell.

Caroline was developing plans of her own, but once she'd thought it over she nodded her assent, "Of course, I'll fetch colours and brushes with me too."

Kitty beamed, for she knew that painting was a pursuit young ladies were supposed to master and her own efforts so far had been nothing other than infantile. Besides which she realised that Mrs Schilling was a *proper* lady who would make the perfect role model for her.

"It's not like Sarah to miss an occasion like this," pointed out Caroline, changing the subject.

"Indeed not, but since young Harry was removed from her care she has become very despondent."

"She'll be feeling his loss deeply, which I can well understand for he's such a fine boy," put in Marian.

"How is Drina taking his departure, for she was a particular friend of his, I believe?" Asked Elizabeth.

"Oh, she intends to marry Harry," replied Catherine Esprey who had spent some mornings at the Martin Hall schoolroom helping Sarah.

"She could do a great deal worse," smiled Marian, wondering how Elysia would take to the idea of her daughter marrying well beneath her own station in life.

Elizabeth dropped her voice to little more than a whisper and said, "I hope all is quiet at Martin Hall now."

"I thank the Good Lord that our troubles are over and pray that we have no such further excitement for the rest of our lives," returned Marian with some force.

"Two dead and a policeman wounded, such young men too," Eliza shook her head.

"One of our own footmen was stabbed to death before he even knew he was in danger from that awful Corsica fellow."

"You've all told me that England is much more civilised than America and that gunfire isn't allowed here," accused Kitty who was still bemoaning the loss of her own pistol.

"*Hush*, child," returned Elizabeth from the corner of her mouth.

"Wasn't this Corsica fellow a close associate of Elysia?" Asked Caroline.

"I believe so, but there was far more smoke than ever there was fire," replied Marian, who was always ready to believe the best of everyone.

"Though Elysia had more than a business arrangement with him, or so it's said," put in Eliza, fishing for tittle-tattle.

Catherine Esprey pricked up her ears at this, but thought it best to keep quiet in case she was sent from the room.

"Richard says that gossip about Elysia is rife at Westminster, though no one dares to come out with an accusation publicly," returned Marian.

"Why ever not?" Asked Elizabeth who loved a good scandal.

"To avoid expensive court cases and the certain loss of their shirts," returned Marian.

"What ever happened to the police inspector?" Queried Caroline, changing the subject.

"The poor man had to shoulder all the blame for the shambles and was reprimanded by the Commissioner himself, besides which his retirement was brought forward, though it was imminent in any case."

"Though I'll wager he was not incompetent," put in Elizabeth.

"He wasn't demoted, was he?" Asked Caroline.

"No, thank goodness.   Charles and I met Inspector Mason several times and we think very highly of him, the probability is that he was given a task which he had no hope of completing."

"He was put on the block to take the blame," suggested Caroline.

"It certainly looks that way."

The ladies sipped *aperitifs* thoughtfully for minute or so and then Caroline asked, "Where's Jane got to?  I was sure she'd be here for she never misses."

"*Ah*, She's gone off on an important mission with Guido," informed Marian with a wink.

"Do tell," encouraged Elizabeth.

"Jane's uncle wishes to meet Guido."

"Is he the one who's the Earl of Bowleas?"  Queried Elizabeth.

"Yes, and he insists that young Turner is to be known within the family as *Guy*."

Caroline thought for a moment, "Jane won't put up with that," she paused dramatically before continuing, "*unless* her son is to become heir to the title."

"Exactly so."

"Though Guido taking a title will be against everything Jane stands for," pointed out Elizabeth with some strength.

"*Ah ha*, but surely you recall the story of the Trojan Horse?"

"Joining the aristocracy by stealth and changing things from the inside, you mean."

"From the very top to the very bottom, my dear."

"So Guido will become the Ninety-ninth Earl of Bowleas," Elizabeth shook her head at the very idea of it.

"Oh, no, he'll only be the Sixth."

"I expect Jane will return as soon as she can, pleased to be shaking the dust of the aristocracy from her feet," suggested Caroline, who in fact was fishing for further information.

"I doubt it, for the current earl wishes *Guy* to become familiar with every facet of his inheritance. Then there's also the question of the boy's education."

"Eton I expect," said Eliza.

"No, I believe that the Earls of Bowleas have been Wykehamists since the school was founded in the Fourteenth Century... Or perhaps it was the Thirteenth," replied Marian.

In her mind, Caroline had been shaping a plan to spend time with Richard, but now that she knew that *both* Jane and Helmuth would be absent for a prolonged time, this opportunity couldn't be allowed to pass without decisive action and; hopefully, one or two romantic trysts.

"*I wonder...,*" she whispered to herself.

"Wonder what?" Asked Marian.

"Oh, nothing much, just a random question which flitted through my mind but didn't pause to await an answer."

*****

"You do realise, I suppose, that marriage to so young a person will undoubtably end in disaster," Roderick Villiers was not happy that his friend was about to leave the theatre to become; of all things, an undertaker.

"There's a wide age gap between yourself and Roberta too," pointed out Solly.

"*Ah,* but Bobbity and I were destined for each other, our union had always been written in the stars had I cared to look," Roddy glanced upwards reverently.

"And here's me thinking that it had a lot to do with Frank Turner grabbing you forcefully whilst you were dead drunk."

"Exactly, as I've said, our future was inscribed on tablets of stone."

"Then how do you know that the same will not apply to myself and Millie?"

Roddy gave the appearance of thinking deeply before he shook his head sadly and replied, "It's your involvement in *trade* that trouble me most."

"Treading the boards is a trade too, and a far less reliable one at that  – especially in so out-of-the-way a theatre as the *Civic*, in which all the actors bar three are amateurs."

"*Enthusiastic* amateurs, though, Solly, that's why we've been so successful."

"Your own brother-in-law is very enthusiastic, though he's nothing other than a disaster on stage," reminded Solly.

"Forget about him and think instead of the talent we have nurtured here."

Vasey shook his head forcefully, "The time has come for me to move on."

"But as an *undertaker*," cried Villiers plaintively.

"Burying the dead in as dignified way as possible is a worthy occupation, besides which I'm no snob and am delighted that my future is a far  brighter one since Millie agreed to become my fiancée."

Villiers sighed and then declaimed, *"O sweeter than the marriage feast, 'Tis sweeter far to me, To walk together to the kirk with goodly company,"* he clapped his hands to his chest.

"Shakespeare again, I suppose."

"No, Coleridge, but I beg you to remain within our *goodly company*, stay with me..."

"That's impossible," replied Vasey steadfastly.

"*I need you*," appealed Roddy, clasping his hands in front of him.

Solly smiled sweetly before replying, "Though you've still not repaid what you owe me.  Remind me, for how many years has this debt been outstanding?"

"A mere trifle, you shall receive what you are due as soon as the bank opens in the morning."

"It's Sunday to-morrow," pointed out Solly dryly.

"Then the day after, without fail, every penny I owe you shall be returned."

"With no interest added I expect."

"Of course you shall have what's due to you and above the current rate too," promised Villiers openhandedly.

Vasey smiled knowingly, but then shook his head, "It's no good, Roddy, my mind is made up and I'm determined to marry Millie. Without her I would be fearing the onset of a miserable old age."

"Oh, do not misunderstand me, for I've no objection to you finding happiness; even so late in life with the adorable Miss Hopper. However, what appals me is the idea of so fine an actor as yourself reduced to conducting funerals."

"My future will be secured, for Mr Hopper has no heir other than his daughter. With Millie I can look forward to a prosperous future because one thing is certain – there is never a shortages of the dead to bury."

Villiers said nothing for a moment, but then struck a theatrical pose and dropped his voice dramatically, saying "You will soon discover that the call of the theatre cannot be denied by one of its favourite sons."

"I am *even like the deaf adder that stoppeth her ears which refuseth to hear the voice of the charmer: charm he ever so wisely,*" declaimed Solly in his deepest and most authoritative tones.

Villiers was brought up short, his expression a combination of annoyance and puzzlement, but eventually he admitted, "I fear that I cannot recall the source of your quote."

"The *Book of Common Prayer,* it's well worth reading as there is some very fine poetry in it."

"I beg you, reconsider, think of the fine times we've enjoyed together…"

Solly shook his head and laughed, "My ears shall be deaf to any such request, for I'll be living very comfortably at the home of my in-laws, rather than in the cramped attic room through which draughts blow from every direction."

"Though what of your art, dear boy, your art *is* your life."

Solly smiled widely before suggesting, "In future I expect my finest performances to be played out in the marriage bed."

*****

At precisely eleven o'clock in the morning the Martindale Colliery Band; brought overnight to Winterbourne, began to play Handel's funeral march from *Saul*.

Ahead of them a full company of the 39th Regiment of Foot, with reversed rifles, black arm bands and shakos masked with black crepe, began the slow march which was to lead the whole procession to Wright's mausoleum. This had been constructed in the park, on a slight prominence looking towards the main gates of Winterbourne.

Behind the band there came a hearse containing the huge, elaborately carved coffin within which lay what little remained of Sir James Hannibal Wright. The horses were bedecked in black and long, streaming feathers of purple decorated both animals and vehicle.

Immediately behind the hearse came an open landau in which Elysia Scott-Wilson, the Marchioness of Studland, sat alone, erect, pale faced and completely dressed in black, though her jewellery of jet gleamed dully in the weak spring sunshine.

Several more carriages carrying national and county worthies followed, after which the whole population of Winterbourne and the surrounding countryside marched solemnly.

"Butter wouldn't melt in her mouth, she's turned herself into the authentic picture of filial rectitude," suggested Tom Harrington as he pointed toward the leading carriage.

Mister Hill thought it would be wiser to say nothing, so he nodded and merely grunted, before replying, "Lots of big names have turned up,"

"Many more have stayed away though; some of whom were happy to accept favours from Wright whilst he lived, the marchioness is not at all happy about that."

"I suppose you organised the military escort?" Suggested the lawyer.

Tom managed to reduce a snort of laughter to a cough before he said, "She originally demanded a gun-carriage, a troop of the Household Cavalry and a full battalion of the Grenadier Guards."

"Oh, dear, then you must have failed her," Hill enjoyed the idea of this.

"She's a powerful woman who's also wise enough to know her limits."

"Of course," Hill nodded sagely and then remarked, "I see that Lady Wright is not with us, it has been remarked upon."

"No, she went home to New York a few weeks ago."

"One would have expected her to attend nonetheless."

"Elysia telegraphed the news to her."

"Then she has no excuse," snorted the solicitor, "she should have attended."

"She will have received the telegram only a day or two before the event," replied Tom, deadpan.

Hill managed to disguise his amusement by snorting into his handkerchief.

Just then the procession turned through the park gates and came into sight of the final resting place of Hannibal Wright. It had been built in the style of Classical Greece, sporting polished white columns; which looked like marble but were not, and an imposing set of steps leading to the portico.

"*Jesus*," whispered Harrington, pointing towards a statue of epic proportions which stood on a plinth at the top of the steps, "Whatever is that monstrosity?"

"It is a very fine likeness of Sir James as a young man," informed Hill, surprised that his companion had asked so obvious a question.

The commemorative statue they were discussing stood in a similar pose to that of the Colossus of Rhodes. However, its legs were a fraction too short whilst the extended right arm was too long though still noticeably shorter than the left one. The head and face bore no resemblance to that of Wright at any age and what was supposed to look like hair blowing in the breeze had ended up as a series of crooked spikes.

Tom smiled and said lightly, "It's probably the likeness he deserves."

Towards the rear of the procession; following the carriage of Sir Charles Martin and his lady, marched the colliers and ironworkers who were there to represent the people of the town which had been the brain child of Hannibal Wright.

"It was good of Elysia to arrange trains for so many to attend," said Marian.

"I suppose so, but myself, I would much preferred to have remained at home – I feel a complete hypocrite as I despised the man."

"He's dead now and so should be shown some charity," she replied very softly.

Charles grunted, "He never showed any compassion for those he robbed and cheated and his many crimes went completely unpunished."

Marian said nothing for a moment and then whispered, "Though he died alone in an awful black hole."

"Who put him there, though?"

"Why we know it was Corsica."

Charles laughed bitterly, "Elysia was behind the whole thing – and no doubt the disappearance of the German woman had something to do with her too."

"Then by now Sir James will have met his Master and has had to answer for his crimes," returned Marian.

"Were that to be the case then the fires of Hell are burning so much the brighter as we speak."

They sat in silence for a short while and then Marian said brightly, "Though you got the better of him in the end."

"You mean I'm alive and he's dead?"

"No, you took Martindale back from him, retrieved your children and forced him to agree to your divorce. Hook, line and sinker to you, I should say."

Charles smiled and nodded, "By, God, I did too and ended up with the kindest and most beautiful woman I'd ever set eyes on."

Marian put on a puzzled look, "Who is this paragon you speak of?"

In reply he flung convention to the wind and kissed her, this action was immediately encouraged by the cries and claps of the miners and ironworkers who were following close behind the carriage.

Lady Martin turned to nod and smile at them whilst Charles raised a hand a hand in salute too.

Then head of the cortege reached the mausoleum and shortly thereafter a thousand or so bobbing heads joined it to play their part in the service of comital.

Two hours later, after a long and tedious service conducted by a bishop; who was deeply in the debt of the marchioness, the important mourners arrived at Winterbourne for the funeral luncheon. Those less grand were well fed and watered in a nearby; though out of sight, marquee.

"Can't we take a train to London and return home tonight?" Asked Charles.

"No, certainly not, Elysia is putting us up at Winterbourne, you'll like it there for it's a beautiful house and we'll be treated like royalty," Marian wasn't going to take no for an answer.

"Do you think we'll come out of Elysia's house alive?" Asked Charles half seriously.

Marian turned on him, "Even though we've both had difficult times with Elysia, she had changed since then."

"Don't you think she played a part in the disappearance and death of her father?"

"I can't believe that she's a patricide."

Her husband said nothing for a few moments and then offered, "I can show you documents which prove that Wright was a traitor to his country as well as being a ruthless and murderous man of business."

"Whatever he was or may have been had nothing to do with his daughter."

"The touch of pitch."

"Blaming the child for the sins of the father? That's not like you, Charles."

"If only I had never become involved in the winning of coal and left things as comfortably rural as they were a mere dozen years or so ago."

"In which case Caroline would now be the mistress of Martin Hall and I would probably have married some farmer's boy."

Charles smiled and kissed her again, not caring about the glances of the people nearby, "In which case my life would have been immeasurably the poorer."

She kissed him back once and then said, "As you have no proof whatsoever of Elysia's involvement in anything illegal, then perhaps we may take up her offer of a comfortable bed for the night."

Charles hummed and hawed for a while but eventually nodded his agreement. He knew that his first wife had provided sustenance and accommodation in the village for the Martindale people and he now intended to return home with them the following day – in fact as soon as he'd taken breakfast.

Across the dining room, Tom Harrington was squeezing lemon juice on to a slice of smoked salmon when he was interrupted by the marchioness herself.

"I'm sure my papa would have been delighted with the send-off we gave him," asserted Elysia.

"Indeed, Sir James couldn't have organised better himself."

"You didn't think it was overdone?"

Tom shook his head, "Certainly not, for your pa' was a larger than life fellow and his funeral demonstrated the truth of that."

"What of the statue?" She asked her eyes sparkling with mischief.

"A very fine likeness," put in Mr Hill swiftly, desperate that he should keep the favour of his employer whose generosity had ended the money worries he had suffered over the wild spending of his wife and two very expensive daughters.

Tom could bring himself to do no other than nod positively.

"I think the way the sculptor's managed my father's leonic head and flowing hair is its crowning glory," continued the marchioness.

"Indeed, I've never seen such lifelike hair created in stone," said Hill.

"Rugged, like the man himself," added Harrington, though unwillingly.

Elysia looked around and saw that none of the other guests were taking any particular notice of them, "You're nothing other than a pair of sycophants," she accused.

Hill; in a minor panic, coughed, "Never...," he began."

"Oh, shut-up Hill," cried Tom, "can't you see the lady's making fools of us."

Elysia laughed loudly, but as soon as she noticed that she had now drawn attention to herself, she sniffed in a ladylike way and put on an expression of deeply felt grief.

"The statue is *awful* and I planned it to be so," she stated.

"Why on earth would you do that?" Hill was genuinely puzzled.

"Because she was made in her papa's mould, the perfect daughter," explained Tom, who then had great difficulty in hiding his amusement from the other mourners.

A little over a mile away in a secluded, sheltered glade amidst which a small garden had been created stood a grave stone inscribed as follows:-

*In Loving Memory of*

*Johnie Corsica*

*1831 - 1866*

*****

"It was very good of you to invite us to take tea with you," Viviane Duncombe smiled across the china at her hostess, Elizabeth Esprey.

"Indeed, especially as we're virtual strangers," added her brother.

Eliza returned the smile, but she wasn't at all fooled by this pair of upper class vagabonds, "We're delighted to play host to any members of the Shafto family."

"We are only distantly related to them, though," laughed Percy, whilst thinking that Eliza; even though she was on the wrong side of forty, was an exceedingly attractive woman.

"Blood is blood, whether it's thick or thin, for the bloodline is everything," put in Colonel Esprey with some positivity.

Elizabeth smiled sweetly at her husband for she knew that his own line of ancestry was a very short one indeed. Not that she felt in any way his superior for she wasn't even sure who her own mother had been. However, she was absolutely certain that her mama would have been found at the very bottom of the social heap.

"Mrs Nicholson has great strength of character and I truly admire her," put in Catherine Esprey.

"Well, said, my dear," the colonel clapped lightly and smiled, he being delighted with the way his Catherine was turning out to be everything he wished for in a daughter.

Percy surreptitiously studied the Esprey girl and found her wanting in most respects, however, she was likely to have access to the money he desperately needed, so he supported her enthusiastically, "Indeed yes, where would the British Empire be today without *character*."

"It would be as dead as that of Rome or Greece," suggested Viviane who wished her brother would get down to business.

"You were in the army too, I believe," the colonel smiled at his guest.

"Much lower in the scheme of things than yourself, sir. My career holds nothing of interest – why, I never once left dear old Blighty's shore."

"Though not through lack of trying," put in Viviane quickly.

"Your brother was very wise, my dear, there were many times during my service in India that I wished I'd had the option of remaining safely at home."

Percy nodded towards Catherine and then said to the colonel, "I'm afraid I made something of a *faux pas* when I rudely intruded upon your daughter at the hunt."

"He did indeed," added Viviane who was pleased that her brother was at last moving in the right direction.

"Really? She's never mentioned it," replied Esprey.

"It was nothing much," returned Kitty, "I hardly noticed."

"I was very gauche, for when I saw such a young girl perched atop of a very large and lively horse, I thought I'd pass on a word or two of advice and so approached her when I had not the right to."

Catherine laughed, "Once the hunt was off I left Mr Duncombe well behind."

"On the awful nag I'd borrowed there was no hope of catching her," smiled Percy with a rueful shake of his head.

"In fact my brother really ought to make an apology to Mr Kent too."

Percy cursed inwardly, but smiled and said, "Yes, I got a little hot under the collar and wasn't as polite as I was brought up to be."

"Mr Kent is a fine fellow, he taught my daughter to ride properly and he's made a damned good job of it," informed Esprey.

"Not only that, but, believe me, the butler of Martin Hall is a man I'd think twice about before I upset him," returned the colonel's lady.

"Were I ever to be in danger accompanied by my dear papa and Mr Kent I would fear nothing," added Catherine.

"Though the whole situation at the hunt ended amicably," Viviane tried to smooth over the edges.

"Perhaps I should apologise in person," suggested Percy.

"The Martins are a very hospitable family, though I'd put in your card first," advised Jervis Esprey.

"No need," jumped in Percival, "we've already visited there."

"Though only briefly, "Viviane sighed inwardly and wished her brother had been as dashing during his army career as he was as a civilian.

"I'm sure you'll be made welcome by all the local families," said Elizabeth, who had decided to reserve her opinion of the these people until she'd known them longer – much longer.

*****

Elysia Scott-Wilson strode into the entrance vestibule of Forest Hall accompanied by her solicitor Mister Hill, who was looking very prosperous as he had been officially appointed her one and only man of business.

"This is looking much better," she remarked after glancing around.

"I'm not yet sure what the total amount spent is, stonemasons, builders, carpenters and decorators are all clamouring for their money."

"Mister Corsica didn't bother much with what things cost," put in Kevin O'Dowd who trailed well behind his betters.

"Pay them what they've asked for and be done with it, after to-day I wish to shake Forest Hall from my mind forever."

"Do you plan to sell, ma'am?"

"No, for that would mean having to return the two ugly sisters to Winterbourne and I've no desire to share dinner table chit-chat with them, no, not even for once a week."

"Fine ladies though they are," returned Hill, who always tried to keep a foot in both camps.

"Aye, they are that," added Kevin whose fondness for the Scott-Wilson sisters had continued to grow.

"Are the antiquarians here?" Asked Elysia.

"Awaiting your pleasure, my lady."

A few minutes later, in the refurbished drawing room, Horace Nelson and Rufus Plantagenet rose to their feet and bowed low to the marchioness.

"I hope that you've found everything here to your satisfaction," she said.

"Indeed so, ma'am, the priest hole is now prepared and ready for our investigation to begin," returned Rufus Plantagenet.

"*Meticulous* investigation," corrected Horace Nelson.

428

"The members of our association are fully prepared and cannot wait to begin," continued Plantagenet.

"Though only to those specialists amongst them who have been invited to view," Nelson put in quickly.

"Allow in as many as you care to," Elysia spoke easily, "my sisters-in-law welcome company at any time."

"You are too, *too* kind, my lady," again the historians bowed in unison.

"Aye, the lasses like company," nodded Kevin, who by now had an intimate knowledge of both sisters.

Plantagenet smiled and turned towards the marchioness, "We much appreciate your support, ma'am, and very much deplore the offensive and negative articles which in the past have appeared in the low-brow press."

"The *Gutter* press," put in Nelson quickly, before continuing, "Which we hope you realise was none of *our* doing."

Elysia smiled very broadly and shrugged her shoulders, "I'm afraid the fault was mine, as I so readily trusted Corsica."

"Who I understand was most abrupt and rude when you first made enquiries," put in Mister Hill, who was delighted that he would never again have any need to fear nor associate with the Corsican brigand.

"I'm afraid to say it, but at the time of your initial enquiry I had not recognised that my man of business was already well on his way to insanity," said Elysia.

"All's well that ends well," nodded Plantagenet."

"Indeed, perhaps you would care to inspect our work, once we have something to display," invited Nelson.

*I think not,* thought Elysia, though she merely said, "I may be rather busy in the near future, but I'm sure that any visitors you recommend will be welcomed by Lady Flora, her sister and of course Mr O'Dowd, who continues to be my agent here."

"*Special* agent," put in Kevin, keen to maintain his status.

"Oh, yes, Mr O'Dowd is very special," smiled Elysia, whilst thinking, *the swine had better be.*

*****

"Hugh told me that your poor wife is ill in bed, so I've brought some flowers for her," Lucy Greenwood simpered as she was led into the Brass breakfasting room.

"That's awful good of you," replied Douglas who never thought that his nephew's girlfriend was capable of showing such sympathy.

"It's nothing, they're just spring flowers, the best I could find at this time of year."

"You'll take a coffee, maybe," invited Brass who was feeling somewhat depressed as he'd already lost one wife and now his second was looking very ill indeed.

"Why thank you, Mr..," she began but he interrupted her.

"Call me Dougie, everyone does."

"Except Mrs Brass, perhaps," she smiled and continued, "A coffee would be most welcome after my climb up the ridge from Martindale."

"Of course," cried Brass going to the door and calling out for refreshments to be served.

"Look at the state of my boots," clucked Lucy, who at the same time had raised her skirts to expose a pair of perfectly clean, high heeled boots and a shapely stockinged calf.

Douglas was a sharp businessman who also had a good grasp of character reading and knew perfectly well the direction this visit was taking.

"If you take them off I'll have my gardener's boy buff 'em up for you."

Lucy dropped her skirt and shook her head primly, "They'd just get dirty again when I hike back home."

"I'll take you down in the trap," he found himself offering without thinking about it beforehand.

"That's very kind, though I did come to visit Mrs Brass."

"And so you shall, though afterwards you shall travel home in better style than you arrived."

Half-an-hour later, after a leisurely coffee, Lucy was taken by a maid to see Arabella, who lay in bed very pale and wan.

"You're the last visitor I expected to see."

"Well, as I'm nearly family now I thought it my duty – my Christian duty to visit."

"I'm not sick, I'm with child."

431

"You don't look very well, though. Can I get anything for you."

"For what reason do you suppose Douglas pays the servants far more than they're worth?"

Lucy nodded and realised that this interview wasn't going to be as easy as she'd hoped and changed tack, "You must be missed awfully at *Brass Shilling.*"

"I'll return next week," Arabella had never liked the look of Lucy Greenwood and she liked her even less as she hovered around faking concern.

"I do like the costumes you and your sister design."

Bella merely nodded and smiled weakly.

"Do you machine the originals yourselves?"

"What do you think?"

"Is there anything I can do or get for you?" Offered Lucy.

"I have everything I need."

"What about Dougie? Is there anything he *needs,*" as she spoke her lips formed a simpering smile.

"*Mister* Brass requires nothing."

Lucy noticed the emphasis which had been put on Douglas' title, but ignored it, "Oh, as I'm nearly family, he insisted that I should call him *Dougie* – everyone does, apparently."

Arabella passed a hand weakly across her forehead, "Oh, go away, I'm feeling rather faint."

"Of course," Lucy replied as she backed out of the room hoping that it would be Brass himself who would drive her home to Martindale.

*****

"Are you sure your parents do not object to you forming a friendship with a sailor man?" Phil Butterfield asked as he strolled with Miss Grainger through the Martindale woods.

Violet pulled him to a halt with a gentle jerk of her arm, "Of course not, they're delighted that you're showing an interest in me."

"Even though I've nothing much to offer you at the moment?"

"You forget the one important thing my parents perceived from the moment you were introduced to them."

Phil shook his head and looked puzzled, "What could that possibly have been?"

"You're a *gentleman*."

"Though I have no fortune."

Violet laughed, "You're what they've always wanted for me, which could never have been provided by any of the other bachelors in Martindale."

"It's true I was brought up as a gentleman, though I have none of the trappings of one."

"That doesn't matter to my parents and even less to myself, for I love you and will accept no one else as my partner in life."

"Though I will not see you again for some time and I've a long climb to make on the navy ladder."

"I *will* wait for you, no matter how long you may be away."

Phil took her in his arms and kissed her cheek.

"You can do better than that," she said as she pulled him behind a tree and kissed him hard on the lips.

"It will be very difficult for me to leave you behind, but I must go," he whispered a few minutes later.

"I know that."

"I'm determined to make a go of the navy and the captain has promised that if I continue to shape up as well as I have so far, he'll try to have me rated midshipman. The first lieutenant is keen to teach me navigation too."

"You've no need to explain yourself to me, I know you're clever, kind and; as a bonus, handsome too."

Philip's face became pink with embarrassment, "You're wonderful," he paused and then his expression became serious, "though should someone else come along while I'm away, I'll understand that you can't wait for me."

"There can be no one else other than you."

"It could be a long time before I even see you again."

"There will be *no one else* – just make sure you write frequently."

"Once a week, regular as clockwork, but you do realise there are no post boxes at sea, so my letters will reach you in batches – eventually."

"That's all right, I'll read one a week until you come home again."

"I'll number the backs of the envelopes so you'll be able to read my letters in their proper sequence."

"Goodness yes, I don't want to read that you've found a new female friend and then learn from an earlier letter that you had in fact adopted the ship's cat."

He kissed her again and hoped fervently that she'd still be waiting for him once the exigencies of the service allowed.

*****

"The post has arrived, sir," announced Simmonds as he entered the office of Richard Turner.

The MP nodded and grimaced as he already had a pile of unopened letters before him, none of which he expected would prove to be of any importance.

His secretary dropped a weighty bundle of mail to join the rest of the jumble which was spread across the desk of his superior. However, he kept hold of one letter, sniffed it and said, "This one appears to be from a lady."

Richard sighed, "Is it not from my wife?"

"No, sir, I'd recognise her handwriting at once, very untidy it is, so it's not from her."

"In that case it'll be from a female relative of one of my electors complaining that sixpence is worth less than a farthing these days and what am I going to do about it."

As his expression made plain, Simmonds doubted this explanation.

"Oh, just throw it down with the others," Richard had had enough of his clerk's curiosity, though he had to admit to himself that his own interest had been aroused too.

Simmonds did as he was told, nodded and departed, though not without raising his eyebrows as high as they would go.

Once the sound of his footsteps had disappeared into the room across the corridor, Richard picked up the mysterious letter and saw immediately that the handwriting was that of Caroline. He opened it, wasting no further time.

*Blanchwell,*

*Butterby,*

*Martindale,*

*County Durham.*

*My dearest,*

*I cannot tell you how much my heart is trembling as I write this; I shake so much that I can hardly put pen to paper as I'm being assailed by successive waves of joy, doubt, pleasure and fear.*

*I'm sure you'll know that Jane has taken Guido to visit her uncle Quintin and will not be returning to Martindale for some weeks. What you may not know is that Helmuth is currently escorting his sister to America, where he will remain for at least a full month. You may also be aware that Grace owns or has an interest in* several properties in America; namely her house at Gettysburg as well as Cardinal Woods and a share of the Knightsbridge plantation, both of which are in Virginia.

Helmuth is particularly keen to check on how work is proceeding to make Knightsbridge profitable once more and this could take him even longer than he thinks – not to mention the time crossings of the Atlantic take.

I don't need to explain what this could mean to us – to our relationship which has for so long has been unconsummated. The question now is:- Are we to take advantage of this rare opportunity or not? Is the time ripe for us both or not? Should we take a chance which many never arise again, or are we to continue to frustrate our deepest desires?

Should you agree to an assignation I am determined that it should not take place at either the Old Hall nor Blanchwell, for servants gossip and are fully aware of <u>everything</u> we do, it's rather like living in an extremely comfortable prison! Besides which, I doubt that either of us would have any wish to defile our marriage beds.

However, I believe that I have a solution. You may remember the cottage at the edge of the Blanchwell estate which I rented to your brother for the use of the lady who is now his wife. I paid a visit to it yesterday and found that Rosemary has left it furnished and in good order. Were you to agree, this could be our rendezvous and if all goes well we may be able to meet several times in complete secrecy and security.

Should you be willing to risk all for my love, then return to Durham as soon as you receive this letter. After allowing time for my message to reach you, I shall *visit the cottage I've suggested and remain there from one o'clock every afternoon for a full hour. I shall continue this routine for five days.*

*Should you fail to join me, I shall realise that you are behaving far more sensibly than am I and so will attempt to forget how close we once were.*

*Caroline.*

Richard wiped a bead of sweat from his brow, thought for a second and then shouted "Simmonds, I need you at once."

After which he tidied his desk as best he could and reached for his overcoat which hung nearby.

Then office door opened and the clerk appeared, "May I be of assistance, sir?"

"Yes, I must go out and may not be back for some days," returned Richard as he stuffed the letter from his lover into his pocket.

"Perhaps you've forgotten that you have a very long list of appointments."

"Cancel them, cancel them all."

"*Cancel,* sir?" Simmonds shook his head, his expression lugubrious.

"Very well, *postpone* them all."

"Should I say that you are ill?"

"No, tell them I've never felt better in my life."

"Yours must be very urgent business, sir," curiosity radiated from both his tone and in his expression.

"Indeed yes, it is important business which I should have attended to years ago."

*****

Harry Nicholson was nothing if not stoical, for even though he had been swept away from the place and people he most loved, he carried on with life as best he could. However, he sighed long and hard as he approached his new home which was the *Northumbrian Piper* inn, not far from Whylam and just off the road to Newcastle.

This public house was owned (or tenanted, he wasn't sure which) by Mr Donald Moncur who had agreed to take in his mother and himself. His mother had been introduced to the regular customers of the inn as the new housekeeper of the establishment, though it was self-evident that she was also required to share the landlord's bed.

Harry's own accommodation was very cramped and lay in a small room (not much larger than a closet) at the bottom of the cellar stairs. It tended to dankness, the walls ran with water and the sour smell of the nearby beer barrels filled the already damp air.

"After spending the night breathing in alcoholic fumes I'm surprised I wake up sober," he pondered to himself.

On top of this, his nearest neighbours were a sizeable colony of rats which scurried, squeaked and scraped the whole night long. He couldn't stop himself from wondering how long it would take them before they decided to share his bed.

His thoughts were interrupted when he realised that he had reached the junction where the pit road met the main road. Looking towards the inn, he couldn't deny that Moncur had chosen a good site for his business. The tavern had been created from the shells of three cottages which had once housed labourers from long defunct iron workings.

Very soon after his arrival it became obvious to Harry that the landlord had no intention of marrying his mother and as soon as he tired of her she'd be sent on her way without so much as a thought nor a penny piece. He was also aware that when that did happen the pittance he currently received for separating stone from coal for endless hours a day would not be sufficient to succour himself, never mind his mother too.

He had no doubt that he would develop into as efficient a collier as his father had been, but realised that success would depend upon the result of a race between himself developing the colliery skills he needed against the falling level of desire Moncur possessed for his mother. He knew also that the road ahead of him would be a long one. First of all a team of hewers would have to take him on as their putter, after which he'd be ready to work at the coal face. Once he'd cleared these hurdles he was certain that he would begin excavating enough coal to provide for both his mother and himself.

"Is this to be my future?" He asked himself glumly, thinking of the enticing prospects which had awaited him at Martindale, when he lived there his future had looked bright.

He sighed again as he thought of Sarah and Elinor and how much he missed them. There he had enjoyed a comfortable bed and reliable meal times with good food and a sufficiency of it.

Though most of all he missed the access to books he had had at the *Education Association*, books of every description which he had devoured, often reading well in to the night.

He was then brought back to reality when his ears caught a strident shout from the doorway of the *Northumbrian Piper*.

"Harry, get yourself in here, there's work to be done before the next shift comes off."

The speaker was Alice Moncur, a tall, gangly girl of about twenty years of age whose red hair was pulled back in the tightest of possible buns and whose eyes were as sharp as the tilt of her chin.

"Haven't you a meal for me first?" Harry's bait tin had contained only half a crust of bread and a sliver of mouldy looking cheese.

"Owt y'get here has to be worked for."

"I understand that, how could I not? Though it should be obvious to you that without proper food I won't have the energy required to make money underground."

She snorted her disdain, "Why, ye don't even work the seams yet."

"I will though, and sooner than you may think."

Alice pondered for a second and then said, "The pa' o' one of your workmates was in this morning, talkin' about you."

"Oh? Who was that?"

"The da' of Gus Macdonald, he said that his son Ally made you run off and hide."

Harry couldn't help laughing, "I've never fled from a fight in my life, though I've never started one either."

"That's not what Gus told me."

Nicholson sighed heavily, "Ally suggested that my father had killed an ironworker and I pointed out that the reverse of that was the truth."

"Then y'tried to hit him and he drove you off."

Harry shrugged his shoulders, "Have it anyway you wish, though I still must be fed before I'll be willing to lift a finger."

For a few seconds it looked as though Alice was going to cause a rumpus, but then she smiled and said, "Gus was always a liar and I don't doubt that his lad takes after him."

"I'll not fight unless I need to, though I won't be browbeaten nor bullied either."

Alice turned back towards the *Northumbrian Piper*, saying at the same time, "Fetch a couple of firkins up from the cellar first and there'll be fried bacon and cabbage waiting for you when ye're done."

"Suits me," replied Harry as he followed in the landlord's daughter's footsteps.

✱✱✱✱✱

"Lady Wright is not presently at home," Murdoch the butler of Isis Hall sniffed haughtily as he spoke.

"I didn't expect her to be," returned James Watkins.

"Then perhaps you'd care to call once her ladyship has returned from New York."

"No, I believe I'll come inside now."

The butler nodded to the pair of footmen who waited behind him and they began to move forward, ready to eject this interloper from the premises.

Jim smiled sardonically as he handed the butler a letter, "This is a directive from the Marchioness of Studland," he informed.

The colour drained from the butler's face and he immediately waved back the advancing footmen.

"You'll find that I'm to be in charge here as the legal representative of the marchioness," nodded Watkins with obvious relish.

Murdoch handed back the letter and nodded positively several times before inviting, "Please come inside, sir, I'm sorry for the delay, but I've had no word of this change of ownership..."

Jim cut him off abruptly, "There has been *no* change of ownership, for from the moment her father died Isis House has belonged exclusively to the Marchioness of Studland."

"Though what about Lady Wright, when she returns she'll..."

Again the butler was interrupted, "Now that the remains of Sir James have been found and interred the instructions he left in his last will and testament are legally valid, binding and in force. In it he left *everything* he had to his daughter with no mention at all of Mrs van Leyden."

Murdoch nodded and wondered if his position was now in jeopardy.

"Lady Scott-Wilson has placed me in charge here, where I shall also be residing. My first instruction is that every exterior door lock is to be changed – arrange for that to be completed by tomorrow night."

"I see, sir, but it may take a day or two longer than that."

"By nightfall tomorrow, or you shall lose your comfortable situation here the day after – and be packed off without a reference to your name."

"Of course, sir, I'll see to it at once," the butler turned and set off in a less that stately way.

"*Wait,*" ordered Jim, "the marchioness has a further important and urgent instruction."

"It goes without saying that whatever her ladyship requires she can rely upon me."

"The marchioness has instructed that under *no* circumstances is Gertrude van Leyden ever to be allowed to enter Isis House again – if necessary you are to set the dogs on her."

"But she's Lady Wright now, the wife of..."

"*A dead man,* whilst the marchioness is very much *alive* and determined to have her way."

It was apparent to the butler that the fire-power of the marchioness was much greater than that of Sir James' widow.

"It shall be exactly as her ladyship has ordered, sir."

"On top of which, Mrs van Leyden is never to be referred to again as *Lady Wright*."

"Yes, sir, I quite understand."

"Good, now I'd best be shown to the finest of the guest rooms after which it will be time for luncheon."

The butler nodded, hurried off to make arrangements and it wasn't long before the rest of the household were made aware of what a foul mood he was in.

Jim Watkins smiled to himself as he considered that the luckiest moment of his life occurred when he had been plucked from the street into the hansom cab of Elysia Scott-Wilson.

*Though it didn't seem so when Corsica had me hanging by the neck*, he shivered as this thought passed through his mind.

*****

Charles Martin's favourite time of day was when he got into bed with his wife, this was especially the case if it had been a particularly tiring and worrying one. This precious interlude didn't automatically lead to a session of love making, nor to a period of stroking and petting, for it was a time set aside for relaxation. It was a time to unwind in the company of the person he loved most in the world and to discuss with her the events of the day and also his hopes for the following one.

445

Marian stretched and place her hands behind her head, closed her eyes and sighed contentedly.

"Safe in bed at last," she whispered.

"Secure in our own, private fortress, time to be together without the need to give a single thought to anyone or anything else."

"The whole house is quiet too and that makes a change."

"No policemen running around in search of homicidal lunatics."

She shuddered at this thought and then suggested, "In future we should insist that the stable yard door be securely locked before we retire."

"You know we can't do that for it's in constant use, it would be a great inconvenience to the servants who have to be up and about long before we are ourselves," pointed out Charles who was always adverse to change in the long established routines of Martin Hall.

"Though this open portal in our stout walls appears to be a magnet for those who wish us ill. I'm sure you will recall that as well as Corsica, Augustus Love entered that way too."

"The damned fool received the shock of his life when Fraulein Kleist laid into him," the memory of it made Charles smile.

"Though I was his intended victim," Marian shuddered at the thought.

"Then the idiot contrived to set the hall ablaze."

"Poor Frank's life changed that day – the burns he received have never healed."

"A handsome face ruined," Charles shook his head sadly.

"Though you had the courage of a lion that night, you saved my brother's life and were injured yourself in the process."

Charles leaned across and kissed his wife tenderly, "At least now Frank has found a woman who'll return his love. He's so well settled that you needn't worry about him again."

"Though I cannot avoid worrying continuously about everyone and over everything," sighed Marian.

They lay in each other's arms for a while and then Charles suddenly remembered, "Oh, by the way Richard's back in town."

"Is he? I thought he would be far too busy running the country to have any time to spare for boring old Martindale."

"As did I, but I had a word with Kent this afternoon and he'd been talking to the station master who told him that our Member of Parliament had arrived at lunchtime."

"*Really?* What on earth is he doing back here, it's not as though Martindale is likely to provide him with any useful information regarding the current condition of the army."

"I'd best put the gamekeepers on full alert," put in Charles slyly.

Marian took her pillow and belaboured her husband with it, "You impish rogue, you know full well that Richard never poached anything larger than a hare."

"Jane is away too, so we'd best invite him to dinner. Perhaps a fine, freshly caught salmon, followed by jugged hare and a haunch of venison," Charles continued mischievously.

Again Marian took up her pillow and set about her husband. Charles defended himself as best he could and once she tired of berating him, he took her in his arms and kissed her again before saying, "Richard ran poor Dunnett ragged, poor man was out in the woods every night and rarely even caught sight of his quarry."

"It must have been galling for Joe when you allowed my brother to go free once he'd been nabbed."

"I wasn't very popular with the 'keepers at the time, but I was never very concerned over the theft of a few hares and the odd game bird."

They laughed together for a moment and then Marian had a sudden thought, "Perhaps Richard is making a discrete visit here and won't wish to be interrupted."

"For whatever reason?"

"It could be a state secret," suggested Marian.

"Half of Martindale will know of his presence in the town by now."

"This is true, though I'll send word to the Old Hall for him, he's bound to turn up there sooner or later."

*****

Richard was running late, for he'd gone to the wrong cottage and had been much disconcerted when he was greeted by three small girls who'd grinned and laughed at the look of surprise on his face the moment they had popped into sight.

He'd returned their smiles and nodded to them before he set off in the opposite direction, wishing to be well away before the tenant came out to ask him what he was about.

"The trouble with infidelity is it carries with it a morbid fear of discovery," he muttered to himself as he galloped away.

Twenty minutes later he found the correct cottage and as he dismounted and was fastening his horse to the gatepost was disappointed to find that Caroline had not appeared to greet him.

"*Damn it*," he murmured to himself, "she's given up and gone home." At first, he looked about disconsolately for sight of her, but then felt a wave of relief, for he knew that this affair was bound, sooner or later, to bring great unhappiness to two families.

"Perhaps it is for the best that she's given up," he whispered to himself just before the door of the cottage opened and Caroline appeared.

"I'm sorry," he apologised quickly, "I took a wrong turn."

"I thought you must have changed your mind," her face was flushed and her lips were damp whilst her eyes were shining with love and the desire for him she felt.

As soon as he came close enough she took his arm and led him inside and straight into the bedroom where they sat together on the mattress.

"We've waited a long time for this moment," she whispered.

"Far too long," he agreed, "I…,"

She cut him off with a kiss whilst at the same time entwining her arms around his neck and drawing him closer.

He returned her kisses and pulled her hard into him, the sweet, musky scent of her fuelling his desire. Then, with little further ceremony, he pushed her into the mattress and began to run his fingers across the mounds of her breasts.

She pulled away momentarily and asked in a whisper, "Is this *our* moment at last?"

He answered her with a hug and a powerful kiss which he continued with until she had need to pull away from him to take breath.

"Wait," she whispered after a few minutes as she climbed from the bed and faced him directly, her eyes conveying to him as words could not how much she wanted him.

Richard stretched out his arms, "Come back to bed," he ordered gently.

She smiled shyly and then began to take off her clothes, slowly, one item at a time.

He soon noticed that she was not wearing any item of corsetry and a vision of Jane publicly burning her own underwear flashed into his mind and left behind it feelings of serious doubt over what he was presently engaged in.

"What's wrong," Caroline had noticed the change in his demeanour.

"Nothing," he smiled weakly, his throat became very dry but he knew that he could not let his first love down again.

Though her eyes were still expressing puzzlement, she dropped the last item of her clothing to the floor and stood before him naked.

"I suppose you're disappointed as I'm no longer the fresh young thing of ten years ago."

"You are as beautiful now as you were then," he replied, his throat made dry with passion.

She then displayed herself to him; with no vestige of coyness, moving subtly so that light and shadow enhanced every intimate part of her body.

At the sight of this he could wait no longer, he reached up and pulled her down into his arms and this time his kisses were full on, hard and determined.

She allowed herself to follow his lead and soon lay spread across the bed whilst his fingers and tongue caressed every part of her body.

"This moment has haunted my dreams for so very long I can't believe it's come at last," cried Richard huskily.

"I never thought we'd ever be together," she replied as she stroked his cheeks and smoothed his hair.

Then he pushed himself down her body inch by inch, kissing her flesh all the way, until he was able to manoeuvre his tongue into her most private place.

She gasped and for a moment her body stiffened before relaxing again and gave in to her need for this, the most natural of human responses.

As he nibbled and licked and sucked at Caroline he was suddenly overcome by a feeling of great consternation. Images of Jane and his children going about their business having no idea that he was currently engaged in the act of betraying them.

"What's wrong?" Asked Caroline as at the same time she pulled her body away from him.

"Nothing," he was too embarrassed to tell her the truth.

She sat up and sighed, "You're feeling guilty," she accused.

He nodded his agreement and then shook his head at his own indecisiveness.

Caroline sighed and then for some reason in her mind she was transported back to the Nebraska prairie. She remembered it had been herself who'd taken command of the assault on the pursuing slave hunters. It was she who had frightened the wits out of them by mercilessly offering them the stark choice of life or death.

The same decisiveness she'd shown then overtook her once more and with a combination of lust, anger and determination she pushed Richard flat on to the mattress and straddled him, forcing his penis deep into her opening and pushing up and down on it with ever increasing passion and speed.

It wasn't very long before Richard's mind was full of nothing other than a hard, unstoppable desire for her.

A few minutes later they were both sated and Caroline allowed herself to fall beside him, breathing heavily with one hand caressing her forehead. She was still breathing heavily and wondering what it was she had done. Upon which twisting, dead-end road had she placed herself now?

"Well, we've managed it at last," he said once they both got their breath back.

"Haven't *I* just," she replied.

"Shall we meet tomorrow?"

She thought for a moment and then said in a business-like way, "I shall be here, though I doubt that you will be."

He took her into his arms and they lay together for a long time, until he began to make love to her again. This time it was he who was in control and their movements took on a perfect rhythm, each seeming to know instinctively what it was the other desired and who then wasted no time trying to fulfil that desire.

Eventually, exhausted but happy, they lay in each other's arms and enjoyed the moment before the inevitable feelings of guilt came thudding down upon them like so many boulders.

## Message from the author

Thank you for reading this novel and I hope you enjoyed it. Should you have the time and inclination, a review on Amazon would be much appreciated by me, especially were it to be a positive one.

My 2021 novel (God willing) will feature the characters featured in my 2019 offering *How Far Is It To Dunkirkr?* centred on their activities just before and after 6th June, 1944. However, it could be something completely different.

Printed in Poland
by Amazon Fulfillment
Poland Sp. z o.o., Wrocław

62564612R00255